DEDALUS EUROPE 1992

editor Aysha Rafaele

The Architect of Ruins

Translated from the German by Mike Mitchell

THE ARCHITECT OF RUINS

Herbert Rosendorfer

with an introduction by John Clute

DEDALUS/HIPPOCRENE

Published in the UK by Dedalus Ltd,
Langford Lodge, St Judith's Lane, Sawtry, Cambs, PE17 5XE

UK ISBN 0 946626 91 X

Published in the USA by Hippocrene Books Inc,
171 Madison Avenue, New York, NY 10016

US ISBN 0 7818 0001 3

Distributed in Canada by Marginal Distribution,
Unit 103, 277 George Street North, Peterborough,
Ontario KJ9 3G9

Printed in the UK by Billings & Sons Ltd,
Hylton Road, Worcester WR2 5JU
Typeset by Cygnus Media Services, Redhill RH1 6HB

First published in Germany in 1969 by Diogenes Verlag, Zurich
as *Der Ruinenbaumeister*
© copyright Nymphenburger Verlagshandlung GmbH
in F A Herbig Verlagsbuchhandlung GmbH Munich 1980

Translation © copyright Mike Mitchell 1992

A C.I.P. listing for this title is available on request

DEDALUS EUROPE 1992

At the end of 1992 the 12 Member States of the EEC will inaugurate an open market which Dedalus is celebrating with a major programme of new translations from the 8 languages of the EEC. The new translations will reflect the whole range of Dedalus' publishing programme: classics, literary fantasy and contemporary fiction.

From Danish:
The Black Cauldron – William Heinesen
The Dedalus Book of Danish Literature – editor W Glyn Jones

From Dutch:
The Dedalus Book of Dutch Fantasy – editor Richard Huijing

From Dutch / French:
The Dedalus Book of Belgian Fantasy – editor Richard Huijing

From French:
The Devil in Love – Jacques Cazotte
Angels of Perversity – Remy de Gourmont
The Dedalus Book of French Fantasy
     – editor Christine Donougher
The Book of Nights – Sylvie Germain
Le Calvaire – Octave Mirbeau
Smarra & Trilby – Charles Nodier
Monsieur Venus – Rachilde

From German:
The Angel of the West Window – Gustav Meyrink
The Green Face – Gustav Meyrink
The Weird, the Wonderful & the Fantastic: Gustav Meyrink's
     Golden Treasury – editor Maurice Raraty
The Dedalus Book of Austrian Fantasy: the Meyrink Years
     1890-1930 – editor Mike Mitchell

The Dedalus Book of German Fantasy: the Romantics and
    Beyond – editor Maurice Raraty
The Architect of Ruins – Herbert Rosendorfer

From Greek:
The History of a Vendetta – Yorgi Yatromanolakis

From Italian:
Senso (and other stories) – Camillo Boito

From Portuguese:
The Mandarin – Eça de Queiroz
The Reliquary – Eça de Queiroz

From Spanish
The Dedalus Book of Spanish Fantasy – editor A R Tulloch

Further titles will be announced shortly.

THE TRANSLATOR

Mike Mitchell is a lecturer in German at Stirling University. His publications include a book on Peter Hacks, the East German playwright, and numerous studies on aspects of modern Austrian Literature; he is also the co-author of *Harrap's German Grammar*.

Mike Mitchell's translations include *The Works of Solitude* by Gyorgy Sebestyen, and Gustav Meyrink's novels *The Angel of the West Window* and *The Green Face*. He is currently engaged in editing *The Dedalus Book of Austrian Fantasy: the Meyrink Years 1890-1930*.

Introducing:

Herbert Rosendorfer

The Architect of Ruins

At last. Now we can begin properly. Some of the work of Herbert Rosendorfer, who was born in 1934, and who became a district court judge in Munich in 1967, had already been available in English before 1992: *Deutsche Suite* (1972), translated by Arnold Pomerans as *German Suite,* had appeared in 1979, and *Die Nacht der Amazonen* (1989), translated by Ian Mitchell as *Night of the Amazons,* had appeared in 1991. But these two books, despite the fleering and carnival brilliance of their presentation of the lunacies of Nazi Germany, conveyed to readers – surely deliberately – a sense of surreal entrapment, of civilization's endgame interminably prolonged. Natural enough, one might think, for an author who spent his childhood in the coils of nightmare. All the same, this obsessive gnawing at the poison cud of remembrance also conveyed – perhaps inevitably – a sense of Rosendorfer as a man caught staring backwards into the black hole of World War Two, unable to escape. So it is, in view of this misprision, a great relief to come upon his first novel, in Mike Mitchell's eloquent and joyful translation, and to see how wrong it was possible to be, and to begin at the beginning.

Der Ruinenbaumeister (1969), which Mitchell has deftly rendered as *The Architect of Ruins,* contains the germ of all of Rosendorfer's work, like a dream. It is a tale of escape into story-land, a discourse about stories, a story about stories within stories within stories: like an onion that makes one smile. Whether or not the book itself represents a long and exceedingly complex dream experienced by the narrator as a series of stories told to him over the course of a few minutes in real time as the train he has boarded carries him and six hundred nuns in the direction of Lourdes, the reader can perhaps decide. But if the reader *does* end up thinking that *The Architect of Ruins* represents a dream, s/he will have also to decide whether or not the narrator – ensconced as he was on a hurtling night-girdled train with a lunatic sneak thief under his seat, and hundreds of females in mysterious all-enveloping habits round about him – is himself caught in the intersections of a larger dream, from which he fails to awaken into a new self only because the last page of the novel intervenes, leaving him with us. For myself, the question can be shelved for the moment. It is perhaps enough at this point to say that *The Architect of Ruins* is *like* a dream.

The narrator, who is never named and who gives no sign that he himself has any intention of going to Lourdes, has boarded a train full of nuns who are bound there. From under his seat, a criminal on the run grabs his foot and asks for sanctuary, which is granted, and begins to tell his story, after indicating that some of his experiences resemble those described in G. K. Chesterton's *The Club of Queer Trades* (1904), a collection of stories which may in fact – like most of the fiction he wrote between 1900 and the outbreak of World War One – constitute a set of dreams. Indeed, the tone and pace of the *Architect of Ruins* – pellmell but preternaturally calm, deadpan but hallucinatory – very closely resembles at times that of Chesterton's masterpiece, *The Man Who Was Thursday: a Nightmare* (1908). In any case, the fugitive under the seat tells the narrator of a previous career as the inventor of an automatic cleaning device which utilizes bugs capable, because of the tiny rubbers attached to their feet, of cleaning rooms very delicately indeed. This venture fails, and he goes into the funeral business, but oversteps the mark when he makes sculptures out of the corpses. The police then invade the compartment, take him away, and the inspector, who remains, describes to the narrator some of the fugitive's further exploits. At the same time the narrator finds himself gazing at a piece of paper which the ex-corpse-sculptor has left behind. On this paper he can see a mysterious pattern of dots. Or holes. Déja vue suddenly afflicts him. He has been here before. Here. He is on a sunlit road, which runs alongside the wall of a vast and infinitely bosky country estate. He goes through the gate. The novel proper – or the dream – now begins; or continues.

He reaches the cool water. An old man, who has been dancing

on the greensward, and whose name is Daphnis, gives him some chilled beer and tells him the story of King Natholocus of Scotland, which is broken off when two mechanical dwarves, who have the secret to each other's wind-up mechanism and who are therefore inseparable though they hate one another, undertake in surly fashion to show the narrator the route to the temple. But before he can reach his destination he boards a steamer, where he finds Dr. Jacobi, who will soon tell him of his Alpine experiences hunting a great wyrm or dragon; Don Emanuele Da Ceneda, who will soon tell him of the search for his beloved Stellidaura which has kept him alive for centuries, though this tale is broken off, only to be resumed later, more than once; and Dr. Werkenbarth, the architect of ruins, who tells him immediately the story of the dwarves, and describes to him the vast cigar-shaped underground shelter, capable of housing huge numbers, which he has designed in order to preserve the human race. A man known as Alfred arrives to tell a tale. The steamer continues to move noiselessly through the night. Within some of these stories nest inner stories. The cast then disembarks. They see Nankeen and his troupe of half-naked dancers, who disappear – like some White Rabbit and its progeny – down what seems to be a rabbit hole. It is, of course, the entrance to the underground cigar. The cast follows Nankeen inside, because the war has started. We are one-third the way through the novel, and going deeper.

The style more and more reminds the reader of Jules Verne's insanely methodical recounting of his Extraordinary Voyages, many of which convey one through subterranean Crystal Palaces, through tunnels half-choked by the brass veins of immense machineries whose brows thrust through the floors and walls, until we reach the central chambers or Winter Garden where the President resides, close to the levers of power. We also think of *Metropolis* (1926). The narrator – we are now compressing the tale – inevitably, therefore, meets President Carola deep within the heart of the cigar. He finds he is now a Senator. He is escorted to his bedchamber, where he meets Spring, his attendant, who reads to him the first scenes of a new version of *Oedipus the King;* these scenes are entirely taken up with a Tristram Shandy dialogue between two guards that serves as a potentially interminable prelude to the tragedy itself, which will never be reached. But the narrator falls asleep. On awaking, he tells Spring that he has had a dream. In this dream he feels as though he had toppled upwards into the infinitely large universe of which our galaxy is but a cell, or perhaps downwards into an infinitely small universe within the atoms that live within the atoms. "Still trembling from the horror," he says, "I found myself in a large and elegant house. It was a Monday." In this house live a retired castrato – music figures through *The Architect of Ruins*, just as it has in Rosendorfer's own life – and his seven nieces, whose names begin Do, Re, Mi, etc. Each niece tells the narrator a story. It is the *Decameron*-like heart of the novel. By the end of the sixth story – the seventh is delayed – we are in its closing pages.

At this point, furore and chaos threaten. Ahasuerus the Wandering Jew – whom we have met – now dies, which means the world is ending. Alarums and battles supervene. But the narrator survives, even though a socially conscious dramatist named Uvesohn – it is a jibe on Rosendorfer's part at Uwe Johnson – makes use of his own play to make a ponderous point or two. He rises like a bubble, hearing a few more stories as he rises. Before he reaches the temple, however, he sees Ahasuerus revived, and Dr. Werkenbarth is made Director of Public Ruins for the quality of his work. The puzzle of the sheet of paper covered with dots – or holes – is solved, but the mystery only deepens. The nuns debouch for Lourdes. The novel has ended.

So the outside story, the story told by the narrator himself, the story of his adventures underground, returns full circle. There is no secret about this, and little suspense. Very carefully, whenever the reader might baulk like a horse refusing a blind jump, Rosendorfer calmly and lucidly lays down a cue to notice, a breadcrumb to follow through the forest homewards, for it is none of his intention to construct a labyrinth whose every turning, like a grammar of nightmare, leads the reader deeper and more inextricably into a state of unknowing. His is a labyrinth of return. It is in this that *The Architect of Ruins* differs so markedly from books like Gene Wolfe's *Peace* (1975), which is a posthumous fantasy whose narrator's constantly broken-off stories carry him deeper and deeper into the sphinx chill of a fully realized death; or Robert Irwin's *The Arabian Nightmare* (Dedalus, 1983), whose protagonist sinks deeper and deeper into dreams the ultimate narrator of which – for the protagonist is soon fathoms and aeons adrift from any control over his own story – is almost certainly the Devil. But the narrator of *The Architect of Ruins,* even lying in the arms of President Carola at the bottom of the Jules Verne cigar after the last invasion of the spiders of the enemy from the skies above, never loses his way for more than a moment or two. He does not turn into a nightmare fish in the black waters of unknowing. For he himself is not the creature fish, but a fisher. He is a fisher of stories.

Because there is no exit from *The Arabian Nightmare,* images from Luis Buñuel's *Exterminating Angel* (1962) tend to ghost the mind's eye of readers who've seen the film, and who remember the huge Narrenschiff of a cast which cannot exit the room, cannot escape the story being told about them. Rosendorfer's first novel evokes different Buñuel films, *The Milky Way* (1969), or *The Discreet Charm of the Bourgeoisie* (1972), or *The Phantom of Liberty* (1974). In these films, just as in *The Architect of Ruins,* the emphasis shifts from souls in Hell who cannot find a storyline which will let them out, to the nature of Story itself. The pilgrims of the first film; the survivor flotsam of the second who cannot finish a meal but who will not perish from the earth; the innocent folk of the third who disappear whenever the story-telling camera leaves them: like the dozens of characters who prance and dream through the stories that make up the bulk of Rosendorfer's album novel, their importance to us – and their blamelessness – lies in the fact that they are *being told*.

Later, in *German Suite,* President Carola may turn into an appalling Princess who fucks an ape and refuses to suckle the human child she bears. But now she is innocent of all that, and leaves not a wrack behind when her story turns. She does not, however, seem to die. In a novel about the nature of Story, deaths come – as in Wolfe's novel – when the tale is broken. Time and again, in *The Architect of Ruins,* a story may stop midway through, and we may fear the haemorrhage, the seeping of all the frail concinnities of telling into the stone labyrinth; but then – it may be a hundred pages later – the story will return to us, and be completed, and become whole. Time and again, this does happen. President Carola, and Dr. Werkenbarth, and Ahasuerus reborn, attend upon their tales, and that is the important thing about *The Architect of Ruins*. We do not know, or care, whether Herbert Rosendorfer's novel is a dream, or not a dream. We do know, and care, that it is whole.

Herbert Rosendorfer

THE ARCHITECT OF RUINS

Herbert Rosendorfer

THE ARCHITECT OF RUINS

Anyone getting on a train in which six hundred nuns were setting off on a pilgrimage to Lourdes would be happy to find a compartment to himself, even if he did notice an odd quiet whistling noise and, even worse, a faint cold, stale smell.

Probably the light bulb, I thought to myself; bulbs are like swans, they sometimes sing before they die. I put my case on the luggage rack and opened the window to rid the compartment of all trace of the sweaty feet of the previous occupant. But as the train set off and I sat down and stretched out my legs and tucked my feet under the seat opposite they were gripped tight and held fast.

I dropped my newspaper, the shock took my voice away and I instinctively tried to kick myself free. When I think back to what went through my mind in those fractions of a second, I must admit that my first thoughts were of a boa constrictor.

It was, however, a human being, a man. He was wearing a herringbone tweed coat that was much too heavy for the time of year and much too long for his short body and had incredibly distended pockets, as people do who carry all their belongings with them everywhere. For the moment, though, all I could see was his head, which he stuck out from under the bench.

"Help an unfortunate persecuted man," he whispered, "a victim of his profession."

"Let go of my feet," I said.

"Pull the blinds down over the window to the corridor", the whisper continued, as he shoved my feet away from him.

I hesitated, but then pulled down the grubby fabric of the roller blinds which, on trains, run in little steel tracks and are operated by an awkward leather flap; they tend to catch you by surprise as they shoot straight back up with a noise like a football rattle. Usually there are three blinds altogether: one on the window in the door and two narrower ones on the windows to the right and left. When you have the second one down, the first one shoots back up. Acrobatic contortions might manage to get two of the blinds to stay down for a few seconds. But the slightest little pull on the third sends at least one rattling back up, as if some devilish mechanism had been tripped. Obviously these blinds have been designed with a three-handed man in mind.

When I finally had all blinds fixed down, the man crawled out from under the seat and sat in the corner of the compartment, enveloped in his grubby coat. He was unshaven, his lips red and moist. He kept on whispering, "Thank you, thank you for helping a man pursued."

"I hope", I said, and found I was whispering too, "that it is not the police who are pursuing you."

"I am a victim of my profession", he said. By now I had formed the impression that he had a very sore throat and was incapable of speaking any louder.

"Yes, but burglars who are pursued are also, in a certain sense, victims of their profession."

"I wouldn't have disturbed you at all, believe me, if you hadn't kicked me in the stomach", he said, somewhat offended. "I'm sorry", I whispered back.

"What did you say?"

"I'm sorry", I whispered, bending down to him. He smelt of beer.

"That's all right", he said. "You see, I haven't a ticket."

"I can imagine."

"And certainly not a first class ticket."

"And if the ticket collector should come?" I whispered.

"That's why I asked you to pull the blinds down – the ticket collector will assume you are asleep and knock on the door with his punch before he comes in. When he does, I will disappear immediately. It would be better, too, if we put the lights out."

He stood up and switched off the light. The compartment was illuminated by the tiny blue bulb and, from time to time, the officially-recommended minimum lighting of the sleepy stations we happened to pass.

"A burglar, you think?" he whispered. "No, no. I have had much more recherché professions. I am not the victim of one profession; to be precise, I am the victim of several professions. It runs in the family. We all have ... my brother for example – do you know *The Club of Queer Trades*?"

"Chesterton", I whispered.

"My favourite book. I could add several chapters of my own to it, even without counting my brother. Once, for example, I took the lease on a ladies' sunbathing establishment –"

"Oh là là!" I whispered.

"Yes, that's just what I thought. The previous owner had had a special wall built in the ticket office; from the outside it looked like an ordinary wall, from inside it was a window through which you had a view of the whole sunbathing area. But not many young women came, and even fewer prettier ones – they take their clothes off in other places! No, mostly it was fat old women or skinny old women. They rolled around on the grass like a tangle of albino salamanders and waggled their gnarled old women's toes in the sun. After only a few weeks I was dreaming of ..."

With a noise like a whip-crack one of the blinds shot up and cut off his story. As nimble as a ferret the ex-proprietor of the ladies' sunbathing establishment slipped back under the seat but reappeared as soon as he realised what the cause of the noise was. I pulled the blind down again.

"I can't go on like this much longer", he whispered, a little out of breath. "There, just look at that."

He handed me a grubby piece of paper. All there was to see on it, as far as I could tell in the light from the blue bulb, was a number of little dots.

"What is it?" I whispered.

"My brother ..., but first of all let me tell you how I made my invention. It was while I was in prison –"

"So I was right", I whispered.

"It's not what you think, really; I'm not a criminal. I was in prison because a few times I had spent the night, not completely sober, I must confess, on building sites or in ruined houses. Once

I made the mistake of choosing the garage of a police station. In the middle of the night a policeman peed all over me – not on purpose, I wouldn't dream of accusing the police of a thing like that, I'm sure it wasn't on purpose. I shouted ... But all that's beside the point. – Anyway, the prison was full of creepy-crawlies and it was those bugs which gave me the idea of the automatic cleaning device. If – this was my idea – if you were to attach tiny india rubbers to the feet of the bugs and then let them loose in the room, they would crawl all over the place and rub away the dirt. Bugs are very light in weight, I grant you, so they could not exert much pressure on the rubbers, but they are very determined and crawl around a lot, often in the same area, the frequency was the key. So I drew up plans for a bug attachment to fit the rubbers to their feet. As soon as I had served my sentence I got together with Pussifoote – do you know Pussifoote?"

"No", I whispered.

"Sorry?" he whispered back – the clatter of the wheels over the rails was very loud.

"No."

"You never know. – Well, our first experiments were with dead bugs and then with live ones. But once when I was out of the house that cretin Pussifoote carelessly let all our laboratory insects escape. They crawled everywhere, including over my plans and designs; they erased the lot. When I got back I found my life's work had been destroyed –"

"So you murdered him?" I whispered.

"Pussifoote? Of course not –"

There was a knock at the door which was immediately flung open – but the ex-proprietor of the ladies' sunbathing establishment and bug-tamer was already under his seat. It wasn't the ticket collector who appeared, but the buffet attendant. He was selling refreshments. I ordered two beers.

"Two?" asked the attendant. "Don't you mean one large one?"

"No", I whispered – "No", I said, "two. Two large ones, if you insist."

The attendant poured them out, I paid him, he saluted and

disappeared.

"That's remarkably decent of you", whispered my travelling companion as he crawled out of his hiding place. "How did you know I liked beer?"

"Just an idea."

He took a deep draught. "No, I didn't kill Pussifoote; not quite, anyway. But I did have a good deal of contact with corpses after that. You see I had another innovative idea: an organisation for tailor-made funeral ceremonies. It was somewhat more complicated than the eraser bugs. To understand it you have to have some knowledge of business operations."

"Well, yes", I whispered, "– but tell me: when the buffet attendant put the light on I had a closer look at your piece of paper. What do all those little dots mean?"

"The dots are holes", he whispered.

"Really?" I picked up the piece of paper again.

"They *represent* holes. But more of that later. My funeral organisation was based on the fact that people like to have a splendid funeral, but don't like having to pay for it when they are alive. The fact that rich people in particular tend to be extremely miserly was an added plus for my plan. I drew up contracts with old, rich people – the more infirm they were the better. I guaranteed them the magnificent funeral they desired: wreaths, boys scattering flowers, funeral orations, virgins in mourning, choirs, armies of uniformed pallbearers festooned with flowers and medals, 21-gun salutes, a ballet in black, tableaux vivants representing striking scenes from the life of the deceased ... I even had a composer of funeral anthems under contract. All that is enormously expensive, of course. But that didn't bother the rich old skinflints because they didn't have to cough up anything while they were alive. They – naturally I only took on clients of sound financial standing – merely had to make me a legacy drawn up by a solicitor to cover the sum. If I had really put on the whole pantomime I would have made a profit of roughly three to four percent. But I used to get in touch with the heirs and waive the legacy for ten percent. I was usually given the corpse as a bonus. ... Do you remember those sculptures made of lard you used to see in every butcher's window?

They were often pigs dressed up as butchers carrying a ham over their shoulder with some appropriate pattern carved on it, or the date of the founding of the firm or something of that kind. – No? – I used to make sculptures like that from the corpses. It was almost all clear profit ..."

A second gulp and his beer was gone.

"My mistake was to give way to my artistic ambitions. I exhibited a couple of abstract butcher-pigs in the gallery by St Stephen's Cathedral in Vienna and –"

The door was thrown open, without anyone knocking. My ex-bathing establishment proprietor, bug-trainer and lard-sculpture window-dresser was back under the seat in a flash, but his foot was just caught in the beam of a powerful torch before he could pull it out of sight.

"Come out of there, sir", said a firm voice. "Police."

The light was switched on. Two men, obviously plain-clothes policemen, were in the compartment. With a groan my unknown companion crawled out from under the seat.

"I've only just met him", I said.

"You seriously thought friend Einstein here had a first class ticket?"

"*I* don't own the railway?"

"You can't prove anything, you bloody pigs –"

The younger of the two policemen raised his fist, but the older one restrained him.

"Wait a bit", he said. "Well, friend Einstein, first you travel without paying and then you insult a police officer. Have you got your papers on you?"

My companion spent a long time rummaging round in the inside pocket of his shabby coat. I noticed how his eyes kept darting nervously back and forth; he searched and he searched ... suddenly he leapt up onto the seat and pushed down the window with one hand whilst pulling the communication cord with the other; the train immediately braked sharply, throwing the two policemen off balance so that they fell on top of each other on the seat; I was thrown forward onto the policemen. My companion had obviously worked out the effect of his move precisely and took advantage of the confusion to swing nimbly out of the window.

Before the officers of the law had had time to disentangle themselves and rush to the window he had disappeared in the blackness. The six hundred nuns screamed. The younger policeman blew his whistle. The corridor was jam-packed with further policemen, ticket collectors, buffet-car attendants, other railway officials and countless passengers who were merely curious. The older policeman had difficulty transmitting his orders. The train had to wait. Outside, the police combed the embankment and the immediate vicinity of the train, but the search was pointless: as far as the eye could see the railway was surrounded by rugged country with trees and thick scrub, and the night was dark with only the new moon. I also had the impression that the policemen were none too keen to stray far from the train, presumably so as not to be left behind. The search was soon called off. The nuns calmed down. We continued our journey. The passengers in the corridor returned to their seats and only the older policeman was left with me in the compartment. He needed a statement from me as a witness. I gave him a full account of everything that had occurred, including what the stranger had told me, and the policeman wrote it all down. Then I had to sign it and the policeman sent one of his subordinates, who had stationed himself outside in the corridor, to the buffet car. "Would you like something as well?" he asked

I ordered a coffee and the inspector – I assume that was his rank – four Frankfurters and a beer. Obviously he regarded himself as no longer on duty. "You've no objection to my staying here?" he asked.

"Be my guest", I said.

He made himself comfortable on the seat where, a few moments ago, Einstein had been sitting.

"Waste of time and money", he said. "That's in confidence, of course."

"What has he done?"

"I shouldn't really tell you."

"Well, he doesn't seem to be a murderer, more a bit mad."

"As I said, a waste of time and money. Mad? Any criminal who knows what he's doing pretends to be insane when he appears in court; it's their only defence when there's an open and shut case against them. Some are so good at pretending to be mad that they actually do go mad. But him? Is he mad? That's ..."

His assistant brought the beer, the Frankfurters and the coffee, and was dismissed.

"We couldn't believe our eyes", the Inspector went on with his mouth full of Frankfurter, "when friend Einstein popped up with this 'Panorama Show' as he called it. How he obtained a licence is a mystery to us. His 'Panorama Show' consisted of nothing more than five or six wooden boxes with an eyehole; when you put a coin in, a series of pictures was shown. You also had earphones with background music and explanations to go with the pictures. From the very start we were convinced that the rogue had some sets of obscene pictures, but we could never catch him. He's not only got a nose for everything connected with the police, he knows just about every cop in the district. Whenever one of us appeared, it was always 'Our Alpine Wonderland' he was showing, or 'A Day in the Life of a Fire-fighter' or 'Highlights of the Helsinki Olympics'. I have to confess that we were so desperate to catch him showing obscene pictures that we missed the ploy behind the whole thing: the eyeholes were so low down on the machines that the customers had to bend down to see through them. According to our statistics eighty-five percent of the male population keep their wallets in their back trouser pocket. With their attention distracted and their rear ends poking up in the air, they would have been an easy target for a much less skilful pickpocket than friend Einstein. But, as I said, we missed it because we only had one thing on our minds – obscene pictures ... Until today, that is. One of his customers – who would have imagined it? – had a mousetrap in his pocket; it was set and it caught friend Einstein's fingers ... He's nobody's fool, though. He cleared off straight away and jumped on a train that was leaving. We just happened to be around, still after the obscene photos. A few of my men wanted to jump on after him, but I said, "Stop! That's one of his tricks, I know him of old. He'll jump straight out the other side and quietly slip onto another train whilst we're turning the first train inside out at the next station." So, "Stop!", I said, "friend Einstein is bound to be in this train", the Inspector pointed to the floor. "Of course, when we saw the six hundred nuns I nearly had kittens. It would be just like friend Einstein, I said to myself, to lure a nun to the toilet, steal all her clothes and wander round the train as a Mother Superior, possibly even collecting for some African mission, whilst the poor nun is sitting stark naked on the toilet, too embarrassed to call for help. So we had to check all the nuns – very awkward indeed! We did find a few priests dressed up as nuns, but no Einstein. After we had searched the whole train this was the last compartment we came to."

What are nuns' passport photos like? I wanted to ask. It is a question that has long puzzled me and here was my chance to settle it. Did nuns allow themselves to be photographed in the officially-approved pose with their hair uncovered, the right ear showing? And if so, wouldn't that make them unrecognisable? But the inspector was already standing up and saying goodbye. We were approaching the next stop. All the policemen were getting out there to go back and look for 'friend Einstein'.

If, I thought to myself as I leant back in my seat, toying with the grubby piece of paper that Einstein had left me, if, after he had jumped out of the window, he were to jump right back in, a little farther down the train, for example, and then ... A nun went past in the corridor – ? – perhaps I was mistaken, perhaps she didn't have a five o'clock shadow, perhaps she hadn't winked at me.

I puzzled over the drawing or writing or whatever it was supposed to be on the piece of paper. This is what it looked like:

The dots are supposed to represent holes? I thought. At that very second I was struck by the realisation that I had already lived through this moment before. I closed my eyes. Was it in a former existence? In this one? Or was it a prophecy? It is what is called the 'double twist', a kind of inner second sight. I thought hard ...

The bright sunlit road (where it came from I had no idea) ran past the wall of a country estate. Behind it were tall, spreading trees ten times as high as the wall; like a river in spate, the greenery foamed above the narrow strip of brick.

The pale line of the wall seemed to carry on into infinity. Set into it between two pillars of the faintest red, the gate was like an immense black seal – not one with a coat of arms, but with the convoluted initials of some polyonymous prince of the baroque period. Its weight, obviously the stress had been wrongly calculated, had made one of the pillars lean over and the one side that did open had scraped out a quadrant in the fine gravel of the drive.

The gate swung shut behind me, reuniting the princely initials which now, seen against the road outside shimmering in the full glare of the sun, looked like the seal appended at the bottom of some yellowing parchment conferring privileges which had long since lapsed.

I turned towards the park. Not a sound, apart from the gradual diminuendo of the vibrating gate, disturbed the pale blue of the midday silence stretched above the trees.

I soon came to a path branching off between low yew hedges. Their scent – we are accustomed to associate it with graveyards where twigs of yew stand evergreen in the consecrated water of the little marble vases by the graves – their scent had been concentrated to an unusual degree by the branches of the chestnut trees which joined over the narrow path like the roof of a pergola, or like the waves meeting over the head of a drowned man. There were only delicate little scraps of sky to be seen; its blue, of such intensity it was almost white, peeked almost playfully through the branches. On its way from the white-blue sky down to me under the spreading chestnuts the light went through a kind of transmutation of the kind alchemists used to dream of: it turned to gold. The leaves that, here and there in the depths of the foliage, were struck by a single golden ray, shone like precious fish or like veins of gold, perhaps fool's gold, in dark green crystal mountains.

A further branch of the path led me to a small monument, scarcely the height of a man. In a grotto beneath the shady vault of the chestnuts, on a marble plinth in a grove of dark trees and surrounded by yews clipped into spheres, was a Mourning Spirit: one wing was missing; one elbow was resting on its knee and a laurel wreath drooped over the edge of the plinth from its listless hand. I went up to it and bent down to read the inscription but saw that the letters had broken off. All that remained were the holes in the stone where they had been fixed. The Spirit, who perhaps had once mourned the death of a child princess, had nothing now to mourn, mourned himself and his meaningless-ness, had become Mourning itself ... (as sad as a forgotten word in a dead language, mute, lost without trace in the depths of time, immortal in its oblivion).

As it continued it soon became clear that the path I was following had decided to give up the idea of being a path at all; a thin depression trodden into the dark earth, edged and someti-mes completely overgrown with moss, it twisted left and right. Spreading bushes blocked the view, though more as a game than in earnest. The park was turning into open woodland.

The path did not seem to want to be followed, but I stuck to it obstinately. As it now led downhill, I increased my pace, and waved my arms about – joining in the game – to part the bushes blocking my way. Finally I sensed the ground beneath my feet becoming softer and damper, the moss thicker and, the farther I went, lusher.

When I pushed the last twigs aside I saw that the woods had given way to parkland again. Before me lay a lake, as calm as a flawless slab of polished black stone, set in a circle of weeping willows, with soft, close-cropped grass lining its refreshing banks.

Across the lake, peeping out from the trees like the face of a beautiful countess beneath the hood of her silk cape, a round temple with six pillars stood among clumps of marsh grass on a small hill. I went over to a bench of weathered stone resting against the thick trunk of a willow a few yards away and sat down. Under the canopy of the overhanging branches I was about to indulge in a silent daydream when I heard the gravel of the path behind me crunch as if it were being whirled up at regular intervals. I turned round.

An elderly gentleman with arms outstretched was performing pirouettes and jetés in a stately rhythm. He flexed his knee, pointed his foot, flung his arms down to his sides or up above his head, stretched, bent, stepped – all in a repeated pattern. I was completely still, less so as not to disturb him than because of the feeling of harmony which enthralled me. Finally the dancer noticed me. He paused, seemed undecided and then walked up to me, as rhythmically as before he had danced. I stood up, the apology already forming itself on my lips.

"Good day, sir", he said; obviously the intrusion was not unwelcome.

"Hello", I replied. "I'm afraid I must have disturbed you."

"No need to be afraid", he said, "you have arrived just at the right moment."

He bowed; I had taken my hat off and, as he was not wearing one, I did not put it back on but laid it on the seat.

"Do sit down", he said, "and excuse me a moment. I'll serve you right away, if you don't mind."

I sat down and watched him as he solemnly took a few steps along the short grassy bank, knelt down and pulled a cord that was attached to a little jetty. At the end of the cord two bottles emerged from the water. He untied them and came back to me, a bottle in each hand.

"You arrived just at the right moment", he repeated, handing me the bottle containing the dark liquid. "I hope it's cool enough. You take this one. *I* drink light ale in summer."

I explained that he should not have gone to all that trouble on my account, as I was quite happy to drink light ale in summer, though I did admit to a general preference for all things dark. He immediately offered me his light ale, which I refused.

Cool droplets of water ran down the bottles and moistened our hands, and it was the knowledge that not one of those droplets had managed to penetrate the glass and water down the contents that enriched the sense of harmony that filled me – and, visibly, the dancer – until my whole being vibrated in a rich accord of delicate feelings and inner peacefulness.

After we had drunk the beer he took off his shoes and socks, rolled up his trousers to his knees, went over to the jetty and dipped his feet into the water. I followed him and did likewise. And while we sat there under the huge canopy of the weeping willow that trailed its branches in the water like a curtain made out of flickering strings of oval pearls, the branches parted and a swan appeared out of the web of sunbeams and glided into the soft shade of the willow. The water rippled gently and it was mirrored in delicate reflections that dappled the willow from its crown to the tips of its branches and gave the pearl curtain the illusion of movement.

We waggled our toes in the water and I felt I ought to engage him in conversation in order to repay the refreshment.

I began by saying how strange and extraordinarily sad I found it that the little monument had lost its inscription, so that now no-one would know what the nameless Spirit on the plinth was mourning.

"There is no such monument in the whole park", said the dancer.

I was rather surprised at the brusqueness of his reply, but even more at the fact that he, who even seemed to have been expecting my arrival, should not know the monument. I told him so.

"You would be quite correct in the assumption that I know every tree and every grotto in the park. I'm rather surprised that you of all people should try to tell me about a hitherto unknown monument. Where was it you thought you saw it, roughly?"

I pointed behind us.

"That's the least likely place", he said.

I held my peace.

"The only thing in that direction is the summer residence of King Nathalocus."

As I had only brought it up to pass the time, I did not insist, but thought a change of subject appropriate:

"Who is King Nathalocus?"

"King Nathalocus is dead. A long time ago he ruled over Scotland and fell victim to the jealousy of an evil witch."

"How did that come about?"

"You're interested in the story?" The dancer took a little volume that looked very old out of his pocket and opened it where a bookmark had been inserted. "I expected that and came prepared. Listen." He began to read:

At about the time of the Emperor Decius there ruled in Scotland a king by the name of Atrich. This king was a tyrant who had no thought for his kingdom but rather spent his nights and days kissing and caressing the ladies of the court; in his cruel lechery he mocked the noblewomen by compelling them to wait on him unclothed at table – and elsewhere; he would have several stable wenches baked in a pie who, when he had nibbled and licked his way through the crust, danced on the table before him. Whilst he gave himself over to these and other lewd practices, Queen Bertha his wife, a witch, slaked her lust on the scullions and Moorish footmen of the palace, that one may search the whole of history and not find their like for wanton lasciviousness.

Two youths alone from the noblest houses of the land, Lord Nathalocus and Lord Findoch, had kept apart from the dissipation of the court and had withstood the wiles of the witch Bertha who lusted after them both for their manly beauty.

It is no surprise that, in a realm where the king concerned himself more with peasant trollops, whom he forced naked noblewomen to wait upon, than with his treasury and his army, there was soon a group of discontented nobles who, at first behind closed doors and then loudly and in public, demanded the King should be deposed. When the King refused to come to reason and continued in his swinish ways more boldly than ever, the disgruntled lords finally chose Nathalocus and Findoch as their leaders and marched on the royal palace.

When the King, whose sole army consisted of piefuls of stable wenches and naked ladies – he had, you will recall, completely neglected military matters – saw that he was surrounded by his enemies, he despaired, and before the fortress was captured he took his own life and several of his strumpets down to Hell with him.

Now Nathalocus and Findoch, with that modesty that was their noblest virtue, each wanted to yield the throne to the other as successor to the evil Atrich. As there was but one King of Scotland at any one time, the two lords, whom the other nobles had left the choice, agreed to decide by lot, and it fell upon Nathalocus. Thus Nathalocus became King of Scotland at the time of Decius, the cruel persecutor of the faithful. The new King remained bound in love to his friend Findoch and set him at his right hand.

But the witch Bertha had, by means of her magic powers, escaped unnoticed from the palace. She changed her appearance; telling no-one who she was, she set up her house in the woods and was soon famed throughout the kingdom as one who could tell the future, read it in the lines of a hand or in the stars, and could use her powers to ward off ills from any animal. And so it happened that news of the great witch reached the court, where Good King Nathalocus ruled with his bosom friend Findoch. And the King decided to send to her to know what the future held in store for him.

Who better to entrust with this task than his faithful friend Findoch? So the King sent him to the witch, and when he stood before her she saw – she, of course, knew who he was – that her hour had come. With baneful mien she questioned the trusty Findoch, ...

The dancer put the book down and looked at me in silence for a while.

"Tell me", he said eventually, "have you come to discover the secret of the 'Nameless Mourning Spirit'?"

"No", I said, "I saw the monument purely by chance and didn't imagine there was anything secret about it. I thought you didn't know it?"

"For certain reasons", he said, "I am vowed to silence. There –", he pointed to the temple on the other side of the lake, "while you will not learn what the Spirit means, I'm

31

sure they will be able to help you."

"But, really, I didn't come here because of the monument. — It doesn't seem far to the temple, though ..."

"You have to go round the lake. As far as the distance is concerned, however, it's easy to be mistaken."

I looked at him thoughtfully.

"It won't be a tragedy if I don't reach it", I said.

"Good", he said. "I'll accompany you a little way."

We put our shoes and socks back on, rolled our trousers down again and I followed the dancer, who set off away from the shore of the lake and pushed his way through the sloebushes. Sooner than I had expected we reached a broad gravel path.

Just as he was telling me which way to go I noticed two small men, no more than two feet high, standing motionless and staring at us.

"Oh!", said my companion turning his head away. He seemed to have become uneasy, jittery. "The figure-of-eight painters. Do excuse me, I have business elsewhere. You'd better ask those two the way. — Farewell."

"But the story of King Nathalocus of Scotland?"

"Some other time", he said. "My name is Daphnis the Dancer. You'll almost always find me near the weeping willow by the stone bench ... And now, farewell."

He disappeared into the sloes like a man diving into water.

The dwarves were standing under the reclining statue of some deity, the spirit of a spring or bridge. They were hand in hand, and yet, in spite of this fraternal posture, their eyes were the eyes of mortal enemies bound together. I approached them. I was embarrassed at being so much taller than they were so I addressed them in the politest manner possible:

"Hello", I said. "Mr Daphnis, with whom, my dear sirs, you just saw me, assured me that you —"

"I don't care tuppence", said one of the dwarves, "what Mr Daphnis assured you!"

"*We* don't!" added the other.

"So there!" the first went on. They stared at me with a hostile look, as if they were expecting an answer which they knew in advance would be another provocation. In the circumstances it was not surprising that I had some difficulty in finding a reply.

I thought for a while and decided to rely on the truth. "I would very much like", I said, "to find my way to the round temple that you can see from this side of the lake."

"We don't care tuppence about what you would like, nohow", said the first dwarf. Because of the general feeling of guilt a person of normal stature has when confronted with a midget, I found I could not descend to insults. As I was trying to concoct a reply the dwarves continued to stare at me fixedly, then, still holding hands, they suddenly turned on their heels, and set off in the direction of a bridge which, broader than it was long, crossed an outlet – or possibly an inlet – of the lake. I was uncertain what to do, but the second dwarf turned round, without letting go of the hand of his brother – at least that was what I assumed the relationship between them was, although I didn't consciously use that word – and shouted back to me:

"If you want to find the way to the temple you'll have to follow us, you ninny!"

I followed hesitantly. When the two reached the bridge they appeared to be turning off along a rough track that led along the watercourse. Again the second dwarf turned round, stuck his tongue out at me and said – I could scarcely understand what he said because he kept his tongue stuck out as he spoke:

"That way –"

He described a semi-circle with his head, using his tongue as a direction marker, as it were; it pointed over the bridge.

Hand in hand, and without looking back at all, the dwarves disappeared among the tall rushes.

I soon reached the top of a small rise from which there was an extensive view. The lake was hidden behind wooded hills. What one could see from this point was not parkland, but open countryside. Whether it was because I was on an open hilltop or because it was now the afternoon, I could feel a gentle breeze, so gentle it was hardly even a breeze, more the caress of the soft air. The towering inferno of the midday heat seemed to have burnt itself out. In a thousand ever-changing colours from the richest velvety green to a shimmering lavender-blue, the tree-tops shaded into the distance, becoming fainter until they hovered like a gauzy film over the horizon.

Below me, at the foot of the rise, was a river. Only a short stretch was visible, where the path led down to the water, and there, too, half hidden by the trees along the bank, was the little steamship ...

"That was Schizion and Pythicles", said Weckenbarth, the architect of ruins – he was Senior Adviser on Public Ruins –, "the figure-of-eight painters."

"Mechanical dwarves", added Dr. Jacobi.

"Not human beings, then?" I asked.

We were sitting in wicker chairs on the afterdeck of the little steamship which was so low in the water that the rail was scarcely knee-height above the surface. Its two-storied superstructure ran the whole length of the ship; it was supported by cast-iron pillars and the sides were made of alternate sheets of glass and enamelled metal, with wrought-iron panels between. Desultory plumes of smoke wafted from the two almost perpendicular funnels, which were painted green and reinforced with occasional brass rings. We were on the roof of the first storey – on the lower deck.

"Not human beings", laughed Weckenbarth, "but hostile brothers. A somewhat eccentric engineer, or so the story goes, wanted to construct a mechanical servant. He designed it as a dwarf because, as we all know, giant robots tend to turn against their masters. Dwarf robots may well do that too, but they're easier to deal with. To start with this engineer – Quirk was his name – constructed two prototypes, neither of which was perfect. But before he could combine the positive qualities of each of them to create the ideal dwarf, he died. At least before that happened he managed to make a virtue of necessity and linked them to one another: each runs for twenty-four hours when it's wound up. The mechanism of one dwarf always runs down when the other still has twelve hours to go and each mechanism has a device that causes it to wind the other one up at the appropriate time. They are technological Siamese twins, chained to each other, although each envies the other for the good qualities the other has that he lacks. Only they know how to repair each other, only Schizion and no-one else, not even Pythicles, knows how Pythicles works, and vice versa. If one of them were to refuse to wind the other up when it was time, he would only be destroying himself, and in order not to risk their lives – or, rather, their mechanisms – they have to keep fairly close to each other all the time. Together they are almost the realisation of perpetual motion, only the eventual wear and tear on their components means they will gradually grind to a halt. Separate them and in twenty-four hours at the most they would be dead – or, rather, broken."

"Interesting", I said.

"Exemplary", said Dr. Jacobi.

The other gentleman, Don Emanuele Da Ceneda, the fourth in our group, whom I merely mention to note his presence, said – as he had done all along – nothing.

"They are employed by a man called Riedl", continued Weckenbarth, "as figure-of-eight painters."

"Figure-of eight painters?"

"Riedl is an eccentric", said Weckenbarth. "I'm not acquainted with him myself, but my brother used to work – occasional economic necessity, you know – for a few months each year in Riedl's factory. Riedl runs an acetylene works, though runs is something of an exaggeration, it's more the opposite: he is doing everything to try and run the factory *down*, but it's no good because he enjoys an almost complete monopoly. I can give you an example: Riedl is extremely sensitive to noise. As he loves farming, he keeps hens, but only old hens who don't lay any more – and don't cackle either. Once a month, so my brother told me, the whole factory was shut down and the employees, forty in all, had to line up in a row in the field behind the factory and scour it for stones, so that Riedl's cow wouldn't hurt her mouth when grazing. To return to his sensitivity to noise, though: no-one was allowed to start a lorry in the factory grounds, they had to be pushed by hand until they were out of hearing. Once a customer left his car door open with the radio on and it came to Riedl's ears – literally – and the driver was immediately informed that Riedl had decided he could do without orders from that particular company.

However, Riedl is also keen on sport. As well as archery, he is an avid rollerskater. He had one of the machine-shops in the factory cleared so that he could practise rollerskating. There is a huge figure of eight painted on the floor which Riedl tries to negotiate on Sunday mornings, in the sole presence of the factory foreman, Leinharting, who is paid double time to applaud particularly well-skated figures of eight with enthusiastic – discreetly enthusiastic – cheers. It was to paint these figures of eight, and to renovate them later on whenever the managing director had worn them away, that the mechanical dwarves were employed. That's why they are called figure-of-eight painters, it's quite straightforward. My brother", he said, "could tell you a whole series of stories about Riedl."

As imperceptibly as the afternoon had gradually given way to the evening twilight, the steamer had left its moorings.

The long shadows of the trees cast by the setting sun almost reached the opposite bank, leaving a narrow, uneven strip of water to glow reddish gold in the dying light. The heat of the day was a memory, only its peacefulness remained. The bushes swayed gently in the soft breeze. The branches of the weeping willows swayed in the scarcely perceptible current. Wherever a gap revealed some still sunlit clearing with lush grass and stone benches, it would not have surprised me to see a shepherd weeping for his lost Phyllis or a group of shepherdesses dancing to a rigadoon played by a crafty but otherwise harmless satyr on the mouth organ.

"The still of the evening", I said, after a pause during which all had been silent – which convinced me that they shared my feelings – "if it would only remain so, that our souls might be held in repose for all eternity."

"What do you mean by that?" said Dr. Jacobi after a further pause.

"Nothing", I said. "I meant – mean is wrong – it *seemed* to me, contemplating this evening, as if it were the peace that passeth all understanding, the primal condition of the world, the eternal, deep and unruffled joy of content, or something –"

"But the world is not eternal?"

"I didn't mean to imply that."

"Well", said Dr. Jacobi, and made a brief gesture to indicate that his remark was intended to finish the equally brief discussion, "I would not like to be counted amongst those of whom it is written that they deceive the people by saying, 'The time is come'."

"But that very thing", said Weckenbarth, "would be a sign that the end of the world is nigh."

"Yes", said Dr. Jacobi, "the false prophets. I do not feel it is my place" – he looked at me earnestly, placing his hand over his heart – "to interpret Holy Writ, but as you have raised the question ..."

"Nothing was farther from my mind, Dr. Jacobi."

"Of course not", said Weckenbarth, "but we can't keep avoiding the subject for ever. Theory" – here he turned to me – "is not for me; practical matters, that's my field. Dr. Jacobi, he's your man for theory. Nothing against theory!" He laughed and patted Jacobi on the shoulder. "Dr. Jacobi... ?"

"Well", Dr. Jacobi looked at me, "if you compare the Gospels, you will notice that three are in full agreement –"

"Only three?" asked Weckenbarth.

"The fourth has nothing to say on the matter", said Dr. Jacobi, "– that three are in full agreement: the disciples asked the Lord about the end of the world. The Lord ignored the question about the precise moment and merely counselled them to be watchful. As always, He made His meaning plain through a parable. In this case, if I remember rightly, amongst others through the parable of the wise and foolish virgins."

"That means", Weckenbarth took up the argument, "that there will be an end of the world."

"Yes", said Dr. Jacobi, "and when they pressed Him, the Lord did not leave them completely without indications. We are meant to know when the time is near. These indications are: –"

"A thousand years yet not a thousand years", I said.

"That is a saying which I have not found in the Bible, nor the one that the dispersed Jews would not return to the Promised Land until –"

"Both apply to the present, though", said Weckenbarth.

"But – are you assuming then that the end of the world is nigh?" I asked.

"Not perhaps quite *nigh*", said Dr. Jacobi. "The Lord – to return to the Scriptures – gave a number of concrete indications of the imminence of the end of the world: the sun and the moon shall be extinguished and the stars fall from the sky. The sense of that is presumably that the rotation of the earth will become irregular. The fires and floods that are mentioned point to that interpretation. But, as I said, all that comes immediately before Christ's return, with the Angels' first blasts on the trumpet, so to speak. Other, less immediate clues, I have already indicated: the false prophets. Oh, and before I forget: the Gospel must be proclaimed to all nations. Proclaimed! – It doesn't have to have been accepted."

"That condition", said Weckenbarth, "has been fulfilled. We checked with the Holy Office."

"Well", I said, "that condition really goes without saying. If people aren't given the chance to choose the true faith, then –"

"True, true", Dr Jacobi dismissed my comment. "But listen to the theory we have worked out about the false prophets: the false prophets preach a doctrine of their own, a convincing one, they perform miracles and imitate the Lord. Who does that apply to, today? Who performs miracles today? There aren't any miracles any more, you will say ... But", he laughed, "the false prophets, that is to say the false prophet, there is only one and he is too clever to use the word miracles, or then only ironically. He says, 'I need no miracles and yet nothing is impossible to me.' That is why they all flock to him ... You still can't guess who it is? I'll tell you a few of his 'miracles', compared with which the loaves and fishes and the raising of Lazarus were harmless tricks. Through this false prophet you can speak here and be heard a thousand miles away; there is even another 'miracle' by which you can be seen. He can preserve your face, your voice, and anyone who so desires can see and hear you after your death. He can make you fly through the air, and even eat, drink and sleep there; he can perform a million calculations in a second. He can make a mouse grow as big as an elephant and he can fly around the moon. He can make gunpowder from air, paints from bitumen and paper from rubbish ... Are all these things not miracles? – Excuse me for going on, you have long since guessed what I'm getting at – the great false prophet who performs these miracles is technology. They all have one little snag, though: you can, if you are patient enough, come to understand how they work. But that, say the scientists, is the greatest miracle, the fact that they are not miracles at all. Oh, those who follow the false prophet are the blindest of all – for the last two hundred years it has been fashionable – they think it is completely safe because *everything can be explained* ... The blindness of enlightenment."

Weckenbarth turned to me. "Dr. Jacobi has written a book with that title", he whispered.

"Technology", said Dr. Jacobi, "has become a false god with its own rituals, prophecies and legions upon legions of priests. Which is not to say that all technologists are its blind priests –" quickly he turned to Weckenbarth "– here is a man of technology who has not been seduced by the false prophet."

Weckenbarth gave a shy, embarrassed little laugh.

"We – that is, our good friend Weckenbarth", Dr. Jacobi continued, "has turned technology against itself. But he is the person to tell you about that."

Weckenbarth still had an embarrassed smile on his face at the praise. After a certain amount of modest protestation, he began:

"Our starting point was the assumption that survival is important. Recent developments in weapon technology, so-called 'superbombs' and the latest armaments, which one can scarcely call weapons in the traditional sense – I'm not allowed to say anything about them at this moment – mean that it is quite possible for mankind itself to spark off the End of the World, and mankind means the generals and the generals means chance. Our second assumption, then, was the depressing recognition of the fact that the End of the World is technically possible – technically, mind you – at any minute ... Even if you only look at the relatively harmless bomb on Hiroshima, there were people, Japanese, who ... you must understand, I'm a technologist and I call a spade a spade – who simply evaporated. Death by evaporation; from man to steam in –" he gave the briefest of whistles – "one second flat. Given that – but here we're back with the theory. Dr. Jacobi, wouldn't you like to continue?"

Weckenbarth was silent and for a while Dr. Jacobi said nothing, either. He began his exposition with a question:

"Do you believe in life after death?"

" – Yes", I said.

"Do you believe in Heaven and Hell?"

"I haven't thought about that for a long time."

"We –", he pointed to Weckenbarth, Don Emanuele Da Ceneda and himself, "we believe in them. Not in the form of a fiery Hell with lots of little souls being poached in cannibals' cooking-pots, as they teach children; not even", he smiled, "in the rather less crude version that Dante describes. We believe in the separation of Heaven and Hell rather in the manner of – Weckenbarth, you tell him the parable."

"After lift-off a spaceship, with all its booster rockets and so forth, has to reach a certain speed before it can escape from – for simplicity's sake, let's say from the terrestrial sphere."

"The speed", I said, "must be great enough for it to overcome the earth's gravitational pull."

"Yes, but that is not the important point here. This is: *once it has left the terrestrial sphere, a rocket retains the speed it had at the moment it entered 'space'*. That's it; there is absolutely no way the speed can be changed."

"And it is the same with the soul", continued Dr. Jacobi. "– I have written a book on that as well." With visible satisfaction, he flicked some cigar ash off his waistcoat, though without noticing that it landed on his trousers. "You believe in life after death. I say: consciousness after death. And is it not reasonable to believe that our consciousness after death should depend on the state of our consciousness *before* death? You should think about that ... or read my book ... Do you know", he went on quickly, "how I would like to die? At one of those moments of sublime pleasure, listening to the adagio from the Prague symphony, for example, or to the first movement –", with tears in his eyes and a touching solemnity he gave the complete title, "– of the Quartet in D minor for two violins, viola and cello, Opus posthumus, known as 'Death and the Maiden'. I imagine

I would be transformed into one of those ethereally joyful melodies of Mozart or Schubert and resound from eternity to eternity." He smiled again in an attempt to control his emotion. "For me, Mozart and Schubert are the twin peaks of music. – And yes", now he was laughing, "I've written a book about that too."

"It is in order to grant Dr. Jacobi that final wish", said Weckenbarth, "and to save many others from being surprised by death, from an *accidental* death –"

"From death as a waste product of the holocaust, so to speak –", interrupted Dr. Jacobi.

"– such as the death by evaporation of the Japanese, it is to allow them to come through the end of the world – which, in our opinion, is nigh – unscathed and to soar into the hereafter in a state of complete mental and spiritual harmony, that we have –"

"– he has –", said Dr. Jacobi.

"– built a tower. Well, 'tower' is misleading, 'inverse tower' might be more accurate, a tower that goes down into the earth. Just imagine a gigantic cigar going straight down into the ground; only a one hundred and twenty-fifth part of it is above ground, and that part is as high as the dome of St Peter's in Rome – right down to the last millimetre, we attach great importance to symbolism! The whole thing is pretty extensive."

"And costs a pretty penny!" said Don Emanuele Da Ceneda, who must have been listening to the conversation after all.

"Yes, true", said Weckenbarth in a tone full of the satisfaction of problems solved and difficulties overcome. "But then the 'cigar' has room for a good three million people."

"And for my instruments", said Dr. Jacobi; "a Guarneri and an Amati – an Amati cello of somewhat dubious authenticity, but still – and a viola by Albani ..."

"He came from the South Tyrol, like me", I said, just in order to say something.

"Weckenbarth will play the second violin", said Dr. Jacobi, "Don Emanuele the viola" – Don Emanuele Da Ceneda sketched a bow – "I myself will play the first violin."

"I would not only be willing, but very grateful if you would allow me to take the cello."

"The quartet we have in mind is extremely demanding", said

Dr. Jacobi gravely.

"And unfortunately", I gave a sigh, "the first movement in particular. If only the last movement were the most difficult, when it came to the crunch we wouldn't get that far ..."

A steward went up to Weckenbarth and they held a whispered conversation. He then whispered to Dr. Jacobi. Dr. Jacobi put his head on one side, whistled softly and was for his part about to whisper to Don Emanuele, but he just said, "Me too, me too."

Weckenbarth leant over to me, "Would you like chicken or would you prefer fish?"

"I'm quite happy to go along with the rest."

Weckenbarth nodded to the young man, who bowed and left.

"Perhaps you would be interested to hear a few technical details on the construction of our giant cigar", said Weckenbarth to me.

"Yes", I said. "The outer layer the thickest ferro-concrete possible, I assume –"

"Quite the opposite", said Weckenbarth, "the outer film is so thin you could push your hand through it: specially treated aluminium foil. The age of mechanised warfare is past – no more atom bombs or helium bombs, they can easily be neutralised. No, there is a new strategy. As I said, I cannot reveal the details ... However, what it does mean is that the world will not end in the way envisaged by Brother Emman –"

"Who is Brother Emman?" I asked.

"Brother Emman? You don't know the story of Brother Emman? It happened in the first year of the pontificate of John XXIII; in actual fact Brother Emman was a paediatrician in Milan by the name of Bianca. In 1945 he received through occult channels a message from his dead sister to the effect that as a result of human error an atomic bomb would be set off and destroy most of mankind. It was to occur before the 1960 Olympic Games.

From that moment on Dr. Bianca called himself Brother Emman, founded a sect, for which he even created a special language, and, with the help of a so-called 'Book of the Prophet Jesaja', worked out the precise minute the catastrophe would take place: Bastille Day 1960, at 1.45 p.m.

Over the years he established psychical contact with the cream of the world's dead writers: Demosthenes, Lao Tse, Dante, Petrarch; finally he managed to reach the Angel Gabriel who put him through to some heavenly being – precisely what kind was not said – who went by the name of 'Logos'. From these contacts Dr. Bianca learnt that the accidental atomic explosion would cause the earth's axis to tilt through forty-five degrees so that all the land would be flooded by the sea. Only the Tibetans – who else! – would survive, less because of the wall of the Himalayas than because of their notorious mystical protection. Perhaps there was something in Dr. Bianca's conclusion that a world in which the Tibetans were the sole survivors would not be much of a place. He bought a house – there was money aplenty from the contributions the members made to the sect's funds – on the slopes of Mont Blanc, above Courmayeur, and called it 'Gehavonise' which, in his private Esperanto, meant 'To the Glory of God'.

In the spring of 1960 Brother Emman made his final preparations. He had food, blankets, medicines and coal delivered to Mont Blanc – on credit, wherever possible, as he was firmly convinced that with the end of the world all his debts would be written off. Motor cars were towed up with barrels upon barrels of petrol. His debts were running into six figures when, at the beginning of July, Dr. Bianca realised that, for all the petrol he had stored, the cars would be of dubious value in a postdiluvian world. As another nought on the end of his debit balance seemed an irrelevancy, he quickly had three motor boats, one sailing yacht and countless inflatable dinghies sent up to Mont Blanc. Perhaps it was the picture that appeared in every newspaper of the yacht in full sail on the glacier below the Aiguilles that sent a tremor of disquiet out from Brother Emman's small group of the elect through the whole world. The one who suffered most from the universal trepidation was, of course, the operator of the cable railway at Courmayeur. The rush – the precise figures have been recorded: it was 550 from Italy, 151 from France, 108 from Britain, and so on, down to the 99 from China and one from Liechtenstein – was too much for him and he collapsed with a nervous breakdown.

In Bologna the Church of St Anthony had to be closed on the morning of 14 July because of the crush of people wanting confession. In London a quiet little Chelsea pub called 'The Armageddon' was overwhelmed with a similarly violent crowd drawn as if by magic. The Mufti of Syria delivered a public condemnation of the prophecies of Brother Emman as being contrary to the teachings of Islam. On the morning of 14 July a woman from Athens rang up the Vatican and asked to discuss the End of the World with the Pope.

The whole affair was given a disturbing touch by the fact that on the night of 14-15 July there was in fact a mild earth tremor recorded in the Mont Blanc area. But that was all. When, on the 15 July Dr. Bianca broke the seal and came out of 'Gehavonise', the first thing he was confronted with was a horde of scornful journalists – who, by the way, would have been unjustly saved had he been right – and then by an even greater horde of creditors. Fortunately for him, he managed to cross the frontier into Italy where he was immediately arrested and thus managed to escape his disciples, who wanted money from him to get the motor boats taken back down Mont Blanc.

He was given three years, for fraud. Afterwards he emigrated. Where? To India, of course."

Dr. Jacobi laughed. "I can still see the picture in the newspapers: a somewhat stocky, somewhat mature woman in knickerbockers – one of Emman's disciples – blowing a trumpet to call the faithful to the end of the world that didn't take place."

"A poor substitute for the Last Trump", I said.

"Which we, for our part, intend to drown with a string quartet", said Don Emanuele Da Ceneda.

"Let us hope", I said, "that the Last Trump and our quartet are in the same key."

"But my dear Sir", said Dr. Jacobi, "we will be playing in D minor. Can you imagine the Last Trump in that key?"

"When I think", said Weckenbarth, "that our salvation ... on the other side ... depends, at least in theory, on our having four instruments available; and, even more, that we have to rely on none of us making a mistake in all the excitement so that we don't stumble over into the afterworld on a discordant note ...

Would it perhaps not be safer to practise some beautiful *a cap-ella* part-song, say the madrigal 'Luci serene e chiare' by Luca Marenzio?"

Dr. Jacobi laughed. "One of us could always have a sore throat! And anyway, with the four of us, the best we could have would be a barber-shop quartet; I hardly think 'Chattanooga choo-choo' would be the ideal vehicle for our journey to the afterlife!"

"That's enough for now", said Weckenbarth. "The world's not going to end today."

"Certainly not before dinner", said Don Emanuele Da Ceneda.

"Let us not be too facetious", Dr. Jacobi gave an amused and slightly malicious smile, "there are other possible scenarios besides our theory: the fungus of humanity is spreading over the planet; there will come a point – and it is not very far off – when it covers the face of the earth completely, and at that point the fate of our poor old world will be sealed."

"Wouldn't it be possible to calculate the time it will take for that to happen?"

"Well, yeees", said Weckenbarth, "except that we do not know to what extent the parameters will be affected by the 'population reversal initiative'."

"Population reversal initiative?" I asked.

"At first glance it does seem odd", said Weckenbarth, "that the impulse for this initiative should have come from the Department of Music at the University of Munich, but that was the case. However, I anticipate:

The increase in the world's population is like an avalanche or, to be more precise, takes the form of a geometric series: if there are six million today, tomorrow there will be twelve, and twenty-four million the day after tomorrow – and that is not taking into account the fact that people are living longer as well. Even assuming all possible advances in food technology, there is an upper limit to the productive capacity of the earth. I needn't go into the anarchy that would ensue if it were reached ... It was to forestall such a situation that quite early on attempts were made to introduce a programme of population control, and it was *India* that led the way. Whilst other countries were still granting large families tax allowances and child benefit, India had already introduced a tax on children. To have two children was a luxury. With the introduction of this tax the money poured into the state coffers and it was used – that is, that part that did not go to grease local palms – for grants to those who voluntarily allowed themselves to be sterilised. People who had been sterilised were given preferential treatment and were given, besides the grants, all the best jobs. The Civil Service was reserved for those who had been sterilised. Senior ranks in the army, the top positions in the yoga academies, in brief, all the lucrative posts with the best openings for bribery and corruption, even, eventually, the diplomatic service, were in the hands of eunuchs. A new voice was heard in the concert of nations – the Indian castrato.

Sooner or later it was bound to happen that the West – which has, as you know, a weakness for all things Indian – would follow the same course. And, as I mentioned at the start, it all started in the Music Department of the University of Munich which was thus indirectly the unlikely cause of Uncle Heino's – a cousin of my mother's – Oedipal tragedy.

You will be aware that in Germany shortly after the so-called First World War there began a movement we can call the 'Handel Renaissance': musicians began to excavate the apparently inexhaustible goldmine of baroque music which had been sealed off for some time. Music groups were formed which played on viols, on theorbos, on the baryton and even on the hurdy-gurdy. The organ-builders removed the pneumatic chests that the so-called progressive nineteenth century had had installed in the Silbermann organs. There was only one musical form that it seemed impossible to restore to its original glory – but that was the one in which baroque music had found its fullest expression: opera! And the reason for that was one single, minute aspect: the Italian baroque opera stands and falls with the castrato! It is only the genuine castrato voice that can cope with coloratura passages and other demands on lung capacity that are beyond any female soprano.

The fact that it was impossible to produce an opera in Munich

– if memory serves me right, the one in question was Pergolesi's *Olimpiade* – with the original voices, led an ingenious lecturer in the Music Department, a Dr. Mitterwurzer, who was not thinking of an immediate realisation, but of a more distant future, to approach the Federal Ministry for Family Affairs. Switching from musicology to Malthusianism, he published a long paper depicting the dangers of overpopulation. One appendix to this epoch-making work mentioned the reappearance of the castrato as one of the desirable consequences of the new population policy.

Long after his death, Mitterwurzer's ideas were being realised on a scale he would never have envisaged. Although the impulse that had led to the whole development was long since forgotten, the Cathedral Choir School in Regensburg had become the leading school for castrati. Every year they opened the Festival in Bayreuth – you may not be old enough to remember this, but it used to be devoted entirely to the works of a Saxon composer popular in Victorian times, called Robert Wagner – with a gala performance of *Olimpiade* in remembrance of Mitterwurzer.

All that had nothing to do with my unfortunate uncle, Heino Pramsbichler. My uncle was merely one official in the bureaucratic network which the new Department of Family Development established throughout the country. There were medical sections, which developed and supervised the programme of sterilisation, and administrative ones, to which my Uncle Heino belonged, which carried out the countless bureaucratic procedures thought necessary, issued the various certificates and paid the not inconsiderable sum which, on the Indian model, the government had set as an incentive for voluntary sterilisation.

'Sterilisation' was much too straightforward an expression for a German government department to use. The technical term was 'deovulation' or 'despermification', depending on sex. My uncle was Executive Officer in the Deovulation Section, later Chief Executive Officer. Year in, year out he performed his duties without the least suggestion of a black mark appearing on his record. This meant that once he had reached a certain age – the age by which the Ministry assumed all interest in matters of sex had disappeared – he qualified for transfer to the position of Post-operational Scrutineer. The procedure for 'Deovulation' was as follows: the person in question – the 'deovulee' to use the official term – went to an authorised doctor who performed the operation and then placed his official stamp on the loins of the deovulee. The latter then went to the Deovulation Section where the stamp was checked by the Post-operational Scrutineer, cancelled and the incentive paid out.

The Scrutiny was a somewhat embarrassing procedure and took place in an office with two sets of doors. My uncle was in his fifty-eighth year and in his twenty-third in government service when, one afternoon, Emma Holzmindel appeared in the line of recent deovulees. Uncle Heino did not look up, he was still completing the papers for the previous case and he merely said, 'Sit down'. Emma sat down.

'Name?' Uncle Heino still did not look up.

'Holzmindel; Emma Holzmindel.'

'Age?'

'Eighteen.'

Uncle Heino did look up. He saw a girl with reddish blonde hair and a generous figure. A flattish face, broadish cheeks, somewhat pale – but that was probably the result of the recent sterilisation – and a fascinating birthmark right on the edge of the lip which gave the corner of her mouth a captivating nuance of melancholy. Her whole person had a physical presence which conjured up thoughts which were anything but chaste.

'Fräulein –' Uncle Heino gulped, 'Holzmindel, will you take your clothes off please.'

'What? Again?'

'Nothing to worry about. I just have to check the stamp.'

Fräulein Holzmindel stood up, turned round and undid a zip down the side of her dress. She performed a kind of belly dance to make the dress slip to the ground and then stepped out of it in her red, cut-away high-heeled shoes.

Uncle Heino sighed.

'Sorry?' asked Fräulein Holzmindel.

'Address?'

'16, Bolland Street, first floor, on the right.'

48

Emma had unbuttoned her blouse and let it float to the ground. Like two exotic blooms peeping over the rim of a rather narrow vase, her shoulder blades and other adjacent curves overhung the white lace bodice. She turned round.

'More –?'

How many persons of – more or less – female sex had he already examined unmoved? It must have been fate itself that had eaten away the pedestal of his steadfastness and pitched him head first into the delicious foaming surf and swept him off to the alabaster cliffs of fleshly desire – do you not agree, Dr. Jacobi?"

Dr. Jacobi scratched his chin. Weckenbarth continued:

"Like two richly decorated goblets foaming at the brim, the lacy cups of her bodice could scarcely restrain the downy pink flesh ...

'More –' asked Emma.

Uncle Heino came to with a start. 'I – I have to check your stamp.'

Emma undid her bodice. Uncle Heino's head was reeling: amidst the glories that were exposed to his view was the fascinating birth mark from the right-hand corner of her mouth repeated just at the top of her left breast.

How many stamps had Uncle Heino scrutinised without any thought other than for official procedures?

'The stamp', groaned Uncle Heino. 'I still can't see the stamp.'

One last scrap remained, scarcely larger than a handkerchief, filmy as a cobweb, moulded to the contours of her body. Not without difficulty Emma pulled it down over her thighs and dropped it on Uncle Heino's desk.

Now the purple stamp was visible.

'Over there –' with an exhausted gesture Uncle Heino pointed to the sofa covered with white waxcloth.

With a graceful flick of the ankles, Emma divested herself of the red high-heeled shoes.

My uncle took out his government-issue magnifying glass ...

After Emma had left he locked up his desk, even though it was only half past four, tidied away the remaining files and sent a message to the deovulees waiting outside that, due to a committee meeting, office hours were finished for the day. Those outside, all of whom had an appointment, muttered amongst themselves and went home. As one of them made an official complaint, Uncle Heino received a reprimand from his superior. But Uncle Heino no longer cared a fig for an official reprimand."

Weckenbarth paused. From behind us came a series of blood-curdling grunts. I swung round. A negro wearing an apron that reached from his chin to the ground and brandishing a bloody knife was rushing towards Weckenbarth. The shock of it paralysed me so that had he been a murderer I would not have even been able to warn him. But it was only the cook, who had slaughtered the chickens and had come to fetch Weckenbarth to the kitchen.

Weckenbarth excused himself: only he knew how to prepare the right stuffing for the chickens, so he would have to interrupt his story. But he would continue it during and after the meal.

With quiet determination Dr. Jacobi insisted on accompanying him to the kitchen.

"My dear Weckenbarth, you always take too much cummin. You imagine you are dealing with turkeys." So I remained alone with the gentleman who had been introduced to me as Don Emanuele Da Ceneda and who, as you will recall, had hardly spoken more than a couple of words all afternoon. He came over to me and said, "If you know nothing about stuffing chickens either, I suggest we stay on deck until dinner. I have something to tell you."

He took my arm and drew me over to the railing. The ship's engines had stopped. The paddles were still, but white foam still flowed out from beneath them to mix with the large patches of delicate algae. Had there not been these patches of algae on the dark waters, splitting at the bows and then flowing calmly past in easy, sweeping movements to meet again beyond the stern, I would not have noticed that the steamer was moving.

Don Emanuele looked across to the bank. He was old, very old, perhaps over ninety, I thought. His eyes were deep-set in their sockets. Above them his forehead, with scarcely a trace of eyebrows projected strangely, almost like a porch or, rather, the sharp outline of the peak of a cap.

"Above all, there is a question I want to ask you, *my* question, the one I ask everyone I meet", his melancholy gaze was fixed on the water, "but which no-one has yet been able to answer. Do you" – he looked up at me with tears in his eyes – "do you know Stellidaura?"

Had it not been for the deep – and deeply moving – seriousness which shrouded him, I would have thought the question was intended to amuse or even antagonise me.

"Who is Stellidaura?" I asked, after a moment's hesitation.

He slumped onto the railing as if he had been hit.

"You neither", he groaned. "I shall never find out."

"I'm terribly sorry", I said, "but if you could perhaps be a little more precise I might ... I do know a lot of people ..."

"I cannot die", he said and laughed in self-mockery, "and Stellidaura, she is long since dead; but how did she die, how? – O Stellidaura, my angel, what torments may you have suffered, O Stellidaura, my angel ..."

He stood motionless for a few minutes, his gaze turned up towards the heavens. Then he turned back to me. "She spoke in the dialect of Naples, that is all I know of her, except that she was as fair as if she came from Paradise itself, and of a purity beyond even what Paradise knew. Stellidaura ..."

"When was the last time you saw the lady?" I asked. I thought practical details might take his mind off his sorrow. "Perhaps that might lead somewhere?"

"It was in Venice", he said "during the Carnival of the year seventeen hundred and seventy-four."

He paused and then, without paying any attention to my understandable surprise, without noticing it even, he began to tell the story of his Stellidaura:

"It was in Venice during the rule of Alvise VI. The great days of the Republic were long since past. The Corsican, to whom she was to fall victim, had already been born. The glory of Venice was fading, its fame had become notoriety, and where once great merchants had exchanged goods from all over the world disreputable characters from both hemispheres now hawked the fruits of sin. The old families had exhausted themselves. The death of some embittered greybeard who perhaps, in his youth, had taken part in the defence of Corsica, expunged many a noble name from the Golden Book of Saint Mark. Even if there was still a Mocenigo on the throne in the Palace of the Doges, even if the white-robed nuns still played the divine concerti of Gabrieli and Vivaldi in the courtyards of the convents along the shores of the lagoon and the people in the theatres still laughed at the antics of Pessarino and Brunetta, the city was in the implacable grip of a choking web of secret intrigue which now and then rose to the surface – spreading instant terror that was, for safety's sake immediately forgotten again – in the grey shapes of its henchmen who dragged its unfortunate victims before bloodthirsty courts and down into damp dungeons whence there was no escape. And the people, led on by ne'er-do-wells from the five continents who pursued their chicaneries behind the mask of carnival licence, danced above the cells where the unfortunates lay, danced and laughed, though the laugh stuck in their throats, until – until the corrupt, ever-present, never-mentioned police struck once more ... and they danced that most furious of dances, the dance over the volcano, round the palaces, churches and bridges, up and down the silent, stinking canals which gleamed with the phosphorescence of decline and decay.

But, to return to my story: I am a Jew, but I have been baptised, though not until my sixth year; I took the name of the Bishop who baptised me.

At the age of twenty I was ordained a priest in my home town and followed the study of literature and rhetoric in the 'Province', what was left of the Venetian possessions on the mainland that they used to call 'terra firma'. After I had completed my studies I was drawn, like everyone else, to the capital, to the Queen of Cities, to Venice.

On the recommendation of my patron, the Bishop, I obtained a position as tutor to the children of a Senator. As I succeeded in gaining the trust of the lady of the house, the position turned out to be lucrative, without my having to exert myself overmuch, nor restrict my comings and goings.

I could wander freely round the city, just like any Venetian or, rather, like anyone in Venice, concealed behind my half-mask and wearing the dress and the sword of a nobleman. There was no trace of the priest in my clothing – confronted with the blaze of emerald, turquoise and gold silks, which were still to be had on the Rialto, how could any young man with a healthy sense of his own worth not be led into vanity?

That was the least of my sins ... In that year, during which not one of my thoughts turned to God, I never once said mass and I took a mistress. She came from one of the noble families of the Republic that had come down in the world; her name was Angiola Tiepolo. A little older than I, she had limbs of alabaster that made her look like a Venus by Veronese, the erotic sophistication of a she-devil and a capacity for jealousy beyond all imagining.

Angiola lived together with her brother Bajamonte, who occupied a few minor, unpaid positions at court and who, as you will soon see, was as deeply involved in intrigue as the rest of the minor nobility. Their palace, in the vicinity of Santa Maria della Salute, was spacious enough to have accommodated thirty lords and ladies in a manner befitting their rank, but as Angiola and her brother were now its sole occupants, it had become home to flies, spiders, rats and all the stray cats of Venice. With the help of a few well-beaten servants they managed to keep the vermin and the cats at bay in a few of the rooms. The rest were abandoned to the dust, which rose in slow pirouettes to the dilapidated, gold-framed portraits of their ancestors on the rare occasions when someone set foot in the abandoned galleries. The marble mosaic of the Tiepolo coat of arms in the grand entrance hall of the palace was now encrusted with moss and dirt.

When my mistress commanded me to move into the palace – the better to keep an eye on me – a regular military operation was necessary to clean up one gallery for the bed where, as the nights were spent in all manner of pleasures, I slept during the day – apart, of course, from interruptions for the lessons I had to give in the Senator's house.

Bajamonte Tiepolo was a bloated young gentleman whose

attitude towards me was from the very first one of hostility. He was two-faced, spiteful and lazy and, moreover, only attracted to his own sex. Far be it from me to reproach him for it, especially as there was another passion which had him in its pernicious grip: gambling.

Day and night he gambled in the dens of the Ridotto, and Dame Fortune was constant towards him – he always lost. Gradually he had gambled away everything of value that he and his sister possessed. Thereupon he had squandered the money that foolish friends lent him, and thus was compelled to spend his days, when he was not haunting the gaming tables, cursing and swearing as he hid in the Palazzo, trying to avoid the attentions of his creditors.

Whatever the reason, his attitude towards me was one of hostility; he required me to address him as 'Your Excellency' – to which he had no right – and he took from me any money that I was careless enough not to conceal from him. He and his sister – this was the only matter in which they were united – had me, a young, inexperienced, credulous provincial, in their power.

I did not even notice the full extent of their tyranny: infatuated as I was with the devilish Angiola, I felt that her alabaster limbs repaid all debts, and more.

And so it continued for several months. At twenty-four I found this dissolute life suited me perfectly. Then the end of the Carnival season began to approach. With the first stroke of Ash Wednesday the Ridotto and all the casinos would close. Whilst out in the streets the masquerade of deception and seduction whirled towards its furious climax, 'His Excellency' was seized by the grotesque notion that he had to win back the entire amount he had gambled away and which he owed to all and sundry within the next few days. He gambled like one possessed and kept on losing.

Finally, after he had literally gambled away his sister's clothes, he rushed around the house in a frantic search for something to pawn. The only thing he could find was my bed. I placed myself in front of it and said, 'Your Excellency –'

He drew his sword and would certainly have run me through if his sister had not held him back. In a fury of rage, and jealous of every second he thought wasted if he was not at the gaming table, he was close to killing his own sister, but she hissed something to him which I was not supposed to hear and which, because of the distance between us, I did not hear.

Don Bajamonte Tiepolo let his sword drop, gave me a blank stare and disappeared.

'What did you say to him?' I asked Angiola.

'Off you go, off you go and find some money!'

'But I've no idea where, my angel.'

'Fool!', now she was hissing at me. 'Don't you understand: if you value your life, go and find some money. I told my brother that you can make gold. Off you go and come back with a hundred sequins or he will kill you, and me too!'

A hundred sequins – that was my salary for a whole year, a fortune; where could I find them? Had the devil offered me the secret of making gold in return for my miserable soul, in my desperation I would have agreed to the bargain. But what should I do? I left the palace to go to my café, where I was allowed credit. I had *one* lira in my pocket, one single lira, and that I gave away, in an inexplicable fit of defiance, to a beggar who was sitting in the Via San Trovaso.

I did not even glance at the beggar, one of Venice's thousand beggars, and had already walked on a few steps when he said with a soft but remarkably penetrating voice, 'Thank you, sir, and I know that today is the most important day of your life.' It pulled me up with a jerk. I turned, looked at him, hesitated and then asked what he meant by his remark. In place of an answer he gave me a visiting card – just imagine, a beggar with a visiting card – and said, 'Come and visit me; I think you will not regret it.'

Pensively I made my way to the café where the divine Conte Gozzi was also a regular visitor. I spent a few hours there with some friends and forgot my miserable situation in the witty conversation. But when the evening came and my friends left one by one my desperate position came back to me. If I only had some money! Best of all, I would have liked to return to my village immediately, repentant, turning my back on everything, giving up all thought of Venice. Immersed in these contrite thoughts, I saw a gondolier enter the café. He looked round as if he were searching for someone, gave me a close look and then a hesitant, inquiring wave. I assumed my mistress had sent him for me, as was often the case. I stood up and followed him. Outside was a gondola into which I climbed and in which, to my astonishment, I found a lady – in elegant but remarkably simple dress and, like myself, masked. It could not be Angiola!

'My God', said my unknown companion in a voice that was graceful, but at the same time trembling with fear, 'my God, who are you?'

'That is what I am asking you', I said, 'you sent for me.' She sat there in fearful silence, not knowing what to do. In the meantime the gondolier had quickly started to propel his gondola in the direction of the Grand Canal. –"

We were interrupted. For some time a steward had been standing behind us giving discreet coughs without either Don Emanuele or myself – who was as deeply engrossed in listening to his story as he was in telling it – really noticing.

"Supper is served, Reverend Father."

"In that case I will postpone the continuation of my tale of woes", said Don Emanuele. We went down the companion-way to an oval saloon whose walls and floors were covered with rugs. There Dr. Jacobi and Weckenbarth were waiting for us. We joined them at the table.

Weckenbarth turned to the steward, "Don't forget that Mr. Alfred wants *two* chickens, and a larger helping of curry sauce."

"Who is Alfred?" I asked.

"Now whose story shall we continue over dinner", said Weckenbarth in a genial voice, "that of my Uncle Heino or of your Stellidaura, Don Emanuele? – I would be very surprised if you had not made good use of the time Dr. Jacobi and I –"

"As I am sure that you", said Don Emanuele with a hint of irritation in his voice, "will not want to miss your usual game of cards with Alfred, there will scarcely be time for your story after dinner whilst we –" he waved in my direction, "can retire to the upper deck at that point." "In that case", said Weckenbarth, "– now where was I? Oh yes, Uncle Heino had not only recorded Emma's address and date of birth on the official form, but also noted it down on a piece of paper which he slipped into his wallet although that was entirely superfluous – there was but one thought throbbing in his brain like a ground-bass: '16 Bolland Street, first floor, on the left' ...

Number 16 was a large old building with dilapidated, white-painted windowframes and a wooden porch that had for years given supposedly temporary protection to the draughty entrance. There was a police station on the ground floor. At first Uncle Heino – all dressed in his Sunday best – had not the courage to enter the building. Only after an hour's wait did he go past the peeling gloss paint of the stairs up to the first floor. On the door on the left he read 'BELLONI', on brass, and underneath, on a simple aluminium plate, 'Holzmindel'. They were obviously subtenants of the Bellonis. Uncle Heino turned round and tried to visualise the lay-out of the flat so that he would be able to locate its windows from the street. Then he heard the sound of doors and footsteps from the flat. Quickly he ran up to the second floor. Now there were voices ... a few seconds later the door opened and she came out – she, Emma. Wearing a pale blue poplin coat, she turned round in the doorway to shout, 'I'm in a hurry, in a hurry –' and raced down the stairs. Uncle Heino raced after her.

Emma caught the tram with a second to spare; so, with a fraction of a second to spare, did Uncle Heino. It took them to the centre of the town. There Emma got out and went straight to a fairly large hostelry. Uncle Heino, as cautiously as if he were leading a reconnaissance patrol, peeped in through the long windows. It was a beer hall and at this time the room with its niches and parlours had few guests. Emma hurried past the tables until she disappeared behind a pillar. Uncle Heino paused to work things out, then he left his observation post, went into the beer hall and wandered round as if he were looking for the best seat. All the while, however, he kept the part of the room behind the pillar under observation. Eventually Emma appeared and served a customer with beer. Uncle Heino's deduction had been correct: Emma was a waitress. With a feeling of satisfaction he turned round and took a seat at a table that was obviously not part of Emma's domain; for the moment he wanted to keep a low profile.

In the course of the evening – Uncle Heino had his dinner there – he became acquainted with a printer called Sperlmann; a chemist, who every evening studied the menu carefully and then ordered sardines on toast; and finally a man called Franzi, who had a number of fingers missing from each hand, from which Uncle Heino quietly concluded that he worked in a saw-mill. Without realising it, Uncle Heino had joined a group of regulars who obviously had no objection to him sitting at their table, which suited him down to the ground since he did not doubt that these gentlemen would know Emma and that he could learn something about her from them.

It was well on into the evening that Uncle Heino, somewhat tipsy as the three pints of brown ale were well beyond his normal ration, set off for the ladies lavatory. Franzi, the presumed saw-mill-worker, took him by the arm and led him in the right direction. Uncle Heino judged this to be the right moment to mention Emma to his new friend.

'That Emma', said Uncle Heino; 'she's a bit of all right, she is.'

Franzi said nothing.

It was only later, when the beer hall was almost empty and after a further two pints poor Uncle Heino's stomach was beginning to heave at the mere sight of the beer, when the chemist and then Herr Sperlmann had both left and Franzi had obstinately insisted that the musicians should come to their table and accompany him in a song which he rendered with more feeling than accuracy – the only thing Uncle Heino could remember about it the following day was that it kept going on about 'my turtledove' –, it was only later that Franzi turned to Uncle Heino and said,

'Which Emma d'you mean, which one?'

Uncle Heino told him.

'But that's Bobbi', said Franzi.

– Aha! thought Uncle Heino, she's Bobbi to her friends; and he decided from now on to think of her by that name himself. He did not learn anything else, he had his hands full refusing a large beer that Franzi was insisting on buying for him. Franzi was just beginning to feel insulted when a newspaper vendor appeared and that diverted his thoughts from the round he wanted to buy. Franzi bought a copy of the morning paper and, in spite of his missing fingers, neatly folded it into two paper hats, which he and Uncle Heino popped on their heads and wore on the part of the route home that they shared. When they went their separate ways my uncle had to swear he would come back the next day, which he would have done without the oath, though not, of course, because of Franzi.

This went on for a whole week. The beer he had to buy for his new friends, whenever it was his round, and all the extra expenses of his new lifestyle exhausted his monthly budget without bringing him any nearer his goal; on the contrary, his cunning strategy of moving from table to table so that he would penetrate Bobbi's territory as if by chance foundered on an apparently insurmountable obstacle. When, after a week and a half, my uncle sat down at a place a few tables away from that of his new friends, Franzi made a great fuss and dragged him back to his regular niche, uttering loud reproaches which cast serious doubt upon his sanity.

Uncle Heino was desperate. But then, the following week, the miracle occurred. The waitress who normally served at the regulars' table fell ill. Bobbi deputised for her.

That was on a Monday. Instead of working his way through his in-tray, Uncle Heino had spent the whole morning writing 'Bobbi – Bobbi – Bobbi' on a hundred sheets of official notepaper: in capital and small letters, in Gothic and Roman, covering the whole page with one, long cursive line or with a thousand tiny, precise shorthand symbols. Someone saw to it that a sample selection was delivered to the Head of his Department, who took the opportunity to order Uncle Heino to see him after work and deliver a very, very severe reprimand – his second, you will remember! The worst thing about it was that Uncle Heino made it plain that the opinion of the Director of the Deovulation Office meant little to him.

In the evening the aforementioned 'miracle' was ample compensation for his professional misfortunes. Uncle Heino was overwhelmed by the sight of Bobbi – who clearly did not recognise him – standing in front of him and asking him what he would like. She was wearing a black dress and a little white apron with a tiny pocket right over the spot from which he had removed the oval stamp of the deovulation doctor ... When his friends appeared he said his misfortune at the Ministry had made him feel physically unwell and used it as an excuse not to drink too much. – An inexperienced seducer, he told himself, needs above all a clear head.

Once again Uncle Heino and his friends were the last to leave. As ever, the chemist was the first to leave followed by Herr Sperlmann, then finally – by this time Bobbi was already taking the cloths with the blue and white lozenge pattern off the tables and replacing them with the upturned chairs – Franzi started his pre-departure ritual. As was his habit, almost, it seemed, a hygienic compulsion, he rinsed out his mouth with the last of the beer, spat it out onto the floor – 'In memory of all dead masons' he always said as he did so – and turned to Uncle Heino:

'Off we go?'

'Yes – no', said Uncle Heino, 'I'm going to wait a few minutes.'

'What for?'

'Just wait.'

Franzi was surprised but already too far gone to argue. As always, he embraced my uncle and the landlord, who was checking that the waitresses cleared away properly, and left. Uncle Heino had deliberately left paying until now. Bobbi came to the table now with his bill.

My uncle took out his wallet. The state of its contents gave a shock to his whole system, as if he had plunged into a vat of boiling lead: he could pay his bill, but the plan he had devised in the course of the evening demanded far greater resources than he had at his command! – He decided nevertheless to put it into operation, if on a reduced scale.

'Bobbi', he said, 'have you far to go?'

'Not too far.'

'I'm going your way.'

'How do you know?'

'I'm going your way whichever way it is.' – You can see that Uncle Heino definitely needed his clear head to produce such blandishments.

Bobbi smiled. She examined Uncle Heino and clearly came to the conclusion that the offer of a lift home would not entail any great risks ...

'By car?'

'Of course.'

Bobbi quickly cleared away, took off her apron and put on a leather jacket.

'There', she said, 'that's me.'

Uncle Heino pushed himself up from his seat, put on his hat and led the way out. There he waved down a taxi.

'A taxi?' said Bobbi.

'When I'm out drinking', said Uncle Heino, 'I never drive myself ...' – a so-called Swiss-cheese-lie: the only part you can rely on is the holes.

His instruction to the taxi driver was his *tour de force*:

'16 Bolland Street', he said.

'But how ....?'

Uncle Heino's only reply was a blasé shrug of the shoulders.

She bombarded him with questions but the only answer he gave was a smile. If however, he promised, she would allow him to see her home the next evening, then he would explain. But not in the taxi, he added; he would take the liberty of inviting her to a late-night café.

Bobbi's response was rather vague. They had already reached Bolland Street. Bobbi got out, thanked my uncle and quickly disappeared.

The long taxi journey, to one end of the city and then the other, consumed the one large banknote Uncle Heino had been keeping at home.

Uncle Heino spent a restless night wondering how he was going to finance the presumed pleasures of the following evening.

In the Ministry he asked for an advance. With a scornful smile, his Head of Department reminded him of what had happened the previous day and refused.

Uncle Heino had a lodger. Her name was Frau Firstenhaar, she was about sixty and ran a newspaper stall in the park. Now my uncle knew that Frau Firstenhaar – with that natural distaste some people have for the banks' incomprehensible, dubious, one might even say amoral, dealings, with all their accounts and numbers and marble counters – kept all her savings in the house. All he was going to do, Uncle Heino told himself, was to borrow a small sum from her – without her knowledge, of course, since the old skinflint would never knowingly have lent anyone a penny ... With a duplicate key, to which, as her landlord, he assumed he had a right, but of which Frau Firstenhaar had no knowledge, he unlocked her room and looked round. Where would such a dim-witted old maid keep her money? He felt under the mattress – nothing; in the vases, in her pillow – nothing; there was nothing behind the pictures, nothing in the hollow statuette of the Virgin Mary, nothing in the miniature guitar hanging on the wall and nothing under the magpie's cage. In the cage? Uncle Heino lifted a corner of the flowered cloth.

The bird woke up immediately and said, 'What is gold? Cold, lifeless stone.'

With a look of distaste on his face Uncle Heino let the cloth fall back over the cage. There was a rattling noise. My uncle swung round – but it was only Frau Firstenhaar's pride and joy, a musical clock which, on the hour, rattled off the tune of the chorale 'Prostrate before Thy majesty lies the Christian host' from Michael Haydn's 'German Mass'. The clock stood on top of the sewing machine. – The sewing machine! – Beneath the cover of knobbly woollen crochetwork Uncle Heino found a small drawer, which he prised open – nothing. On the other side of the sewing machine was another drawer with a well-worn tea caddy in it ...

When he opened the box the contents took Uncle Heino's breath away. He had to sit down on a chair that had an antimacassar of similar woollen crochetwork. It was a staggering sum. – And the old bat lives in a furnished room and is so mean she makes her coffee as thin as lemon squash! But it's probably too much to expect of a person to change from being a miser to a wastrel at the appropriate moment.

He took a hundred-Mark note ... after a brief hesitation he took another.

'Two hundred should be enough, and of course I'll pay her back at the end of the month, with the usual rate of interest.'

Uncle Heino closed the caddy, the drawer and the door and went on his way.

Bobbi was more eager to learn his secret than he would have expected, he had no problem getting her to accompany him to a late-night café after she had finished work. A jukebox filled the café with such an uninterrupted stream of noise that the only way Uncle Heino could tell her his secret – and one that filled him with a delicious tremor – was to move up close beside Bobbi, put his lips to her ear and whisper the promised explanation.

His account of how he came to know where she lived was long and involved, with much circumlocution and flowery phrases.

Bobbi's reaction mystified Uncle Heino. She thought for a long time, very hard and very seriously, then gave him such a searching look that he flushed to the back of his bald head, and then she laughed, a full-throated laugh but inaudible because of the jukebox. She bent down to Uncle Heino's ear and said, 'Let's go.'

They decided to go to another, quieter place. There was only one possible bar. Uncle Heino was glad he had taken both hundred-Mark notes ...

That evening he spent every Pfennig of the money he had borrowed from Frau Firstenhaar. The little that remained after they had left the bar was spent on a bottle of champagne that he bought at the railway station to take back to his flat. After the third glass Bobbi – scarcely fifteen feet from where Frau Firstenhaar lay and separated by only two walls from the woman who, all unknowing, had opened the gates to paradise for Uncle Heino – gave a parody of the striptease artist they had seen earlier in the bar. Morning was already breaking when my uncle was vouchsafed an experience which, apart from a slightly incestuous youthful indiscretion, he had until then only enjoyed in his dreams ... how does Boccaccio put it? 'He tilled her garden right lustily and they changed horses four times as they sped along love's highway'."

We – and that included Weckenbarth, who demonstrated a remarkable skill in eating and talking at once; his explanation was 'years of training the will according to the Tibetan system' – had eaten our fill of the delicious curried chicken. Now the steward was standing behind Weckenbarth and whispering to him again.

"He can wait a little", said Weckenbarth. "Tell him I'm in the middle of a story."

The steward disappeared. Whilst the servants were clearing away, we lit our cigars and Weckenbarth continued:

"Around the hour when Uncle Heino was normally fortifying himself for the rest of his morning's work with half a roll covered in Co-op cheese spread, he awoke in bed beside the unclothed waitress, Emma Holzmindel, known to her friends as Bobbi.

In order to be able to offer her a suitable breakfast, he had to take out another loan from Frau Firstenhaar. He slipped past the magpie to the sewing machine where, as on every hour, the clock was playing the chorale 'Prostrate before Thy majesty lies ...' '... Frau Firstenhaar', sang Uncle Heino gleefully.

That Wednesday was the first evening that Uncle Heino did not spend with his new friends in the beer hall; on the one hand because Bobbi intended to come straight back to him after she had finished her work, and on the other because he was afraid that through some stroke of ill fortune he, who since he had entered the Civil Service had never had one day's unexplained absence – even when he had been ill he had dragged himself off to work to obtain his Head of Department's permission to return home – might be seen by colleagues in the beer hall or on the way there.

In the afternoon, after Bobbi had left, Uncle Heino lay down for a sleep. Around eight o'clock there was a knock at his door.

It was Frau Firstenhaar.

'If I'm disturbing you – good evening –', said Frau Firstenhaar, 'don't hesitate to say so.'

There was no one – as you will understand – whom Uncle Heino would have found more disturbing than his creditor, who by now was clearly aware that she was one. Drugged with sleep, he tried to work out an excuse.

'I have something to ask of you.'

'Oh yes', said Uncle Heino.

'It's rather embarrassing', said Frau Firstenhaar, and put a white envelope on the table.

'Please sit down' – the best thing, thought Uncle Heino, would be to say I have no time.

'You see, I've no time just now', he said.

Frau Firstenhaar bent forward and whispered,

'There are thieves in the house!'

'That's ridiculous, Frau Firstenhaar ...'

'And I know who they are.'

She thinks there's more than one? thought Uncle Heino, somewhat relieved.

'And who is it?'

'Not it – she.'

'She?'

'That Frau Woschek on the second floor.'

Frau Woschek was an elderly woman who, after her drapery store had gone bankrupt, took as her second husband an artist who left her with two children from his first marriage. Frau Woschek's stepson made his living by signing his father's paintings with names that ensured they sold for inflated prices but, since he did not find this activity entirely fulfilling, he spent many hours pursuing his passion for rat-hunting. Once he had peppered Frau Firstenhaar's calf with shot – with malicious intent, Frau Firstenhaar maintained, but the accusation did not stand up in court. Frau Firstenhaar took some comfort in the fact that shortly afterwards he had indeed been sent to prison for causing a painful injury to an expert who had declared one of his late father's pictures, which the young rathunter had boldly signed 'Rembrandt', a forgery; but that did nothing – like all her kind, old Frau Firstenhaar assumed that blood will out – to lessen her grudge against Frau Woschek.

'Frau Woschek on the second floor?' Uncle Heino shook his head dubiously. 'What has she stolen then?'

'Four hundred marks!'

'Who from?'

'Me!'

'It's a bit of a cheek', said Uncle Heino.

'It's a crime!' said Frau Firstenhaar.

'In that case ...', said Uncle Heino reflectively.

'I have with me', said Frau Firstenhaar, 'an envelope and a sheet of paper. I intend to report her to the police, and that son of hers!'

'But he's behind bars –'

'All the same.'

'Good', said my uncle after a while. The relief had cheered him up no end. 'I assume you would like –'

'Yes', said Frau Firstenhaar. 'You are, in a manner of speaking, an official.'

'Not in a manner of speaking; I *am* an official.'

Frau Firstenhaar handed him paper and envelope. 'Who shall we address it to?' she asked.

'Hmm – to the Archbishop's Palace', suggested Uncle Heino.

'Are you sure? I would have thought to the police?'

Uncle Heino drew close to her and whispered in her ear:

'You still trust the police!? After they let old Woschek and her son get away with shooting you in the leg! Don't you realise?'

'No. What?' asked Frau Firstenhaar innocently.

'That cunning old Woschek has bribed the police!'

The penny dropped.

'There you are', said Uncle Heino.

'But why the Archbishop ...?'

'Stealing is a sin, isn't it? And do you think Frau Woschek could bribe the Archbishop?'

So the letter with – Frau Firstenhaar insisted on it – a more than detailed description of the facts plus a comprehensive analysis of Frau Woschek's character was addressed to the Episcopal Palace. Uncle Heino promised to deliver it himself. Frau Firstenhaar thanked him warmly, even if, deep down inside, she was still not entirely happy with the way the matter had been dealt with.

'Do you', said Uncle Heino at the end, – he had been tingling with anticipation for the moment when he could casually put this apparent afterthought – 'do you keep any more money in the house?'

'... No.'

'Ah', said Uncle Heino. 'Otherwise I would have recommended you to put it in a bank.'

'Never', said Frau Firstenhaar.

'So that Frau Woschek wouldn't find it – if you did have any more.'

'In that case I'll take it with me to the stall', said Frau Firstenhaar, appalled at the thought.

'That would be right up old mother Woschek's street.'

'Why?'

'Because it would be there all night with no one to guard it.'

Uncle Heino's arguments had brought Frau Firstenhaar close to tears.

'But I don't want to put money in any bank. Banks are so ... so ...'

'I know hundreds of banks.'

'So?'

Now was the moment: 'I could deposit it in our Ministry Bank', said Uncle Heino; his inspired invention of a 'Ministry Bank' worked wonders.

'Only', said Frau Firstenhaar, 'if I don't have to pay interest.'

'– Pay? On the con..., er, don't worry, I will have a word with the Ministry's Bank Inspector. We were at school together. It would be best if you brought me the money right away.'

So Uncle Heino opened an account with a bank. The account was in the name of Heino Pramsbichler and was overdrawn within six weeks.

It was a Tuesday again. An unsuccessful attempt to secure a

secret loan from Ministry funds had led to his dismissal. Over the last few weeks he had shown such a casual attitude to his work that he immediately aroused suspicion when he suddenly started to work late, claiming he had to do overtime. It was only the fact that no actual loss had been incurred, and his many years of blameless service, that saved him from legal proceedings

It was with an uneasy feeling inside that Uncle Heino made his way home for the last time.

Frau Firstenhaar was waiting for him. With a sigh my uncle tried to think of a new excuse as to why there had been no progress in the campaign against Frau Woschek. But Frau Firstenhaar wanted some of the money she had deposited with him, in order to have a repair done to the newspaper kiosk. Uncle Heino tried to talk her out of the repair. In the course of the argument she discovered the letter to the Bishop still lying on my uncle's desk. – Without a word Frau Firstenhaar picked up the letter and walked out.

At half past eight, rather earlier than usual, Bobbi arrived.

'Is this your day off?'

Bobbi looked serious as she sat down in silence on the couch.

'Aren't you going to take your clothes off?'

Bobbi had got into the habit of getting undressed the moment she came into the flat and serving my uncle a tasty snack – dressed only in a scrap of linen for an apron and a stiff waitress' cap.

'I don't feel like getting undressed ... And you won't either', said Bobbi, 'when you hear what the doctor told me –'

'What doctor?'

'I'm going to have a baby.'

It took a few minutes for Uncle Heino to recover from the shock.

'That's impossible', he whispered.

'Why?'

'You've been – you've been deovulated –'

Bobbi laughed.

'Don't laugh!' To find something, after all the trials and humiliations of the day, on which he could vent his justified anger was like balm to his wounded soul. 'The Ministry will have to pay. The Ministry! The deovulation can't have been properly carried out. Or the doctor will have to pay compensation. It'll be no problem finding out who he is. I'll look it up tomorrow at the office ...' he gave a start, there would be no *tomorrow* in the office for him, '... anyway, the state will have to pay. From today onwards I will have nothing more to do with the state. The state must pay in full!'

'But I haven't been deovulated, darling.'

'– ? –'

'It was my sister Emma', said Bobbi, 'lots of people get us mixed up, we're twins you see. I', now Bobbi laughed out loud and fell back among the cushions, kicking her legs in the air, 'I haven't been deovulated ...' Then she slipped her clothes off.

Standing on the sofa, she was just tying the linen apron round her waist when Frau Firstenhaar popped her head round the door.

'Oh', she said, gave a smile and closed the door behind her.

Uncle Heino rushed out after her. She had already disappeared into her room. 'Who said you could come in without knocking!' shouted my uncle.

'You didn't knock just now and anyway, I *did* knock. Only you were so involved in your – in your orgy that you didn't hear.'

'Orgy you say, orgy?! That's my fiancée you're referring to!'

'I', said Frau Firstenhaar, taking the letter to the Bishop out from under the tablecloth, 'I want my money back.'

'The money –' hissed Uncle Heino, 'oh, so that's it, the money, the money ...'

'Herr Pramsbichler!' Frau Firstenhaar retreated, clutching the letter to her breast.

Uncle Heino grabbed her by the throat and forced her down into the chair by the sewing machine.

'You too', gurgled Frau Firstenhaar. 'You've been bribed by that Woschek as well –'

Uncle Heino pressed harder and harder. Frau Firstenhaar fell to the floor, but my uncle only let go when, with a shiver of horror, he thought he could hear her vertebrae crack under the pressure of his hands ... – but it was only the sound of the musical clock getting ready to play 'Prostrate before Thy majesty lies ...'

Uncle Heino hurried out of the room.

'What was it', asked Bobbi, naked.

'I told her what I think of her.'

'That's cheered you up?'

'Oh', said Uncle Heino, 'I feel I can breathe again now that I've told her what I think of her.'

The following day – Bobbi was still asleep – Uncle Heino crept into Frau Firstenhaar's room. She was lying in the same place and position he had left her in the previous evening. Uncle Heino felt her pulse. Then he turned her head from side to side – it moved easily through a hundred and eighty degrees. Had it really been the sound of her vertebrae? Uncle Heino took out his penknife and scratched his lodger's skin. No blood appeared. She was definitely dead.

Quietly Uncle Heino stood up, went out and locked the door carefully. Then he took his hat and a sheet of paper and went to the newspaper kiosk. There he fixed the note to the blinds; it said: 'Closed due to bereavement'.

Uncle Heino did not have an easy time of it during the following months. Soon Bobbi's little snacks were a thing of the past – it was not only that in the natural course of things she grew less attractive, became pop-eyed and lost a few teeth, she also became irritable and, after she had moved her regular domicile – to borrow a phrase from Uncle Heino's officialese – from Bolland Street to Uncle Heino's flat, kept on nagging him about getting married.

But Uncle Heino had no intention of getting married, especially as now he had to survive on Frau Firstenhaar's modest pension.

In order to be able to collect the pension from the post office, he had forged an authorisation on which he had copied the signature from the letter to the Bishop which he had collected from the room together with the magpie two days after Frau Firstenhaar's decease.

He gave the bird to Frau Woschek. To the door of Frau

Firstenhaar's room, however, he attached a padlock and told Bobbi that the occupant, who had gone on an extended visit to relatives, had put it there before she left.

After a few days an unpleasant smell began to spread through the house. At first it was only noticeable in the corridor, then everywhere in the flat, and finally even out on the stairs. Even hours of airing could not get it out of their clothes. Bobbi felt sick when she came into the house. Uncle Heino said it was all due to her pregnancy.

Less in order to get rid of the smell than because it seemed a good idea, which had been gradually forming in his mind, Uncle Heino made one final visit to Frau Firstenhaar's room. He avoided looking in the direction of where she lay.

He pocketed the keys that were still on the table where Frau Firstenhaar had put them. Then he set about – naturally he had chosen a time when Bobbi was out at work – filling every gap around the door with a special felt strip. He even remembered the keyhole. As a final touch he knocked a pane out of each of the windows to allow the smell an easy exit. And the smell did indeed disappear almost completely. The whiff that was left was so faint that you were not quite sure whether it was really there or whether it was merely a malodorous memory of the nightmare weeks.

He used Frau Firstenhaar's keys to reopen the newspaper kiosk, ran the business in her name and, with no objections at all from either clients or suppliers, bought and sold cigarettes, newspapers and soft drinks.

Bobbi was understandably surprised at this, but he explained it away by telling her that the kiosk had always actually belonged to him and only been leased by Frau Firstenhaar. Now, since her unseemly behaviour that evening, he had cancelled the lease.

Bobbi accepted his explanation, but her curiosity was now focused on the room, which, because the old woman had added an extra padlock, she was convinced must conceal something mysterious. Uncle Heino airily gave all sorts of explanations – a different one for each provoking question.

As she went on asking her questions, asking and asking, day

in day out, and pointing out the contradictions between all his different answers, he finally told her she had no business in the room and that was that.

Once more it was a Tuesday, this time in early March – Bobbi was in the fifth month of her pregnancy – and, as had become his habit, Uncle Heino left the flat at half past seven to go to the newspaper kiosk. When he came to open it he found that he had forgotten the keys. On the key ring were also the keys to the room ...

Although he turned round on the spot and set off at a run for home, he met the police before he was half way there – without, of course, them recognising him away from the kiosk, which was where they were expecting to find him.

Bobbi had found the bunch of keys or, rather, had seen him forget to transfer his closely-guarded treasure from the pocket of yesterday's trousers to today's. In a few seconds she had the right keys in her hand and entered Frau Firstenhaar's room. The sight brought on a miscarriage.

Frau Woschek had heard Bobbi's piercing screams and – curiosity can give any woman the strength of a Goliath – had broken down the door of the flat. She helped Bobbi, called an ambulance and, more importantly, the police, who immediately set off for Uncle Heino's or, to be more precise, the late Frau Firstenhaar's kiosk.

What then happened is quickly related, but is the really remarkable part of Uncle Heino's story:

He had with him an umbrella and a briefcase, in which he was carrying his usual packed lunch and the cash float. He watched the police pass him, paused briefly for thought and then took a tram to the station. There was a train leaving for France immediately, but my uncle worked out that it would be eight hours before it reached the frontier. He waited an hour for a train to Italy which would reach the Austrian frontier considerably sooner than that. The cash float was sufficient for a single to Bolzano with a little left over. He used the spare cash to pass the time until the train left in a news theatre where he saw a film on the marine biology of Schleswig-Holstein and another on aluminium production.

Once more Uncle Heino's deductions were correct: the police had not counted on such a rapid, unhesitating escape. He had no problem crossing the frontier.

He did not leave the train in Bolzano, but stayed on until the conductor threw him off in Verona.

Initially Uncle Heino lived on half-ripe fruit that he stole at night from gardens, later in broad daylight from market stalls. When the hunger became unbearable he ate in restaurants and simply left without paying. He lost his hat when he tried to copy a tramp and jump up behind onto a lorry that was driving past. He exchanged his briefcase for a new pair of soles on his shoes. An unkempt beard made him unrecognisable. He was arrested a few times, but pretended to be deaf and dumb so that identification was impossible.

The sole item he clung onto was his umbrella – we will see why.

He slept in barns and stables, in garages and boathouses. For a while he travelled together with some gypsies. It was in a cart in which a peasant from the Campagna was taking pigs to the Eternal City that he bumped along the Via Flaminia and through the Porta del Popolo – the same route that Goethe had taken.

The city – the great City, the only City, the pattern of cities, the eternal, holy URBS ROMANA, the heart and soul of the world, the mother of cities – embraced Uncle Heino, in spite of the fact that he made his entrance in a cart with pigs, on a bright spring day with her domes glittering in all their glory, with the silver banners of her fountains waving over the colonnades in the breeze, with her steps and basilicas, her majestic obelisks, her marble Emperors and saints, who, with arms outstretched in gestures of greeting or blessing, called out to the stranger dazed by its celestial, cloud-enthroned uniqueness, '*Salve* ... you have come! You have come where all roads meet. You have reached your goal. Bow your head – there is but one misfortune that can befall you: not to bear the fullness of joy of being in Rome.' " Weckenbarth interrupted his narrative – "Well, something like that – you must excuse me if I allow myself to be carried away a little, but when I think of Rome, like all architects of ruins I ... – Yes, yes", he said angrily to the waiting steward, "Mr. Alfred will have to be patient."

The steward whispered excitedly.

"I see", said Weckenbarth and, turning to Dr. Jacobi,

"The other one is there already."

"Well then, off we go", said Dr. Jacobi, "otherwise Alfred will shoot through the wall with impatience."

"But what happened to Uncle Heino?" I said.

"A few days later", said Weckenbarth as he stood up, "he was arrested by the Swiss Guard trying to plant his umbrella in the Vatican Gardens. Uncle Heino told the whole story to a German Dominican who was brought in as interpreter – as interpreter from German German to Swiss German. The Dominican obtained permission for him to plant his umbrella behind a shed in an out-of-the-way corner of the Gardens ... – he came to see me years later and confided the whole story to me, under a vow of secrecy.

Uncle Heino was already dead then.

The Vatican had not delivered him up to earthly justice though, for reasons you can well imagine, the Dominican did not go into details. I assume he was given a false name and sent to a monastery. Until the Dominican turned up we, that is his relations, had heard nothing of him. We do not know where he was buried, either. For the police it is another unsolved case ..."

"And did the umbrella flower?" asked Dr. Jacobi.

"I assume it would have been in the newspapers –"

We too – that is, Don Emanuele and I – stood up. Dr. Jacobi had left already. Weckenbarth followed him.

"A remarkable story", I said.

"My story is even more remarkable", said Don Emanuele.

"I am sure it is", I said, "and I am burning with impatience to hear how it goes on. But tell me something first: what are the others going to play?"

"Bridge", said Don Emanuele.

"Weckenbarth, Dr. Jacobi, Alfred – if I might be so familiar – and who else?"

"Oh", said Don Emanuele, "an evening guest, whom we can

only entertain when we are in motion. It is so that they can play bridge with him that they – Weckenbarth and Dr. Jacobi – have hired this boat. In a house it wouldn't be possible, do you see?"

It was completely dark when we went back up on deck. The boat glided through the night with no more than a soft gurgling noise. We lay down in deckchairs and wrapped ourselves up in black and yellow tartan blankets. Don Emanuele put out the lantern, so that it would not attract midges and moths, and now – the moon had not yet risen – we were lying under the awning in complete darkness. The air was filled with the chirruping of the crickets from the bank. As he continued with his story, Don Emanuele's voice seemed to come from another world.

"So I stepped into the gondola, which immediately pushed off and in which I found an unknown, masked lady ...
'I beg of you, please leave the gondola!'
'You surely do not want me to drown?'
'But what do you want? Please leave me alone.'
There was something strange about her voice. Up to this point the adventure was unusual, but not particularly remarkable: I had stepped into the wrong gondola – one mistake, two apologies, and that would have been the end of it. What was it that held me back, that made me think of ways of starting a conversation in order to give me a reason to remain there? It was her voice, which had a note of sorrow, the sorrow of one who has been abandoned, the fear of one who is being pursued, although my unknown companion no longer seemed to be afraid of me.

In the hope that she, too, would reveal her identity, I took off my mask and introduced myself.
'I cannot give you my name', she said. 'Do not think me impolite, but', she added quickly, 'I would not even have revealed it to the man for whom the gondolier mistook you.'
'But you will not be able to conceal where you come from, every word you speak says 'Naples'.'
'Christ have mercy on me', she whispered, 'is that true?'
'Well', I said with a cheerful air, 'perhaps not to everybody, but certainly to one whom you have wounded to the heart with your angelic voice ...'

With a sigh she sank back into the cushions, incapable, since she had not met the person for whom the gondolier had mistaken me, of deciding what she should do. I was now sure I was embarked on an adventure and was determined not to let the opportunity slip.

'Madame', I said, 'you are in sorrow, in pain. Let me be the one to comfort you. Fate has brought us together, some higher will turned your gondolier's eye on me. Allow me to stay in this gondola, where I will kneel at your feet.' But she just looked away.

'Who knows, Madame, whether the man with whom your gondolier confused me is not at this moment unfaithful –'

She gave a soft cry. But I went on talking, prattled on that now she had been so treacherously abandoned it was my duty as a gentleman to stand by her, and so on ... Mostly I kept repeating myself in different words, and each new embellishment was more threadbare than the last. Understandably it did not get me very far. When I paused to search through my exhausted stock of empty phrases she merely asked:

'Why do you torture me so? Why do you not leave the gondola?'

The truth slipped out before I knew what I was saying,

'Because I find it impossible to believe I shall be denied your closer acquaintance, since chance has brought me into your life. If I fail, I shall know as little rest as you do. You possess a secret which will torment me for the rest of my life.'

'Unfortunately' – she spoke with a hint of the vivacity which, under normal circumstances, probably illuminated everything she did and said – 'you have omitted to surround yourself in mystery; perhaps then I might have become curious about you? As for myself, I possess nothing –'

With that last remark she was clearly beginning to flirt.

'Then you can tell me your name.'

'No'. Now she even gave a little laugh. 'Is it so rare in Venice that a lady prefers to remain unrecognised? Assume I am the wife of – a Procurator of the Republic and was about to meet my lover ...'

'You are not from Venice.'

'A Venetian Procurator could have a Neapolitan wife –'

'So you really are from Naples?'

She gave another laugh. At the same moment the gondola bumped against the canal bank and my unknown beauty was once more as melancholy as she had been at the start.

'Oh dear', she said, 'here we are.' She corrected herself, 'Here I am. Now you have no choice but to get out.'

'We could let the gondolier row us up and down a little, sample a few sweetmeats –'

'What can have put that idea into your head!'

'If not today, then perhaps tomorrow?'

'Who knows where I shall be tomorrow.'

'You are leaving Venice?'

My unknown companion gave me her hand. I kissed it silently and when I looked up again I saw that she was crying.

'Wait tomorrow at the same time and in the same place where the gondolier found you today', she whispered. Hurriedly she left the gondola and disappeared through a gateway. My first thought was to follow her, but then I realised what her final words had been. I would respect her desire to be alone; I would see her tomorrow, or at least hear from her! But until then, I knew, the hours would pass as slowly as if I were in purgatory. How differently did everything turn out, oh Stellidaura, how differently ... "

Don Emanuele paused. The moon had still not risen. We heard loud laughter from the cabin of the unknown – to me at least – Alfred.

"You never saw the lady again?"

"No, or rather, yes, I did see her again, but much happened before that. Have you forgotten that I had a mistress?

So: I did not follow my unknown beauty, but stayed in the gondola and reflected on what had occurred. Then I asked the gondolier whether he knew the lady.

'No, signor.'

'To whom does this gondola belong?'

'To me, signor.'

'You ply for hire?'

'Yes, signor.'

'Where did the lady get in?'

'Here, signor, and I was supposed to row you back.'

The gondolier knew nothing. I had him take me to the Palazzo Tiepolo. When I arrived, I remembered that I had no money left, to pay the gondolier. I told him to wait and went into the house. The first person I met was our fine Don Bajamonte. Scarcely had he seen me than he drew his sword and shouted,

'Where is the money?'

'One thing at a time, Your Excellency. First of all, would you be so good as to pay the gondola that brought me here ...'

'So you have no money?'

The threat in his voice left no room for doubt.

Trapped, I spun him the tale his sister had invented that afternoon.

'Your Excellency! Do you imagine I can make gold as easily as dung? I had to obtain certain ingredients, and they were expensive enough; it is only fair that you should pay for the gondola.'

'Show me the stuff you bought.'

'Certainly, Your Excellency, if you want them *not* to produce any gold. You see, they cannot be exposed to the light.'

He tossed two lire to me and asked,

'When will the gold be made?'

By tomorrow, I reckoned, I would be able to find some somewhere, even if I had to pawn my own bed, so I said,

'Not before sunset tomorrow. – But if you know of a better alchemist?'

With an oath, he turned on his heel. I went out and paid the gondolier. As I entered the house again Angiola was coming down the stairs. She was trembling.

'It would have been better if I had saved myself the lie I told my brother, that you can make gold', she screamed at me. 'If he had cut you down this afternoon you would not have been able to be unfaithful to me this evening. It is long past midnight! Where have you been?'

'In the café.'

'In the café, in the café', she mimicked, 'I sent a thousand times by a thousand servants and you were not there! Oh, how unhappy I am –' and with that one of her outbursts of jealousy began which were constant variations of the same theme: amid curses she would shower pity upon herself and on me all the wrongs, imagined or real, she had suffered at the hands of former lovers. To interrupt such a tirade was to take your life in your hands, and until that evening I had always followed that precept. Now however, I could stand it no more and when she repeated her question, 'Where have you been, where have you been?', for the hundredth time, I replied,

'In some other café for once.'

She grabbed an inkwell that happened to be near and threw it at me. I managed to raise my hand swiftly enough to save my face, but the splintering glass cut my hand – blood, mixed with ink poured down. Angiola, who could not stand the sight of blood, shrieked and fled.

I bandaged my injured hand as best I could, indifferent to the physical pain and with thoughts only for her, my unknown beauty. The more Angiola's behaviour disgusted me, the purer, more divine appeared that unknown angel. I despised Angiola, and I despised myself for having been her lover.

I fell asleep – what my dreams were like, you can imagine. The cut on my hand must have burnt dreadfully since the ink had penetrated below the skin, but I felt nothing ... The fact that the wound did not lead to blood-poisoning, that I survived, like a somnambulist so to speak, I ascribe to the supernatural force of the thoughts of Stellidaura that filled my body and soul."

The moon had finally risen. Silver, sickle-shaped reflections played over the gentle waves and in the tree-tops.

Perhaps without realising it himself, Don Emanuele had started to hum a simple melody to himself – probably the memory of some song that was connected with the events in Venice. Contemplating the moon, my thoughts too turned lyrical and I recited:

O night, tho' dark, yet art thou fair:
All busyness thou bringst to rest.
Clear of eye who thee calls blest,
Who honours thee, of judgment rare.

Suddenly, from Alfred's cabin – to whom I had not been introduced, I even suspected he was being kept hidden from me – came loud shouting. Two voices, one of which I clearly recognised as Weckenbarth's, kept on repeating the same words, presumably terms from bridge, they were unknown to me; Alfred – I assumed it was he – spoke quickly, in a blustering voice and in a foreign language, and Dr. Jacobi's voice – he was scarcely comprehensible at the best of times, anyway – cracked as he screamed and continued with a series of inarticulate, though crisp, sounds. The distinguished bridge party had audibly broken into a rather vulgar argument.

As if he were ashamed of them, Don Emanuele quickly resumed his tale,

"So full of blissful yearning was my sleep, so full of delight my dreams, so cruel was my awakening. My hand was sore and the whole misery of my wretched situation came over me. What comfort was it that I reproached myself for being the cause of my misfortunes, a degenerate, a renegade priest, who had not said mass for weeks, nay months?

To be honest, my self-reproaches were not entirely genuine. It was not remorse and good intentions that were my comfort, but the thought of her, of her whose name at that moment I did not even know.

I did not doubt that I would see her again that evening, but what would happen then? How could I win her, given the complications of my present situation, which I would, moreover, have to conceal from her if I did not want to lose her respect?

The first essential was to find money. The only way seemed to be to ask the Senator's wife, whose son I taught, for a further advance. It is probably superfluous to say that by then I had received my pay for months to come. Therefore I dressed and went to the house although no lessons were due that day. I explained the situation to her, using an excuse which was probably just plausible.

She was about to leave the room to fetch the casket where she kept her money, when she noticed my bandaged hand and, in sympathetic tones, asked me how it had happened. This time my lie was so clumsy that she was struck by a contradiction with my excuse and – her polite interest was painfully embarrassing – pursued the matter. I became entangled in an ever-expanding web of lies, which I had to invent in order to back up earlier ones. Eventually I was reduced to weaving in a thread of truth here and there so that in the end my explanation had not only become completely unbelievable, but also more dishonourable than it really was.

'What?' asked the Senator's wife. 'You say you were thrown down the steps while saying mass in San Simeone Piccolo by my husband's sister-in-law's cousin, Bajamonte Tiepolo, and landed on the chalice? I did not realise you knew that capon, Bajamonte Tiepolo. It's true we are related to people like that, but that does not mean we have anything to do with them,'

'No, no', I interjected quickly, 'not him so much as his sister –'

My employer's wife gave a little scream, as if she had been stung by an insect, and drew back, as if she could see the marks of some loathsome infectious disease on my face. Not only did she not give me the advance, she fired me on the spot – to save her son from being infected – and barred me from the house for good.

The Senator, I later learnt, had once had a brief but very tempestuous relationship with Angiola, that had brought him into contact with a certain secret sect and almost led to his banishment from Venice.

However that may be, my only hope of obtaining money had been dashed and I did not dare to return to the Ca' Tiepolo; I wandered about the city in desperation. Turning out my pockets to see if there were not by chance some coin I had overlooked, I found the card the beggar had given me the previous day.

In such a daze that I was grateful for the least sign of hope, I had the absurd idea of asking the beggar to return the lira I had given him. I rushed to the part of the city where he lived and when I reached the address I was astonished to find a large mansion. I knocked, fully expecting to be told I had made a mistake, or that a trick had been played on me. The door was opened by a well-dressed old man whom it took me some considerable time to recognise as the selfsame beggar who, the previous day, had given me this address, which was obviously his own. He, on the other hand, recognised me at once and seemed pleased to see me again.

He asked me into a spacious room, magnificently furnished. Along the walls in a pedantically straight line stood a number of black, iron-bound chests. In the middle of the room, on an inlaid table, was a small chest – modelled on the others, but bound with gold.

The old man clapped his hands. A beautiful and chaste-looking girl appeared, indeed, so beautiful and chaste did she seem that, had my thoughts not been fixed on *her*, I would certainly have fallen violently in love with her soft grace. She called the old man Papa and asked what he wanted.

'Bring us some chocolate, my child', he said. – You must realise that chocolate was at that time the most elegant drink there was. – When his daughter had left, the old man said,

'As you will learn the whole story anyway, I can tell you this straight away: the one disadvantage of my existence is that I can keep no one to wait on me personally. Servants for the kitchen and so on I have in plenty, but none of them knows me. A personal valet would almost certainly sooner or later find himself in the embarrassing position of being asked for alms by me outside some church or other ...', he gave a merry laugh, 'so my daughter waits on me.'

We chatted about this and that, and I did not dare to bring the conversation round to the only thing that concerned me: that one lira.

The young girl served the chocolate and the old man began to tell me his story,

'My name', he said, 'is Odoardo Eugenio Zaparini and I come from a family of organ-builders; my father, my grandfather and my elder brother Adam Orazio were all organ-builders.

I was fourteen years old when my father died, after a life during which he had created many famous and melodious instruments, and I was put into the care of my brother, who was considerably older and already enjoyed a wide reputation. He was sought after all over the Republic to build organs, above all here in Venice itself. The Council even passed a law forbidding him, on pain of death, to leave the Republic. They were jealous of other cities having organs from his hand. It almost cost him his life when he was caught being smuggled out in a salt barrel among the luggage of the English ambassador, who wanted to send him to London to build an organ for the great composer Handel. He was only saved by the fact that a monastery, which admitted exclusively ladies of the aristocracy and which refused to go without its Zaparini organ, had one of his instruments awaiting completion. Later on he managed to make good his escape, from Belluno in the foothills of the Dolomites, and returned to Silesia, where my grandfather Adam had come from. He died there, years ago now, held in high esteem as an organ-builder and in low esteem as a loud-mouthed, obstreperous drunkard ...

All the time he had me under his thumb, instead of initiating me into the family secrets, he kept all my father's and grandfather's notes hidden from me, presumably because he was as jealous of his reputation as the Republic itself, and feared I might display some inborn talent for organ-building. He forced me to enter a monastery, having destined me for holy orders.

But in the narrow cell the paternal blood within me began to thunder like a bass stop every time my fellow inmates talked of my brother's fame. The nearer the day approached on which I was to take my vows, which seemed to me a fate worse than death, the more troubled became my nights. Waking and dreaming, I saw visions of gigantic organs which would send my fame coursing round the world on a storm of sound from a thousand pipes. I saw myself with my organs cast down the Kingdoms of this world, Republic, Emperor and Pope, I saw myself rule the whole planet, and finally I saw my mighty works bring down heaven and hell, leaving only myself with my organ pipes rising above the ruins of heaven.

The last night before I was to take my vows I called upon – I do not dare to pronounce his name until I am finally redeemed – I called upon *him* ...

The whole monastery was in uproar as the cloud of pitch and sulphur rolled, as thick as porridge, through the passageways.

But I held onto my pact, which guaranteed that every commission would be completed with ease and would result in an unparalleled masterpiece. My rise to fame would be inexorable and, as was expressly stipulated, beside it that of my brother should pale into insignificance, even ridicule. I had, moreover, made it a condition that I should be rich, rich beyond the dreams of avarice – and what in that might appear as greed, turned out to be my good fortune, for which I praise God. For instead of what you might call an expiry date for my soul, the agreement was that with the millionth sequin that I received for my work, for any task I undertook or in recognition of any service I had performed – in money or kind, in goods or estates – I should descend into hell.

The wording of that clause of the pact would have done credit to the sharpest legal mind:

Legacies, assignment of debts – everything had been thought of, from the rates of exchange into and out of foreign currencies to the snail shells the Chinese use to pay for their edible worms, and all written down in my own blood! Everything had been thought of – apart from charity, for he, the Master of the Nether World, cannot imagine in his arrogant pride that there are men for whom giving is its own reward.

At first I did not notice this point at all. Nor did I make much use of my ability to build organs without training or effort. I believed there would be time enough for that later; moreover I was suddenly showered – you may well laugh – with legacy upon legacy from all kinds of aunts and uncles. My priority was to spend my way through them. First of all then, I *lived*, at least that was what I thought, and lived in such a manner that within a short time I would have gone to hell, pact or no pact. My iniquities were legion. Did I keep accounts during my dissolute life? Of course not – one of the pupils I had soon attracted looked after that.

It was the day when an old woman brought me two sequins – one I had lent her, the other I had demanded as interest – it was the sight of that shameful sequin of interest that suddenly filled my heart with fear, with sacred, saving fear: I knew – heaven surely told me – that sequin was the millionth! I drew back from the old woman as if from a scorching fire and cried, 'I do not want it! Keep the money! Away! Away!' And I felt the powerful wing-beats of my guardian angel returning ... I discovered the loophole in the agreement and decided to live on charity from then on.

At the beginning I did not find it easy. But gradually I became accustomed to a frugal existence; often I received ten or twenty lire in a day, three times as much as I needed to live on. And in the course of the twenty-eight years that have passed since then, it has built up into the wealth you see around you.'

He stood up and opened the chests one after another. They were full to the brim with coins, arranged according to denomination.

'All I have to do is to be sure not to accept a single lira, except in charity. And before the money is used to buy anything, it has to be given away. I gave it to my wife, then, since she died, to my daughter: you see, the moment I bought something to the value of at least one sequin I would be on my way to hell because it would not have been given to me, I would have bought it ...

Thus my situation forces me to do good. Everything you see before you belongs to my daughter, Fiametta, apart from the money itself, and that, too, will be hers after her marriage.'

I enquired politely how his plans were proceeding in that respect and learnt that Messer Odoardo had chosen me for his son-in-law – as long as his daughter, he added, found me reasonably acceptable. Since my arrival in Venice he had, without my knowing it, observed me and had come to the conclusion that I was the right husband for his daughter.

'*Me!*' I cried.

'Yes, you.'

'And you have observed me since I have been here in Venice?'

'Every step.'

'Then', I said, 'either you have not observed me very well or your choice of me is completely incomprehensible. I am' – I started to list my faults – 'an unworthy priest, I am in the clutches of a jealous courtesan, I have just been dismissed from my employment ...'

'I know all that', said Messer Odoardo calmly, 'and I know that you are good.' I threw myself to my knees before him and covered his hand with tears and kisses, at the same time insisting that I could not fall in with his plan but asking permission nonetheless to be allowed to call him father.

It must have been a sore disappointment to him, but he immediately composed himself, embraced me and said,

'Why is it impossible, my son?'

What answer could I have given this noble gentleman, this man of such innate goodness, who was prepared to shower me with blessings, other than the truth?

I did not need to tell him, he knew everything. There was but one thing he did not know, the depth of the wound Stellidaura, whose name at that point I still did not know, had made in my soul. I confessed it all to him, and that it was impossible for me even to think of another woman.

'Well', he said calmly, although his disappointment was audible, 'one day too late. I said yesterday that it was the most important day of your life —'

'I remember', I said.

'And I thought that would so arouse your curiosity that you would come the very same day ... but I see that even so, it was the most important day of your life.'

'We are forgetting: I am a priest', I said, 'I couldn't have married her anyway.'

'It could be arranged', he said. 'If the worst came to the worst, you could have moved to Geneva and become Protestants like my forefathers.' With a sigh he let his head droop.

Warm tears welled up from within me. I kissed his hand and sobbed that I had come to ask no other favour than the lira I had given him the previous day. His eyes were damp, too, but he was composed, and it was with a gesture of goodwill, not of contempt, that he gently pushed me away from him and took the little box from the table, the miniature money-chest.

'Open it', he said, calmly.

I opened it and there I saw, nestling on a cushion of velvet, a lira coin. 'It is the lira you gave me yesterday. It was to bring you good luck. I had thought that this little box would be the noblest of dowries that I could give you and my daughter: the symbol of your good heart. But take it now and go with my blessing. May this one lira bring you the happiness you dream of, that is all I can wish you.'

I took my leave of him and hurried to my café. It was certainly not by chance that there on the board was a note from some gentleman – an Englishman, the name is irrelevant – challenging anyone to a game of draughts for money. The Englishman was there in the café. I offered to play at twelve soldi a game. I did not dare to risk the whole lira ...

I won, at first slowly and then with ever-increasing rapidity, so that when I left the Englishman, whom I promised a return match the next day, I had twenty-four ducats in my pocket. I hurried to the Ridotto. What I had not dared to do with my lira I would now dare with the ducats: I joined in a game of *Ombre*.

You won't be familiar with the game. It is supposed to come from Spain and is extremely complicated. I always bid *Solo*, that is the boldest *Chicane* of the game, and I tell you, two out of five times I drew the *Spadille*, the *Manille* and the *Basto* – they are the top trumps – from the stock ... That all means nothing to you, but perhaps it will give you an idea if I tell you that the only reason I was not accused of cheating was because half the Ridotto was gathered round me and no cardsharper's trick would have escaped all those expert eyes.

When I had won four hundred sequins I announced I would take the bank at Faro. Immediately everyone around joined in to bet against the bank, to pit their luck against mine. They lost ... Not counting the pawn tickets and God knows how many IOUs, which I threw away, my winnings amounted to the sum of six thousand sequins. And I would have gone on winning if there had been any gamblers left willing to bet against me.

But I suddenly noticed that among all the coins the lira, my lira, was missing. I had marked it by scratching a cross below the belly of the Lion of St. Mark. Feverishly I turned out my pockets, but could not find it. I went outside; the Venetian night lay like a heavy curtain over the city. Then I felt a shock as of physical nausea, I was rooted to the spot as if molten lead had been poured into my belly and everything went black, blacker than the Venetian night: in the frenzy of gambling I had forgotten the rendezvous in the café! Like one pursued by the Devil, I rushed there, my whole body tingling with self-reproach. It was too late, of course. Yes, they told me, hours ago a gondolier had been there looking for someone. He had left without finding him. No one knew anything more.

I ran on, took a gondola, ordered the gondolier to row me this way and that round Venice, in there! – no, here, follow that gondola, no, go back, this archway, that archway ... and then back to the café, perhaps ... I wanted to be everywhere at once. I searched every theatre, ran to and fro until my feet would carry me no longer. Finally, it was my last hope, I returned to the café; when it closed I made my way back to the Palazzo Tiepolo, all hope gone, cursing myself and the money, for which I had missed my only chance of seeing her again.

Don Bajamonte was waiting for me, his sword drawn. I did not give him time to speak, but tossed the money to the ground at his feet.

'May the One who sent the money come to fetch you, Your Excellency.'

He ignored me and fell on the sequins like a hungry dog on a bone, then disappeared – doubtless back to where I had won them and where he, in even less time probably, would lose them again.

I went to bed, fighting off Angiola's loathsome embraces. My eyes ached, each tear was a burning torment; yet eventually I fell asleep.

Early next morning I awoke to shouts from 'His Excellency'. I had obviously been mistaken, the lucky coin must have been amongst my winnings after all, for Don Bajamonte, contrary to his usual misfortune, had only managed to lose half the money. His sister was demanding the rest in order to be able to pay the most pressing debts. He, however, was trying to force his way into my bedroom to make me use my magic arts to replace the half he had lost – the end of Carnival was near, and that meant the end of gambling in the Ridotto.

I slipped out by a side door and wandered, without hope or comfort, through the streets of Venice. By a happy chance and contrary to my usual habit, I went to my café around midday to be greeted by the news that an hour ago a gondolier had been looking for me and would return with a message in an hour.

You can imagine how this news revived my spirits! Impatiently I waited for the hour to pass. It was the gondolier I had seen before, he was pleased to find me there and asked me to accompany him. He told me that he had searched for me both the previous day and that morning, and that the unknown lady asked me to go to a discreet house in the Giudecca. I told him to take me there.

She welcomed me, and for the first time I saw her unmasked. I had expected to be greeted with reproaches, but she overwhelmed me with her warmth, her tenderness. She wasted no words on my absence the previous day, which she must have found impolite, even hurtful. However, she did seem uneasy, troubled. I begged her to tell what it was that was weighing on her mind.

'That I cannot do', she said, 'not yet. But I have not asked you here without reason. This I can say: I am being most cruelly persecuted. One sign, one word from a spy could mean my ruin. There is not one moment when I can feel sure that the sbirri are not about to apprehend me and carry me off.'

I assured her that as long as I was by her nothing could happen to her – the sort of nonsense one says on such occasions. But she went on:

'I must continue to flee. Where I come from you have already guessed. What you cannot know is why I have flown here, to the very city where tyranny and bloodthirsty intrigue hold sway, where half the population lives from spying on and denouncing the other half. Perhaps – if you agree to my plan – there will come a day when I will be able to tell you, along with the whole strange, sad story of my life, on which some curse seems to lie. One thing only I will say: I came here because of a man I hoped could save me. It was his emissary my gondolier mistook you for. But he has betrayed me, perhaps even gone over to my enemies; that is the most terrible part – I am not sure of anything in this labyrinth of dangers ...'

She cried, and I tried to comfort her. Still sobbing violently, she continued:

'I do not know why I trust you. Some angel seems to have sent you. Help me ... Flee with me, take me to be your wife, if you do not find me repulsive. Everything I have – it is not much more than my poor life – shall be yours.'

I threw myself at her feet. 'You love me? I am the happiest man under the sun. I adore you ...'

She interrupted me and laid her hand on my arm. 'I trust you; you will protect me and I will be a good wife to you.'

'I do not even know what you are called?'

'Stellidaura', she said, 'and there is only one condition: you must never ask me about my life before we met.'

Nothing simpler, I thought. How old might she be? At most, twenty-two. She can't have much to hide. – At that time, my friend, I did not realise just how much a woman can have been through at twenty-two.

'Where shall we flee to?' asked Stellidaura.

'To Geneva', I said. 'We will have to become Protestant; I, too ...'

'You too? Are you being pursued as well?'

'I am a priest', I said.

'And presumably you haven't two soldi to rub together?'

'Precisely', I said.

'It makes no difference', said Stellidaura, 'and it is a not a bad idea at all to become Protestant. That would never have occurred to me. We must flee this very night.'

'This very moment, if you want.'

'No', she said, 'there are matters I must settle which will take a few hours. Be here on the stroke of eleven and be booted and spurred, as they say. And not a word to anyone, I need hardly say that, need I?'

I stood and made to kiss her hand. She offered me her mouth.

It was a kiss of friendship, of that there was no doubt. Would Stellidaura's affection turn to love? Of that I had no doubt, either. A woman of twenty-two cannot live for long without love, or so I thought. But my brain was wrestling with other matters: to Geneva ... what would we live on? I could speak neither German nor French. How could a runaway priest earn money? The more I thought about it, the more the objections piled up.

Deep in thought, wavering between love and all kinds of misgivings, my first visit was to a church, then to my café and finally, towards evening, to the Palazzo Tiepolo. Fortunately Don Bajamonte was not there. Angiola made a scene which left me completely cold. I turned my back on my former mistress and went to my room.

My love for Stellidaura, the lure of adventure and, not least of all, my own wretched situation here in Venice: it all persuaded me to ignore my misgivings. Perhaps a lucky star would guide us to a place where our love could blossom despite all adversity. With a light heart I secretly packed my things – and few enough they were, just some Latin classics and my beloved Petrarch – and told the gondolier, unsuspecting fool that I was, to row me gently through the canals to the Guidecca. I wanted to arrive on the stroke of eleven and take her in my arms ...

It was in a joyful mood that I glided along through the masked revelry of Venice that night just before the end of Carnival; I returned the exuberant greetings of the colourful harlequins on the banks and bridges that were garlanded with lanterns; bubbling over with happiness – and with a tinge of sadness because I was about to leave it all behind for ever – I blew kisses back to the fair Columbines in the mystery of shadowy rooms behind delicate balconies; I sang to the sound of the mandolines as squares full of wild dancers in fancy dress slipped past; and in the water of the canals the reflections of the brightly-lit windows and the lanterns which bedecked the façades danced to the rhythm of a barcarole. I felt, unknown and insignificant as I was, that I could embrace this great city, dying, and yet so magnificent in the costumed pageantry of its delightful citizens, dying and yet immortal: Venice.

Oh, my friend, I cannot describe a mood composed of such contradictory feelings: I believed Stellidaura was mine, joyfully I wanted to follow her and leave Venice, the city which, in that very hour, I saw as the pearl in the oyster of the world, the city I would love for ever. What should it profit me that I should conquer the whole world if I were never able to set foot in Venice again? In spite of the joy in my heart, in spite of the exultation on my lips, I had tears in my eyes.

The nearer we came to the Guidecca, the more distant became the noise of the Carnival. All was quiet. At the stroke of eleven I arrived at the inconspicuous house, but instead of Stellidaura, it was the landlady who greeted me with pitiful wails: half an hour ago the secret police had forced their way into the house, had confiscated Stellidaura's belongings with grotesque formality and dragged my poor angel, who had put up a mute and desperate struggle, to a gondola draped in chains which had swiftly disappeared into the night.

O Stellidaura!

In answer to my questions the old woman told me that in the house and on the way to the gondola they had not beaten Stellidaura, but then, when the gondola had pushed off, her screams had been audible for miles across the water. And behind the windows, where they drew the blinds as soon as the chained gondola appeared, all the people had secretly made the sign of the cross for the poor soul of the beautiful lady; more, the old woman whispered to me, they could not do for her.

How well I knew that! For all my desperation, there was nothing I could do for Stellidaura either, except make the sign of the cross for her poor, beloved soul. I felt I wanted to ... even today I dare not think of my mood as I made my aimless, indeed pointless, way through the noisy, happy crowd. I put on a red mask with a long nose to conceal my tears, but they ran down my cheeks, wetting my lips, whilst before and behind and above me Scaramuccio sang songs of love and death in Venice, sweet as the nightingale, fresh as the breeze from the Lagoon and as bitter as the tang of seaweed ...

Under the velvet sky of a Venetian spring night, surrounded by the bubbling cadences of the serenades, jostled this way and that by the exuberant crowd, I searched for the gates of the underground prison.

But who knew where the cruel, venal and beyond all measure corrupt judiciary of this Republic, which was already decaying before it died, kept their victims and tortured them and, so to speak, executed them by dissection? Walls I could have assailed, but a gigantic, thousand-headed, invulnerable jellyfish?

It was a long time, you can believe me my young friend, before my hatred was transformed into pure sorrow. I became restless and since then have wandered all over the world. The Republic, that poisonous jellyfish, collapsed not many years later. I was in the desolate and almost deserted city when it trembled before every French drummer-boy instead of the sbirri. The Seat of the Doges had become the dependency of a foreign power, and where once Harlequin had brought smiles to the faces of the Venetians now French officers drafted the pathetic remnants of Venice's youth to perish on the frozen fields of foreign dishonour. Where the Ridotto once stood was now a brothel for the occupying forces, and the cells of the state prisons were filled with provisions for the maniacal expeditions of the stunted fool spewed out by the revolution in Paris to empoison the whole of Europe.

I found no trace of Stellidaura. You too", he turned to me, "whom I asked, just as I ask everyone I meet, have not heard of her. It will remain an eternal, leaden mystery that robs me not only of my sleep, but also of my death ... O Stellidaura!"

He fell silent.

I was so moved, I remained silent too – what could I have said? I stood up and went slowly across to the railing. Lost in thought, I watched a flare rise above the treetops and burst into a shower of red stars that slowly sank back down. A midsummer night's festivities here in the park? I wondered in surprise. Then a shot rang out. From Alfred's cabin came a babble of excited voices. Suddenly Don Emanuele was standing beside me.

"For God's sake, hurry! Hurry!"

He dragged me through a small door and along an iron walkway.

Gradually a pale, yellowish glow began to illuminate the night sky. "The time has come", said Don Emanuele; he was panting as he ran and I suddenly realised that it was not from the exertion but because he was in the grip of an emotion which infected me as well – fear.

"The morning?" I said anxiously, uncertain whether I should

feel hope or not.

"There will be no more morning, no more day. Hurry up or we'll be too late."

From the horizon to the zenith there appeared in the sky regular stripes of a more intensive, but still pale yellow.

We had reached the bank – how, I could not say. "That way!" Don Emanuele pulled me to a small ramp from which two flights of stone steps led down, between balustrades ornamented with statues, to an open space around a fountain. The fine stonework surround had been desecrated with piles of earth and rubble. The displaced water sent streams – some narrow, some broad – coursing over the gravel. Old chestnut and beech trees had been felled, hastily and carelessly by all appearances, and they had knocked statues from their pedestals, overturned marble benches and crushed delicate stone balustrades. A gigantic towering object, alien as if it had irrupted from another dimension, dominated all things that grew and blossomed. It was a kind of gleaming silvery dome, which in both shape and colour vaguely recalled a Zeppelin stuck at right angles into the ground.

We ran down the steps towards the silvery object.

"Don't touch!" shouted Don Emanuele.

We hurried through the undergrowth round the side of the object, that now looked to me more like a circus tent.

"You mustn't be surprised", panted Don Emanuele, "if it turns out that we're too late."

We stumbled on. There was a sort of fishy, sweaty stench. Don Emanuele gave a grunt – of approval, it seemed to me.

Suddenly we came to a clearing. The freshness of the surfaces where the trees had been felled showed that it, too, was of recent origin.

A group of some thirty girls appeared. They were all wearing the scantiest of briefs (actually they were just stars covered in paste diamonds with rays spreading out round their hips and buttocks) and black fishnet tights, with feathers bobbing up and down on top of their heads; each clutched an ostrich-feather fan to her bosom. They were being driven across the clearing by a man in sports trousers and a black roll-neck pullover.

They were hurrying towards an opening in the gigantic tent. This opening or doorway narrowed to an acute angle at the top; with a hissing noise it started to shut in a seamless join.

"Thank God", said Don Emanuele, "nearly, but not quite."

We rushed along behind the girls towards the gap in the tent. It was already quite low down when we reached it and the last of the girls had had to crawl, but Don Emanuele still took a few seconds to look round. I shall never forget his expression: it was his farewell to the world.

I was grabbed by the feet, pulled to the ground – grazing my elbow – and dragged into the tent. Then Don Emanuele thrust his head and shoulders through the gap; I gripped one arm, the man in the roll-neck pullover the other, and we pulled Don Emanuele in. The wall closed behind him, red with the sizzling, scorching heat.

The girls pressed together in a huddle, trembling with fear and wailing, "There are more to come, the others are still outside ..."

A man in uniform appeared and said, with a shrug of regret, "We cannot open the door any more. I'm sorry. Anyone still outside is lost. Would you please give me your names?"

The man in the roll-neck pullover explained they were some of the artistes from a variety show. They had been rehearsing, which accounted for their dress, or rather, undress. He was, he said, the impresario, Nankeen by name.

"First name?"

"Just Nankeen, no first name."

The man in uniform was not asking out of politeness, they were formalities that had to be gone through. We too, Don Emanuele and myself, had to give our particulars. "Unfortunately", said the man in uniform, "only a fraction of the space in the bunker is taken. There is room for roughly three million. So far a mere ten thousand have completed registration! It just all happened too quickly."

When Don Emanuele gave his name the man in the uniform grovelled. Apologising for not dealing with us straightaway, he trembled with excitement as he wrote down our details.

"Herr Weckenbarth?" asked Don Emanuele.

"Of course, of course", said the uniform, "he's downstairs..."

"Then presumably Dr. Jacobi too ..."

"Of course, of course ..." – his obsequiousness rather undermined his credibility. He gave the impression he would say yes to anything Don Emanuele said.

"It would have been too awful", Don Emanuele said turning to me, "if they, of all people, had not been able to reach the bunker. – Take us to them", he said to the lackey, or soldier.

The girls and Nankeen had been taken off to the right by another man in uniform. A long, dimly-lit corridor led away in either direction along the curve of the bunker. On the inside wall were steel doors with porthole windows as in telephone boxes: they were doors to the lifts.

We went to the left. With an odd-looking key the man in uniform opened one of the doors and ushered us in, following us into the cabin of shiny, punctureproof metal. A heavy plate of the same metal slid across the door and on the indicator, a kind of long thermometer with black and red markings, a column of mercury began to descend from level to level.

Our uniformed guide gave an obsequious laugh when he noticed how I was fascinated by the 'thermometer'.

"There are one thousand and sixteen floors – No! don't lean against the wall!"

Startled, I looked round: the wall behind me was growing brighter and brighter, first a dull white, then light blue, then greenish until finally it seemed to become transparent, a swirl of shimmering greens, as if we were travelling through an empty aquarium.

"This metal", he explained, "is one that glows cold. It glows because of the high speed of the lift which we do not feel because of the pressure equaliser." The mercury column stopped by one of the red marks about a third of the way from the bottom of the 'thermometer'.

The metal wall slid to one side, the man in uniform opened the door and we stepped out onto a scaffolding of black bars that encircled a large area of empty space, as wide as the dome of a cathedral and dimly lit.

"We haven't quite managed to get everything completed",

said our guide. "Follow me, please, it will be quicker this way, rather than taking the link-lift."

We stepped out into the murk of the immense void and crossed the echoing planks. The immensity of open space was not oppressing, on the contrary it gave one – or me at least – a feeling of security: one thousand and sixteen floors of which this area here was perhaps only one; we must be safe in the womb of the earth, safe from any kind of danger.

A short ladder led to a door. The man in uniform rang a bell. A second uniform appeared. The first explained briefly who we were, saluted and left. We followed the second. He was surly.

"Are Herr Weckenbarth and Dr. Jacobi here?" asked Don Emanuele.

"Yes", said our surly guide without turning round.

"Thank God for that", said Don Emanuele and took my arm with a relieved, almost jaunty gesture.

We passed countless doors and went along various corridors, all of which were carpeted and cheerfully and brightly lit. There were niches with large and not always very tasteful vases containing evergreen plants. We met no one.

Finally we came to a kind of glass-roofed winter garden with a spiral staircase leading up to a book-lined gallery. Here our surly guide told us to sit down in the leather armchairs and disappeared. After some time a third man in uniform appeared, a Chinaman, who grinned and lisped something incomprehensible. Since as he did so he pointed to a high, padded double door, we entered to find ourselves in a cloakroom. As we had no coats to deposit there, we went on through several lobbies with revolving doors until we came to a smoking-room with a fire blazing in the grate and three men chatting over port. Dr. Jacobi and Weckenbarth, who were sitting facing us, both put their glasses down with a laugh of relief. The third stood up – presumably the mysterious Alfred.

Two mannikins scarcely two feet tall, who had been sitting at the back of the room with sullen expressions on their faces, now also stood up and disappeared through a concealed door.

"Now", said Weckenbarth, "we must see that we get down in time for lunch."

"How on earth ...?" I said. "It was late evening when Don Emanuele finished his story and at most two hours can have passed since then ..."

"Time", said Weckenbarth, "is not quite the right word any more. Due to some of the technical aspects of the arrangements time is – how shall I put it? – somewhat the worse for wear in here, absolute time, at least. Not that it was intentional, but certain measures we had to take meant the distortion was inevitable. But time as a measure of bodily function, time calculated by the alternation of hunger and sleep, relative time – that, of course, remains."

"Oh, I see."

"Well, it is difficult to explain something you don't understand yourself."

"Don't clocks work any more?" I looked at my wrist-watch. It said half past one.

"Of course the clocks work. A radio can still work when the transmitter has broken down ... that is roughly the way to think of it."

"But my watch says half past one – is it half past one here, or not? Somewhere it must be half past one. Where has the time that *was* half past one disappeared to? *This* half past one here. Is it half past one outside?"

"Possibly."

"But not certainly?!"

"The question is academic. We are separated from the outside by a difference greater than any imaginable in the world that was."

"What?"

"Does it mean anything to you if I say, to put it in simple terms, 'dispositional parallax'?"

The others had noticed our discussion and broken off their conversation to listen. Now Don Emanuele too enquired about lunch.

"Through there", said Weckenbarth.

We rose. We went through a small door opposite the one the mechanical dwarves had disappeared through into an oval room containing a sofa-bed with the sheets turned back and a washbasin. I asked Dr. Jacobi if I might wash my hands.

"Of course", he said. The others went on ahead.

"If I have to go for more than two hours without washing my hands, my brain and my senses stop functioning."

In a cool stream of water I rinsed off the fragrant foam into the basin.

"Such is my awareness of my unwashed hands that the longer I continue in that state, the more every other feeling, every mood, every thought is paralysed by it, so that finally, if I am denied the opportunity of washing, I lose control, I am no longer myself, not myself nor any other human being, but an animal; I am transformed into a single organ that is focused on one thing alone – the nearest tap and bar of soap ... in mystical terms presumably something like guilt ..."

The dripping of the water from my refreshed hands was blissful. I took the laundry-stiff, white towel and gazed mindlessly into the mirror as I dried them.

"That", I continued, "is why I am incapable of climbing a mountain or, rather, of enjoying climbing a mountain. Before you reach the top and can enjoy the beautiful view, or whatever makes up for all the effort, there is so much mountain you have to lay your hands on and not a drop of water ... even the majesty of the Dolomites would fall to move me if my hands were dirty!"

"Ah yes", said Dr. Jacobi, "mountaineering ..."

It was only now that I noticed the window reflected in the mirror. A window! I remembered where we were. The window looked out onto a park. Behind a balustrade with two sphinxes facing one another was a diagonal line of young poplars interspersed with low yew-trees clipped into cones which threw long shadows in the evening sun. I was perplexed: only the yew-trees threw shadows, not the poplars ...

"Dr. Jacobi!" I cried, turning round. He followed my gaze and laughed.

"Did our theatre give you a surprise?"

"What theatre?"

"We are in one of the boxes of the theatre. It is probably not yet finished either! Nothing has been finished in here."

I went to the 'window' and could see the whole set: a pastoral scene tinged with blue.

"Well the shadows of the poplars certainly haven't been finished."

"Shadows or no shadows, there will be no plays performed."

"Why not?"

"Who is going to act?"

"The chorus girls maybe?"

"Who?"

"Just before us – Don Emanuele and myself, we were the last in – a troupe of chorus girls and their impresario came into the bunker."

"Then you had better book this box so that you can wash your hands before the great experience; otherwise it might be the same as mountain climbing."

"Do excuse me", I said. "I hope you did not object to my remark. Are you a mountain climber yourself?"

It was an innocent question and Dr. Jacobi laughed out loud.

"What, me a mountain climber? No, no, I have only once taken part in an excursion in the mountains."

"And you didn't enjoy it?"

"A strange experience", said Dr. Jacobi, "it was a long time ago and I was, it goes without saying, much younger. It came about through a cousin of mine; he belonged to the Knights of St. John and there was some connection between the Order and the man who was organising the expedition – yes, it was a regular expedition, not just a common-or-garden outing! It was the connection I have mentioned that procured me an invitation – normally one had to pay if one wanted to join these expeditions, and the prices were not low. The cost of such an undertaking was enormous. Sixty bearers had been hired and vast amounts of equipment and supplies were required.

The village we set off from belonged, as did the whole area including, of course, the hunting rights, to my host. The sixty bearers, all of them sturdy lads from the village, were mostly illegitimate sons of the Count's father, or sons of the illegitimate sons of the Count's grandfather. – As Roda Roda says, a seigneur who knows his rights will make his own dependents. – So there were sixty village lads to accompany us. Each one carried a rucksack and, in addition, either a rope, part of a tent or a pole. Apart from the tents, food and equipment they transported a dismantled howitzer plus ammunition. We carried our own binoculars – we, that was the three young counts, Heinrich, Severin and Balthazar, Count Severin's wife, Countess Wilhelmina, myself and a few other guests, mostly of the paying variety. On top of that there were the ghillies and the mountain guides.

On the first day we followed relatively civilised paths to a hunting lodge that belonged to our host where beds had been prepared for us. In spite of the general tiredness and the intense cold, hardly anyone slept. Everyone was talking about the coming ascent. The great hero was a huntsman called Jamie. He it was who had discovered the cave we were heading for and he had to repeat the story of its discovery several times.

Then we played cards for a long time and drank so much that the expedition's schnapps supplies had to be supplemented from the cellars of the hunting lodge which led to protests from the resident gamekeeper.

We set off early the next morning, around three o'clock. Neither moon nor stars were to be seen. The wind blew ice-crystals in our faces as we struggled through the knee-deep snow. All around was unrelieved darkness.

During the night the cannon had been assembled since, so it was said, it would have been impossible to carry out this complicated operation in the primitive conditions higher up. I could see nothing, but I could imagine how difficult it must have been to pull the piece of artillery.

Some stormproof lanterns were lit, but the storm immediately blew them out, so a long rope was unrolled, one of the ghillies took the leading end and all the members of the expedition followed him one after the other, keeping one hand on the rope. The path was steep and I lowered my head like a bull to brace myself against the wind. Sometimes I looked up, my scarf tight across my mouth, and I could see the leading huntsman holding the lantern, that would flare up for a few seconds as the wind blew it back horizontally like a pennant, as he looked for the track.

101

At first all we did was climb – for an eternity. Now the wind blew from the front, now it buffeted us from behind. Sweating, in spite of the fact that most of my limbs were frozen, one hand clamped to the guide-rope, nose encrusted with ice, I followed the man in front, and my mind was similarly clamped on one thought: Will we ever get down? But for the moment we were going up ...

At least after a while, after the first of the many eternities we spent on our feet that day, it began to get lighter. A strip of sky above what were presumably the eastward ridges turned grey. At the same time, or so it seemed to me, it became colder. I could see now that we were making our way up a narrow mountain valley. Black rocks covered with glassy ice piled up on the left and the right and from the saddle, where the valley merged with the still-dark sky, the storm wind whistled down unimpeded. I looked back: a long chain was zig-zagging up the valley. I was a link in the chain, the eighth. At the very rear some of the young villagers were dragging the little cannon along behind them.

After a few hours of ascent we rested. Against the backdrop of a massy, motionless, slaty bank of cloud covering the sky above us, frayed streamers of light-grey cloud poured over the mountain-tops. The head of the valley still seemed as far away as ever. A small barrel of schnapps was handed round and everyone had a slice of cold beef, bread and a plate of potato soup, which had apparently been cooking in the portable field kitchen at the back of the line as we marched along. Unfortunately, before I had time to insert my spoon the soup was blown out of the plate and flew through the air in a flat curve. I suggested to another of the party, number seven in the chain in front of me, that the sun would probably rise now that it was becoming lighter. No, he said, it would soon be night. I had lost my sense of time as well as that of direction. That narrow strip of brightness in the sky, that had been the day!

After the rest we continued our climb. It grew dark again so that I had no idea whether we did finally reach the head of the valley up there in the clouds.

I had already given up thinking or hoping anything when we eventually reached a mountain hut where the cowherd stayed in the summer with part of the Count's herd of cattle. The hut had been prepared in advance for us. The wind still whistled through gaps between the planks the size of your finger, but I was just happy that it did not blow the soup out of my plate, only caused a gentle swell. After the meal we had schnapps. I soon lay down and wrapped myself up in a few blankets and slept rolled up like that, slept in spite of the noise of the others, who again sat up until late into the night boasting of exploits to come and playing cards. I can still see today how a card, which one of the players was holding, ready to play it, was ripped from his hand by a sudden blast, whirled up against a gap in the wall, folded in two and sucked out into the icy black inferno. The result was a violent quarrel – it turned out that no card in the pack was missing.

When I woke up I seemed to be lying in milk: there was thick fog all around. I made the mistake of taking my hand out from under the blanket to look at my watch; as I did so I happened to touch the ear of my neighbour, who was still asleep. At once my finger froze fast. I did not realise this and tried to pull it away. He gave a roar, kicked the blanket off his foot and froze his toe to a beam. We had to use a blowlamp, which was brought along for precisely this kind of occurrence, to free my finger from his ear and his foot from the beam.

Because of these little annoyances it took some time to get started that morning, but also, as I was pleased to see, because even the huntsman who was in charge of the party was frozen fast to the schnapps barrel by his moustache.

Then snowshoes were handed out – large fan-shaped sheets of some woven material which we strapped to our boots. When I took my first step out in the snow I sank in up to my neck, but I was hauled out with a winch, which they had had the foresight to set up in advance. It was explained to me that the purpose of the snowshoes was to make the holes you sank into bigger and therefore more easily visible: a normal hole the size of a man would have immediately been filled in by the wind. The local term for the frozen bodies of such mountaineers which reappeared in the spring was 'ice-turds'.

So we set off once more on our march through the beautiful

and mysterious winter landscape of the high mountains. As the light increased, so did the fog. It only lifted for one hour, when an infernal storm swept up the valley, and now my fearful gaze could see that we were still making our way between the black, ice-encrusted rocks crowned with huge cornices. The head of the valley seemed no nearer.

I will not bother you with a description of the further adversities we somehow overcame before we finally reached the notch in the sky. The view of the mountains all around was magnificent. The light grey scraps of cloud rushing across the dull sky were now below us. As far as we could tell, given that our eyes were encrusted with the ice-crystals that the storm constantly blew in our faces, it was possible to climb even higher.

I noticed the leader of our guides discussing matters with the elder of the younger counts, pointing this way then that until they finally did indeed decide on a route that continued to climb. We scrambled, or rather crawled on our bellies, up a dreadful snow-covered ridge. On either side smooth snowslopes, larded like a saddle of mutton with haphazard, gristly rocks, but otherwise incredibly vast and slippery, fell steeply away into the seething cauldron of icy mist.

We had our stop on the ridge. As this time the field kitchen was at the front, I had to pass back seventy plates of rice pudding, always making sure to hold them vertical against the wind, thus cunningly putting its malevolent strength to some use as it kept the pudding stuck to the plate. One false move and the precious pudding would have plunged down into the icy cauldron. I finally received my helping which I ate sitting astride the ridge and holding the plate vertical. Then the empty plates were passed forward and we set off once more.

I was already beginning to fear that we were going to spend the night on the ridge, but finally it took us to a pigeon-breasted plateau covered in snow which fell away gently at the edges into all kinds of cracks and crevasses: here it was decided we would bivouac. The howling wind, the swirling mist below us and the endless banks of cloud from which white peaks rose like islands – it all gave me the feeling the heights were dangerously unhealthy.

Although they all looked the same, the peaks aroused great enthusiasm amongst my companions. They shouted names at each other, 'Goiter Fell', 'Hen Comb' and 'Buttock Crag'.

I crept into the tent the guides had erected, as wet as if I had had a bath in my clothes, as weary as a fly in November, and so cold that I felt I was about to fall apart. I wrapped myself up in my blankets, that is, I folded the frozen blankets, that were as stiff as a board, roughly into my shape and slept in this icy envelope. My companions, however – and the young counts joined in – began to bellow out songs in praise of the somewhat vague ideal of the mountain wanderer. They were accompanied by a guitar; that noble instrument ought to be banned for the hiking classes. I do not need to describe to you my melancholy memories of Vivaldi's guitar concerto, of Venice, of spring. I swore an oath that, should I ever come down from here alive, I would never venture beyond the tree-line again.

My tiredness did not prevent me from lying wide awake, tormented by dismal thoughts. You probably did not register the site on which we had bivouacked: our tent was on a narrow, sloping, snow-covered plateau. Just beyond, as I had unfortunately not been able to avoid noticing, the plateau ended in a steep precipice broken by jagged rocks dripping with icy sweat. Whipped up by the stormwind, sulphurous streamers of mist flew past like the spray from breakers crashing against seacliffs. They swirled and writhed until a stronger blast blew them whirling up to even greater, crueller heights, where we were to follow them in the morning.

Although at that moment my life seemed meaningless to me I was still devilish afraid that some clumsy movement might send me hurtling helplessly towards the void. It was not death that frightened me but the seconds before it: the moment when the sharp, damp, cold rocks would slit open my clothes, my skin, the moment when, naked and bleeding, I would still have a few seconds to live in the howling maelstrom of ice ... purgatory fire would have been paradise compared with it. O fire! – Dante must have taken part in a similar mountain expedition before he depicted the innermost circle as a desert of ice.

Enough of that. Eventually I did manage to sleep. This time it was not the noise of departure that woke me but Mijnheer Cuypers who the whole time had been number nine in the chain. He told me that it had become even colder and that when they wanted to distribute more schnapps, they discovered that even that had frozen in the barrel. Mijnheer Cuypers was not an invited but a paying guest. He felt the expedition was well worth the thousand Dutch guilders it had cost him. He found the mountains, he said, a grandiose spectacle, but what delighted him more than anything was the comradeship. It was the tenth expedition he had been on. He suggested we should be on first-name terms, and promptly used my first name without waiting for me to agree. However, it was a familiarity which I only had a short time to take advantage of ...

Our departure was held up by a vain attempt to unfreeze one schnapps barrel. One measure at least increased our comfort: we no longer had to cling onto the rope, it was tied round our waists; they expected the wind to be stronger at some of the exposed passages that lay before us. It was this convenience that was the death of Mijnheer Cuypers. After we had been climbing for some time I felt a violent tug on the rope and only just managed to cling on: Mijnheer Cuypers had lost his foothold and was swirling out from the cliff face in the wind like a balloon on the rope between number ten and myself. It took a long time before we managed to haul him in, by which time we found that he had frozen to death; the cause, according to Count Severin, was the lack of schnapps.

'Losses were anticipated', he added. 'Who was it? Mijnheer Cuypers? As he only came this far his widow will get half of the hunting fee back. Of course, we'll have to deduct the expenses for carrying the body down.'

Transporting the corpse brought problems on which the expedition almost foundered. None of the ghillies or the lads from the village wanted to carry the unfortunate Dutchman; not for fear of contamination from the decomposing body – it was as cold as in a freezer – but out of superstition. 'Carry a dead body?' whispered some, 'A Protestant?' added the even more cautious ones ... Finally a solution was found: we could not prepare a hot meal before we reached the plateau we were heading for, so Mijnheer Cuypers was rolled up and packed into the field kitchen like a soused herring. When we reached the plateau he would be given a provisional burial in the snow until we set off back down. Even the most superstitious – the superduperstitious as one might say – were happy with that.

We finally reached the spot we were making for after surviving countless other dangers. I have forgotten the order in which they occurred, but once, I remember, we had to don crampons to crawl over a sloping ice-field with a surface like a ballroom floor and a devil of a camber. By this time the storm had relented – perhaps we were above the storm-line? Clouds and mist vanished. The sun appeared. In spite of that it was so cold that our breath froze the moment it met the air and stopped our mouths with a plug of ice. The magnificent mountain scenery was bathed in golden light and looked, so they told me, like fairyland ... Unfortunately I could not see much because I was blinded by the snow. Later on there was an avalanche which almost took the howitzer with it. Then there was a shower of rocks and we had to put helmets on which were so heavy that they pushed our snow-goggles down to our chins. Finally we had to jump over awesome crevasses – which, if one is to believe the experts, are almost as majestic as a Gothic cathedral inside. As they were said to be merely *almost* as majestic as Gothic cathedrals, this only reinforced my determination to stay below the tree-line in future, to keep well away from crevasses and stick to cathedrals.

As I said, our goal was a corrie of snow and ice with a diameter of some two hundred yards. The dragon we were hoping to slay was supposed to have its lair in a cave in the slope at one side of the corrie. The greater cave-wyrm is, as you will be aware, an eastern variant of the Alpine dragon.

After the tent had been erected in a spot with some protection, the howitzer was trained on the cave entrance. Fires were lit and lookouts posted. We retired to the tent. The waiting began.

The dragon did not appear.

The lack of wind meant that the smell of sweat in the tent

quickly began to become overpowering. One unwashed person stinks: several unwashed persons do not just add their personal body odours, they multiply them. I am astonished that the mountain air manages to stay so pure, given the large number of climbers. The storm, even my fear on the nasty little plateau, were pure joy compared to that stench. Hanslick says somewhere that Tchaikovsky made it possible to hear music stink. Up there, as truly as I am sitting here, the stench of my companions took on acoustic form, though I will not go into precise musical details, just in case you happen to be a Wagnerite.

I volunteered to go out on watch, took my rifle and my blankets and settled down in a snow-hole. By the entrance to the cave we had tethered a ram that had been brought specifically to serve as bait.

Everyone waited.

Where the blowlamp had failed, the superfetation of body odour succeeded: the schnapps barrel thawed. There was schnapps to drink. The lookouts lit pipes. The stars shone. There was no sign of the wyrm. The night passed.

The next morning the whole camp was electrified by a shout: a trickle of greenish smoke was coming from the cave.

'The wyrrrm', exclaimed Jamie, who had discovered the cave, 'Aye, 'tis he.'

Count Severin, the boldest of the hunters, decided that the ram was too far from the dragon's cave. The dragon would not scent the ram from where it was tethered at the moment, he declared. Since, because of the greenish smoke, no one else was willing to approach the cave Count Severin volunteered to go and try to drag the ram closer to the cave by himself.

'Oh, Severin, don't do it!' pleaded the Countess.

'Bugger off', he said.

They were his last words to her ...

Scarcely had the intrepid Count taken a few steps than a rumbling sneeze was heard from the cave. Instead of one, there were now two thin streams of smoke rising into the air.

Count Severin strode down into the corrie and up the other

side. The sneezing stopped. We saw the Count grasp the ram with both hands and; clearly in a rage, he screamed something across to us and tugged at the ram, but it must have been frozen fast. Like lightning a pale, greeny-grey, nose-like object shot out of the cave, gave the Count a shove so that he fell down in the snow, and disappeared again.

'The wyrrrm, the wyrrrm!' shouted Jamie.

'Let go!' we shouted to the Count.

But now the Count was frozen fast to the ram. In spite of that he managed to pull himself to his feet. Quickly the dragon appeared from the cave and gave him another shove; enormous picturesque whorls of greenish smoke rose up into the sky. As the snow did not melt, we assumed it would be cold smoke, but probably poisonous. The ghillies were all shouting at once:

'Fire the howitzer!' – 'Nae, nae, ye'll shoot the Count!' – 'Fire, ye ninny, fire!'

They were all trying to push each other away from the howitzer. Meanwhile the dragon was repeating its rapid thrusts – it looked like a gigantic bird pecking at a tiny seed. Before we came to the conclusion that it might be best to fire the gun after all, the cave-wyrm had bitten off one of the Count's legs. With a deafening, thousandfold echo, the shell whizzed out of the mouth of the howitzer. The whole corrie was filled with steam and smoke. When it cleared we could see a small, black hole outside the cave where the shell had plunged into the snow. The dragon was pulling both the ram and the Count by the latter's one remaining leg into its lair.

Solemnly – they removed their hats – the two younger counts decided there would be no quarter given to the dragon at all. They took the feathers from their hats and handed them to the Countess, swearing they would not wear them again until the dragon was dead. Unfortunately the ram had been lost and they had not brought any spare bait. Eventually someone had the idea of using Mijnheer Cuypers.

'Good idea', said Count Heinrich; 'in that case we'll reimburse his widow half the hunting fee in full.'

Afterwards, lunch had been taken in the meantime, we encountered some technical problems – the beast was now replete and needed a stronger lure than before. If, however, we were to push Mijnheer Cuypers' body any farther into the cave the dragon would not have to emerge sufficiently to present a target! What to do? We decided to tie Mijnheer Cuypers, whose corpse had been slit open from top to tail, to a long rope. Thus we could deposit him in the cave and then wait for the right moment to pull him away from under the dragon's nose. The body was covered in a thick layer of grease so that it did not freeze to the rock.

Two bold young ghillies cautiously pushed the bait into the cave and then ran the rope back – supporting it on wooden poles so that it would not freeze – across to the other side of the corrie where it was attached to a winch. The howitzer was reloaded. We all lay in wait ...

When we had neither heard nor seen anything of the dragon for the whole afternoon, the whole night, the following morning and well into the afternoon, the two surviving counts decided that it was time for new measures. Two further bold young ghillies, goaded by references to the heroism of Count Severin and encouraged by the promise of a bonus, lit torches and, carrying a supply of firework rockets, set off for the lair. They clambered over the raised rope, waved back to us and disappeared into the dark cave.

The wind had got up again. Yellowish drifts of cloud covered the sky. The rising wind sang – later on it howled – through the cliffs surrounding the corrie. For a long time we waited, breathless and full of trepidation; not a sound, not a murmur. Suddenly a ball of fire came whizzing out of the cave, burst into a number of red balls which in turn burst into many blue stars before exploding into myriads of green sparks which the wind whisked up in decorative spiral patterns – clearly one of the huntsmen had set off a rocket aimed in the wrong direction.

Again we waited while nothing more happened. Night began to fall. The wind blew scraps of mist round the corrie. Then – the ghillies must have learnt how to handle the rockets – there was a peal of bangs and crashes from within the cave. The noise inside must have been deafening, a whole bundle of rockets all set off at once in what was presumably an enclosed vault! Not surprisingly the two ghillies immediately came rushing out of the cave.

'What is it?' called those waiting across the corrie, 'what is it?'

'The wyrrrm! It's coming', shouted the two.

And there was the cave-wyrm! One of the two huntsmen stumbled over the rope because the others had already started to pull Mijnheer Cuypers toward them. But the dragon showed no interest whatsoever in Mijnheer Cuypers. It just stood there blowing green smoke into the scraps of mist. One of the bolder of the huntsmen shot the dragon in the eye with his rifle; the eyes were the only part of the dragon that we could distinguish, for the rest it was just a large shapeless lump looming out of the twilight and the green smoke. The glowing eye which the huntsman had aimed at blinked. The nostrils stopped emitting smoke and seemed to sniff the air. On our side of the corrie everyone was running backwards and forwards.

'Fire!' roared some.

'Get out of the way!' shouted others to the ghillies on the other side.

The two who had entered the cave as well as those who had waited at the entrance started to dash back across the corrie as fast as they could or fled for cover behind boulders or snowdrifts. The extra-bold huntsman fired off another round at the dragon's eye and then joined in the dash to safety. The dragon, one eye now blinking continually, opened its mouth. It was like looking into a furnace – yellow and red flames let off poisonous fumes whilst a forked tongue the size of a largish flag flapped to and fro.

And then the beast gave a roar ...

A loud roar, very loud and very long: not only did one of the huntsmen, otherwise a strong, healthy lad, suffer an instantaneous personality-change – he came to believe he was St. George –, but most of the others were rendered tone-deaf for the rest of their lives. We were sure we felt the mountain tremble with the roar and – as true as I'm standing here before you – for a few seconds the storm was diverted in a different direction.

The dragon leapt down from its cave to the floor of the corrie.

From its nostrils came smoke-rings the diameter of tree-trunks. One eye was still blinking. Its tail thrashed from side to side, causing a snowstorm. Mijnheer Cuypers, rope and winch were all flung high over the jagged cliffs of the corrie.

'NOW!' someone shouted.

His jaw jutting out with determination, his pipe clenched between his teeth, one eye closed tight and the other, on which our lives depended, screwed up and almost closed as well, the best shot among the huntsmen aimed the howitzer, adjusted the gun a little this way and then a little that way, lowered his head and suddenly pulled the trigger. Compared with the dragon's monstrous roar, the boom of the howitzer, usually so loud, seemed like the pop of a champagne cork.

The dragon froze.

Then it slowly rolled its eyes, snorting more than ever. One eye went lifeless. The greenish smoke was presumably the way a dragon bleeds, because of its high body temperature it has gaseous blood.

'Tis deid, tis deid!' shouted the village lads, but no one dared approach the dying dragon.

It grew as hot as a smithy. The life-gas poured out of the dragon's body in a hissing jet. The wound opened out, presumably due to the internal pressure of steam, until finally a column of green steam rose up as high as a church spire at which the wind tugged and teased. All around the dead monster the snow melted, and where it did not melt it was stained green.

Finally, when the jet of blood-gas subsided and only came hissing out in green puffs, like a steam engine, the carcass began to give off leaden black smoke. Soon the dense smoke enveloped the monster's body and settled in the corrie, swirling and billowing. Through the drifts we now and then caught glimpses of the smouldering carcass.

The next morning the smoke had cleared. The dragon was cold and had a light covering of fresh snow. We examined it cautiously. Apart from the countless armour-plates all the rest had burnt down to a spongy, sooty, fatty mass, which disintegrated at the slightest touch. We collected the armour-plates: they were about the size of a man's palm, shaped like a squat pyramid with a pentagonal base, and each ended in a short, curved spine.

Every member of the expedition was given one of the plates as a souvenir. One was to be sent to Cuypers' widow. Of Count Severin there was no trace.

At last we started out on the long-awaited descent. It was scarcely less arduous than our ascent. Every new stage in our descent I greeted as if it were paradise. Looking back, however, at the twilit peaks from the hunting lodge, where we telephoned for the cars to come and collect us, I was filled with pride at the dangers overcome. Nothing is as sweet as dangers overcome, in this case made even sweeter for me by my decision, never, *never* to face them again.

"Herr Weckenbarth wishes to know how much longer they should keep lunch waiting?" Scarcely had Dr. Jacobi uttered his last word than we were addressed by a man in a brown uniform – those we had seen so far had been olive green.

"Lunch!" said Dr. Jacobi.

"I didn't want to interrupt, Dr. Jacobi", I said, "but you did not say where it was?"

Dr. Jacobi, however, had already set off after the uniform and I had to hurry so as not to lose them.

We went along a corridor where chairs had been drawn up beside small bull's-eye windows. As we hurried past I managed to ascertain that they looked into the theatre. Then we went down some stairs into an untidy room where there were many ladders lying around.

"Nothing has been finished", said Dr. Jacobi, "nothing."

We passed through a concealed door into a library or, rather, onto the gallery running round the library half-way between the floor and the ceiling. At first I thought it was the same room I had rushed through with Don Emanuele for our reunion with Weckenbarth and Dr. Jacobi, but when I leant over the balustrade I saw that I was mistaken: beneath me stretched a murky, gaping void – they had not had time to install the floor! The staircase from the gallery spiralled down into emptiness ...

We went past rows of books. They were magnificent works, old and rare, but only painted on the walls.

"An exact copy of the library of the Monastery of St. Gallen", said Dr. Jacobi. "We had hoped we might be able to bring the original. All that is gone now ..."

To my astonishment, the uniform led us down the spiral staircase; he stopped on a small landing in the middle of a painted edition of the 'Encyclopaedia of Classical Antiquity', opened a small door and led us along a corridor with many doors leading off. In a lift we went up a few fractions of an inch on the mercury column.

"That was an illusion, of course", said Dr. Jacobi.

"What?"

"The fact that the indicator appears to show that we are going up. In fact we are going down."

"But", I said, "does that mean that Don Emanuele and I did not go down below ground, but upwards?"

"That again is an illusion", said Dr. Jacobi. "It is all arranged so that if the enemy should manage to penetrate the bunker at least they won't know where they're going in the lifts."

When we left the lift we found ourselves in a hall divided by dark, massive pillars into a smaller and a larger room. The smaller one was dark, the larger one brightly lit. In it was a table around which some hundred people were sitting. There were two empty chairs.

"Please excuse us", I said to Weckenbarth, "I had to wash my hands."

"Sit here, next to me, I have something to tell you. Are you having the consommé with liver dumplings?"

Then Weckenbarth explained to me that I had not been as discourteous as I had imagined. The others, those who had gone on ahead, had only been waiting for a couple of minutes. The farther away people were from each other in space, the less correspondence there was in time. I had been fortunate. It could just as well have happened that Weckenbarth's time, and that of the others, had rushed on ahead by – relatively speaking, of course – two days, and they would already have been tucking into their third lunch.

"What about those at the other end of the table?" I said to Weckenbarth. "They must be a good thirty feet away, do they have a different time from us?"

"Quite possibly", he said.

"So time is all out of shape; is it not possible to bring some system into it?"

"Only with great difficulty", he said. "You must imagine it rather like warm and cold air in a very large room: in an invisible chain of cause and effect set in motion by infinitesimal changes, streams or clouds of warm and cold air move around according to the laws of thermodynamics. That is how time behaves in here. But to more important matters; here in the 'cigar' – we call it that because of its shape ... have I told you about that?"

"Yes", I said, "while we were still on board the ship outside."

"Good. So, the cigar it is, for simplicity's sake. In here there are – not counting the military – some ten thousand people."

"I know."

"How?"

I told him. Herr Weckenbarth was annoyed at the indiscretion, or overstepping of authority, of the first man in uniform and, laying his hand on my arm, whispered something to Alfred, who was sitting on his right. Then he turned back to me and continued,

"Naturally the military have their own chain of command. But the civilians have to be governed as well, somehow or other. We have a President, Carola. We want to organise an assembly to advise her, a parliament so to speak, or rather, a Senate. Would you be prepared to allow yourself to be put forward as Senator?"

I did not know quite what to make of this. Herr Weckenbarth did not really know me at all. Forgetting the corruption of time, I had made his acquaintance at the most six hours ago. Did he find me so impressive that he thought me worthy of the position of Senator? Or was the position of Senator so insignificant?

However that might be, I accepted with thanks, if for no other reason than to have something to help pass the time. Who knew how long we would have to stay in here ...

"Good", said Weckenbarth, "then you are, from this moment, a Senator."

I still wanted to probe a little.

"I presume, Herr Weckenbarth, that you are also a member of the Senate?"

"Yes," he said, "but when I was appointed, although I retained the title, I was, for various reasons, relieved of my duties. However, we will still be colleagues, we can still address each other as 'Senator', can't we?" I did not dare to laugh, even though his serious tone seemed feigned.

Whether I really took it seriously or not, I had to admit to a heightened sense of my own importance when, after lunch, I was led to the first sitting of the Senate, this time by a man in a yellow uniform who was to accompany me everywhere as my personal attendant – this was clearly an honour that went with my new dignity. His name was Spring.

The meeting took place in a large, low hall. I had hoped to see Don Emanuele or Dr. Jacobi among the Senators, but neither the huge, tall, black figure of the old abbé nor the short, lively, skinny one of the doctor – his nose was his most prominent feature – were visible among the twenty or so present. Presumably they were also Honorary Senators, like Weckenbarth.

We all waited a little. The attendants in their yellow livery (all Senators had attendants and all attendants wore yellow livery) drew up chairs for their masters and busied themselves setting out the cold buffet and drinks for the meeting. In the course of the next ten minutes – relatively speaking of course – ten more Senators appeared, but none of them was anyone I recognised.

Then the meeting began. The attendants (I liked to think of Spring as a gentleman's gentleman) left. Another door opened in the wall that all the chairs were facing. Dressed entirely in black and bedecked with veils, Carola, the President, entered and went over, not without a certain dignity of manner, to a lectern where she delivered a long, ceremonious speech of welcome. Her voice was a little too thin and hesitant, too high for such a solemn text. Anyway, I paid very little attention to the hackneyed clichés which lost any claim to be taken seriously by the fact that the lady read her speech from a script.

The President was young and slim, though pleasantly well-developed in appropriate places. Her black dress enveloped her

116

figure right down to the ground – you could not even see what kind of shoes she was wearing. The only jewellery she had on was a necklace of purple pearls which hung down from her gently throbbing bosom to the level of her navel in the well-known catenary curve.

The speech lasted for a very long time.

I looked to the left – there sat an elderly gentleman with snow-white hair and large, slightly protuberant teeth. I looked to the right – there sat a youngish man, a little older than myself, with an infinitely long face: his nose was so far from his chin that you had the impression that he was yawning all the time but, out of a sense of modesty, with his mouth closed. The younger man had all the signs of intellectuality on display: hair brushed forward and shaved right up to the temples, thick glasses with plain and functional black metal frames (obtrusive industrial design, emphatically unemphatic; Meyrink calls it 'plain as lice'), and a roll-neck pullover. Obviously a German writer had infiltrated the Senate. His name was Jan Akne Uvesohn and he was the first to take the floor. Initially when I heard him speak, I thought he was a foreigner, but he was just from the north, from Pomerania. His speech was extemporaneous, without a manuscript, but nearly as long as that of the President. I could not understand the content, and for three reasons: firstly because of his odd accent, secondly because of his confused argumentation (later he supplied us all with a mimeographed copy), and thirdly because I was not listening.

Suddenly I started; everyone had risen. I stood up as well and thus, without realising it, cast my vote. The subject of the vote was whether, as a sign of our Senatorial dignity (in addition to the attendants in yellow livery), we should wear a purple ribbon. Everyone – myself, as I said, included – was in favour. Purple ribbons, two inches wide, nine inches long, with a border of gold braid, were distributed. I would have been in favour of hanging them down from the back of the jacket collar, or from the rear pocket where the Spanish hidalgos used to keep their golden keys. It was decided, however, that they should hang from the top jacket pocket or the second buttonhole down. Everyone attached their ribbon accordingly; only Herr Uvesohn earnestly attached his to his ear.

Then, just as the meeting was about to disperse, I rose to make a speech. I'm sure you will not count it immodest of me if I give the text of my speech – which the others probably listened to with as little attention as I did theirs – in these pages:

"Patres conscripti", I began. This salutation, although doubtless correct, was greeted with surprise and bewilderment. "Patres conscripti! I cannot say whether my feeling is due to a deficiency in my sense of direction or whether it is a result of the general situation here, but I don't know where I am! Since arriving here – there is presumably no point in trying to give a precise time because of the dispositional parallax – I have not found anything by which to orientate myself, I have not found any place where I felt I had been before. I trust that once this meeting has finished my attendant will lead me to my room and, whenever necessary, back here, without my having to bother about finding the way, but gentlemen, we are in a state of emergency! We must bear in mind that we may have to find our way around without servants. Is it not right and proper that we, the Senate, should have a detailed plan of this 'cigar' with its one thousand and sixteen –"

"How do you come to be in possession of that knowledge?" The President interrupted in her high-pitched voice.

"Your Excellency" I said, "a man in a position of responsibility cannot underestimate the importance of knowledge as a means of keeping a situation under control. If the majority of honourable members are in favour of allowing military constraints to outweigh this 'inquisitiveness', and not see it as a necessity, then I will accept that decision, however little I agree with it. I propose we now proceed to vote on whether we should be allowed access to detailed plans of the cigar or not."

After this maiden speech I returned to my seat. Before we could proceed to a vote on my motion a fat Senator with a hoarse voice and a polished bald head rose to speak. He was wearing an obviously expensive but messy suit. "Matters", he thundered, hardly had he reached the lectern, "are not that simple! I know something of these things. Military constraints or not – that is not the question. The fact is that our 'cigar' has not been finished. You all know that it looks roughly like this" – he drew a shape with his hands – "like a cigar. Now the 'cigar' is hollow. From the 'dome', from the highest point that is, a 'thread' hangs, reaching about half way down. At the end of this 'thread' hangs a 'droplet'. We are in that drop. All around us is emptiness. The thread, that is the lift shaft, is our only connection with the dome and our only security. We are hanging in a void, without support. We had to allow enough space or, bearing in mind the dispositional parallax which the previous speaker has already mentioned, enough time between ourselves and the outer walls. It was originally intended to extend this 'droplet' down to the floor of the 'cigar'. Unfortunately it was not completed. 'Droplet', then, is not the right word. It is a drop with the bottom cut off; open at the bottom."

I shuddered with horror.

When I was in the gallery of the painted library had I not looked down into a room without a floor, down, without realising it, into those awful depths? If all this confusion of rooms and corridors and halls and storeys, these one thousand and sixteen floors, were contained within a mere 'droplet', how deep must be the void below? And I had only been separated from it by a frail banister ... I felt dizzy.

"You need have no concern about the strength of the thread. It was calculated for a droplet of about twelve times the size of the one we are left with. And of course the sheath of the lift-shaft contains other things as well, intermediate stops, military installations etc."

"Is it possible", I interrupted, "to see the world outside from the dome?"

"Naturally. But it is dangerous. At least, it is forbidden."

"Even to Senators?"

The speaker looked at the President in consternation.

"Then I would like to propose a further motion", I said. "Senators should have the right to enter the dome from time to time in order to see outside and ascertain the situation there."

"I cannot allow the motion", said the President. "We are not competent to decide on such matters."

The second motion was outside the Senate's remit, then. My first one was rejected, when it came to the vote.

I enquired whether Senators were obliged to attend sessions and was told one could absent oneself as long as one sent one's apologies. I said I wanted to go to bed. That counted as an apology, so I went. Spring flung open the double doors (how did he know I was about to leave?) and followed me. I put my head down and strode on ahead. We passed through a low corridor with a vaulted ceiling and metal walls which was so narrow it was impossible for two people to walk side by side. It was crossed by other such corridors. In the distance one could see that they led to further similar corridors.

It was like a warren through which I strode hither and thither at top speed. Eventually Spring asked me breathlessly,

"Where are you making for, Your Eminence?"

"Eminence?"

"We have to make distinctions. Senators are addressed as 'Your Eminence' – I am *plain* Spring."

I made a mental note to consider whether I should not forbid such disrespectful talk, never mind the dreadful pun. "Be that as it may", I said, "I would like to go to bed. A good servant should have an instinct for things like that."

"Then we have to go that way."

With Spring now leading we hurried on through several more corridors until we came to a vaulted chamber, similarly lined with metal, into which corridors led from all sides. A free-standing ladder took us through a skylight in the vaulted ceiling into a rather more pleasant gallery, from the balustrade of which we could look through windows down into the chamber. We met Mr. Nankeen, the impresario of the variety troupe; seeing Spring in his yellow livery and the purple ribbon dangling from my top pocket, he made obsequious obeisance.

"Ah, our excellent impresario, Mr. Nankeen", I said, thinking to myself what a stupid manner of speech one adopts when one has been made an Eminence. Nankeen, however, beamed all over his face. It is a well-known fact that Napoleon turned people into slavish adherents merely by remembering their names.

"Still wearing our roll-neck pullover and corduroy trousers, are we, Nankeen?" The eminential tone was like a muzzle over my mouth. Was it a virus with which one was infected along with the title? Or—terrible idea—was I a born eminence and only waiting for the day ('day' to be taken with a grain of salt, given the corruption in time) when I could enter into my inheritance ...

"I hope, my dear ..." (don't repeat the name too often, I told myself) "... my dear sir, we shall meet again."

"The honour will be all mine, all mine, Your Eminence."

"And how are your fair charges coming along?"

"I'm sorry, Your Eminence ...?"

"The chorus girls."

"Oh, I see. We're rehearsing a new routine."

"Excellent, excellent. Do let me know when it's ready. Reserve a stool for me for the first night ..." An Eminence, I assumed, must have his connections with the chorus girls.

"Oh", said Nankeen, "that would be a great honour."

"You'll keep me a seat then." I gave him an affable wave. "All the best!"

He bowed silently. Spring and I went on our way. We came to a lift. Spring unlocked the door. We ascended—or descended—and, after a certain amount of toing and froing, came to my apartment. It was less a 'suite' of rooms than a warren. The central point was a parlour with a bed in an alcove. The windows, which had curtains that could be drawn, were like an arcade through which one could see into twelve smaller rooms, one of which was a bathroom; another was for Spring. Beyond this circle of rooms was a further circle of vestibules and foyers, which—I inspected each one—had different exits into the most confusing variety of corridors, stairs and halls. I ordered Spring to lock all entrances.

"Tell me", I said when I had put on the pyjamas he had handed me, "can you get me a book?"

"A book ..." said Spring. "Certainly. Any kind you like. Just tell me what you want and I'll *spring* to it."

"For a servant you talk too much", I said. "A book that won't bore me."

Spring brought me a book in a red cover with a picture of a strangled woman in Greek costume on the cover. *Oedipus the King* was the title. The author's name was Leopold Sagredo.

"Oh", I said, "that's sure to be boring. Read it to me aloud."

I washed my hands and lay down in bed. Spring read and, I must admit, not without dramatic expression.

OEDIPUS THE KING
Tragedy in one Act

'One! Thank God for that', I thought.

"By Leopold Sagredo.

I'll skip the foreword and the long list of *dramatis personae*", said Spring.

"Good", I said.

"The scene is a high terrace on the battlements of the royal palace in Thebes.

Scene One. Two guards.

1st Guard	Without the heat it might never have happened.
2nd Guard	It would have happened in any case.
1st Guard	Perhaps it wouldn't have been so bad; we wouldn't have been so short of water.
2nd Guard	When it happens, it happens.
1st Guard	If the springs hadn't run dry the people would have been able to wash, the flies wouldn't have come; those large flies with the hairy backsides and small wings.
2nd Guard	Some of the springs flow again at night; it makes no difference.
1st Guard	Not any more, not now everyone's got it.
2nd Guard	Not everyone.
1st Guard	Not yet, but they will. Everyone will. There's no way of stopping it, once it's here in the city.
2nd Guard	Not beforehand either. Not ever. There's

122

	nothing we can do.
1st Guard	They've sent a man to Delphi.
2nd Guard	By the time he gets back, we'll all be dead.
1st Guard	Perhaps not us in the palace.
2nd Guard	If not, the man returning from Delphi will bring it.
1st Guard	Perhaps he'll bring an oracle to save us.
2nd Guard	There is no such thing as an oracle that saves people.
1st Guard	The heat towers over the city like a column of oil. The air is dense and sweet, like sugary melted fat. The wind cannot move it, scarcely makes it tremble. In the hot, viscous air it already feels as if it takes more effort to breathe. The air is so dense it's like a wall of glass distorting everything, making it quiver. It's as if you could pick it up in your hands, mould it into balls and throw them at the mice that eat the dead flies with the hairy backsides – that's how dense the air is; you could cut it with a knife.
2nd Guard	It'll get worse.
1st Guard	But dreadful is that moment, when, scarcely has the sun gone down, it turns icy cold for the time it takes to draw breath, that moment when the black, glassy, shimmering, oily column of reek and decay over the city seems to be swept away by the wing-beat of some mighty bird – for a breath and no more. They say it is the Horai come to fetch the souls of the dead, the souls that moan and groan in their dead bodies until sunset.
2nd Guard	They say so, but it's not true. It's the worms, those fireworms – wicks glowing in the wax of the corpse – legions of them under the dead skin, making it move as if it were still breathing. Neither heat nor cold affects them, they multiply unceasingly. They writhe through the

123

	streets in diamond-shaped clusters. Soon they will come over the walls ...
1st Guard	We'll crush them with our hobnailed sandals.
2nd Guard	There'll be too many of them. The Captain has had brooms made so that we can sweep them over the ramparts.
1st Guard	Even if they are swept down, they will crawl back up again. I will crush them with my hobnailed sandals.
2nd Guard	There'll be too many of them.
1st Guard	What if they keep on crawling back up?
2nd Guard	Perhaps they will tire of it after two or three times? They will be consecrated brooms. Tiresias is to perform the blessing of the bristles today.
1st Guard	Do you believe in consecrated brooms?
2nd Guard	I believe in brooms.

1st Guard starts.

2nd Guard	What is it?
1st Guard	A rustling ... can't you hear it? A rustling or hissing or grating or boring or creeping or flitting: to and fro, above us or below us. The greasy air distorts every sound, you never know where it's coming from. Can't you hear it? I'm glad I'm not alone on the battlements!
2nd Guard	I can't hear anything. Perhaps it was only a dove from the doo'cot, stretching its wings in its sleep.
1st Guard	The doves from the Queen's doo'cot are dead. The hot wind killed them.
2nd Guard	Then it was a beetle.
1st Guard	Terrible ... Listen, there it is again!
2nd Guard	You're right. It sounds like someone creeping past.
1st Guard	It's the air: you never seem to be alone. You're surrounded by grubs and beetles and flies. I think the air's gone and all that's left is beetles that look like the eyes in a horse's carcass. But

| | they're very much alive when they crawl across the back of your neck with their fluffy, oily feet ... |
| 2nd Guard | It seems to – listen – it's steps, creeping foot-steps ... |

He goes to look; not as if he is interested, casually rather.

1st Guard	I get frightened when the cold comes.
2nd Guard	The sun hasn't set yet.
1st Guard	It will set. Those moments will come when the icy black wings of night make the heat column of the day collapse.
2nd Guard	It's Creon's mad son.
1st Guard	What did you say?
2nd Guard	Those creeping steps that frightened you – it's Haemon, Creon's idiot son.

Scene Two. Haemon and the same.

1st Guard	*as Haemon approaches slowly.*
	It's no use. You can conquer the fear you feel when you are walking through a forest alone, or when you're in the cellar all by yourself, by singing out loud. Wine and people to talk to will drive away the fear of the awful thoughts you have when you think of eternity. But this fear, when the heat is split by one blow from a sword of icy fire, there is nothing that will drive that away. It must be horrible to die at such a moment.
2nd Guard	Stand up! Salute!
1st Guard	But he's not right in the head.
2nd Guard	An idiot prince is still a prince. Anyway, it's a good idea to behave as if we were always being observed. We are being observed most of the time.

They salute. Haemon gives them a quizzical look.

| 2nd Guard | I think he hasn't even noticed. He doesn't even |

	know what a salute is.
1st Guard	And just listen to him grunt.
2nd Guard	It was the Sphinx, they say, that made him mad.

They stand at ease again.

1st Guard	The Sphinx ... was there ever such a thing as the Sphinx?
2nd Guard	The King defeated her.
1st Guard	I know. But nobody saw her.
2nd Guard	Haemon saw her before he went mad.
1st Guard	So people say ... and the King?
2nd Guard	He defeated her.
1st Guard	It's easy to defeat something that isn't there.
2nd Guard	In your place I'd be a wee bit more cautious. Not because of that. (*He points at Haemon.*) But someone's bound to be coming, you'll see, it won't be a minute before someone turns up. He must have escaped. They never let him run around free.
1st Guard	No one knows what the Sphinx looked like; not even what it was. The Sphinx was ... the Sphinx. That was it. No one saw her.
2nd Guard	Lots of people claim to have seen her. Lots have seen her. None survived. Apart from Haemon, who went mad; and the King, who defeated her.
1st Guard	She never existed.
2nd Guard	The King, they say, hinted at what she looked like: a woman, a gigantic woman with breasts like billowing sails, indescribably horrible eyes, a lion's body of indeterminate colour, like mother-of-pearl but not mother-of-pearl, an unutterable stench and a great thing of a tongue, like a huge, pale toad.
1st Guard	And he defeated her?
2nd Guard	Of course; she doesn't exist any more.
1st Guard	Because she never existed!
2nd Guard	Countless people disappeared; later on their

	bones were discovered in the valley of the Sphinx ...
1st Guard	Yes. Troublemakers, awkward creditors, uncles and aunts who had large fortunes to bequeath.
2nd Guard	But in whose interest would it have been for young Haemon to disappear?
1st Guard	There are rumours going around. Creon married the daughter of Tiresias. Haemon is his son, but not hers. They say that Tiresias is none too fond of his step-grandson; Creon shows more love towards him than to the firstborn of his legitimate union.
2nd Guard	The Sphinx is the just punishment of the Gods.
1st Guard	For what?
2nd Guard	For uncertain things. Perhaps for crimes that are still hidden in the womb of time or which no one suspects. The Gods have no sense of 'before' and 'after'. For them everything is happening at the same time. Maybe occasionally retribution comes before the guilt.
1st Guard	There never was a Sphinx.
2nd Guard	Then there was from the moment he defeated her. If something can be defeated, then it exists.
1st Guard	A great feat of heroism.
2nd Guard	Could you have done it? Then you would be King of Thebes and the Queen's husband.
1st Guard	That old woman.
2nd Guard	The Queen is a magnificent woman. The Queen is a promise of alabaster delight, a woman with hair like a shady curtain on a hot summer's noon, eyes with a scent of dark wine, a mouth like a velvet couch, breasts that quiver like the steam rising from a freshly-slaughtered calf and thighs that tremble like trout in mid-stream ...
1st Guard	How do you know that?

2nd Guard	You hear things.

Haemon starts to climb over the wall.

1st Guard	Stop! (*Runs over.*) Come on, we've got to stop him.
2nd Guard	We haven't been given orders. Princes can do what they like.
1st Guard	*holds on to Haemon, who screams.* Now he's screaming. We can't let him fall off the wall.

Cries from within, Haemon!

Scene Three. Menoeceus junior, Alcaeus and the same.

Men. jun.	Will no one stop my brother?
2nd Guard	Yes, sir!

The guards restrain Haemon.

Men. jun.	An empty-headed lot without a scrap of initiative. (*To the 2nd Guard.*) You, take him back to his cage. And sit there for the whole night, or until he falls asleep.
2nd Guard	Very good, Your Highness!

He leads Haemon away.

Alcaeus	Out here it seems even more sultry, even more sultry.
Men. jun.	Not after sunset.
Alcaeus	Has the sun – has the sun set already, then? No – I'm not sure whether it won't be too chilly for me when the sun sets. I miss my walks in the country. Before we shut ourselves up in here I used to go for a walk every day – nearly every day – under the trees, at twilight. At twilight. It has been three weeks already. I hope it will not last another three weeks.
Men. jun.	They have sent a man to Delphi.
Alcaeus	Huh!
Men. jun.	We have to do something.
Alcaeus	For the people. Everything he does is for the

	people. He should do something for us.
Men. jun.	Perhaps the man will bring an oracle from Delphi to save us.
Alcaeus	You know, Menoeceus, oracles ... I'm afraid I don't think the man is even going to Delphi.
Men. jun.	Where is he going, then?
Alcaeus	I have good reason to believe he has only gone a few hours distance from Thebes. There he will wait for as long as it takes to get to Delphi and back. And when he returns, your grandfather Tiresias will tell him what to say.
Men. jun.	If the oracle can save us, it doesn't matter where it comes from.
Alcaeus	From your grandfather? It is no concern of mine, but I have my reasons, I have my reasons.
Men. jun.	We could do with some rain.
Alcaeus	I wish it would rain, too. Since the day they barred the palace gates, smells have been rising like smoke from the city, from the houses and streets. Like flowers, those smells have blossomed in the heat of the day, have opened like parasols on thin, quivering stalks, like parasols which have sent down colourless, sickly threads as roots into the earth which fight over the last remnants of unspent air and grow into a tangle of creepers made of scent glands, into a gigantic sponge soaked in smells. The sudden cold at night tears them apart, but does not destroy them; it just re-aligns them so that they solidify, like an eruption, like lava.

The smell of the sick, the smell of sweat, the smell of the rats and of decay: they are all starting to form blocks and to force their way, one bulky block on another, through the chambers, up the stairs and along the terraces. The rotting smell of rot. It is said that decay

	purifies like fire – a fine pair of symbols! I wish a democratic rain would come and make everyone smell the same, smell of rain. I love men with bald heads; unlike dogs, they smell sweetly in the rain, like a field of poppies.
Men. jun.	My father! (*Laughs.*)
Alcaeus	I regret that you do not have a bald head, Menoeceus ... there would be nothing more enchanting than a bald-headed youth, even if he were a hunchback like yourself. Your father, Creon, was bald as a youth, around the time I took his sister to wife ..., but his scalp was covered with scabies. He stank. From very early on he had his bald head painted gold. Covered over like that with an airtight seal, the rash gets worse, but it can't be seen. One day, however, the enclosed sores will eat through the skull, because they cannot burst outwards. Your father's brain will rot, the stench will not only come from his mouth – it does that already – but from his nose, from his ears ... until the pus fills his eye-sockets and pushes his eyes out. May the Gods grant it does not happen at the dinner table.
Men. jun.	Every evening he has the gold paint washed off and ointment spread on the sores.
Alcaeus	That will not make any difference, not as long as during the day, under the bronze skin, pus and poisoned blood are fermenting in the holes the boils have etched in his skull ... He loves to let the sun flash off his golden skull for the people. – No, the youth I would love would have a bald and scented pate, like a thigh anointed for a wrestling match.

Scene Four. Hipponomene and the same. Hipponomene appears suddenly, silently.

Hipponom.	(*To Menoeceus jun.*) Your brother Haemon has escaped.
Alcaeus	Nonsense.
Hipponom.	He has!
Men. jun.	They've caught him again.
Alcaeus	And Menoeceus is not interested. I cannot imagine a more pointless piece of news to interrupt us with.
Hipponom.	I'm in the way?
Alcaeus	Darling! These conditions! The overwhelming hopelessness of our situation! Must you provoke me?
Hipponom.	I do not understand this preference for the company of hunchbacks.
Alcaeus	You might catch a chill in the cool night air, darling; the temperature is bound to drop once twilight sets in, it does every day – though even that is not certain any more..
Hipponom.	Hunchbacks are particularly prone to chills. Their blood gets held up in the knotty tangle of arteries in their hump, stays there longer than is good for it and then enters the head, where colds originate, in an icy stream. Go indoors, dearest nephew.
Men. jun.	People also say hunchbacks store surplus intelligence in their humps.
Alcaeus	You'll find it boring, darling.
Hipponom.	Not at all. I'll just sit here and play my mouth-harp. Perhaps the moon will appear ...
Alcaeus	We'll not see it for the stench. (*To Menoeceus jun.*) We ought to murder that woman.

Hipponomene plays her mouth-harp

Men. jun.	From a distance one might take it for the cry of a hen drowning in a not-too-deep well.
Alcaeus	Nonsense! You've never heard a hen.

| Men. jun. | From a great distance – on a high rock, beyond a wood, above the clouds – one might take it for the cry of a hen. Perhaps an eagle might hear it? Hear it and plunge like a bolt of lightning to gouge her eye out? |

Alcaeus sighs.

| Hipponom. | What did you say? |
| Alcaeus | We were talking about poultry. |

Hipponomene continues playing.

| Alcaeus | Unfortunately the eagles will already be asleep. Anyway, they have no ears. There is, therefore, not much hope of an eagle taking your musical aunt for a hen. Three times we have been to Delphi. There the eagles circle over the cleft in the rocks. None of them ever took my wife for a hen or anything else edible – edible from an eagle's point of view, that is. After our third visit she gave birth to your cousin Anaxo, the one with three breasts. That tells you just how useful a pilgrimage to Delphi is. If the man they are supposed to have sent to Delphi really has gone to Delphi, then he'll bring back some similar nonsense with him ... with him ...with ... him ... with ... him ..." |

"What?"

"... with him."

"With him and then what, Spring?"

"Those were Alcaeus' last words Your Eminence, it goes on –"

"So all these aesthetic delights did send me to sleep, after all. I think Herr Uvesohn must be the author."

"You overestimate his talents."

"Is that a way to speak about a Senator?"

I sat up in bed.

"I have been dreaming."

"Of Oedipus?"

"You see what little impression that tragedy made on me; there was no trace of Oedipus in it. No, it was a fairly long and

132

complicated dream. I clearly remember it being a Monday when I was saved. But I don't think that was the beginning. I feel rather as if that was the point when I woke *up,* so to speak, from a lower dream, in one nearer the surface, nearer the here and now. The lower dream must have been horrible; fortunately even in the upper dream all I had was a vague sense of terror vanquished but no real memory of it. All in all it may have been several dreams, one inside another or, rather, one below the other. If I think back hard to the upper, innocuous dream I have the impression there is a hint of a memory of swimming in dark waters, no, of swimming in black light that laps against the edge of the imaginable universe. I would not rule out the possibility that I had come from outside the infinite – that depends on one's point of view, of course – universe where, well, Spring, I don't know if I should say this, where another God holds sway ..."

"You should take a pill or some Epsom Salts. Dreams like that are caused by indigestion, Your Eminence."

"Have you never heard of the esoteric doctrine called the 'Doctrine of the Spatial Continuity of Atomic Structure'?"

"If it's really esoteric, then it's not surprising I haven't heard of it."

"Only the deep proofs are kept secret, the findings are freely available. You know we inhabit a solar system, don't you? One where a number of planets orbit a – relatively – fixed star. At distances that we can calculate, though they are beyond imagination, there are other, countless, solar systems. All these and ourselves – small fry, really – form a Milky Way, a galaxy. But there is a vast number of galaxies, all of them vast – there is no other word for it – vast distances away from us. And all this, insofar as it is material and not the pure emptiness between the stars, consists of varying combinations of chemical elements, molecules, compounds of atoms. For a long time people thought the smallest, indivisible particles were the atoms. But we now know that the atoms themselves are nothing other than tiny solar systems with a certain number of planets orbiting a – relatively – fixed body. There is no doubt that these 'infinitesimal' particles are also divisible. They probably consist of even tinier atoms-within-atoms, which I am sure our scientists would have succeeded in analysing if their work had not been interrupted by this war, or whatever it is. The structure of these 'atoms-within-atoms' would have been determined, but they would only have established that the 'atoms-within-atoms' consist of ... atoms, worlds within ever smaller worlds. And in that case, is there any evidence to contradict the idea that we, our solar system, are only an atom in the molecule of the galaxy? Perhaps these vast molecules, that is our galaxy and the other galaxies we can detect with our radio telescopes, are merely a tiny, perhaps even superfluous, intestinal polyp in the bowels of an unimaginable, extra-universal goose? One movement of that goose and our whole universe would be destroyed – and it is certain that movement will come, some time ... but don't worry, Spring, time varies with space. One second for the great goose could be millions and millions of years for us."

"Yes, but why a goose", said Spring. "Is there any evidence to support that?"

"Oh that", I said, "was only an example I chose at random. Perhaps there – *there* is the wrong word, it's still here – there are no animals. But look: here, in your hair, are thousands of galaxies, millions of tiny worlds: one second for you is millions of years for them. Perhaps a whole world has just evolved, from the seething maelstrom of primeval slime to the raising of the bank rate to four and a half percent due to an unforeseen change in the price of tin ... perhaps on one of the tiny 'atoms-within-atoms' in your eyebrow a Plato is philosophising, a Julia falling in love."

"I'm afraid, Your Eminence", said Spring, who was now looking slightly pensive, "that I find the idea rather uncomfortable. I daren't move. And all that was in your dream?"

"No", I said. "I just feel as if in the last, upper dream I felt as if I had fallen into one of those unimaginable worlds – larger or smaller, I'm not sure which, but certainly terrifyingly different – and been saved by the skin of my teeth. Still trembling from the horror, of which I only had a vague memory, I found myself in a large and elegant country house. It was a Monday – I think I have mentioned that already – and the house belonged to an acquaintance of mine who was spending a week there with his seven nieces. This acquaintance was a retired castrato – can there be such a thing as a retired castrato? – who had been a well-known singer in his day; the Pope had made him a Count. His nieces were the daughters of his sister, likewise a singer. Each one of them – this is in confidence, naturally one doesn't mention it there – had a different father, and the town where each was born represented an important stage in the primadonna's career.

'What a pity', the Count said to me, 'you slept through the croquet.'

He was sitting with the young ladies in the White Room. The wallpaper was patterned, white on white, and the pattern, if I remember rightly, consisted of large roses. Sometimes the roses, sometimes the background seemed brighter, depending on the lighting. The chairs, upholstered in dark, almost black velvet, were arranged around a table covered with knitting, embroidery work, cards and other pastimes for young ladies. Two nieces, Fanny and Laura, were sitting at a small table to one side and were playing dominoes. The Count asked Dorimena to sit between us.

'She will fill in the time between now and dinner by telling us a story', he said.

'Me?' said Dorimena, the Roman niece. 'I have no story to tell. I have not seen life, only read about it.'

'That doesn't mean anything', said the Count. 'People who have not seen life have had more time to think.'

'But I don't think, Uncle dear, I'm a woman.'

'Of course', said her uncle; 'all we want is for you to tell a few lies.'

'But I couldn't tell lies, the most I could do would be to tell you ...'

'Excuse me for interrupting, but it is ages since you told us the story of your unhappy love affair with young Campo Sant'angeli.'

'But that's not true; it wasn't unhappy –'

'Happy or unhappy, who can tell which love is what. Popular psychology calls a love affair unhappy when the lovers are unable to sleep together.'

'Like Romeo and Juliet', I said.

'What do you know', said the Count, 'about what went on between the scenes. But I will allow it. Is it not possible that such love is 'happier' than –'

Dorimena interrupted, 'It was neither unhappy nor happy in that or any other sense. If there was any 'love' – and in that case it certainly was unrequited – it was my love for the cello. It was a love that was –'

'Just a moment', said her uncle, 'I'll have some black coffee sent up.'

It was soon served, in small, octagonal cups. Deep in thought, Dorimena stirred hers a few times and then continued,

'It was a love that fate had destined to end unhappily; I haven't got the hands. My F-sharp in the first position on the C-string was always so out of tune that it gave Campo Sant'angeli a drum-roll in the ears, as he put it – *rullo negli orecchi*. That is, it wasn't really out of tune, except for the ear of the maestro; by the time I first heard of him I was already in the master class at our academy. And when I made my debut – I played the Dvorak – the reviews were not unfavourable.'

'A somewhat poetically inclined critic', said her uncle, 'wrote that she embraced her instrument between her knees like Leda the swan, stroked its neck and coaxed such sounds from it – he could not say whether they were groans of pleasure or the proverbial swan-song?'

The sisters laughed.

'That was rather silly, but I must admit that a woman abandoning herself to such a masculine instrument is quite likely to arouse erotic thoughts – not counting the position one has to assume in order to play it: with short dresses one's knees are often a distraction. When I made my début I made a point of wearing gold lamé trousers.

It must have been around that time that the rumours about the mysterious maestro, Livio Campo Sant'angeli, began to circulate among the cognoscenti. I cannot remember where I first heard his name or who it was I heard it from. The name was just there, though none of the people I knew had ever heard him play. It was the same as with ghosts – everyone knows someone who knows someone who has seen one, but it is difficult, if not impossible, to find anyone who has actually met a ghost himself. Everyone knew someone who claimed to have heard Campo Sant'angeli. One had a friend who just happened to be in Sydney when Sant'angeli gave a concert there: the friend had seen the posters. Afterwards the whole city was buzzing with talk of his fabulous playing. Another knew some people in Zurich where Sant'angeli was due to give a concert which, however, he cancelled at short notice. In spite of the cancellation people still talked of a miraculous talent. A third had actually seen him in Tokyo – seen but not heard. He went into raptures. The maestro was said to give ten or twelve concerts a year in North America. People even listed the cities, cities whose names I had never heard before: Spokane, Topeka, Seattle ... – No one goes to Seattle! A fourth friend had seen a record, brought out privately, not available for sale, in the house of some friends of his in Stockholm. The record player happened to be broken at the time, but the Swedes raved about it. A slight acquaintance of a distant cousin of ours claimed to have been present when Campo Sant'angeli gave a private performance for Casals. For a while afterwards Casals is supposed to have considered taking up the clarinet.'"

"But Casals could play the clarinet", said Spring.

"I know that, but clearly Dorimena did not, and *I* was tactful enough not to mention it.

'Rising', she continued, 'in a crescendo from the pregnant whispers of a few connoisseurs of performance to the thunderous certainty of accepted fact, all this talk naturally went to establish Sant'angeli's fame. Soon there were stories, and extremely contradictory ones at that, of his personal circumstances, of, for example, his fabulous inherited wealth, his obstinacy, his minimal repertoire; the latter reports hinted that in reality he had an enormous repertoire but just concealed the fact – some said from humility, from snobbery according to others. Then came the sudden news he had decided to become a recluse for two years in order to learn a recently discovered concerto by Haydn. As always, there were those who knew better, who said he was not learning a concerto, the music in question was a particular passage in a sonata by Dotzauer. Shortly after that a piece of news exploded like a bomb, or rather it dropped like a lighted match into the tinder box dripping with the kerosene of conjecture that was his presumptive audience. Campo Sant'angeli was going to give a concert in the Arena in Verona. Unfortunately that turned out to be false and some newspapers were already relaying rumours about a concert in Moscow. A few days later, by which time I was already seriously considering travelling to Moscow, posters appeared announcing a concert in Rome!

It was a notable occasion. The programme consisted of one of Bach's solo suites, then the Debussy sonata, followed by a solo suite by Reger and finally the Arpeggione.

I had pulled a thousand strings to obtain a ticket and now, trembling with excitement, there I was in the stalls, surrounded by the cream of the music world.

First of all we waited a good half hour.

Then a rumour in the front rows reached us: Campo Sant'angeli had just arrived. 'It'll take a while' said those in the know, 'he always meditates before he plays.' – 'How long for?' – 'Two hours.' – 'No, he just stands on his head for ten minutes.' Then the news broke over the auditorium: Sant'angeli had donned his tails. The tension rose. From the other side of the concert hall came a denial: no, not Sant'angeli, it was his accompanist who had put his tails on. Some people leapt up and ran nervously round the hall. One old lady, who was said to have heard Julius Klengel play, had a fit. A first aid attendant fainted and had to be carried out. At this point experts still tended to the view that the maestro would play. Then the impresario came onto the stage and announced that the concert would not take place. Our tickets were reimbursed. The newspapers reported the next day that the maestro had sent a bouquet of flowers to the first aid attendant in hospital. But I observed the strange phenomenon that everyone who had been at the concert – if that's what you could call it – seemed to have been bewitched. It was ... I can't really describe it. It was a *happening*. We were enveloped in a haze of charisma.

I decided to have lessons with Campo Sant'angeli, whatever

the cost; I imagined this could be arranged through my – how shall I put it? – connections with the Vatican.' The castrato gave an avuncular smile. 'With them normally you can get anything done ... You can tell how difficult it was to become a pupil of Sant'angeli by the fact that in this case they were of no use, or at least only helped indirectly. Cardinal N., a close friend of my mother's – I call him uncle – went personally to see Sant'angeli's mother, who is a devout widow. He had been at school together with her late husband who was, after all, the father of the virtuoso. But Campo Sant'angeli, although a strict Catholic of an almost other-worldly piety, was strongly anti-clerical. I later learnt that the Cardinal's visit had made him ill for several days. Even the *sight* of a priest could cause nose-bleeds if the weather was unfavourable. Fortunately he never learnt of my connection with the Cardinal's visit, otherwise the intervention of a young friend of the Cardinal who had a high position in the Jesuit University in Rome and at the same time – don't tell anyone else – was a fellow Freemason and in the same Lodge, Transience at the Sign of the Three Pyramids, as Sant'angeli, would have been in vain. So eventually – it all took more than a year – I received a bizarre communication, a card on which was written in large, but nonetheless somewhat feminine, handwriting, *Come and visit me next Monday at 24 minutes past 11, or at any other time that suits you. L. C.* When writing, Campo Sant'angeli obviously did not let himself be constrained by the size of the paper he was writing on: the little card was not just completely covered, in places his large handwriting seemed to have flowed over the edge. The note gave the impression of having been written on a larger sheet and then cut out.

When I finally met him and spoke to him I realised that the rumours were a blend of truth and invention. Inherited wealth there certainly was. He lived in a villa – a villa in the old sense – on that part of the Ligurian coast where it is rocky. On the inland side the estate was shielded by an extensive park, but it was open to the sea. The villa stood on a rocky spit that jutted out into the bay. A large and bizarre rock garden cleverly incorporated the natural strata in its design. From the house steps led down to the sea. At the foot of the steps, shaded by trees, surrounded by grotesque rock formations and the occasional weathered statue or stone vase, a bench had been hewn into the cliff. Above it was a marble tablet, but the inscription was no longer legible. Only rarely, when the sea was rough, did the waves engulf the sandy beach, but the bench and the steps in front of it with a little balustrade had been so cunningly constructed that not a drop ever touched them: Campo Sant'angeli could sit in safety as he watched the sea raging before him like a wild animal on a chain ... But I anticipate. It was only later that I saw this melancholy favourite spot of the maestro. Holding a book open in his hand, he would sit there for hours without reading it at all.

Campo Sant'angeli received me in the villa. He was sitting on a sofa in a black roll-neck sweater, black trousers and bare feet. When he stood up, I saw that he was very short, short and slim. His pictures showed him with very short hair and a closely-trimmed moustache that was not quite shaven clean. His hair was still cut short and his moustache trimmed, but both seemed to me, in some indefinable way, unkempt.

The first few minutes were torture. Campo Sant'angeli merely offered me a seat – well away from his own – and curled back up on his sofa. He covered his bare feet with a cushion. He didn't say a word, he just looked at me. I was not sure whether I should say something, but on the other hand I did not have the feeling that he was expecting me to. He already knew why I was there. So I remained seated for a while and then stood up; he stood up too; he shook my hand and said, 'Bene, tutto a posto ...' and I left. I had not been long driving my Fiat along the dusty country road back towards Rome when a parrot-green Maserati overtook me at breakneck speed and as it skidded screaming into the next bend, Campo Sant'angeli waved to me from the open car.

From that time on I often went to the villa. Sometimes the maestro was not there – it was impossible to get him to agree to a definite time, his standard formula was, 'Come at ten minutes past five, or at some other time' – sometimes he would be waiting on the stone bench; he never said more than a word of greeting, at most a remark about the weather. Now and then I chatted to his mother.

Once when I went he was having a meal – at a most unusual time. He was sitting on a terrace in his black roll-neck pullover with a plate of cheese, olives and grapes in front of him. He went into a long explanation of the natural and soothing quality of this combination of flavours – complemented by coarse white bread and a light red wine – looked at the problem of food from all possible viewpoints, from the aesthetic, medicinal, historical, even astrological and mythological perspectives, discovered all kinds of secret hermetic relationships between individual dishes and kept returning to his praise of the combination of cheese, olives and grapes with coarse white bread and a light red wine. 'At heart', he whispered to me, 'at heart I'm really – see: cheese, olives ... – I'm really a peasant.' In the course of his exposition he had succeeded in finishing off the cheese and the olives, the bread, too, and half the grapes. On the plate were two bunches: one covered in plump grapes and one picked clean to a skeleton. He found it an intoxicating image. He lifted up the plate. 'Look', he said, 'a bunch of juicy grapes and a skeleton picked clean – vitality and decay.' He placed the plate on the balustrade of the terrace in the evening sunshine. He fell into an ecstasy of melancholy when one of the peacocks that were kept in the park jumped up onto the balustrade, plucked one grape, a single one, and strode off.

In the course of time, as was inevitable, I met other pupils of Sant'angeli at the villa. If more than three happened to be there at once, he tended to give a lesson.

During these classes – they cost, I quote, '*15,282 Lire, or whatever you feel like paying*' – Campo Sant'angeli never touched a cello, and I mean that literally. Not only did he not play, he anxiously avoided all contact with the instruments, which were of necessity lying around in the room. He got us to play – 'Play the first movement of Beethoven's G minor sonata, and in particular that one passage in such-and-such a time, or whatever you like' – sometimes he would mumble incomprehensible criticisms to himself. Often when he was indicating corrections he would sing the passage to us or he would spend a long time searching for the right words and then burst out with an image that put it in a nutshell. I remember there was one pupil who was rehearsing the Dvorak concerto. This particular time it was the magnificent entry in B minor, the soloist's first entry in the repeat after the whole orchestra has stated the theme *grandioso* and the cello seems to emerge from the gradually subsiding orchestral frenzy with double-stopping in the high registers. It was a question of dynamics. If I remember rightly the solo line is marked *fortissimo* and is accompanied by oboes: *piano,* violins: *pianissimo,* violas: *forte/piano* and a few other instruments. The problem was how to interpret *ff* and how to play *ff* without producing a screech.

Campo Sant'angeli whistled and sang, thought up this idea and then that, but it was clear that he was not satisfied until finally he said, 'It can screech a little, tremble perhaps. Once on a hot day in the mountains I watched a storm come up. A bank of dark cloud appeared between two mountains. I happened to be looking through a telescope. Above the valley, still in the clear air, not yet caught up in the troubled waves of the storm but borne on the tension in the air, a bird was hovering, completely without effort, high above the pines, a hawk before the storm', he relaxed and sang the passage, he had found it: a hawk before the storm ...

I had been studying with him for about three months when he started to become even moodier, if that were possible. His mother had told us that he hardly managed to get any sleep. He ate very little, drank hibiscus-flower tea and a lot of champagne – and not at all elegantly, out of ordinary tumblers. He would recork bottles of the most expensive French champagne with a twist of newspaper and put them under his chairs like a pub musician his pint. Quite often he drank out of the bottle. He scarcely drove his Maserati any more, we learnt, because he had frequent trembling fits and the fact that he was starting to confuse right and left was highly dangerous. Sometimes his brain would react the wrong way round.

When we, that is his pupils, one day met a stupid person in an extraordinary state of excitement in Sant'angeli's villa – it was his manager – we believed we had discovered the cause of his physical decline. Yes, decline, there's no other word for it: the maestro had agreed to give a concert and now he regretted it. For some reason or other he could not or would not withdraw his consent, at least that was our supposition. And that was gnawing and eating away at him. A particularly forward pupil – this was in September – asked Campo Sant'angeli directly about it. The consequences were terrible: the maestro had a persistent attack of the hiccoughs which lasted for days on end. 'As if at least a Dominican Provincial or a Papal Privy Chamberlain were visiting the neighbouring villa', murmured his anxious mother.

When he had recovered from his hiccoughs and enough pupils were gathered for a lesson the maestro gave a mischievous smile and handed us a poster. It was the announcement of the concert the manager had had printed, but which he had not yet allowed to be released. As he handed it to us he commented, 'It's just the date that's wrong; the concert will be a few days earlier – or later.'

Later on we heard of further subterfuges. Posters with different times were put up at various points in Rome. The programmes also differed and every poster had a different – deliberate – printing error in Campo Sant'angeli's name.

It was shortly before the concert, that went ahead, I remember it precisely, on 6th November. I visited Sant'angeli alone. He was trying to eat a cold chicken and I watched with horror as he kept on attempting to dip a tiny piece of chicken into a bowl of mustard sauce, but did not have the strength to do so. Tired and apologetic, he gave me a smile. In spite of that he was very cheerful and told me it had suddenly occurred to him to conceal the venue, the concert hall. New posters with new versions had already been pasted over the old ones. In all there were six or seven different places where the concert was supposed to take place. Campo Sant'angeli was particularly amused by the fact that one of them was the Sistine Chapel.

Thus the audience at the concert would be a chance gathering of those who happened to have seen the relatively few posters with the correct time and place.

Perhaps there would also be a few there for whom two wrong

posters had led to the right answer, or who in their haste had misread, and yet in a sense correctly read, the posters. The concert was held in the Great Hall of the Palazzo Colonna (the one with a cannon ball from the 1848 revolution still stuck in the steps up to the podium), and at the other supposed venues there were hundreds of people tearing their hair: outside the entrance to the Forum, at the monument to Cecilia Metella, at the Teatro Argentino. Many tried to find the Church of San Meleagro delle Divine ... It is hard to believe, but there is no such church, no such saint even.

We pupils had been given the correct time and place a few hours before the concert. The doors to the hall were closed right on the dot. Groups of students were turned away by the strict attendants. Five minutes later Campo Sant'angeli appeared in faultless evening dress, as close-fitting as a corset and – we were aware of that, of course – performing the same function. Until then I had only ever seen him barefoot, now he was wearing patent leather pumps, so small, so slim and glossy – out of this world, I tell you, the kind of shoes that are kept in glass cases with only faithful retainers allowed to dust them; if men could fly, these would be the shoes to do it in. As it was, Campo Sant'angeli's feet scarcely seemed to touch the floor.

The first item was the G minor sonata by Beethoven. With excitement we witnessed an almost unheard-of event: Janos Starker, who, to wild applause, came onto the stage together with Campo Sant'angeli – Benjamin Britten, who was to play the piano part, was two steps behind them – was carrying the maestro's cello. Whilst Campo Sant'angeli stood there, head bowed, Starker tuned his instrument. There followed a whispered discussion, Britten joining in as well. Then Starker retuned the cello and plucked each of the four strings. Campo Sant'angeli nodded. Starker stood up and handed the instrument – this was the moment none of us had expected to see – to our teacher. He took it, just took it, flicked the tails of his coat behind him, and sat down.

The Sonata for Cello and Piano by Ludwig van Beethoven, in G minor, opus 6, number 2, begins with a G minor chord in the piano part. The cello plays the bass note on the open G-string and then has a longish rest. Campo Sant'angeli had hardly completed the bowstroke when he collapsed, falling forward and knocking the cello to the ground in front of him as he fell. The bridge snapped and hit the still reverberating body of the instrument with a sharp crack: a breaking heart was the thought that flashed through my mind. Of course, it all happened in a fraction of a second. The 'breaking heart' was drowned by the crash of the body on the stage. Benjamin Britten had jumped up the moment Campo Sant'angeli slumped forward over the cello and then fell sideways to the floor where he remained stretched out on his back. The audience leapt up out of its seats as well. I was overcome with horror such as you only feel in a dream. I ran out.

You know, if you read something like that, or if you see it in the theatre or the cinema, you can comprehend it. But if you live through it, you cannot. It was as if this powerful, horrific experience grazed my consciousness like an explosion, making it flicker, perhaps sucking it out of me for that one moment. For one second, death was a palpable physical presence in the room.

Others, however, were less sensitive than I. They rushed onto the stage and grabbed fragments of the splintered cello. Years after they still fetched high prices. For that one single note, that G on the open string, finally established Campo Sant'angeli's outstanding reputation – only for a short while with the fickle public of course, but among connoisseurs it hardened into the certainty that Livio Campo Sant'angeli was the greatest cellist the world has ever heard.'"

"You have a remarkable recall of the details of your dream, Your Eminence."

"Oh, did I forget to mention that the Count gave me a small pink pill to take so that I shouldn't forget my dream?"

"He gave you a pill *in your dream?*"

"In my dream. Of course."

"But it has its effect afterwards?"

"When else?"

"A miraculous dream", said Spring, "or a miracle drug. You must be glad your gigantic goose didn't give you a pill."

"I certainly am! – But wait, my dream isn't over yet. After Dorimena had finished her story, we went into the dining room. Then I played billiards with the Count. The following day the seven young ladies went out riding – and a noble sight they were – whilst I played croquet with the Count. We did not see the nieces again until the evening, when the Count's Neapolitan niece, Renata, told us the following story before dinner in the yellow and gold drawing-room,

'It is a story from my birthplace', began Renata, 'although it starts in Florence, where Messer Domenico Orlandini was born. His father, Orlandini the Elder, who had been a famous opera composer in his time – that idiot Marcello fulminated against him, but for anyone from Naples that counts as praise – was *maestro di capella* at the cathedral in Florence and personal violinist to the Grand Duke.

Young Orlandini, destined both by his father's profession as well as by his own striking talent to be a musician, was sent to Naples which, in spite of my Venetian sister's grin, was even then the centre of the musical world. Moreover, old Orlandini had studied there, and his son's first name had been chosen in honour of his teacher in Naples.

Having received his musical education at the Conservatorio dei Poveri di Gesù Cristo, the oldest and most respected of the Neapolitan conservatories, Domenico had, with a number of masques, vespers and hymns, aroused the interest of the musical world in Naples – and in those days that meant of all Neapolitans. As a result he had been commissioned by the head of one of our richest and most musical old families, Prince Crispo Cursi-Cicinelli, to compose an opera for his son's wedding. As you will know, in Naples we did not distinguish between church and opera composers. It was a common and justified assumption that if a Neapolitan composer had written a beautiful 'Salve Regina', his 'Alcandro lo confesso' would be just as beautiful.

In actual fact, the opera was not to be performed at Prince Gennaro Cursi-Cicinelli's wedding – that was to take place in Salerno, as the bride was a Lombard from the ancient Salernan family of the Gisulfini – but in celebration of the bride's entry into the Palazzo Cursi in Naples.

Like almost every Palazzo of the Neapolitan nobility, that of the Cursi had a private theatre.

The first performance of the opera was a real feast for the eye and ear. Not only because of the presence of the King and Queen, Carlo IV and Maria Amalia of Saxony, as well as the whole assembly of the aristocratic families, but also because first of all a large sum of money had been spent on a completely new libretto – 'Idaspe' – and because secondly the amount lavished on the sets, the costumes, the orchestra and above all the singers went far beyond what was usual even in Naples for such occasions.

Thousands of candles illuminated both stage and stalls, and the young maestro found his breath taken away by the scent of roses and the applause of Neapolitan society as he entered the pit to direct the overture – at that time it was called a sinfonia – from the cembalo. He bowed, blinded by the glare of lights, and when he straightened up again he found himself face to face, at a distance of a few feet, with a beauty more radiant than all the lights, sweeter than the scent of any rose, more breathtaking than the applause of Neapolitan society – the budding bride, Teresa Principessa Cursi, of the line of the Gisulfini from Salerno. Still with a virginal air, as blonde as the blessed Cecilia, she was standing in a snow-white gown, scarcely whiter though than the white of her breast, next to a short boor with a premature paunch wearing a jade-green frock coat with a collection of trumpery decorations: His Excellency Gennaro Maria Aloysio etcetera, Principe Cursi-Cicinelli, the heir to one of the largest fortunes in Naples and her frog of a husband.

As protocol required, Orlandini had dedicated his opera to the Princess. But now, after he had bathed a moment too long in the radiance of the Princess' eyes, he silently but solemnly transformed the formal dedication into an act of true consecration.

I will not conceal the fact that this caused young Orlandini to play a few false notes on the cembalo. In the sinfonia he made the bassoons lose their place. Roxana's big aria was only saved by the quick-witted insertion of a trill by the primadonna, accompanied by furious glances at the maestro – for a moment

Orlandini had sighed instead of conducting. To cap it all, just before the finale he played a completely unexpected solo on the cembalo, a poignantly beautiful fantasia inspired by his awakening feelings which, not surprisingly, caused chaos in the orchestra. Although the horn player, who thought his entry had come, interrupted at one point, it was this improvised piece that made the most impression. For the next few seasons it was expected that every maestro di capella would improvise a poignantly beautiful fantasia on the cembalo before the finale. But the young Princess Cursi requested Orlandini, when she thanked the composer at the ball which followed the opera, to write out the fantasia and bring it to her.

The music for the ball was conducted by another musician, who was in the service of the old Prince, so Orlandini was dismissed. He went home; in his tiny room in the Conservatorio dei Poveri he felt his heart was full to bursting. He could see the Princess dancing in the magnificently-lit ballroom in the Palazzo, he was even jealous of the light around her. He was so engulfed with a feeling of hopelessness that he even toyed with the idea of sending the Princess his head with a note (perhaps stuck into the permanently silenced mouth) to the effect that she would find the fantasia in this head. It was only the vigour of youth – and the practical difficulty of carrying out such a bizarre suicide – that led him to his desk, where he sat down to write out, with a heavy hand, the requested fantasia. He even found some consolation in the occasional addition of more sophisticated harmonies.

But the Princess in the ballroom was no less lonely. Her one consolation was that the ball went on for so long. Afterwards her oafish husband of a few days would be too tired to make his usual coarse advances. And she could spend the whole night talking of Orlandini, singing his praises without anyone finding anything unusual about it – his name was on everybody's lips, he had become the latest fashion and, measured against some remarks by other ladies, her praise was, if anything, cool.

Before the ball had ended she had asked her father-in-law to engage Orlandini as her music-master. The old Prince promised to do his best for, he said, the maestro would probably receive a hundred similar offers the very next morning. Teresa felt her heart sink at the thought, and she trembled as she awaited the return of the messenger she sent to the Conservatorio at six o'clock in the morning.

The Princess' messenger was the seventeenth to arrive. Around half past three one had come from the old Princess Aiutemicristo; ten minutes later it was one from a well-known music fanatic, the philosopher and alchemist, Count Ferrario, and at a quarter past four from the English ambassador, at half past four from Prince Pozzo della Cisterna. From four thirty-five on, when the messengers of Prince Ruffo di Calabria and the Prior of the Knights of St. John arrived together, the messengers usually arrived in pairs, later in packs. If the pain of new love had not robbed him of his sleep, the messengers would have.

He informed the Princess' messenger that he would take the liberty of waiting on her that morning, after mass. The Princess quivered when she heard this reply, which did nothing to reduce her uncertainty.

When Orlandini appeared at ten o'clock, laid the score of the fantasia at her feet and answered her question, whether he was willing to become her music-master, with an 'I will' that was strangled rather than whispered, the young Princess swooned. Several aunts who were present smiled. 'Gennaro's been hard at it!' But Gennaro had nothing to do with her faint.

From now on Orlandini visited Princess Teresa almost daily. On Mondays she had singing lessons, on Tuesdays cembalo lessons, on Wednesdays he taught her harmony, on Thursdays the violin, on Fridays the harp, on Saturdays they played flute duets and there were music lessons even on Sundays: on that day the Princess wanted to be taught the art of counterpoint, of which Orlandini was well capable because our composers are trained in it, unlike the Venetian bunglers. Had there been more than seven days in the week, the Princess would have ended up learning the trombone ...

These lessons took place partly in a music room, partly in the theatre, but as often as possible in a gazebo in the garden. How often did Teresa stand behind Orlandini as he sat at the cembalo, looking at the same score – sometimes a sheet of music can be like the starry sky where lovers gaze indirectly into each other's eyes – and how often, as she breathed in before a trill, did her soft breast brush apparently unintentionally against his shoulder.

But he, his whole being imbued with the sense of the sacredness of his adoration, did not for a single moment dare even consider the possibility that she, who seemed so far above him not so much because of the difference in social standing as because of the halo he surrounded her with, might return his feelings. Where a more experienced man would have guessed everything from a mere fraction of Teresa's attentions, even the fires that burnt on her cheeks did not arouse Orlandini's suspicions.

Teresa, for her part, was confused by the matter-of-fact attitude he maintained for months. At first her only hesitation was for the moral scruples she had to overcome, but now she began to doubt his affection.

Thus they fought against each other, or against themselves rather, against the beginnings of despair, which was wearing them down, until they were finally – how shall I put it: victorious or defeated? It came about in the following way:

The following summer the younger Prince Cursi-Cicinelli was sent on an important secret mission to Madrid. That is he was the rather dim-witted but aristocratic emissary who accompanied the sharp privy councillor, who was to negotiate an agreement between the Kingdoms of Spain and Naples on the succession to the throne. The Prince sent his wife to a country estate. Naturally she was accompanied by her music-master ...

In order to counter the boredom that usually attends a stay in the country, Orlandini had composed a short opera which was to be performed by members of the princely family including Teresa herself. The text was supposed to have been written by a Don What's-his-name. In actual fact, Orlandini himself had put his and Teresa's story into somewhat ethereal verse, in the rather naive assumption that Teresa would not notice. Naturally he arranged things so that he and Teresa played the corresponding roles.

There was one scene at the end of the first act – appropriately it was based on the theme of the fantasia – which ended with a warm embrace, warm but decorous, more a suggestion of an embrace, not least because Teresa had to sing a florid aria. When the curtain fell the two singers found themselves alone on the darkened stage ... later they confessed that they had each said to themselves: now or never. This time there was no aria to hinder the embrace and the fiery kiss which, if you will allow a hackneyed image, threatened to set the décor on fire..

Unfortunately the summer was already coming to a close. They were due back in Naples in a few days time to welcome the Prince who was already on his way home from Spain. It was a breathless happiness they enjoyed, a painful and rather tearful exploration of tender spots, and all in a spirit of youthful honesty: the pair had nothing else in mind than to travel, separately of course, to Rome to persuade the Holy Father to annul the young Princess' marriage; for Teresa, her overpowering love for Orlandini was sufficient canonical grounds. At the same time they wanted to use Orlandini's music to move, indeed compel, the Pope to raise the musician to the rank of Marchese which would remove the difference in rank and clear the way for a marriage. They were so convinced there would be no difficulty in realising this plan that they believed they were justified in jumping the gun – if you see what I mean – as far as the marriage was concerned.

There was not a cushion in the house, no patch of grass in the park, no boat on the lake that was not witness to their love, provided they were left alone there for a moment.

When they then returned to Naples the surprised Prince felt some of the warmth of this fiery passion, enough at least for the son that the Princess gave birth to the following spring to count as his child – if the calculation were done in the right spirit.

The following summer the Prince went with his whole household to another, larger country estate. Again the young Princess was accompanied by her music-master. But the love between her and Orlandini, although as torrid as ever, was less happy, less painful perhaps, but also less pure. It was a sinful passion which found fulfilment in the few nights together in the secluded hunting lodge where they went by separate ways, with a thousand excuses to the others. A year ago they had still believed in the possibility of domestic happiness after an annulment from the Pope, but this year there was no longer any question of that. They knew that all that was left to them was sin, and even if it did not impede their passion, they were still drinking from the poisoned chalice of lost hopes.

It was of course only a matter of time before suspicion was aroused. The old music-master kept an eye sharpened by professional envy on his young colleague. It was impossible that his rival's real success should remain hidden from him for long. He reported his suspicions to the old Prince.

Although nothing could be proved against Teresa and Orlandini, the suspicion alone was enough to unleash a scandal. The Princess was forced to dismiss her music-master. The worst part of all was the formal farewell. He had to come to the table when everyone was present and kiss her hand. She just nodded – 'regally' said the aunts with approval. Of course she only nodded – she felt as if she had been turned to stone. And it seemed a miracle to her that the chain that bound their hearts together did not at that moment glow visibly. Silently both swore to belong to the other alone, yet they never saw each other again.

When the following spring Teresa gave birth to a daughter whom she knew was also Orlandini's child, she left Naples. For sixteen years she lived with her children on the lonely country estate of that first summer, surrounded by the Prince's spies. Carlo, her son, grew up the very image of Orlandini. Her daughter, blonde as an angel and of a heavenly loveliness even as a child, seemed by some magical process to absorb the beauty as it faded from her mother's face: –

The full moon shines down on a calm pool. But the pool is black and does not reflect the moon. The moon wanes just a little and a wisp of a sickle moon appears in the pool. And night by night, the more the moon in the sky wanes, the more the sickle in the pool fills out. And when the last ray of the dying sickle vanishes from the sky, its reflection in the depths of the dark waters ripens to its full glory.

When Teresa, Princess Cursi-Cicinelli, died after sixteen years in voluntary exile, the beauty of her daughter at her death-bed possessed an otherworldly radiance. But her pale forehead already bore the mute sign of suffering to come.

The Prince had sent a father confessor. Whether he was a *false* priest or a false *priest,* he had been charged to report to the long-suspicious Prince – suspicion seems to have been his sole intellectual endowment – the Princess' last confession. And indeed, the Princess confessed her love for Orlandini.

The Prince hired six bravos. The first two strangled Carlo in his father's palace. The next pair set off for Capua, where Orlandini had been maestro di capella for a number of years. The third pair went to the country estate where the Prince knew that his bastard daughter was.

The bravos arrived in Capua at the moment when Orlandini, a prematurely aged but still powerful man who, no one knew why, but the Capuans had become used to it, always wore clerical garb without being a priest, was entering the church where he was organist. It was a requiem mass for one of the parishioners. But Orlandini had heard of Teresa's death. He played the fantasia, for the worthy mourners strains of an alien music they would not have dreamed possible; it throbbed through the church like the scent of unknown, luminous flowers, like the soft light of Persian jewels refracted into a hundred rays, like the eyes glistening on the tail feathers of a sick peacock with the reflection of suns from the farthest corners of the universe, thus it throbbed through the church as Orlandini played the fantasia, and the keys burnt under his fingers. He was incapable of conducting the choir, and left the rest to one of his pupils. He stumbled down the steps from the organ-loft and out into the side porch of the church. There, between the church and the street, the assassins were waiting.

'Was that you, signor, who played the fantasia?'

Orlandini looked at the two bravos.

'I think', said one of them, 'it would be a sin to kill you ...'

The other just silently kissed Orlandini's hand. – You can see how musical we are in Naples, even the professional assassins.

The bravos told Orlandini of the murder of his son and the

planned assassination of his daughter. He set off immediately. Fortunately he reached the estate before the other pair of assassins. There he found the image of Teresa, divinely transfigured, his daughter ...

'My child', he said; he meant to go on to say that he could face all the suffering in the world as long as he did not lose his daughter the very moment he had seen her for the first time ... but he was too moved to speak. When he had managed to calm the storm of conflicting emotions within, he immediately turned to practical matters and explained everything to the young girl. She listened to it calmly, as if she had known all along – or had she known all along?

'What shall I do?' she asked.

He told her to take the coach, in which he had come, and travel to Venice where a younger brother of his – her uncle – lived. Orlandini would get a message to him and he would look after her. He told her the name of an inn where she was to stay and gave her all the money he had been able to gather together in his hurried departure from Capua. I fear, he thought as he watched the coach disappear, her beauty will attract more attention than if she bore a brand on her forehead.

When the assassins reached the estate they found Orlandini instead of his daughter. They had no orders to kill him, so they turned round and left.

But the girl – how else could it be with a plan conceived in such haste? – did not find her uncle in Venice, the reason being he had in the meantime moved to Milan.

Pursued by the desperados hired by the man who, until now, she had assumed was her father, and with the money Orlandini had been able to give her fast running out, she wandered hither and thither through Venice. Finally word did reach her uncle who sent his son to collect her. But the son did not succeed in finding her. Perhaps the gondolier who was supposed to take him to her made some mistake. All that we know is that the Prince's powerful connections saw to it that she was arrested by the sbirri. It is better not to say anything about the rest of her brief life ...'

Renata stopped.

'And what was the daughter's name?'

'Stellidaura', said Renata. 'You look surprised, as if you knew more?'

'A little more tea, please', I said .... – I'll pass over the evening and the night, Spring."

"Oho!" said Spring.

"Not at all 'Oho!' – the nieces had been brought up extremely strictly. Their uncle, with whom they had grown up, had taken great care to stifle any tendencies they might have inherited from their promiscuous mother."

"That means nothing, Your Eminence. On the contrary. The little trollops or the old pander probably just gave you an antidote to the pink pill that only worked for the night ..."

"Is that a way to talk about a Senator's friend?!"

"But you said yourself it was only a dream."

"It's like the 'atoms-within-atoms'. There are dreams and there are dreams within dreams, and we fall from the one into the other and wake up from one into the other. You can *never* tell whether you are dreaming or not. Perhaps while I'm telling you all this, someone up there, in the real world – which could be just another higher-level dream – might shake me and I will wake up –"

"And I will go on living down here in this dream?"

"Yes."

"And what does that make me? A bubble in your dream, Your Eminence? No thank you, Your Eminence. I'm afraid I don't accept the creed you're trying to teach me."

"Perhaps I'll take you with me?"

"I hope to God you can."

"Good – well, I'll jump forward to the next day, the Wednesday. The only change from the previous routine was that the ladies went riding before lunch and stayed out a long time."

"And I wonder where they were all that time, the innocent little lambs?" said Spring.

"The Count and I dined together. Afterwards we all met in the mother-of-pearl room where Mirandolina, who came from Vienna, immediately began her story:

155

'It will surely come as no surprise, since we come from a musical family, that my story is a musical one as well. Actually it's more of a novel, but I find a story is better the more one leaves out. Truth, they say, is stranger than fiction, but it's also much more long-winded, full of superfluous detail. Truth is a block of marble which the artist has to work on before the 'fiction' – I would call it the real truth – is revealed.

Therefore I will keep my story as short as possible, I will sketch in the bare essentials, and if any writer enjoys it, he is welcome to take it and turn it into a full canvas. Moreover, I don't want to keep you up too long, certainly not after midnight; I don't know whether it's a good idea to tell this particular story after midnight.

In Vienna there lived a young man of twenty-three who was imbued with high ideals to an extent one might almost call abnormal for that age: an otherworldly person – let us call him Felix Abegg. He came from a numerous family with anthroposophical tendencies, was a vegetarian and, as is the way with otherworldly people, neglected his external appearance to concentrate on his soul and – this much one must allow him – his mind.

Being genuinely talented in several directions, he had long hesitated between various ambitions. His interest in literature was as great as his love of old languages, and his remarkably willing memory would have made minor branches of scholarship such as law or sociology child's play for him. But greater than everything else was his love of music. While still at school he had developed into a pianist of remarkable technical ability, had taught himself the fundamentals of harmony and counterpoint and provided original and profound examples of his talent for composition. At school he was top of the class in every subject' apart from physical education, of course, well-behaved and popular with his teachers. The highlight of the leaving ceremony for his year was a cantata he had composed for tenor, choir, string orchestra and horn obbligato, which sang the praises of schools in general and his in particular.

They expected, it said in his school-leaving report, great things of him.

Not surprisingly, given his manifold interests, he started to study in two directions at once, piano at the conservatory and classics at the university. Although his knowledge of classical literature and his ability to absorb Latin and Greek, later on Coptic, Egyptian and Hebrew as well, put not only his less gifted fellow students but also junior lecturers in the shade, he gave up classics after a short time, to the relief of the aforementioned junior lecturers, and devoted himself exclusively to music. He took a master-class for piano and studied composition with a renowned teacher, his only problem being that he once set some poems to music which his teacher had already used. In his modesty he would have naturally kept them to himself, but a student of the Lieder master-class had discovered them and insisted on singing them at the end of year concert.

Felix Abegg felt uneasy about the concert; he was afraid that the better his settings were, the greater the chance his teacher would be offended.

But that evening was to see the start, the quiet and unobtrusive start, of something much more sinister ... Were I of a poetic mind, I would have said there was a rumbling of fate.

Present at that end-of-year master-class concert was Brankovic, Gabriel Brankovic, the famous Brankovic, Brankovic the Great.

What you need to know is that Professor Brankovic had never attended a college of music, a conservatory or an academy. He had never been anyone's pupil. Initially ignored by the contemporary musical – so-called musical! – world and rejected by the academic establishment, the success of his writings, which in spite of their demanding style attracted a wide readership among the musical public, had finally forced musicologists to capitulate. There were lectures on his works, he was given an honorary doctorate, and so on until finally he was offered a professorship. Brankovic accepted with manifest condescension. He gave an inaugural lecture on 'Beyond the Academic: the Triumph of Genius', and this inaugural lecture was to remain the only lecture he ever gave. He held seminars, and those not in the university, but in Brankovina Castle where he lived. Incredible stories circulated of strange concerts in the Castle, of performances of the 'Art of Fugue' by candlelight or moonlight in a lofty hall that almost went beyond music, of the pupils going hunting on horseback, and of the fair Lady of Brankovina, Isabella Brankovic, the Professor's sister, who played the cembalo like an angel and rode like a goddess, or vice versa.

Everything that was reported in the Academy about these goings-on was rather vague, since the pupils who were allowed into Brankovic's seminars spent the whole semester as the Professor's guests at the Castle, and even after they had returned to the Academy, they always enveloped themselves in something of the master's otherworldly aura. To jealous fellow-students they just occasionally let slip hints of what they had experienced there, which of course led to the creation of breath-taking, not to mention hair-raising legends; Brankovic himself never appeared at the Academy. At most he might drop in on the Principal. Even the oldest students could not remember Brankovic having attended an end-of-year concert or any other such trivial event.

So it was a sensation when he arrived at the concert unannounced. Even the Principal, who naturally did not attend such – theoretically public, in practice private – events either, had had no inkling of Brankovic's intention. The senior of the professors present welcomed Brankovic who, for his part, acted as if it were the most natural thing in the world for him to turn up unheralded like this. Everything went on as normal, apart, that is, from the increased number of butterflies in the performers' stomachs due to the presence of Brankovic. It was noticed, however, that Brankovic scribbled a few words down in his programme, and some claimed to have seen that it was alongside the note announcing Abegg's Lieder.

All this happened towards the end of January when the winter semester was drawing to a close. Abegg suddenly found himself the centre of interest, or at least gossip. Although otherworldly, this sudden fame would not have left him entirely unmoved if another event had not occurred at the same time – his first love. Yes, your ears do not deceive you: I said 'first love' and we are talking of a young man of our day and age who was twenty-three! Felix Abegg, as he told my mother, who was a close friend, was completely innocent in such matters. He had, of course, read about love in books and knew that people took each other in their arms and occasionally, even, to bed; as, however, serious works of literature – and that was the only kind he read – adopted an attitude of genteel reticence as far as the precise biological details were concerned, he was left with the impression that love must be something holy and sacred, of idealised sublimity.

Somewhat coarse in appearance, not particularly graceful or sociable and without wealth, he was not a natural target for feminine wiles, and thus his literary image had not been corrected by practical experience. It must have been a fateful aspect of his own nature that until the day after that concert he had not felt the need for any such correction, neither with regard to a particular person, nor in general.

On that day one of Abegg's sisters received a visit from a certain Fräulein Frauke Frosch. His sister studied psychology and Fräulein Frosch was a fellow-student. Frauke Frosch was a somewhat plump girl – so much so that she appeared to be bosomless – who imagined her mind was set on higher things; she had just been through an unhappy affair.

In contrast to Felix Abegg – she was about the same age – Frauke Frosch was permanently in love. Although on the one hand a ferocious supporter of total emancipation, or perhaps for that very reason, she was constantly in raptures about the male sex. No fellow-student, no lecturer, no cousin, in brief no person of the male sex who ventured into her proximity was safe from what she called *love,* and had this love showered upon him in the whole range of its meaning. At the same time Fräulein Frosch carefully remained vague in her own mind as to what precisely she meant by it. She liked to hop around in parks at night, doing a dance of love, real or imagined, and on moonlit nights she would pace up and down on the balcony of the student residence, naked apart from a flowing gauzy nightdress.

Frauke Frosch was a very hard-working student. She had devoted herself absolutely to the theory of one of the professors, with whom she was naturally in love, and through a combination of perseverance and half-digested theory she had managed to obtain a part-time post as the Professor's assistant. Her main task was to put out-of-place books back in the right place and to keep an eye on the time for the Professor during his seminars – until one day something better came her way.

At that time the Professor had a case. It concerned an ex-ballet dancer, a young man from a respectable family who – it had happened in Venice and would make a story on its own – had fallen prey to melancholy. Although there was a definite clinical aspect to the case, the young man's mother who, widowed young, well-off and well-connected, loved her only son above all else, had great hopes of psychology and had consulted the Professor.

By then the young man – his name was Alexis Baswaldt – had for several years been lying in a state of more or less complete apathy. First the Professor had prescribed pale blue sheets, later he added music to his therapy: a constant stream from a tape with specially selected items – pieces for a capella choir, the Tristan Prelude, early baroque organ music etc. – washed over the sick man. After that the Professor began to lose interest in the case. He handed it over to his assistant, who seemed qualified through the work she was doing for her thesis on cases linking music and psychoanalysis, *The repression of manic repressions in J. S. Bach, with particular reference to the cantata 'Dearest Lord, when must I die'*.

Frau Baswaldt was glad to see Frauke Frosch. Not only did the assistant have more time for the patient than the Professor, it was plain to see that she had immediately fallen in love – of course – with Alexis. Frau Baswaldt, who did not know who would care for her son after her death, silently put her hope in Frauke Frosch.

It must be said in Frauke Frosch's favour that it was solely her idealised conception of love, and not the considerable inheritance that went with it, that persuaded her to accept the old lady's proposal that she marry her son. The proposal itself had been preceded by countless hints and parallel intuitions before the two women finally clasped hands across Alexis' counterpane and burst into tears.

The Professor had prophesied that at about this time Alexis would have one last moment of lucidity, and since up to this point all the Professor's prophecies had come true, the two women were on tenterhooks waiting for it

The moment arrived. Fräulein Frosch, who, in order not to miss it, had taken up residence in the house, was led into Alexis' room by his mother, carrying a candle in each hand and dressed in a bridal gown of her own design and which reflected her idealised conception of love. Slowly, Alexis Baswaldt opened his eyes. His mother said,

'Look, Alexis, your bride!' Slowly, even more slowly than he had opened them, Alexis Baswaldt closed his eyes. He had understood perfectly what was happening, it was a 'lucid moment' in the true sense of the word. In a relatively strong voice he said, 'No'.

Anything that happened later between Frauke Frosch and Frau Baswaldt and her son is of no further interest to us. As the story I am telling you is a true one, it has the disadvantage that it branches out on all sides – and in front, and behind – into other stories, almost unnoticed, like the shadow of a bird flying overhead, so that the boundaries are very difficult to define in the tangle of stories of which our life consists, that is, in the one and only story that is called 'The Creation'.

You must excuse a little girl like me,' Mirandolina interrupted herself, 'talking all this clever stuff about the world being like a story told by God; perhaps it is a way of understanding the Trinity ... or perhaps just a way that makes it clear to a poor female brain.'

'What do you mean?' we asked.

'Well', said Mirandolina, 'God the Father tells God the Son the story we call 'The Creation', and the Holy Ghost listens to check that the other two forget nothing of what they have once

161

told or heard ...'

'How silly of the philosophers, then', said the Count with a smile, 'to worry that the world doesn't make sense. It's just a story that hasn't been finished yet.'

'Thus every story', continued Mirandolina, 'is a compromise. We have to draw boundaries, artificial and sometimes painful boundaries. Let's leave the Baswaldt affair on one side. You will be well able to imagine Frauke Frosch's mental state: the disappointment about Alexis Baswaldt plus the fact that she had not fallen in love again since then – it was already a few days ago – meant that at the point when she visited Abegg's sister she was particularly susceptible. But you must not think that the mere presence of a man was sufficient to provoke Fräulein Frosch to love. No, she did need a little push, some tiny grain of sand which her passion could transform into a pearl. The fact that Felix Abegg came into the room where his sister was with Fräulein Frosch at about ten o'clock in order to practice would not, of itself have been sufficient to ignite her passion. It was only the delivery shortly afterwards of a telegram for him – Felix was annoyed and still standing there uncertain what to do as he did not like practising in the presence of strangers – that swept the necessary 'grain of sand' into Frauke's soul.

Abegg's mother took the telegram. The Abeggs lived modestly; father Abegg was a devout and honest man whose sole concern was to give his children a decent upbringing on a bookkeeper's salary. Sophisticated matters such as telegrams were unheard of in the Abegg household. His mother immediately assumed some aunt had died, or something similar, although that did not explain why the telegram was addressed to Felix.

Felix opened the telegram. It was from the Principal of the Academy asking him to ring. His sister suspected some practical joke from Felix' fellow-students – it was the end of January and the middle of the Carnival season. Felix, as a serious person, was a likely target for student jokes, and this suggestion paralysed him with doubt. He spent an hour pondering over it, going over suspicions, possibilities and risks point by point before deciding to phone. The frugal and thrifty Abegg family did not have a telephone of their own – such people still existed! He went to the post office to make his call. The Principal was already becoming impatient. Scarcely had Felix given his name than the Principal began to moan about the Post taking so long to deliver his telegram. Felix attempted to protect the Post Office's reputation with a long-winded account of his hour of doubt, but the Principal cut him off with an impatient 'Good, good. When can you come and see me?' The next train from the suburban station went at one o'clock. 'Good,' said the Principal, 'take a taxi from the station; I'll pay for it.'

'May I ask what ...'

'Later, later,' said the Principal, 'it's nothing unpleasant, quite the contrary, quite the contrary. And bring a note of the cost of this call.'

Felix made his way home from the post office in a state of pleasant bewilderment, as if he had been transported to another, higher world. He repeated the conversation to his family, and Fräulein Frosch, the embryo of her young love already growing within her, was all ears. His sister's immediate assumption was that he was going to be sent down from the Academy. The Principal had only said 'nothing unpleasant' to make sure that Felix would come. He, however, did not believe that.

There was still some time to go before the train left. Not only was Felix a vegetarian – and not one like our uncle here who makes it a strict rule only to eat the flesh of herbivorous animals such as cattle, sheep, pigs and poultry, and thus abstains from eating lions, dogs, cats and eagles, his only exception being trout and pike – Felix normally ate nothing at all at lunchtime and, indeed, found the mild feeling of hunger stimulating. Frauke Frosch, pregnant with burgeoning love, already in labour even, for her part also turned down Frau Abegg's invitation to lunch. Thus the two were left alone in the sitting room and Felix began to play the piano after all. His mood demanded something rapturously ecstatic, so he started to play a sonata by Weber but then thought better of it, deciding it would be more in line with his character to suppress his ecstasy. At that moment Frauke Frosch came up to him, pawed the back of his hand a little and said, 'Oh!' Horrified, he pulled his hand away – but no woman had ever said 'Oh!' to him before ... Felix closed the score and began to play, dispassionately, severely, Bach: The Well-Tempered Clavier, Inventions, French Suites and finally – by this time his sister had come back into the room – the *Chromatic Fantasy*.

At first Frauke Frosch had just listened, then she gave a few 'eurhythmic' hops and skips and started to throw her arms about, analysing the music that Felix was playing according to Becking's curves.

His sister went back to her mother in the kitchen. 'Mother', she said, 'something terrible has happened. Felix has fallen in love with Froggie! She analysed the *Chromatic Fantasy* with Becking's rhythmical movements as if it were by Brahms, and Felix said nothing!'

She was right. Felix had said nothing ... and by the time he had got to the Inventions Fräulein Frosch had given birth to her latest love.

One day near the beginning of February, the weather was fine and clear, but also cold, Felix Abegg left the city in Professor Brankovic's specially-commissioned purple Bugatti. The car swept through the streets and along the main road until after an hour they came to the mountains. Road and weather conditions worsened. Leaden clouds descended over the mountains. It became dark around four o'clock and then it began to snow. They passed through the occasional village, but otherwise as night fell the driving snow was too thick to see the lonely farms on the slopes either side of the road. At first Brankovic had chatted to Felix, genially, not at all as one would have expected from his reputation; on the contrary he had shown great tact in the matter-of-fact way he asked about his background, his studies and his plans. Later they fell silent. Brankovic was concentrating on driving and Felix felt tired and huddled up in his winter coat.

Everything had happened in a rush. When Felix had gone to see the Principal he had not been alone; Brankovic was there too. And he had asked Felix, as a result of the Lieder he had heard the previous evening, to join his seminar group – not the next one, no, the current one, although it only had another month to run. Brankovic had only grudgingly allowed him a short time to think it over, had even gone to visit him at home, where he chatted expansively and amiably with his parents. Felix' sister assumed he had homosexual designs on her brother.

Finally Felix had given in, had said his goodbyes and disappeared in Brankovic's car ...

Felix was suddenly woken up by a violent jolting – Brankovic had turned off the road onto a forest track with two deep ruts. On either side of the entrance were square-edged columns of stone. The track was hardly wider than the car and thickly lined with young conifers. Above the tree-tops the storm was blowing the snow in horizontal lines, but down in the forest track the wind was caught and the snowflakes whirled in a witches' Sabbath in and out of the beam of the headlights. Every time the car brushed against a low-hanging branch a load of snow thudded onto the roof. Soon the track became steeper, the trees taller. The engine of the Bugatti roared as it skidded round the many corners. But then Felix heard a different noise, now nearer, now farther away, drawn-out and high-pitched, a howling rather than a roar. At first he thought it was the storm, until he looked out through the rear window and saw glowing points of light, always two at a time, following the car.

At a particularly steep curve the snow had piled up against a stack of logs and blocked the track. The Bugatti was stuck. The wolves, who were now trotting past the car on both sides in a hunched, wary posture, seemed to Felix to be the size of calves, but that was presumably just an illusion brought on by the dreadful night. Their tails whipped like hard brushes against the paintwork of the car.

'Devil take it!' said Brankovic. 'And I thought we would get up without snow-chains.'

'Are they wolves?' asked Felix

'Yes', said Brankovic, opening the door.

Immediately the wind blew snowflakes into the car. The

howling of the wolves was louder than ever. Brankovic said something. Felix thought it was Latin, but could not understand it in the raging storm. The wolves did understand it, however ... They stopped howling, cringed and bristled. Finally they ran off into the dark forest.

Brankovic, clumsily assisted by Felix, put the snow-chains on, and they set off again. The trees thinned out and all of a sudden a high gate appeared out of the snowstorm. The track became broader. An immense black mass rose up before them: Brankovina.

Brankovic drove through the outer and inner gate into the castle courtyard.

'There are still wolves here, then?' asked Felix.

'Mmm', said Brankovic as he got out.

'Excuse my asking, but aren't you afraid of wolves?'

'Well, there are the students here during the semester, but in the quiet periods in between we have this lonely place more or less to ourselves. You see things differently then. And I read old books a great deal.'

Professor Brankovic took Felix' small suitcase out of the car. They walked along under the low arcades to the castle entrance. Brankovic opened the heavy wrought-iron gate and they went up a broad stairway. Felix saw that the walls, otherwise plain, were covered over and over with sets of antlers. Burnt into the bone between the eyes each trophy bore the date of the hunt and the initials of the hunter: J.B., A.B., F.B. – Johann, Alexander, Ferdinand and all the other Brankovics. The higher they climbed, the farther the branded dates went back through the centuries. In the corridors as well, and even between the pictures on the walls of the galleries, were more antlers of dead stags, legions of dead stags from the woods around Brankovina. They must have been gigantic stags. On the second floor the antlers were of even more immense proportions; often they were hung above oak wardrobes darkened with age and threw distorted ghostly shadows across the vaulted ceiling. Felix started when, between the huge branches and points, he saw two eyes glowing.

'Psss!' went Brankovic, and a large cat jumped down.

'The Duke of Lazun', he said.

'I'm sorry?'

'One of my sister's cats. They all have names which, she says, suit them. This tomcat is called Duke of Lazun. He is handsome, evil-tempered and sad.'

So far all the corridors and stairs had been icy cold, and thus it was a relief when Brankovic opened the door to a brightly-lit and blissfully warm room.

'It is already late', he said; 'there will be no one else still up. But supper has been left out for us. Excuse me' – he sat down and pushed his plate to one side. Felix sat down as well and looked at the table in rising irritation: there was a more than sumptuous meal for two: pheasant, carp, eel, slices of roast beef, some stuffed pigeons, ham smoked until it was almost black, a little venison, cold saddle of hare ... finally he discovered to his vegetarian relief some cheese and fruit. Brankovic poured him a glass of red wine and then took for himself what was obviously a special bottle out of a locked wall cabinet – the key hung from the Professor's belt. From its colour it seemed to be red wine. Immediately after he had filled his glass, he replaced the bottle in the cupboard and locked it.

'*Prost*', said Brankovic.

Felix raised his glass. A hand coloured blood-red by the wine was engraved on it.

'Our coat of arms', said the Professor. 'One of my ancestors fought on the Turkish side at the Battle of Kossovo, breaking his oath. He fell, and a year and a day after the battle the hand that he had raised in oath grew out of his grave. His son cut it off, but it kept on growing again, every time it was chopped off – at least so the legend goes. The family adopted the coat of arms as a penance. You'll see it everywhere here.' Brankovic pointed to the mantelpiece, the arms of the chairs, the carpet and the lampshade: everywhere was the hand the ancestor of the Brankovics had raised in a false oath.

Felix had eaten and drunk. Brankovic yawned.

'I'll take you to your room. You sleep down below, in the

other wing, it has a view out across the valley.'

Again they went through long, cold, dark corridors festooned with antlers.

'Those are the oldest', said Brankovic, who had noticed Felix studying the dates. 'That one was killed by the ill-fated Konstantin Brankovic, the one with the chopped-off hand.'

'How can people kill so many animals', said Felix. 'There are hundreds'.

'I've never counted them', said the Professor.

He led Felix into a tiny chamber. However, it was only the space, made by the thickness of the walls, between the inner and outer doors to his bedroom. The room itself was huge. Students who had had it before Felix used to claim it was so big one could just about detect the curvature of the earth. In the most distant corner, tiny as a mouse, stood a bed. By it was a rug made out of a badger skin. The storm rattled the shutters as if hordes of chained slaves were in silent revolt. Abegg read for a while. As he was putting out the light, he noticed that, woven everywhere into the linen sheets, white in white, was the dismembered hand of the foresworn Brankovic.

He slept well. He only woke once – the storm had torn one of the shutters loose which was banging against the castle wall – and gave a start of horror: in the opposite corner stood a man swathed in a creased white cloth holding a black object up in his hand. Felix lit the light – it was the tiled stove. He got out of bed, opened the window where the shutter was being blown about in the wind and, if you'll excuse the expression, made heavy weather of closing it. It must have been in the small hours, it was still completely dark. The storm had not abated in the least and he could not even see the closest trees. In the distance he thought he could hear the wolves.

He slept late, obviously later than the other students – there were six in all – since Brankovic and his sister were the only ones at breakfast with him. The Professor was drinking from his private supply of red wine again. His sister had not touched her plate and left it untouched. Isabella Brankovic was beautiful and still almost young. Considering Gabriel Brankovic's age it seemed scarcely credible that she was his sister. She was as slim as a young girl, had large, dark eyes and red hair, which was always beautifully and elaborately done. One of Brankovic's students caught the essence of her fascination when he said she was the girl inside every lady and the lady inside every girl. If, as today, she was wearing long green corduroy slacks and a riding blouse and, after a hard ride on her favourite horse, she slashed the morning air with her crop as she brushed a stray leaf from her hair, then one felt she was in disguise, and automatically pictured her as a *grande dame,* proud in white lace, a tiara in her hair and her hand in a blue glove lightly resting on the mantelpiece ... If, on the other hand, she was sitting in her brother's *sanctum* in a long, black velvet gown with a high collar, her slim white neck rising like a flower from the black cloth and a string of pearls woven into her hair, and if, sitting erect in the straight-backed chair, one hand was idly caressing one of the tall, lithe retrievers whilst the other played round the edge of her wine-glass, then one could sense in her eyes the smoke in the forest and the mist rising on the moors over which that morning she had been galloping in a wild, exuberant ride.

Isabella Brankovic always seemed to be somewhere outside her own world, always seemed to be merely the reflection of another, invisible sister, and it was the current sparking across the gap between the visible and the invisible Isabella that made men tingle at her slightly absent presence.

She was not only a brilliant horsewoman, she was also an accomplished pianist. And it was probably the imagination of the audience rather than her intention that produced the impression that everything she played seemed to be dipped in ice, frozen—unless, that is, she were performing some sparse, brittle piece which would then sound as if it were consumed by fire.

Professor Brankovic drank his wine. Isabella merely poked at the marmalade with her spoon.

Felix asked after his fellow-students and when the classes were. Of the six students two had stayed on in the city for a few days after the concert. Two others were hunting and staying in a hut on the other side of the valley, towards the frontier. One had already finished for this semester and had gone home for some reason. Only the cellist, a certain Burghardt, was still there, but he had set off early on horseback for the village to have a horse shod. The fact that Brankovic spoke of 'the' cellist aroused Felix' attention. As all the senior students were known to each other, he knew which instruments those at the castle studied as their main subjects. They made a nice little chamber ensemble: string quartet plus oboe and clarinet; as the clarinettist also played the horn and one of the violinists the bassoon – plus Isabella Brankovic as pianist, one could spend a whole semester working through an interesting programme of experimental music. So Brankovic chose his pupils for their usefulness as his own private orchestra. But what about Felix himself? He could not really see what use the Professor would have for a second – with Isabella – pianist. Had he suddenly developed an interest in music for two pianos? But he himself was a good enough pianist to play with his sister, or one of the other pupils, who were all at least tolerable pianists. Was it not natural if Abegg concluded that Brankovic had a genuine interest in his compositions?

For the time being, however, they stuck to chamber music. Nothing was said about classes and Felix did not ask. The other students who, apart from the one who had gone home, came back one after the other, seemed to have no thoughts of tuition or anything of that kind. Thus Felix did in fact spend time playing pieces for four hands with Isabella. She particularly liked the great F minor Fantasy by Schubert, that most romantic of pieces, reflecting a whole bitter-sweet chapter in the story of Schubert's heart. Isabella played her part as if it were something transcribed by magic from a Palestrina mass.

The chamber music only took up a small portion of their time. They generally played for an hour or so, mostly before dinner, sometimes after as well. As the Professor laid no great emphasis on perfection, there was no need to practise, at least for Felix. Now and then he would play in his room, where Brankovic had had a magnificent grand piano installed. The rest of the time was spent in riding.

As already mentioned, Isabella Brankovic was an ardent horsewoman. Abegg, who had grown up in modest circumstances and was quite the opposite of a man of the world, had never been on a horse in his life. At that very first breakfast – Isabella had greeted Felix with a silent nod but submitted his features to a searching examination – her first question was about riding.

'Do you ride a lot?'

'I'm sorry?'

'Do you ride a lot?'

'Where?'

'On a horse ...'

'Oh, I see, no, I've never ridden a horse.'

'Pity. I was going to ask you to come out for a ride with me. Or perhaps we should go shooting?'

Felix was a vegetarian out of conviction. Rather than kill an animal, he was prepared to ride on one. He said he would be happy to learn to ride. Isabella selected a particularly quiet horse for him, and so, instead of studying the art of composition, Felix spent his time at Brankovina learning to ride. Any other place in the world, as will become clear in the course of the story, would have been more suitable for learning the art of composition, as far as there was anything left for him to learn.

Isabella Brankovic's teaching methods consisted solely in getting on her own horse, waiting for Felix to mount his and then making her pupil's horse trot along behind her's until he fell off. This at the beginning he did quite a lot, and each time Isabella burst into loud, but never hurtful laughter. Occasionally she would gaze at him, seemingly lost in thought, and then quickly make some casual remark about the way he was sitting or holding the reins. As she never repeated her instructions, it was usually not until much later that Felix came to understand what she meant by them. Gradually, however, he became a tolerable horseman and capable of going on extensive excursions on horseback through the snow-covered woods, sometimes with fellow students, sometimes with Isabella alone, but never with Brankovic, who obviously did not go riding. As he had stopped falling off his horse, Isabella only laughed when the echo of the horses' hooves on the frosty bridle path loosened a pile of snow on a pine branch which then landed on Felix.

Towards the end of February it became somewhat warmer. The grip of winter was broken. In the valley the snow began to melt. The semester had come to an end and the other students left the castle. One stayed on for the first week in March. Felix asked him what was the done thing about leaving Brankovina. The reply was that Professor Brankovic threw you out with the remark,

'I think you have learnt enough for this semester; don't become too clever, perfection is hubris.'

Felix waited for his cue. It did not come. It never came.

Life at Brankovina grew quiet. Riding across the moors they had to be extremely careful and stay on the narrow paths so as not to end up in the mire. Isabella, who always rode on ahead at this point, could find her way with instinctive assurance, even if they stayed out until night was falling and they could see will-o'-the-wisps on the tallest fence-posts and sometimes a dead tree-trunk half sunk into the mire shining from within. Once they came across the skeleton of a stag.

'You see,' said Isabella, 'if we don't shoot them, the wolves kill them.'

Then – it was in the middle of March – from one day to the next she began to be more talkative. They were riding beside each other along an easy path.

'Do you know', said Isabella, 'believe it or not, a few semesters ago we had a married student here. It was in the summer. My brother allowed him to send for his wife and two children and they stayed here for the rest of the semester. It is such a long time since there were children here in Brankovina', she said sorrowfully, 'a long, long time. The children, a little girl and a little boy, played in the courtyard and in the castle, in all the corridors and halls. One day we noticed that they were talking of a third child, a boy, who was somewhat older than they. We assumed it was childish imagination. But they insisted that they always played tag and hide and seek with another child. They described the child as about nine years old and dressed like a server at mass. Where he came from they did not know, only that afterwards he always disappeared through the same door. We got them to show us the door. They took us to the chapel. The chapel has been locked for many years, since my mother died ... The student's children insisted, however, that the chapel door was always open. We fetched the key. Inside they pointed to the wall behind the altar: that, they said, was where their mysterious companion went. But there was no door there. Led by one of my brother's students with a practical bent, we examined the wall and we did discover a secret mechanism, which by then had almost completely seized up, but which opened part of the panelling. We found a short ladder which led to an enclosed room without windows. There was the skeleton of a child of about nine; around it were server's robes. We had it buried in the village below. After that the child appeared no more.

Strange? The style of the server's robes suggested they must be from the seventeenth century. We consulted various chronicles and found that during the thirty years war the Swedes attacked the castle and cut down the priest and the servers who were saying mass in the chapel. We deduced that one of the servers must have escaped into the little hideout where he was forgotten and, since the secret door could only be opened from the outside, died. Since then the chapel has been locked.'

'I thought', said Felix, 'that was since your mother died?'

'Oh yes', said Isabella. 'Since my mother died.'

'It certainly is strange', said Felix; 'but what seems even stranger to me is for people to believe in ghosts in our enlightened age.'

'I', said Isabella Brankovic, 'saw the Black Cock the day before my mother's death. Have you', she turned quickly to Felix, 'have you seen any hens at all at Brankovina? No. We don't keep any. And yet, when I opened the library door on the day before my mother died, a large, fat black cock came in through the door opposite, crossed the room – I could hear the scraping of its claws on the wooden floor – and went out by the door I had opened. My mother was the last of the line of the Counts of Valdharmin, whose seat was the Castle of Hochalbion in the Tyrol and who were descended from Saint Peter. It was prophesied that the cock that crowed for the second time after Peter had thrice denied Christ would appear once more when the last of the line was about to die. You see? And I saw the cock ...'

In spite of all these activities, Felix had not forgotten Frauke Frosch. Although he was much too shy to tell anyone of his feelings for her – which during the interminable nights at Brankovina he had analysed and long since classified as love – he made an attempt to see her again. He went to the Professor, therefore, and asked for his 'cue', and Brankovic, although with obvious reluctance, allowed him eight days' leave. This was also the first occasion that composing was mentioned between them. The Professor complained that the whole time he had been there Felix had not composed anything.

'How on earth do you know that?'

Brankovic smiled.

It was true that since he had been at Brankovina Felix had not given any thought to a new composition. The fault lay neither with Fräulein Frosch, nor with the effort of learning to ride and the excursions with Isabella. It was a natural break in inspiration, perhaps caused by the change in climate. In the last few days, however, he had once more started to feel the creative urge. On the day after Isabella had told him her story Felix had come across a peculiar phenomenon in the village. He had happened to go there around midday to have various pieces of tack repaired and heard the twelve o'clock chimes. The notes of three smaller bells of different pitch mingled with the chime from the church tower, famous for its big, old bells. The bells were not in phase, but overlapped and shifted in relation to each other, so that the convergence and divergence of the different frequencies created a unique kind of melody, probably only audible at certain points in the village, and Felix determined to find a way of making use of the principle in his music. He sketched out the idea to the Professor after the complaint, made more in jest than seriously, about his lack of productivity. Felix felt flattered by the spurt of interest in his teacher's eyes, though he could not quite explain why.

Although of a very dogged nature – some even called him phlegmatic – Felix seemed to Fräulein Frosch to be a changed person when he came back from Brankovina. Isabella Brankovic's riding lessons were probably not a sufficient explanation. No, there was some other, stronger influence at work which, without his suspecting, had blown away some of his innocence. Now Frauke Frosch set about doing her bit to get rid of what was left of that innocence, at least the physical side of it, in the few days she learnt he was to be in the city ...

I hope that I have put it in a way that is fitting for a young girl, but is still clear enough for you to understand what I am getting at.

Although Fräulein Frosch could, if necessary, promenade naked up and down the balcony of the female hall of residence all night, her room was shared with another student. Therefore she decided to take Felix to the Baswaldt house, under the pretext of showing him a strange and interesting case of mental illness. When they arrived there, however, she led him to her room, donned the bridal attire intended for Alexis Baswaldt and presented herself thus to the bewildered Felix, whose efforts were even clumsier than his first outings on the horses in Brankovina. Some time later and on reflection, however, he had to admit that he had had a sensation as of some mysterious music, coupled with the feeling of satisfaction after a successful concert.

Felix had hardly been in the city for a week when Brankovic appeared, on the pretext – until now he had left it to his colleagues' recommendations – of having to select his students for the coming semester. The first thing he did was to go to Felix' home, where he learnt from his sister that he was spending most of his time in the Baswaldt house. There he more or less plucked Felix from Fräulein Frosch's arms and whisked him off back to Brankovina; he, in contrast to Frau Baswaldt, to whom Felix had been presented as a 'colleague', was quite clear about the purpose of the 'study sessions' in the young lady's room.

In the area around Brankovina there is no real spring. When the power of winter has been broken, the thunder of avalanches announces the short, hot summer. When the bare birches, silver against the flaming orange of the marshy hollows, bend before the hot, dry Foehn wind, when the blackcocks display between patches of snow in sedge still fiery red or blazing yellow from the previous autumn, then the wind blows the last, crumbling snow from the peaks like a pennant against the pale blue sky above the saddle and winter is past, summer is on its way. But there is no spring in Brankovina. That also has psychological effects. The general thirst for erotic activity in nature, from which human beings are not excluded and which in other places is spread over several months, is here compressed into a short time span, into almost no time at all. So the pantheistic feeling of oneness with nature, which the word spring conjures up, is compressed into a nameless longing, impotent and yet thirsting for action, that produces nothing but sighs and only ripens into action in the summer. The days are already longer, but that does not mean the nights are clear of demons: and if this time between times, this non-time in Brankovina, this mere bar-line between winter and summer, coincides with the full moon, then there is an ominous point of intersection between this world and the other.

When Felix returned to Brankovina with Brankovic the wolves were silent, but the moon was full over the valley, which resounded to the ebb and flow of the windstorm – nature's organ, as Brankovic called it.

Felix, a child of the city and as such only appreciative of the pretty, flowery side of nature, was, without noticing it, subject to this contradictory atmosphere in the area, but grasped nothing of the other manifestations of the two worlds surrounding him. Moreover his attention was fully occupied with the attempt to create a synthesis between the mysterious tones his experience with Fräulein Frosch had produced and the acoustic phenomenon of the bells.

As the other students were not expected until the end of May, Felix could not avoid the excursions on horseback which, since the weather was no longer cold and since there was no chamber music, often lasted the whole day. In such cases milk and some strong hard cheese were packed for Felix. Isabella ate some raw salt venison. She washed it down with her brother's blood-red wine.

'After the war', she told him once, 'something funny happened here. You know that we were occupied by the English. In the early days we had to have people billeted on us, as well. They were officers from a Scottish regiment. A colonel, Lord Roslyn, was even related to us. One of the officers refused to believe in our 'room of horrors'. You know about the strange room with an oriel window overhanging the moat?'

They had just stopped in a clearing with a view of the castle, and Isabella pointed out the peculiar seven-sided oriel window in the tower that rose above the rocky precipice.

'Since time immemorial no one has spent the night there and come out alive. When three young officers, slightly the worse for drink, started to wager with the others that they would sleep in the room, we knew it would cause all sorts of awkward problems for us. The Colonel and my brother tried to stop them, but in vain. Camp-beds were set up for them and they told us they would keep their revolvers by their beds with the safety catches off, take it in turns to be on watch for an hour and shoot at the slightest noise. They warned the others not to try to play any tricks on them, as the consequences might be fatal, took a few bottles of wine and locked themselves in. During the night we heard shots.

The next morning the door was forced open. One of the officers was sitting upright on his camp-bed, dead, his eyes wide open. The second was alive but incapable of coherent speech. After various attempts to cure him he was taken to a mental hospital, where he still is, I believe. The third had disappeared. It was only later that we found him, squashed as flat as a flounder, behind an oak wardrobe so heavy it took twelve men to move it.

You can imagine what followed. His Britannic Majesty's

Military Police turned the castle upside down. Months later we were still being interrogated. You must remember that in those days we had hardly any rights at all as far as the occupying powers were concerned, and it was only the intervention of Colonel Roslyn that saved us from a very nasty situation. They do say, however, that the British Army is very reluctant to admit to the affair when anyone makes enquiries.'

'And you call that funny?' said Felix.

'Funny, did I say? I must have been going to tell you about something else. Perhaps the story about my brother and the frog: One day in the forest we found a particularly large frog with a gleaming, gold skin. My brother was struck by the colour and looked at it closely. But the frog also gave my brother a close look and suddenly said, 'Take me home with you, take me home with you.'

Astonished, my brother did take the frog back to Brankovina and put it down in the grass outside the gate. But the frog said, 'Take me into the house, take me into the house.'

My brother took the frog into the house. There the frog said, 'Give me some food, give me some food.' He had a few flies my brother caught for him. Then he said, 'Give me a drink, give me a drink.' What do frogs drink? My brother sent for a glass of mulled Malmsey. Then the frog said, 'Take me with you to bed, take me with you to bed.' So my brother took the frog to bed with him. Hardly were they under the covers together than the frog turned into a beautiful girl – and my brother's wife, who came in at that moment, never would believe the story.'

Isabella laughed.

'Was your brother married, then?'

'Yes', said Isabella. She looked at Felix, and her eyes had an almost reddish glow.

Although tired from the ride, Felix began his composition that night, a choral work called 'The Hours', a setting of a poem by a certain Raimund Berger, whom you have unfortunately probably never heard of. He had the misfortune to be Tyrolese, and, what was worse, from Kitzbühel. In the Tyrol only ski instructors count for anything, poets for nothing. This lack of regard was the death of Berger. So far, so good – or bad. The poem, in short stanzas, consists of prayers for the Hours of a night watch from the ninth Hour through to the ninth Hour again. The first verse,

> O Babel, tower to man's pride,
> God's wrath hath scattered far and wide!
> ...

was sung by the whole choir in unison, to an apparently simple chorale-like melody. In the following verses the voices divided into combinations ever more rich in meaning and harmony. Inversion, regression and complex interweaving built up into a carpet of counterpoint in which, as if by chance, at particular points where the voices converged like carefully-placed knots, there appeared the pattern of a melody that was not sung by any one single voice and yet was clearly audible. Then in,

> At the first hour
> A call resounds and echoes o'er
> The plain: 'This once and then no more' ...

the piece reverted to a powerful unison, which was renewed with each Hour until it reached its resolution at the return of the 'Ninth Hour',

> The long dark night of sin is past:
> On Golgotha – redeemed at last.

Felix had long since worked out the piece, had composed it in his head during the long rides through the forest, with all the subtle play of counterpoint, and had then let it rest in the womb of his remarkable memory until this night, when he set about putting it down on paper, not suspecting that someone else had already done so.

Again the Foehn was raging and tearing at the shutters. Felix sat for a long time at his table writing until, once again, it seemed that the wind had loosened one of the shutters from its catch. He went to the window. Outside – it was a very steep drop, the tops of the tallest spruce trees did not reach the overhang – outside on the narrow window-ledge sat Brankovic. Scarcely had Felix torn open the window than the Professor scurried head first on all fours down the precipice. Felix saw him disappear into the seven-sided oriel window ...

The next morning Abegg woke to find himself in his bed, although he could not remember how he got there. On the table lay the manuscript, completed in a similar, yet different hand.

Felix confronted Brankovic. In the name of Reason and the Enlightenment he demanded an explanation for suchlike medieval Jesuitries.

Brankovic laughed and started to explain that Jesuitism – even as understood by an antiquated Protestantism – had nothing to do with the Middle Ages, but was a reaction against them and therefore ultimately part of the Enlightenment. He did not get very far. Felix, well aware of what he was doing, even in his anger, carefully picked up a vase and threw it in the general direction of the Professor where it smashed to pieces on the stone floor with the inlay of the Brankovic hand.

Brankovic retreated, but only to take some music from the drawer of his desk. He handed it to Felix. It was the score of the Abegg choral work, already published by Schott and Son. The composer was Gabriel von Brankovic.

Now it was Felix' turn to retreat. He went slowly to the door. Brankovic made no attempt to follow him. Felix threw the door open, ran out and down to the stables. It was now that his riding lessons with Isabella came in useful. He quickly saddled a horse and, without a thought for his few possessions left at Brankovina, rode at full gallop down into the village. There he left the horse at the inn and waited for the next bus. Nothing happened. The bus came. Fortunately Felix had some money in his pocket. He got on without let or hindrance and took a seat by the window. Finally the bus left and climbed slowly up the hill out of the village. Before descending to the next, larger valley, it came to a place on a level with Brankovina. At a bend the trees parted to allow a view of the castle: broad and grey, with the seven-sided window stuck on the round tower, it squatted above the slopes between the bare trees as if it were as firmly embedded as everything else around in the space-time continuum.

The bus took him to the nearby market town. From there Felix continued his journey by train. When he arrived home he noticed that he was still clutching the score of Brankovic's supposed composition.

His sister greeted him with the news that Frauke Frosch was ill. He therefore abandoned his rather vague plans against Brankovic and went to see his lover. She was confined to bed in the house of Frau Baswaldt, who had shown a rather touching concern for her. Frauke was a miserable sight, she had lost all her plumpness, could scarcely speak and was incapable of any kind of love at all.

'It's a strange kind of illness', said Frau Baswaldt to Felix in a worried voice. Without any organic symptoms to suggest a cause, she had become weaker and weaker, had been unable to retain her food, had lost all will-power and was prey to terrible dreams.

'Brankovic!' thought Felix. He was filled with a fear which at first he refused to admit to himself; all the arguments of reason paled before it and, like a childhood nightmare, it came to dominate not only his nights, but every day, every hour and every place. At the same time, almost against his will, he felt an unusual increase in his creative power.

He stayed by Frauke's side. Her condition did not deteriorate, although it did not improve either. In those two weeks he wrote a 'Concerto Without Key' for piano and small orchestra. It was based on an old idea of Felix': a one-movement work with a slow central section between two faster outer parts, thus approximating to the traditional concerto form. Without being atonal it was, as its name indicated, in no single key. Its themes all ended up in a void, in a crystal-clear, profound and melodious yet ultimately unfathomable nirvana.

The moment he had finished copying out the piece he rushed round to the broadcasting corporation with it. As an unknown composer he had great difficulty in contacting the producer responsible, but eventually succeeded. Abegg's intention was clear: he wanted the work made public under his name as quickly as possible, in order to prevent Brankovic, who clearly had supernatural means at his disposal, from reaping the fruits of his inspiration and hard work for a second time. He told the producer in charge of modern music a shortened version of his story refraining, in spite of everything, from mentioning Brankovic by name, and asked him to have his work performed.

Although he had claimed he had no time at all to spare, the radio producer heard Felix out without interruption.

'Have you finished?' he asked.

'How do you mean?'

'Your story would make a magnificent opera – but your concerto already exists.' He handed Felix the latest number of a musical journal which contained an article discussing Brankovic's recent works, his first after seven years in which he had published nothing: 'The Hours' for choir and the 'Concerto Without Key' for piano.

Felix was about to fly off the handle, but the producer calmed him down.

'You see', he said, 'we are going to play your concerto, let's call it *the* concerto. Of course we will, all the stations will because it's by Brankovic. You should be pleased – if it was by you, no one would play it. Perhaps you can come to some arrangement with Brankovic regarding the royalties. You have to understand: we too are much more interested in a concerto by Brankovic than one by – what did you say your name was?'

'Abegg', said Felix.

'By Abegg.'

When Felix returned to Frau Baswaldt's he found her airing Frauke's room and rearranging the furniture.

'I'm so relieved', she said. 'In time it would have been too much for an old woman like myself. A friend of my son's has taken Fräulein Frauke away to the country. It's sure to do her good.'

'What?'

'Yes, a dear friend whom we have hardly seen at all since my son has been ill – Alexis danced in the premiere of one of his ballets – Professor Brankovic.'

Mirandolina interrupted her story and took a sip of tea with

Slivovitz from the pearl-grey teacup.

'It's getting close to midnight!' said her uncle in mock horror. He took out his watch and compared the time to that on the large grandfather clock.

'I will happily put up with the appearance of a ghostly server from one of your walled-up hideouts', I said, 'as long as I don't have to miss the end of the story.'

'That can be quickly told', said Mirandolina.

'No, no', said the old castrato, 'take your time. As you will not be finished before midnight in any case, it will be better if you tell us the whole story and we'll stay here together until one o'clock.'

Everyone agreed. The pearl-grey cups were refilled and two more logs put on the fire; we drew our chairs a little closer together and Mirandolina continued:

'You can imagine that Felix Abegg's first thought was to return immediately to Brankovina to liberate Frauke. But then he was gripped by fear and doubt. 'Second thoughts, Satan's thoughts' runs the old saying. Initially man was good, then came the Fall. Men's first thoughts are good, and good men are those who are not put off by second thoughts, by fears and doubts, but find their way back to their first thoughts. Above all Felix was not unnaturally afraid of falling into Brankovic's physical power, if he were to meet him alone at Brankovina. – And who would free Frauke then?

What Felix needed was help. He went to see a friend who had studied law and was qualifying as a barrister. His friend listened with interest and described it as a rather unusual case of infringement of copyright which, however, had not been dealt with by any of the commentators nor decided by the High Court. He offered to help if Felix should take Brankovic to court, but that was all. He did however agree to keep a detailed report of the events Felix had written in a safe place.

Brankovic's high opinion of Felix procured him an immediate appointment with the Principal of the Academy, whose initial benevolence gradually turned to icy disapproval and stony disbelief.

After further unsuccessful attempts Felix returned to his original decision to go to Brankovina. There were two points that spoke for this course of action: in the first place it was already May, the summer semester had begun and the other students would doubtless already be at the castle, therefore he would not be alone. And secondly he had in his possession the means of coercing Brankovic – himself! For in all the confusion, one thing was clear – Brankovic needed him, Felix Abegg, him and his inspiration; and he needed him healthy and willing to cooperate.

Felix went to Brankovina. He got out of the bus in the village and set off up the path to the castle. Although he knew all the short cuts, it took him a good two hours. It was night when he arrived. The moon was full. The weather had changed. The short interval, which hardly deserved the name of spring, was over. It was the first warm summer night at Brankovina.

He found the castle gate open. Was he expected? He went into the courtyard. From inside he heard a piano – Beethoven, the Eroica Variations. This had been the first piece Felix had tried to orchestrate, since he had long been aware that each of the variations seemed made for a different instrument or group of instruments. The inner gate was open as well and Felix went up the staircase with the antlers. The music came from the banqueting hall, where the students normally ate and which had a broad terrace outside. Obviously the music-making hour has been extended, thought Felix, for by this time they had usually started on the cards or the schnapps, or both, unless they were telling stories, as it was too early to go to bed yet.

He went round the outside and slipped onto the terrace. There was a white figure leaning on one of the half columns, which were used as flower pots, and looking at the moon: Isabella. A long scarf of thin silk trailed from her shoulders like a loose sail. Her hair was piled up on her head. The four arched doors into the banqueting hall were open. Inside Brankovic was playing. There was no one else to be seen. A standard lamp by the piano threw four narrow strips of light onto the moss-grown cracks of the stone flags on the terrace.

''Where is Fräulein Frosch?' Felix did not bother to say hello.

Then he saw that Isabella was crying. She turned away and ran down the steps into the garden. Brankovic stopped playing and, his head still bowed over the piano, looked over the rims of his black glasses. He stood up and came out to join Felix.

'What a surprise', he said.

'Where is Frauke Frosch?' said Felix.

'Sleeping', said Brankovic in a friendly tone. 'Have you eaten already?'

'You are a fiend!'

'You do me too much honour', said Brankovic.

'Where are the other students?'

'I am not holding any classes this semester. You could have found that out at the Academy. But you are welcome, of course.'

'That I can well imagine', said Felix. 'But I tell you: I will not compose a single chord, I'll not even think of a single note, unless you return Fräulein Frosch fit and well.'

Brankovic sucked at his lips as if he were drawing on an imaginary pipe.

'You will compose, whether you want to or not', he said. 'I know quite well that you cannot control your ideas and even less can you *forbid* your ideas to turn up in your mind. In certain moods the creative personality is ambushed by inspiration as if it were a band of robbers. You will compose, whether you want to or not.'

'I have deposited a statement containing a precise description of all your devilish tricks with my lawyer.'

Brankovic went inside and rummaged around in a drawer. He brought out an envelope.

'Do you recognise this?'

Felix tore it open. It was the statement he had written. The sheets fluttered down to the floor. He was standing right next to Brankovic. The Professor was a good head shorter than he was and an old man, too. Felix drew himself up and flung himself at him. He tried to grab him by the throat, but Brankovic caught him and threw him to the ground without difficulty.

'I will find ways of forcing you to compose', he shouted at him.

The light in the hall went out and Brankovic vanished.

Isabella was standing by Felix.

'Did he hurt you?'

Felix stood up. He had scraped his elbow and his knee, but he could hardly feel it.

'He has the strength of twelve men', said Isabella.

'He is not just a devil, he's *the* devil', said Felix. 'Where is Frauke?'

'Come', said Isabella, 'let's go in and sit down somewhere.'

They went up to a drawing room in her wing of the castle. Isabella took him by the hand. As their hands met he suddenly realised that during all his time at Brankovina he had never touched her – the Brankovics scorned the handshake. He had a vague idea that he ought to shudder, as if he were touching cold stone, but all he felt was a deep calm. Even when they sat down he kept hold of her hand.

But he still started to ask, 'Where is ...?'

Isabella raised her hand in a gentle but commanding gesture.

'Do you', she said, 'know anything about flies?'

'About what?'

'House flies, ordinary flies? It's the concept of time I am trying to convey. Flies live for only a few days – or at least that's how it seems to us. But to them it seems different, that is, for them, the flies, it *is* different. Their eyes are constructed in such a way that they register every movement of the world around more quickly than it actually is. When you want to kill a fly and try to get it with a quick blow of the swatter, it comes at only one tenth of the speed for the fly, in slow motion, so to speak. That is why flies are so difficult to catch ... but that is only by the way. Just try to imagine: if everything seems to happen ten times more slowly, from the movement of your hand to the movement of the sun, what will the effect of that be? A fly imagines it lives ten times longer than it really lives. But what does 'really' mean – flies inhabit a different *time* than we do; or rather, than you and your kind, Felix Abegg.'

'What do you mean by that?'

'Time exists in a thousand different modes. There is a geography of time just as there is one of place. We are much farther

186

away from each other than we think, even when we are on the same geographical spot. A fly's consciousness of time is altered by a relatively simple mechanism – the structure of the eye. Can you not imagine what an incredible dislocation in time would be brought about by a complex change in a complex mechanism – say in the human psyche?

You see, I know people are surprised that Brankovic and I are brother and sister because they always tend to assume I am his daughter. In fact, I am his elder sister. If my arithmetic is right, he is only three hundred and thirteen years old whilst I am three hundred and twenty.'

Felix tried to let go of her hand, but she kept his in a tight grip.

'I almost gave the game away when I told you about his wife. You remember? Yes? It was almost three hundred years ago. He is the last male Brankovic. It was our parents' desire that he should marry. But I was against it, for I loved my brother, and not with a love a sister should have for her brother. Oh, no, it was a cruel, fiery, satanic love. And I hated the pretty young woman who had been received as his bride at Brankovina with feasts and revels and now shared his bed. And my hatred revived in me powers which my ancestors had enjoyed and which the family had hoped were buried and forgotten. Night after night I spent in the family vault with the dead Brankovics, tearing their bones from their coffins ...

You need not be afraid of me, I only wanted to destroy *her*, my brother's wife. Night and day I tormented her with dreadful apparitions. I drove her out into the forest, to lonely ruined towers, I poisoned her dreams, I made her think she was rotting alive. Everywhere she went she thought she could smell the odour of her own decaying body. The room with the seven-sided oriel window was the bedroom of my brother and my sister-in-law. After some weeks she threw herself out of the window and I had my brother back. But the powers I had reawakened did not go away; worse, they took hold of my brother as well. Chained to each other, we live and cannot die, or we are dead and condemned to live. We inhabit a twilight world. And as is inevitable with that kind of love, it existed on a knife-edge and soon turned to hate; perhaps it had been hate all along and only seemed like love, or at least like desire, to us.

Eventually the powers within my brother became stronger than my own. He controls me. And one day he had the idea of trying to achieve immortality as an artist in order to regain mortality as a man. He thought about it for a long time, but it was more chance that led him to choose music. The chance was the fact that a young composer of moderate talents happened to be staying with us. My brother forced me to suck the thoughts, ideas and, eventually, compositions from him, the moment they had occurred to him. It was easily done since, like most of his successors, he fell in love with me. I did not even need to share his bed every night, as I did with you. His thoughts were constantly hovering round me and so his ideas came to me almost of their own accord ...

As I said, he was a mediocre composer. The result was those pieces – the 'Settings of Poems by Franz Werfel', for example – which, as you know, he later withdrew as not worthy of himself. It did, however, bring him a certain reputation as a composer. Soon we were able to attract more talented young people and milk them, as my brother calls it, in the manner I described. Each one, of course, had a different style, which you can see in the works by Brankovic from that time. A particularly perceptive critic said, 'Brankovic is working his way through the history of music.'

The breakthrough came before the War. A highly talented young man called Magnus Wolf joined us of his own accord. He had new ideas about the way music should develop. From him came the work, the first of a whole series, – you know the one I mean – which aroused such a furore and which enabled my brother to withdraw all his previous music with a grand gesture: 'This is my Opus Number 1.'

Poor Wolf went on composing for twenty years. He was desperate. We kept him locked up and the music composed itself within him, so to speak. After that he was spent. He is still alive, in a cellar cut into the rock. But his mind is a complete blank. So that led to the famous caesura in Brankovic's creative work. We looked for a suitable replacement for Wolf, but without success, all the young composers were writing serial music, and my brother could hardly expect to achieve immortality with that. Then he tried a composition of his own in which he copied Wolf's style, imitating himself, in a sense. You will know the piece, the little miracle play, 'The Copper Buttons'. The reaction of the critics was unexpectedly sensitive, they felt it was somehow not a genuine Brankovic, but just a rehash of his earlier work, a self-imitation. I presume that none of the critics had any idea how close to the truth they were with that. Gabriel immediately dropped the idea of composing himself. That was seven years ago, and then you came along ...'

'I want to see Frauke Frosch', said Felix, pulling his hand out of her clasp and standing up.

'Have you not understood?' said Isabella. 'I love you.' In a whisper she went on, 'Do you know what it means that I can love? I am not asking you to save me, I am asking you to redeem me.'

'Tell me where Frauke Frosch is!'

Without putting out her hands to stop herself, Isabella sank forward, hitting her face against the table top. Her red hair came loose and fell around her head like a pool of blood. The words came with difficulty,

'My brother will tell you that.'

Brankovic was in the library, reading. When Felix entered, he smiled. Felix hesitated, turned, ran to the room where the hunting rifles were kept, loaded one and returned to the library. Brankovic was still smiling when Felix aimed the rifle at him. The report of the shot – Abegg registered the phenomenon without being conscious of it – sounded *disproportionate* in the room, seemed inappropriate to the quiet of the library and turned its spiritual architecture upside down; space seemed to dissolve into chaos and – Felix recalled what Isabella had said about time – to rush through centuries in a fraction of a second. Brankovic alone remained sitting there, sitting there and smiling. There was a hole through the book he was holding in front of his chest. Do you think it was mere chance that it was *The Saragossa Manuscript*?

Hardly had the thunderous echo of the shot died away than Brankovic laughed out loud. He said nothing, just laughed a high-pitched, whinnying laugh that seemed to echo down long empty vaults. But there was another sound there too, a scream, someone screaming. A tormented voice was screaming from far below, screaming for Felix. It was Frauke Frosch's voice. The cellar cut out of the rock! Felix dashed down the stairs, following the voice, but he could not find the dungeon cell where Frauke was being tortured. Many times he thought he was close to her, but in vain, and finally he sank to the damp rocky floor of the underground passageway. Frauke's piercing screams which, scarcely articulate, named the tortures she was being subjected to, were thrown back and forward by the walls with a firm, steady sound, as if it were music, weaving themselves into a Sarabande from a suite in the old style. In Felix' mind the horrible screams were instantaneously translated into vivid musical ideas. He clamped his hands over his ears but inside his head he heard them over and over again, the Sarabande from his new 'Suite in the Old Style' for small orchestra and harp ...

And so it went on for days. Every day on the hour, like the chiming of some terrible clock, he could hear Frauke's screams for a short time and followed them, stumbling through the maze of countless passages, cellars, dungeons. And all the time they were transformed into movements for his new suite – the high phrases for the harp in the Gigue, the beautiful, low passages for solo flute in the trio section of the Minuet, or the harsh staccato of the Rigadoon. And always from above came the sound of Brankovic repeating the pieces on the piano ...

The number of movements – Brankovic later divided them into two suites of nine movements each, as Frauke sometimes screamed in sharp keys, sometimes in flat – will give you an idea of the length and nature of the tortures the poor girl had to suffer.

Abegg had long since given up trying to resist the blood-soaked musical ideas. He just ran blindly round the cellars, blundering in the darkness into corners and doorposts as he pursued his desperate, pointless search.

Then – after how many hours, how many days? – he saw the gleam of light. At that moment Frauke's screams seemed infinitely distant, but he still went towards it. He found a cell that was empty apart from a pile of straw at the back. Felix rattled the bars and suddenly a creature, a naked man covered all over with filthy hair, leapt up from the straw and scurried over to the bars, grinding his teeth. He opened his mouth, as if he wanted to say something, but no sound came out, only an awful stench of rotting flesh that Felix could smell, even though he was a good two yards away.

Felix trembled and turned away. The creature, its eyes wide open, unhappy rather than frightening, leant weakly against the bars. It was Magnus Wolf ...

Felix stumbled back up the stairs. Frauke's screams had died away. One movement, one single movement from the twice nine, was missing from the serene Suite in the Old Style.

The summer night was sultry and oppressive. The sky was covered with a veil of mist. Behind the western mountains and blacker than the night rose a castle of clouds, a celestial reflection of Brankovina. Felix went out into the woods. He had no idea whether he really wanted to flee or not. Did he think Frauke was dead, tortured to death in order to wring from him a serene suite in the old style for chamber orchestra and harp? His mind was a blank, a complete blank as he ran and ran. The storm broke. Dry and stifling, still without rain, the first flash of lightning came. In the pale, electric brightness Felix saw them ... the stags: thousands of stags, skeletons, bones bleached white, were coming up out of the valley across the clearing, singly and in pairs. When they came level with Felix they turned their heads towards him and gazed at him out of large, empty sockets with a look of reproach, as if he instead of generations of Brankovics had killed them.

Now the lightning flashes were coming in quick succession, illuminating the clearing as the dipping shadows of the huge antlers, the silent procession of phosphorescent skeletons, floated across. And the more that passed, the more immense were the ones that followed. It seemed to Felix that the antlers of the last ones were higher than the tree-tops.

Fear struck him like a blow to the head, and he tumbled to the ground. He screamed for human company, for human comfort to help him in this hour. Isabella appeared by him.

'I saw you running', she said, 'but I could not keep up with you, I almost lost you ...'

Felix hid his face in the folds of her long velvet coat.

'Can you see them too?' he said. 'The stags?'

'Yes', she said, 'they have taken their antlers back from the castle tonight. But they still have the initials branded on them. They are ours.'

'The stags are as tall as the trees', said Felix.

'Do not fear', said Isabella, 'I will carry you.'

Felix felt her pick him up and rested his head against her shoulder. He fainted.

When he came to he was in the castle courtyard, his head in Isabella's lap. Her hand – a hand of bleached bones – lay on his. Held together by a tiara with the Brankovic hand in diamonds on it, her red hair was piled up on the bone-pale skull which rose above the delicate Spanish collar of her black gown.

It was light, just before daybreak.

Felix jumped to his feet. The skeleton, which had been leaning against the rim of the sealed well, collapsed. The tiara broke into pieces on the stone slabs, and when Isabella's skull burst open with a dreadful sound, a thin, dry note, a musical theme sprang to life in Felix' mind, the theme entitled 'Requiem' on which the last movement of the Suite is based and which – scholars are divided – either does not go with the rest of the suite at all or which is the perfect conclusion to it:

A smiling Brankovic was standing at the window high above the portal. Felix raised his fist to curse him; he opened his mouth, but all that emerged from his distorted lips was the stench of rotting flesh ... Swiftly, with both hands, Brankovic drew the curtains. The next moment the rays of the rising sun sparkled on the window.'

Mirandolina was silent.

As we did not know whether she was just pausing, or whether the story was finished, we also stayed silent.

'I have finished telling my story', she said eventually.

'The story is finished?' asked Dorimena.

'I said', replied Mirandolina, 'that I have finished telling my story, not that the story is finished. I said before that no story is ever really finished, each one is part of a larger story and consists of smaller stories, some of which are told, others passed over in silence. And whenever you tell any one of the stories, whether you intend it or not, you include the shadow of all the others. The result is that once you have told one story, once you have undone the meshes of the net at one point, you are trapped. You are compelled to go on with the story. And because we ourselves, like all life, are stories, we become the story of the stories.'

As Mirandolina's story had gone on until well after midnight, we all went to bed soon after. Thursday was spent in the usual pursuits, we played a little croquet and in the afternoon, after luncheon, the old Count had sung a few arias by Caldara in his voice which was still beautiful, though it was the beauty of a ruined temple. The music was kept in a cabinet of cherry-wood lined with cool green silk. It contained some rarities, as he pointed out to us, some contemporary copies. In some of the operas from which he sang arias he had taken part in the first performances. It was with a deep sigh that he took out the music for his last aria, a single sheet that was kept in a morocco folder with gold lettering – a manuscript copy of Sesto's aria 'Parto, parto, ma tu ben mio' from *La Clemenza di Tito*. 'I don't know whether you are familiar with this powerful work from the end of his life which one hundred and fifty years of musical ignorance has allowed to fall into neglect. The obbligato clarinet alone raises this aria above all others ... and this copy – touch it with reverence! – has two expression marks and one dynamic, this f here, in Mozart's own hand.' Solveig Sangrail, the English niece, accompanied him on the piano and Fanny, to my astonishment, played the demanding clarinet part. Then in the evening we gathered in the emerald drawing room. The Count had some bottles of old champagne brought up and Fanny, the

Spanish niece, began her story:

'Truly, there is nothing more to be said about Mozart. Fortunate indeed are those to whom has fallen the task of editing his works, collecting his letters and investigating the details of his life. Although not a scholar, I have for a long time felt that the day would come when I, too, could light a candle of my own at his altar. I would not presume to talk about his person, which I regard as sacred, nor about his music – all that my remarks would amount to, indeed, all they might consist of, would be the empty and yet all-embracing phrase: he was unique. What I will do is to kiss the hem of his mantle, so to speak. Thanks to the knowledge I have of certain facts, I can help to clear up an apparent discrepancy in one of his operas. Just like the slaves who bore the pitchers of water from the well to the house where the marriage at Canaan took place – they did not even see the Lord face to face, but handed the pitchers over to the servants on the threshold –, just as these slaves made a contribution within their own limitations to Christ's miracle, so I would like to make my contribution to the miracle that is Mozart.

As you will doubtless be aware, the members of the high aristocracy in Spain are known as grandees. Now, some grandees are grander than others, so that they are divided into classes. I think there were three and the whole thing had something to do with hats; grandees of the first class were allowed to put on their hats in the King's presence before he addressed them – addressed them, moreover, as *mi primo,* which means 'my cousin'. The second rank of grandees had to wait until the King had addressed them, but could then put on their hats and ask a question of the King. Third-class grandees had to keep their hats in their hand whilst they put their question to the King, but could cover themselves before it was answered. Since there were also strict rules about when to take one's hat off and when to put it on during conversations amongst the grandees themselves, and when addressing ladies or prelates, one can imagine that even an only moderately animated conversation at the Spanish court consisted mainly of a non-stop doffing of headgear.

Don Gonzalo – at least that is what I shall call him, I don't know what his real name was; Don Gonzalo, then, – if you like

I'll also make up a fine-sounding title for him: Don Gonzalo de Ullon de Santa Clara, from the house of Barrientes, XIVth Baron of Alcoba – was only a grandee of the third class, although his high psition in the Order of the Knights of Alcantara gave him a status above his class. He had entered the Order at a time when the Knights still had to dedicate themselves to celibacy, and had already been appointed Commander of the Order when the requirement was abolished. Thus he was already old when he had married. After his wife's death – that was already a few years ago at the time my story took place – Don Gonzalo had been granted leave to withdraw from court and lived, sombre and dignified, in the seclusion of his old town house in Seville.

It was only rarely that the old man left the city. Before hunting became too arduous, he used to spend the hunting season with his daughter and a retinue of falconers in a family castle in the interior of Castille. Now he preferred the company of the equally old Prior of the Franciscan Order; sometimes, when it was not too hot, he would sit musing on a stone seat in the garden. Once, and this is the point at which my story starts, he went into the garden at an unusual hour, at twilight. The gravel was iridescent, as if it were giving off light stored during the day, and the row of scarlet-blossomed quinces was as black as if it had been drawn in Indian ink. The old grandee was looking for his daughter.

Doña Anna was sitting on the rim of a small fountain. From her lute came the tones of one of those sets of songs by old Spanish masters, slow, strangely dry and of an almost geometrical severity. She stood up, a little surprised to see her father so unexpectedly appear on the gravel beside the dark branches of the quince bushes. Don Gonzalo asked her to continue playing. He did not sit down, just leant on his stick and finally, his voice trembling with emotion, said that that very day, only half an hour ago, he had received the annunciation of his death. A messenger, he said, a messenger from another world had come to him.

Doña Anna laid her lute aside and asked precisely what had happened.

Haltingly, his voice cracking, the Commendatore told how, shortly after sunset he, Don Gonzalo, had been having his stiff knee rubbed with camphor oil when a monk arrived.

'He neither told me his name', said Don Gonzalo, groaning from his stiff knee or with a presentiment of death, 'nor could I tell from his strange grey habit which order he belonged to. You know, my child, that I have concerned myself much with spiritual matters recently and I know all about holy orders. It was a very distinctive monk's habit that I have never seen! It could perhaps have been one of the Olivetan Anchorites, they are very rare and scarcely seen in this area, or just possibly one of the Armenian Order of Humiliati, but they are extremely reclusive. He said he had been sent by someone I knew and he offered me a monument for my grave ...'

'And?' said Doña Anna.

Their brief conversation was interrupted by three – given the circumstances could it have been any other number? – blows on a distant door.

'That will be them', said the Don Gonzalo.

A while later a servant came running and met father and daughter already on their way back into the house: he announced the monk and four men with a crate.

The monk was waiting in the gloom of the entrance hall, seeming to be almost completely wrapped up in the oddly-cut habit of coarse cloth. Behind him stood four men with a huge crate. The monk murmured a blessing. The Commendatore sighed and ordered lights to be brought. Soon the entrance was illuminated by pine torches. Don Gonzalo wanted to have the crate taken to his bedroom.

'From now on I will sleep under my own memorial', he said.

The monk warned them, however, that the floor might break under the great weight and so Don Gonzalo decided for simplicity's sake to have it erected there where it was, on the ground floor. He gave orders for it to be unpacked. The monk murmured again. The Commendatore bent down towards him.

'Aha', he said.

It was a question of payment. Don Gonzalo sent for his personal valet who also functioned as his almoner, so to speak. In the meantime the Armenian Humiliant, or whatever he was, insisted on giving the Commendatore and, when he discovered who she was, Doña Anna as well, his blessing. Doña Anna in particular he gave a thorough blessing to and kissed her several times on both cheeks. When the valet returned with the cash box the Commendatore counted out the price demanded and handed it over to the monk. The monk mumbled to himself; the Commendatore gave him four more coins – for the bearers – and then another – for the crate; finally the monk ordered them to break open the crate. He told the servants with the torches to stand back a little and the bearers smashed the slats to pieces, revealing a roughly life-size statue of a man with a beard. Choking back his tears, the Commendatore looked on the statue.

'Not', said Doña Anna, 'a very good likeness.'

The monk interrupted quickly:

'Now all you need is to have the plinth made, Your Excellency.'

'That can be done in half a day', said the Commendatore, bade the monk farewell and went up to his room.

After they had all left, Doña Anna made the servants gather round with the torches and gave the statue a sceptical examination.

'Not', she repeated, 'a very good likeness. One thing, though,' she went on, 'one thing is remarkable: it does have the same little wart on the left side of the nose ...'

Doña Anna would have done better to look out of the window into the narrow street outside the house. Perhaps she would have become even more sceptical if she had seen the monk take just a few sedate steps before dismissing the bearers and then putting his fingers into his mouth to give a piercing whistle. Immediately a young lad led up two horses. The monk picked up the skirts of his habit and leaped onto one, the lad onto the other, and they set off at a gallop in order to get out of the city before the gates were closed. Outside the city, perhaps fifteen minutes hard riding away, was an inn. There the monk jumped down off his horse, threw the reins to the lad, flung the habit to the ground as he walked towards the door, and went in. Inside Don Juan was waiting.

The name Juan is anything but rare in Spain. If I were to be charitable and call all Spaniards who were neither peasants nor servants *Don,* then in those days there were bound to have been thousands of Don Juans. But as I have been talking of a Commendatore who had a daughter by the name of Doña Anna and who lived in Seville as well, then you will hardly have to rack your brains to think who the Don Juan in the Spanish inn near to the walls of Seville might be. And yet I do have to explain to you who it was: it was not your common or garden Don Juan or Don Giovanni, but Don John of Austria; or rather, it was both of them in one and the same person. It was my mother who bequeathed me the knowledge of this quirk of history, which she came upon through some mysterious connection.

Da Ponte's inspired libretto of the libertine who gets his just desserts goes back, via some rather tortuous cultural genealogy, to a presumed play by Gabriel Tellez, who called himself Tirso de Molina and to whom 'El Burlador de Sevilla y convidado de piedra' is ascribed. He, for his part, is supposed to have made use of an old legend for his play, the legend of Don Juan Tenorio, who was said to have lived in the XIVth century and been chamberlain at the court of Peter the Cruel of Castille. Others say that Tirso de Molina used the story of a certain Don Juan de Mañara, or combined the two stories, which anonymous monks had already written down before him and performed in the monasteries as a cautionary tale.

Just imagine, the story of Don Juan in a Spanish monastery, perhaps even in a convent and performed by nuns: actors and audience must have shuddered with envy at so much depravity!

But all that, unfortunately, is mere speculation since Tirso de Molina, if he it was, used neither the *auto sacramentale* of an unknown poet-monk nor the two legends, but the life of Don John of Austria and, as we would say today, his private life at that. What is still not certain is whether he deliberately chose Don Juan Tenorio in order to portray through him – not long after Don John of Austria's death, by the way – the remarkable misdeeds of the royal bastard and victor of Lepanto, or whether Don Juan himself hid behind the mask of the legendary Don Juan Tenorio in order to be free to seduce his 1003 Spanish ladies, before his half-brother, the gloomy Philip, sent him to the Netherlands.

I have long been surprised that my secret has remained a secret; all it needs is someone with a keen eye to compare a few dates. It all fits, like the halves of a coin that has been cut in two. Can you imagine a better Don Juan than Don John of Austria, the son of the Emperor Charles and Barbara Blomberg from Regensburg. On the one side the imperial blood burdened with the morbid legacy of his grandmother, Johanna the Mad, on the other a love child, tainted with the stigma of bastardy, which at the same time gave him carte blanche? Without a rank that counted in court protocol, below the grandees and yet the brother of the King, who admired, envied and loathed him, all at the same time? The glorious victor over the Turks, the adventurer who set out to win himself a kingdom in Tunis and who died so young at the siege of Namur, supposedly of the plague?

After he entered the room of the mean little inn where Don Juan was sitting waiting Leopoldo de Badajoz, better known as Leporello, first of all kissed his master's hand and then took the purse with the money he had received from the Commendatore and handed it over, though not before he had skipped around the room for a while, singing and shaking the purse like a castanet, and received a kick in the backside from Don Juan for his pains.

'Idiot', said Don Juan, 'how can you make such a song and dance about the money. Do you want the cut-throat of an innkeeper to know we are in funds?'

'My Lord', said Leporello, 'even if money were as soft as snow and as invisible as air, an innkeeper, and especially this innkeeper, would know within a few...'

He had not finished speaking when the innkeeper entered the room, rubbing his hands and with that shifty yet unctuous expression on his face which innkeepers, waiters and such people have kept down to this very day. Don Juan was about to pre-empt the demand for payment with a barrage of oaths and curses, when he noticed a girl behind the innkeeper.

'Aha', said Don Juan, 'you have a third daughter, have you?'

'No', said the innkeeper, 'that is my wife, my second wife,

Your Honour; she has been spending a few days with her parents in ...' – he named some place, let's call it Alcala or El Pedroso. The anger left Don Juan's face, which softened to a smile. He walked past the innkeeper and out to his young wife. The innkeeper did not leave the purse out of his sight. Don Juan quickly threw it to Leporello saying, as he shut the door behind him,

'Pay mine host what we owe him, Leporello, and I'm sure you know some jokes and stories to keep him amused ...'

With a sullen look on his face Leporello tossed the jingling purse up into the air in front of the innkeeper's nose a few times then caught it adroitly in his hat. He turned the hat inside out – it was empty.

Upstairs – it was, as I said, a pretty wretched inn and all that separated the upper rooms from the lower was a thin deal floor – steps could be heard.

'Look', said Leporello. He reached inside the innkeeper's trousers and pulled out the purse.

'How much do we owe you?'

The innkeeper named the sum. Leporello dropped some coins into the innkeeper's outstretched hand, but noticed that he was giving the ceiling a suspicious look as something crashed to the floor upstairs.

'Count it', said Leporello.

The innkeeper turned his attention back to the money to check it – and found an egg in his hand. Leporello gave a laugh. Then from upstairs came a rustle of cambric followed, when sufficient cambric had rustled, by a soft delicate sound, not unlike the sound of a steak being gently tenderised, accompanied by a gurgling and a purring, at which Leporello grabbed a guitar hanging on the wall and began to sing a song – very loud – about dishonest innkeepers. You know the song?

Came a falcon from Toledo
Met a crow ... etc

The innkeeper chased Leporello over tables and benches shouting, 'I want my money and none of your devilish tricks.'

He threw the egg at Leporello, but hit a picture of Saint Isidore, giving him a second halo. Upstairs a clearly large and fairly old piece of wooden furniture began to creak, the rafters seemed to bend. Before things temporarily fell silent there was the sound of a gentle slap.

'If the Inquisition ever found out about that!' said Leporello. The innkeeper had gone stock-still at the sounds from above. 'Found out about what?' he asked.

'That you throw eggs at your patron saint! If they did, the only use you would have for that money would be to pay for the wood for your own auto-da-fé.'

The innkeeper swore and wiped off the superfluous halo with the sleeve of his jacket.

'He's crying tears of gold, is your patron saint!' said Leporello. 'It must be a miracle!'

The innkeeper wiped off the golden tears as well.

Upstairs the creaking started again, once, twice, then gradually, almost imperceptibly, becoming faster and louder.

'Oh dear', said Leporello, 'the rats.'

'That's no rat', said the innkeeper, about to rush out. 'I know what your master's up to.'

'Hey presto!' said Leporello, and there was a gold coin on the table. The innkeeper hesitated. The creaking upstairs continued. Slowly the innkeeper inched towards the gold coin.

'Wait a minute', said Leporello, 'and it'll turn into a frog.'

The innkeeper grabbed the coin and pocketed it.

'And here is another where that came from', said Leporello, putting one on the window-sill. 'How many did you say we owed you?'

'Three', groaned the innkeeper, 'and one for the horses.'

'Usurer', said Leporello, 'and when I think that all I need to do is to tell the Inquisition that you throw eggs at Saint Isidore ...'

In the meantime the innkeeper had secured the second gold piece. He held it tight, examined it closely and nibbled at it.

'All right', he said, 'the horses are free, but I want my third gold piece.'

'Feel on top of your head.'

The innkeeper did so; there was the third gold piece.

The groaning of timber proceeded *stringendo* and *crescendo* until it was so fast and loud it was almost like a galley in a storm, then ... you remember that thrilling moment in *Tristan* when the whole orchestra swells and swells into a thunderstorm of notes and then, just when you are expecting the final crash, comes – calm. So it was here: the thunderous creaking and groaning, a sharp cry, and then nothing.

The innkeeper rushed out, Leporello after him.

'Look!' he shouted.

The innkeeper, one foot already on the stairs, turned round. Leporello sent a gold piece rolling across the floor straight down a mouse-hole.

'We can't let the oats for the horses go unpaid just for Saint Isidore's sake.'

The innkeeper hesitated, then ran to the mouse-hole and began fumbling around in it. Before he had found the gold piece, Don Juan came slowly down the stairs, humming a tune.

'What is the matter?' he said.

'A gold piece has fallen down a mouse-hole', said Leporello. ('Your Excellency!' he whispered ...)

'What's all this whispering about, Leporello, is there something else wrong?'

'No', said Leporello, 'it's just that Your Excellency has no breeches on.'

'How careless of me!' said Don Juan. 'Just imagine, my good sir, if your wife had seen me like this.'

He covered his nakedness with his hat.

'Stop excavating that mouse-hole and leave the ducat for some distant descendant to find; who knows, they might have need of it. Leporello, give the innkeeper another, and another; tell him to bring his best wine, I'm in a good mood.'

The innkeeper scratched himself in embarrassment, stood up and went down to the cellar.

'Your Honour, the thin planks of the bedroom floor have cost us two gold pieces.'

'How much did you get for the last of the apostles?'

Leporello named half the price he had been paid. Don Juan

gave him a box on the ears. Leporello admitted to three-quarters, swearing by his mother's eyes that that was all, received a further box on the ears, confessed to the full sum and swore another oath – Don Juan was already raising his arm – this time by the golden tears of Saint Isidore, that that was truly all. Don Juan was so amused by the invention of a new attribute for the saint that he forgot to ask Leporello how much he had got for the crate ...

'Come and join us in a glass of wine, there's a good fellow, I've just completed some profitable business', he said to the innkeeper when the latter appeared with the bottle. At first he just sat there, suspicious and taciturn, but towards midnight, stimulated by Don Juan's condescension and Leporello's stories, he offered them his very best wine on the house. He whistled, his young wife appeared and, as she received her husband's instructions with her gaze modestly lowered, she quietly slipped Don Juan his breeches. The innkeeper ordered her to bring a bottle from such and such a shelf. His wife went and returned with a dusty, pot-bellied bottle. Then she was sent out again. As she turned to go Don Juan took a fork and caught the bow tying up her skirt at the back. The bow came loose, the skirt fell down. You know that it is only in the past few decades that women have worn undergarments of any kind and so you can imagine what was revealed. The innkeeper's wife shrieked, Don Juan gave her a slap on her bare bottom, the tipsy innkeeper laughed and Leporello thought to himself that he had heard that gentle slap once already that day ...

The men were enjoying themselves so much that the hours passed in a flash; the innkeeper brought up older and older wines from deeper and deeper cellars and later his wife and two daughters danced a, let's call it a fling. For decency's sake I will not go into details, suffice it to say that for the duration Saint Isidore was turned to the wall. They were all in rather high spirits, even the innkeeper. You must remember that Don Juan was not only a great seducer of women, he could charm men as well. That evening his charm sparkled like a Chinese firework display because he was not only celebrating another conquest but looking forward to the next – Leporello had told him about

Doña Anna, whose discovery was a piece of pure serendipity accompanying the sale of the last of the apostles. No sooner had he heard of her than Don Juan had decided to go to Seville that very night to find a breach in the wall surrounding the garden of the Ullon town house. So they set out shortly before four o'clock. Their departure was considerably less complicated than their arrival had been. Whilst now all Don Juan had to do was to finish his glass and shake the innkeeper by the hand, their arrival with the four massive crates, each weighing at least a ton, accompanied by a regular caravan of mules, bearers and their assistants, had been quite an affair. That's right, four crates, Leporello had replied to the innkeeper's concern about his thin floorboards, and he should count himself lucky that they had already sold two-thirds of their original supply. The twelve almost life-size stone statues of the Apostles – they had been bought up from a monastery that had gone bankrupt – were a wedding present from an uncle to Doña Elvira when she married Don Juan in Burgos. The ceremony, by the way, had been carried out by Leporello in the same habit he had used for his visit to the Commendatore ... When Don Juan had fled after the wedding night, Leporello had insisted they take the twelve Apostles with them as their own, well-earned property. He intended to turn them into cash, but that, as they discovered, was not so simple.

In Valladolid he tried three monasteries without success before he found a fourth, where the Prior was prepared to take two of the statues. In his monastery the chapel was being repaired and clumsy stonemasons had damaged Saint Peter and Saint James the Less so badly that they had to be replaced.

All right, Leporello had said, but you must see, Your Grace, that the ten Apostles that are left will not be worth anything like as much as the complete set. I will have to charge more for the two than two twelfths of the total price..

The Prior paid.

In Olmeda Leporello offered the remaining Apostles for sale as the 'Ten Commandments'. An old alms house warden bought 'Lechery' and paid, having heard the same argument, more than a tenth of the whole.

The next step was difficult, but fortunately in Coca Leporello found an almost blind Hidalgo and managed to palm one of the 'Nine Muses' off on him in the twilight. In Segovia he was touting the 'Eight Winds' around, and they had to cross the high passes of the Sierra de Guaderrama with the 'Seven Deadly Sins'. A buyer was found for one of them in Madrid.

'Six', said Leporello, 'is an awkward number', and racked his brains for a long time until he came up with the slightly far-fetched 'Six Sons of Uranus'. They were put on sale in Toledo. From then on the numbers and the transport became easier: they arrived in Cordoba with the 'Five Senses', and it was a somewhat lighter caravan that stopped outside Seville with the 'Four Elements'. Leporello managed to palm 'Water' off on the owner of a brothel and continued his rounds with the 'Three Ages' then, after he had sold one to a notary called Don Basilio, 'Morning and Evening'. 'Morning' was bought by a widowed Duchess, because it reminded her of her late father confessor. All that remained, then, was 'Evening', formerly the Apostle Bartholomew who, in the course of a truly protean career, had been in succession 'The Fourth Commandment', 'Clio', 'Anti-boreas', 'Falsehood', 'Iapetus', 'Smell', 'Spring', and 'The Age of Iron'. He had a wart on the left side of his nose. This gave Leporello the idea of looking for a man with a similar wart. A barber provided the information and set him on the trail of the Commendatore Don Gonzalo d'Ullon.

'I would not like to have to go through that again', said Leporello when he had sold the last of the Apostles. 'It was a piece of luck that the Prior in Valladolid took two – I would not have known what to do with eleven ...'

Well, as I said, their departure took much less time than their arrival. The last bearer was paid off – he was given the last mule. Then Don Juan and Leporello rode back into the city. Shortly after the gates had been opened again they reached the house of the Commendatore and Don Juan left his servant – here, there, no rest day or night, he muttered to himself – to wait under an archway whilst he climbed over the wall ...

The rest you know, but now you also know how it came about

that the Commendatore had a monument so soon after his death.'

The Count, who had spent a long time in Spain, said nothing. He just grinned to himself and drank another glass of champagne. Did I imagine it, or was there a touch of sadness in his smile."

"It would be a good idea", said Spring, "if you ordered me to believe all this. That is, I don't believe the story anyway, but you could order me to believe that you dreamed all that. I dream now and then and sometimes it gets pretty wild, but at the most I fly through the air on my bicycle, or something like that. But too much is too much. No one can have such a detailed dream."

"The little pink pill, Spring", I said, "don't forget the little pink pill."

"Then your friend should have given you a pill for me, too, one that would make me believe in your pill."

"Do you find my stories boring?"

"They're more interesting than cleaning shoes", said Spring.

"So it came to the Friday. The weather had taken a turn for the worse and we had to stay in the house. After dinner we sat in the gold and yellow drawing room.

'It is a pity that my story has never been told by one of our great writers', said Solveig, the English niece, after we had settled down in the ingle-nook; she took a sip of her Irish coffee and looked out of the French windows into the rain-darkened park, 'he would have made it into a long family novel of great social significance. A family novel that would have the great advantage of describing two very different families, who came together in one particular – or, rather, in two particulars, the two heroes of my story – and were swept away in a maelstrom they had unleashed themselves. It is an exceptionally sad story, and a Christmas story at that; for a title I would suggest 'In the deep midwinter'.

'Oh', said her uncle, 'you could have called it 'A Christmas Carol', then, if that title hadn't been booked already.'

'It's no laughing matter', said Solveig. 'As I said, it's exceptionally sad; in fact, it's the most unchristmassy Christmas story imaginable.'

'At least it seems to be a musical story from the title.'

'Only peripherally, only in one crucial factor, but one that is not of very great musical interest. I didn't intend to begin with this, but the only musical aspect of my story, in fact the only musical aspect of the two families, was great-uncle Nestor Bilberry. In spite of his name, great uncle Nestor was the youngest of three brothers and twenty years younger than the next of the three. He was born in Madagascar where great-grandfather Sir Alexander Bilberry spent nine years as her Majesty's Consul – not exactly the crowning point of a great political career, especially when, like Sir Alexander, you have already been undersecretary of state. Nestor Bilberry was a composer. He had studied with Vincent d'Indy, but his success was moderate, to say the least. For some decades he had been known as the great white hope of English music because of his tone poem, 'Wuthering Heights'. Having inherited a fortune, he lived off it in Paris. For that reason, and because his marriage with Blanche, a daughter of the younger Nicholas Forsyte, remained without issue, he, and therefore music, made only fleeting appearances in the glorious history of this distinguished family. To this family also belonged, among others, Nestor Bilberry's niece, Miss Mary-Anne Rosalind Bilberry, known as Molly, who had married Mr. Arthur Sangrail and thus become the mother of the two heroes of my story, Nicholas and Clovis.

It is – that is how I intended to begin – a Christmas story; nevertheless It starts one hot afternoon in July in a country churchyard.

A procession of serious-looking ladies and gentlemen of various ages was following a coffin. At the head of the procession, in front of the coffin even, walked two delightful little page boys of five and six years old with thick blond curls which gave their faces a delicate touch, but without disguising the hint of masculinity which sent all the ladies, especially mothers of young daughters, into raptures. The boys were dressed in gold brocade with large white lace collars and, as was the family custom, they were scattering black roses, since it was their great-uncle, Sir Thomas Albert Bilberry, First Viscount Semiquaver, who was being buried. The First Viscount was the middle son of the aforementioned Sir Alex Bilberry and the pages' mother's uncle. It was in this Bilberry that the family's rise in society had reached a glorious, but unfortunately final, climax. He had taken silk, won a seat in the Commons when still young, been made a High Court judge and was for a number of years Viceroy of the Crown Colony of Grand Botti in the Aldives, or somewhere. The heat out there had preserved his wife – from the Rummy branch of the aristocratic Campbell family, she was lady-in-waiting to the Queen and was called Adele – like a dried prune, but her husband had withered in it and died soon after he returned home. Following the family tradition, the youngest members of the family – in this case, as I said, Nicholas and Clovis – were scattering black roses at the funeral.

Whilst the family was gathered round the grave, the page boys were allowed to take a back seat during the speeches. Thus they noticed a dark-skinned, grey-haired gentleman in black, so stocky he was as broad as he was tall, with a slim lady in a very short dress. The dark gentleman grinned and gave Clovis something that looked like a toffee. When the speeches were over and the page boys were handing each of the mourners a rose which they cast – heads bowed, therefore deeply moved – into the open grave, Clovis gave Lady Camilla Bilberry-Semiquaver, the late Viscount's daughter-in-law, née Lady Montague-Belfort, the toffee instead of a rose. Deeply moved, that is without looking at it, she threw it into the grave.

It was a firecracker.

The dark gentleman and the lady in the short dress had to leave by themselves and they didn't come to the funeral banquet, although no one – this was Clovis' later line of reasoning – could have seen that *he* was the one who gave me the firecracker.

A few days later, shortly after Clovis had been let out of the wooden cage in the attic – you can see that the children were very strictly brought up; the cage dated from the time Mr. Arthur Sangrail, their father and a ship's engineer, had tried unsuccessfully to breed one-eyed pekinese – the following dialogue took place between the two brothers, Nicholas and Clovis Sangrail:

'Do you know why the Viscount died?' asked Clovis.

'He had stomach ache.'

'No; because I sang a Christmas carol in July.'

'Oh', said Nicholas.

'Yes', said Clovis. 'Aunt Martha told me that if you sing a Christmas carol during the year someone dies.'

'People are always dying,' said Nicholas.

'Someone in the family!'

'When is *during the year*?'

'I don't know exactly; not at Christmas, anyway.'

'Would November be *at Christmas*?'

Clovis hesitated.

'Hmm; I don't know. It works in July anyway. Last week when I was up here' – the boys were in their favourite hiding place, the pekinese cage in the attic; you can see how easily the strictest upbringing can go wrong – 'I sang 'In the deep midwinter' and already the Viscount's dead.'

'But it could just as well have been me who died' said Nicholas.

'I'm sorry', said Clovis, 'I didn't think of that.'

'That's all right', said Nicholas, 'we got away with it this time. But from now on any singing of Christmas carols during the year will be done together. That's the only way we can be sure we don't sing each other to death.'

They gave each other their word of honour.

'If there's any justice', said Clovis, 'it ought to be Aunt Martha's turn next. She told me about it.'

'Do you think it will work with 'Away in a manger' as well?'

'I think any Christmas carol will do, not a particular one.'

The funeral of Mrs Barbara Sangrail, the mother of Arthur Sangrail and second wife of his father, Charles Sangrail – he had been a barber in Newcamp-on-Ooze who, thanks to his marriage with the said Barbara, née Quail (daughter of a bank manager who had a country house in the vicinity of Newcamp and used to have his moustache trimmed by the old barber, John Sangrail) had managed to develop the junk store he ran on the side into an antique shop, eventually into an art gallery – this funeral was manifestly middle-class: no page boys, no black roses. It poured down, and everyone commented that they could not remember a colder August. Uncle Simon Pettifogger, a bank clerk and cousin of Arthur Sangrail, lost his galoshes which stuck in the soft ground in the graveyard.

'Grandmother Sangrail doesn't really count', said Clovis as the cold August rain drummed on the roof.

'Why? Wasn't she part of the family or wasn't she a some-one?'

'Oh, she was both, but she was ill already and had been for so long she would have kicked the bucket even without our Christmas carol.'

'What a way to talk about your grandmother!'

'Let's sing another one and see if anyone dies who isn't ill already.'

Not only the two boys, not even older members of the family – if it had interested them – were able to check whether Mrs. Alfred W. Hobnob, née Jennifer Sangrail, the wife of Hobnob the well-known boxing promoter, had ever been ill or even what she died of. Mrs. Hobnob was the daughter of Ebenezer Sangrail (a great-uncle, that is, of Nicholas and Clovis). He had been a master baker who had emigrated to America, whence he retur-ned to Newcamp accompanied by a rather common American wife with a dreadful Polish name, only to disappear shortly before the War. Arthur Sangrail, the ship's engineer, suspected his Uncle Ebenezer was a spy. The obituary notice was the first thing anyone heard of the existence of his daughter. Nothing more had ever been heard of Great-Uncle Ebenezer Sangrail.

'Oh, we're sure to get a card announcing his death as well', said Clovis, with a wicked smile on his face. His father had no idea what to make of this obviously childish answer. But the boys made their way up to the attic, where they sang 'In the deep midwinter' again.

This time Clovis was in a decidedly bad temper at the burial.

He was beside himself with fury, mainly because he only had himself to blame for the disaster: the funeral of Mrs. Julia Pettifogger-Sangrail, the mother of the bank clerk, their Uncle Simon, the one who had lost his galoshes, was held on – of all days! – Clovis' birthday. It was a cold October and it was followed by a particularly stormy and unpleasant November, during which Mrs. Cordelia Sangrail, née Coot, died in childbirth – it would have been her seventh. Aunt Cordelia was the wife of Uncle Jack Sangrail, Arthur Sangrail's elder stepbrother from the first marriage of the ex-barber, later antiques dealer, Charles Sangrail, from Newcamp; on their marriage she had added a mill to the fortune Jack had inherited from his mother and his father's business, which he had transferred to London.

'I'm not sure', said Clovis, 'Aunt Cordelia isn't really family, only by marriage.'

'And anyway', said Nicholas, 'we've been having such bloody awful weather this November, it might count as Christmas already.'

'Shall we have another go?'

'Let's have another go.'

And, indeed, no one died, apart from Sir Lanfranc Baffle-Aspik, who had married Aunt Sarah Sangrail, the youngest sister of their father, Arthur. He, Sir Lanfranc, was Chairman of the Board of a bank and was so proud that he would have nothing to do with the Sangrails. Only Uncle Simon Pettifogger, who was a clerk with that same bank, attended the funeral for a combination of business and family reasons, and lost his galoshes again, this time in the slush.

As was to be expected, no one died in December. That year, to the complete bafflement of those around, the two boys were less interested in the Christmas celebrations themselves than in the time after – Boxing Day, Hogmanay, New Year's Day, Epiphany – throughout which, there being no need for concealment at that season, they ran round the house singing Christmas carols at the top of their voices. No one will be surprised that their singing produced no effect, except that Aunt Martha fell ill in the middle of January.

Aunt Martha's condition showed some improvement towards the end of January. The boys sang their hearts out and in February she had a serious relapse.

'It's her age, fifty-two', said Uncle Jack, 'you can tell when a woman's never had a husband.'

February was not yet over when Aunt Martha was restored to normal health and even more than normal maliciousness.

'It seems', said Nicholas, 'as if February counts as part of Christmas.'

He was wrong, as it turned out, but at the time he could not know – the family only heard around Easter – that it was in February that their father's brother, Major Cœnwulf Sangrail, his wife Æmilia née Bigwig, plus three or four native bearers, had been eaten by a tiger in India, where Uncle Cœnwulf was stationed.

'It's too far away', said Clovis, 'but at least Uncle Petty won't lose his galoshes at *that* funeral.'

The burial of Mr. Orfric Pettifogger was simple and of no consequence, just as the corpse, while alive, had been of no consequence, not only for society at large but also for the Sangrail family in particular, apart from one quite remarkable circumstance – but first I will have to tell you who Mr. Orfric Pettifogger was. He was a great-uncle of Nicholas and Clovis who had married into the family – he was the widower of the aforementioned Aunt Julia who died in October, and the father of the bank clerk, Uncle Simon. Old Mr. Pettifogger had been janitor at the bank where his son Simon rose to be a clerk; years before, an accident while stoking the central heating boiler had led to the loss of both hands. After that he was made commissionaire and became very skilful at operating the door-handle with his teeth. As Sir Lanfranc had remarked, when this redeployment was decided upon, he had to bow when anyone came, anyway ...

When Orfric Pettifogger lost his teeth as well he was granted a pension, thanks to his connection with the Chairman of the bank.

Inevitably Uncle Petty lost his galoshes, a particularly smart pair, in the graveyard mud that was all churned up under the March snow.

It was this funeral that saw the reappearance of the dark-skinned gentleman who was as broad as he was tall and who had given Clovis the firecracker at the funeral of Thomas Albert, First Viscount Semiquaver. That was – you will recall – at a ceremony for a member of the boys' family on their *mother's* side; how would the dark gentleman behave at the interment of a distant relative, a janitor and commissionaire at that, on their *father's* side? He was once more accompanied by the young lady who this time, however, followed the coffin and was wearing a black dress, albeit an extremely short one. 'She was wearing black knickers as well', said Nicholas later, 'I saw them when she bent over to throw earth into the grave. She must have been in specially deep mourning!'

That year there was so much snow in the late winter – or early spring – that it was easy to think of February and March as still being Christmas. And since Aunt Martha's health, after a further relapse, seemed to be on the mend, the two boys lost interest in their game and turned to other things.

'It gets boring', said Clovis, 'when you sing yourself to death and instead of Aunt Martha someone you've never heard of dies, someone who didn't even have any hands.'

'What do you expect', said Nicholas, and, humming 'In the deep midwinter', pointed out of the window where the frosty winds were indeed making the first blossoms and tender shoots moan.

It snowed again during Holy Week, then on Easter Saturday came warm heavy rain which washed away the snow, turning all the paths around the house – the boys were staying with their parents on the estate of their grandfather on their mother's side, the shipping magnate Nicholas Bilberry – into a quagmire. It was an old house of red brick with tall chimneys and lots of eaves and gables. There was a wall of the same red brick outside the park surrounding the house. Nicholas Bilberry, the son of Sir Alex Bilberry, the Consul in Madagascar, had used his inheritance from his mother to buy into a shipping company, then married the daughter of the Company Chairman; later he dabbled in steel and the like. In contrast to his father and his second brother, Thomas Albert, First Viscount Semiquaver, he had not had anything to do with politics; he retired fairly early from business to devote himself to collecting ancient Greek and Roman statues. The shipping company and the steel he handed over in perfect running order to his son, Alexander Oswald Algernon Bilberry, whom the boys used to call 'Uncle Biscuit' because their father used to mutter something about Oswald really taking the biscuit.

Grandfather Nicholas Bilberry had two children, Uncle Oswald, the Biscuit just mentioned, and Mary Anne Rosalind who, as I said, had been known as Molly in her youth and, as wife of Mr. Arthur Sangrail, had produced Nicholas and Clovis. When Oswald and Molly were children the big house on the estate had only been used for a few weeks each summer. Even as a child Molly had hated it and her father's favourite joke on family occasions was to remind her of what she had said, namely that she hoped her parents would not die before her because she didn't want to inherit that awful house, that was infested with mice into the bargain. Later, after Nicholas Bilberry had retired from business, he and his wife lived in the house all year round. Soon it was crowded with a host of plaster gods and heroes, which did not make the house any more attractive in the eyes of his daughter Molly. I will not conceal the fact that almost all the originals of these plaster casts had had to be sold soon after Uncle Biscuit had taken over the firm; the success, even if only a *succès d'estime,* of his slim volume of poems, *Good Night, Sweet Swans, Good Night,* was not matched by his success in the world of business.

'It'll get better', said his mother, 'when he gets married.'

But it was a long time before he married, and when he did it was only to a divorcee, Adelaide Thompson, née Crow, who presented him with a son from her first marriage, Herbert Baldwin Thompson, and persuaded him to go on a retreat for some time to an Indian monastery. She talked vaguely of union with the Karma. The expedition had naturally cost a pretty penny, but in spite of that it had been something of a disaster, due to an extremely hairy, scrawny, grubby Head Guru – Oswald used to tell people later that he reminded him of a flea he had once seen under a microscope. Oswald Bilberry was understandably somewhat piqued to discover that in practice Adelaide's union with the Karma took, despite the undoubted spirituality of the Head Flea, what appeared to be a remarkably physical form.

'What do you know about it!' Adelaide had said. 'The practical study of the sacred books of love is also part of the Karma.'

So Adelaide and the Head Guru worked their way through every chapter of every sacred book of love. Once – even Oswald was impressed – the union with the Karma or, to be precise, the Head Flea, took place whilst performing cartwheels. By then Oswald had come to terms with the fact that this particular chapter of the Karma was studied in the presence of all the monks, who sat around in a circle singing incomprehensible songs. What he could not come to terms with, however, was the fact that on the rare occasions when she allowed Oswald to exercise his marital rights – without cartwheels – she would say, at the slightest outbreak of passion on the part of her husband:

'Take care! Don't forget you are dealing with a Vessel of God!'

It was considered pretty certain that the Head Flea was the reincarnation of Buddha, or someone similar. There was always some important ceremony or other to stop Oswald setting off home and putting an end to these spiritual exercises. Once Adelaide's son Herbert had to be initiated into some mystery of God knows what degree. His head was shaven and a long needle – completely, they were assured without any danger or even pain – pushed through his leg. The poor child screamed horribly and his little leg bled. Unfortunately he had been initiated at slightly too high a degree, said Adelaide earnestly. The second time Oswald decided to leave the Head Guru immediately announced he was going to walk on water. Even Oswald was interested in that, so he stayed. He was to pay dearly for the decision, literally. All that the spiritual Hindu managed were the introductory prayers and meditation. The whole thing took place in the swimming pool of the Provincial Health Club. After his meditation Mandavarananda, or whatever he was called, went to the edge of the pool. He put one foot firmly on the water. That went quite well. When, however, Mandavarananda put out the other foot, he fell straight into the water and disappeared beneath the surface. Oswald had to repay the furious crowd of spectators, who had been cheated out of their miracle, their money back, or they would have lynched him along with the monks. That evening the monks held a complex ceremony of purification since Mandavarananda had come into contact with water.

After a year Oswald, Adelaide and little Herbert returned to England. First of all, however, Oswald had to pay for a cinema for the monks, as an aid to meditation.

That, then, was Uncle Biscuit, though to be fair, one must wonder whether it was not Adelaide Bilberry-Crow who better deserved the title 'Auntie Biscuit'.

Ever since Nicholas Bilberry had, as I have told you, retired from business it had become traditional for the family – that is, Oswald with his wife and their son and Molly Sangrail-Bilberry with her husband and children, occasionally also their nephew from the ennobled line of Semiquavers – to spend high days and holidays in the large red house in the country. The dislike of the grandparents' house had been inherited by the third generation. In constant fear of Centaurs and Laocoöns, which, especially at night, peopled the galleries with ghastly-white creatures but which even by day could suddenly stretch the stump of an arm or a leg out of a jungle of foliage plants or from behind heavy velvet drapes, the boys fled to the park or, as at home, up to the attic.

As already mentioned, it was a very rainy Easter after a fall of snow shortly before. Nicholas and Clovis were standing in the doorway leading out into the garden and looking along the path, which had soaked up the rain like a sponge; it disappeared even before the first clump of laurels behind a wall of heavy, vertical rain. The rain had set in, as they say, and the raindrops bounced up off the terrace and spattered against the third, even fourth panes of the glass door like the rattle of gunfire.

'With the path like that, Uncle Petty wouldn't be the only one to lose his galoshes', said Clovis pensively.

'It's a long time since we sang a carol', said Nicholas, 'and it must surely be unchristmas now.'

'Let's go through the kitchen to the attic. In there they're arguing about money.'

The boys slipped through the kitchen, taking the opportunity to collect a few biscuits on the way.

'They're not arguing about money, they're arguing about Aunt Adelaide.'

'But she's just left.'

'Precisely.'

'I would be sorry', said Clovis as they clambered up the steep stairs – also flanked by plaster casts –, 'if Herbie were to die, especially after they stuck that pin in his leg in India.'

'I shouldn't worry about that, he's not a real cousin, not a cousin at all, actually, he's not one of the family. He's called Thompson, and if he's to die, then it'd have to be a Thompson singing the Christmas carols.'

Hardly had the boys got to the end of the first line of 'Silent night, holy night' than came their first surprise: from down below they heard a short, sharp bang. They rushed downstairs, the second line still on their lips, so to speak, and found Uncle Oswald on the floor in the hall. That is, they deduced from the golden brown quilted smoking jacket that it was Uncle Oswald, as there was hardly any of the head left. He had shot himself – the little pistol with the mother-of-pearl handle was still clutched in his hand – through the mouth. As the bullet had also struck a plaster statue, which was not difficult in this house, and the statue had exploded into a cloud of chalky powder, everything looked as if it was covered with a thin dusting of flour. A copy of the Venus de Milo and an aspidistra both had a fairly regular pattern of brownish-red spots.

Naturally the other members of the family came running too. Their grandmother, Mary-Anne Bilberry, threw herself on her son. Molly quickly led Clovis and Nicholas away. Arthur Sangrail picked up something that Oswald must have been holding in his other hand. It was a copy of *Good Night, Sweet Swans, Good Night*.

'I bet', said Clovis, 'that we'll miss out on the Easter eggs this year.'

He was right. But the boys found plentiful compensation in the police, who came to take statements from everybody.

As far as the literally explosive effect of their singing was concerned, Nicholas and Clovis attributed it not only to the fact that Easter is especially unchristmassy, but also that 'Silent night, holy night' is an exceptionally christmassy Christmas carol.

Although Uncle Biscuit's death rated a brief mention not only in the Times Literary Supplement but also, unfortunately, in the official bankruptcy lists, no expense was spared over his funeral. There were, however, a number of regrettable and unpleasant incidents. In the first place a bicycle race was taking place ... no, I'll have to go back a little. The family vault of the Bilberrys was not in the town nearest to the country estate, but in Tanguilf-upon-Ooze, which was the area the Bilberrys came from. So Uncle Biscuit was delivered there. Arthur and Molly Sangrail had gone home for a few days and would then travel direct to Tanguilf from London. The plan was to drive to Tanguilf, arriving in the evening, spend the night in the so-called best hotel in the town and start the funeral procession from there the next morning. 'My God!' somebody recalled, 'wasn't it poor old Oswald who said when the Viscount was buried, many more funerals here and we'll be taking the bedbugs from this so-called hotel home with us ... not suspecting that he would be the next?' The luggage was already stowed in the car and the family sitting down to tea, when Mr. Hobnob was announced. Their father was just admitting to himself that the name did remind him vaguely of something when a rather short but exceptionally skinny young man entered, wearing canary-yellow shorts and a jersey the colour of pig's blood with 'Dunlop' written across the front.

To make matters brief, it was Jeremiah S. Hobnob, the son of Jennifer, the cousin of Arthur Sangrail and daughter of the missing Ebenezer Sangrail, who, you will remember, had recently died in America. He was a professional racing cyclist and was taking part in a race round England that had just reached London, where they had a rest day. He was using this day, said Hobnob, to trace his mother's family. He was invited to take tea. He did somewhat disturb the quiet tea party, since he kept hopping as he drank his tea. He had to keep in training, he explained, so he hopped round the table doing low knees-bends and not unnaturally spilling tea on his pigsblood jersey. He dashed the family's hopes that he would soon hop out and onto his bicycle by declaring, after he had heard of the sad occasion of their journey to Tanguilf, that he regarded it as his duty to join them. So Mr. Hobnob accompanied them, even though he had to sit still in the car. He asked them to call him 'Uncle Jerry'. During the journey he told them funny stories from the world of professional cycling, the point of most of which was that somebody, whom Uncle Jerry knew well but who was unknown to his audience, on some occasion, the funny side of which, as it was drawn from the world of cycle racing, needed extensive explanation, had said something – and to make the joke clear, Uncle Jerry had to explain precisely what the person in question would have been expected to say.

'There is one thing to be said', remarked Arthur Sangrail later, 'for someone telling long-winded jokes – he can't tell that many.'

In Tanguilf the lashing rain lashed, if anything, even harder. When the family set off – as a group, since everyone was staying in *Tanguilf's Premier Hotel* – for the graveyard, which was situated below the town, there were already quite respectable torrents running down the sides of the roads. Uncle Jerry caused quite a stir in his canary-yellow shorts and pigsblood jersey – he had no other clothes with him, of course – even though he took a modest place at the rear of the procession.

The entrance to the graveyard was flooded and they had to use a side gate, to reach which everyone – the pallbearers with the coffin, the mourners with their umbrellas and Uncle Jerry in his blood-red jersey – had to wade through a water-meadow and clamber over a barbed-wire fence.

Clovis and Nicholas scattered sodden black roses over the soft mud of the path, a triumph of tradition over the elements. The rain on the coffin was like the drumming of skeletal fingers. Water poured off the wreaths. When the vicar, looking up, as was his habit, and, pointing to the sky, opened his mouth to say the beautiful words, 'Verily I say, ye shall see him again, not on this earth, but in Heaven', he swallowed so much water that he had a coughing fit and needed medical attention. In the interests of justice it should be mentioned that Uncle Jerry who, as a racing cyclist, was used to wind and weather, maintained a dignified posture throughout.

When the vicar returned, he announced a hymn; everyone was to join in.

'Come on', said Clovis, ' 'In the deep midwinter' ...'

To their horror, they noticed that the dark-skinned gentleman with the lady in the short dress had obviously heard them and gave them a wink as he joined in. The effect was devastating. When Nicholas Bilberry, the father of the dead man, stepped forward to the grave he slipped – there were also people who maintained he jumped deliberately – and fell, not with a thump, no, with a splash into the grave which by now was almost full of water. He was fished out without great difficulty, but he was already dead.

Such an event naturally gave rise to a splendid legend, but for the moment everything was higgledy-piggledy. Some people were trying to do this, others that: loosen grandfather's clothing, fill in the grave, remove the wreaths, shovel the earth, try artificial respiration, pray ... Finally they agreed to bear the corpse back up to the town – out through the side gate of the cemetery, over the barbed wire and back across the water-meadow. Alone and astonished, Clovis and Nicholas remained by the grave, which was by now beginning to overflow with the torrents of water from the paths. This time the dark-skinned gentleman and his lady, her tight, slime-green dress already starting to shrink, did not have to leave alone, but accompanied the solemn – if that's the right word – procession. Uncle Jerry accompanied them: his sharp eye had registered that they were uninvited mourners and he had introduced himself. Together the dark-skinned gentleman and Uncle Jerry lifted the lady over the barbed wire. Her dress split.

'Look', said Nicholas, 'whatever she had on underneath must have split before.'

But here, too, the American Uncle showed he was a true gentleman. Looking away, he took off his guaranteed weatherproof, pigsblood jersey and pulled it down over the lady's head. It was not much shorter than her dress had been when dry.

Nicholas and Clovis had, as the saying goes, taken Uncle Jerry to their hearts.

'I'll never be able to drink tea and hop at the same time like him,' said Clovis, spilling half a cup over the carpet.

The boys were delighted that he had promised to come back to London when the race was finished, and see them again.

Molly Sangrail, who usually did not read the newspaper at all, now studied the sports section every day, but could not find the name of Jeremiah Hobnob anywhere.

'That'll be because he's not winning', said Arthur Sangrail, and the boys decided that until Uncle Jerry returned they would not only not sing, so that he wouldn't fall into a gorge or somewhere, they would *positively* not sing, so that he would win. It all fitted in quite well anyway, because the boys were following a long-term plan. Nicholas, much against his will, had started to learn the recorder at school. Clovis, the younger brother, had listened to him practising and pointed out that it might be safest not even to play the tune of a Christmas carol, during the year. Nicholas, his musical ability not even up to the simplest of carols, muttered:

'I wish the teacher belonged to the family', and threw recorder and music into a corner.

But Clovis managed to talk his brother into experimenting with the effect of instrumental Christmas music, perhaps even duets. Their parents were astonished when Clovis demanded a recorder too. Soon the boys were to be heard practising for hours on end in sweet accord.

That summer things happened thick and fast. The story becomes so entangled, so matted that I really don't know in what order to put the events.

The next thing to happen was that the dark-skinned mourner with the lady who wore the short dresses came to see Nicholas and Clovis' parents. They were returning Uncle Jerry's blood-red jersey and, as it was tea-time, there was no polite way round asking them to join the family. He – he told the boys to call him Uncle Manda – was wearing a suit with large checks; so large were the checks, in fact, that his suit almost resembled a medi-aeval herald's costume with trouser legs of different colours which also appeared, inverted, in the coatsleeves. She – Aunt Julie was her name, said their mother with a vinegary smile – was wearing a green turban on her head. That was her major item of dress, for the rest she was more or less clothed in two rows of tassels held up by two thin straps.

'Fat old Uncle Manda', said Nicholas later, 'sat on that chair, the one we half sawed through the legs, and it didn't give way.'

'If we had started singing ...'

'Too dangerous, you never know, Uncle Jerry might have been attacked by a bear.'

'The bike race doesn't go to Siberia.'

'Let's practise our scales.'

Downstairs their delighted mother let her crochetwork sink to her lap and said:

'The boys obviously take after Uncle Nestor, the musical one who lives in Paris.'

(The composer, you will recall, of the tone poem 'Wuthering Heights'.)

Uncle Jerry did actually return, not as victor, but unharmed. He came in mufti, so to speak, in a normal, if somewhat gaudy suit, and sat down to drink his tea, except when the children pleaded with him to drink it hopping round the table. After a few days – the boys had taken up singing again – he disappeared. At the same time it was noticeable that their mother was also missing. Their father's sister, Aunt Martha, came into the house and started cooking and sewing and tidying up and moaning; after a few days their father threw her out again. The boys heard that she had had a relapse – the same illness she had had in the spring – but she didn't die.

'Just wait until Whitsun and we can play 'Ding dong merrily on high' as a duet, then she's for it.'

The house was crowded with Bilberrys and all sorts of people, there was a constant toing and froing. Grandmother Bilberry, her eyes brimming with tears, said to the boys:

'You poor things, you'll never see your mother again ...'

Although only an aunt by marriage, Camilla Semiquaver sobbed even more and rambled on about a great misfortune through which they had lost their mother.

'A terrible, terrible disease', said Lady Camilla, 'perhaps the most terrible one there is.'

Once, when for a change it was quiet in the house, their father took the two boys by the hand and said, in an unusually deep voice, that their mother had lost her life in a car accident.

'And where is Uncle Jerry?' asked Clovis.

A box on the ear was his reply.

'I don't know whether all this about Mummy has anything to do with our singing,' he said later. 'I think probably not. There's something fishy about the whole thing. There's not even been a funeral.'

The hubbub gradually subsided leaving, as a kind of deposit, a new household in the parental or, the anagram is more appropriate, paternal home. It consisted of people who first of all just dropped in out of curiosity, then came back and eventually stayed: Aunt Senta Flare, the sister of the bank clerk Simon Pettifogger – he of the disappearing galoshes –, and now Arthur Sangrail's housekeeper, her husband, Mr. Anthony Flare, an out-of-work bassoonist whose ambition was to open a variety theatre, and their daughter, who turned out to be none other than

Aunt Julie, the lady who wore the short dresses. And it was not long before the arrival of Uncle Manda, his full name was Thomas Radama Mandabonatave, who immediately fell out of favour with the two boys because he was allocated the attic where he installed all kinds of easels and quantities of painted canvas, then set about covering further yards of canvas with paint. There was also the stump of a marble column that the removal men carried up to the 'studio', as it was now called.

The boys knew of a secret entrance to the former attic. Once when they crept in they saw Uncle Manda, in a bespattered velvet smock, painting with several brushes in his hand and one gripped between his teeth. Aunt Julie was sitting naked on the marble column, holding up a slipper.

'Odd, that slipper', whispered Clovis, 'and Daddy's sitting there smoking a cigar.'

The mystery of the slipper was soon revealed. It happened during a party one summer evening that was given less by the owner of the house, Arthur Sangrail, than by his guest, the artist Thomas Radama Mandabonatave. It was the same day as the boys, taking stock of their progress on the recorder, decided that they were ready ...

The boys disobeyed orders and watched the guests arrive from the landing, hiding behind aspidistras and peeping between the banisters. It was a hot July evening and for several days now the air had been oppressive. Even when darkness fell there was no relief. The atmosphere was ominous, and not only due to the climatic conditions. It was due in part, certainly, to the noticeable distance between Arthur Sangrail's guests and those people invited by Uncle Manda. One fellow-artist, for example, a gentleman in a striped shirt, had given Uncle Teddy – Sir Edward Alexander Bilberry-Semiquaver, now Second Viscount Semiquaver – a somewhat hearty slap on the back and intimated that he found it decidedly amusing to meet a man whose father, the First Viscount, had once sentenced him to four years in prison.

The hostess was Julie Flare who, together with a feather

turban, naturally wore a very short and very décolleté dress.

When all the guests were assembled Manda announced that he was now going to present his latest work to the public, a painting that had been acquired by his landlord and patron, Mr. Arthur Sangrail. Everyone gathered in a semicircle round the sofa and Arthur Sangrail pulled a cord to reveal the picture of the naked Julie Flare, though on the painting, instead of the slipper, she was bearing aloft a torch.

There was applause and the model drank a toast to her portrait. Then it happened.

The boys had gone up to their room and played their two-part carol. Had they not hurried back to their place in the gallery, they would have missed seeing the fruits of their musical labours.

When everyone joined in the toast of the half-naked Julie to the completely naked one, the Second Viscount turned away and put his glass down on the sideboard.

'What's the matter?' asked Arthur.

'If you take that female into your house,' said the Second Viscount, 'then that's your business. She is, after all, vaguely related to you. And you can hang that awful daub up there, if you insist, although I do think it's not in very good taste, hardly two months after Molly, who was ... is my cousin, after Molly ... but this performance here, to be compelled to take part in ... to have the gall to make us party to a vulgar show like this! I call it an insult to the family.'

'And may I remind you', said Arthur, likewise putting his glass on the sideboard, 'that Mr. Mandabonatave, the artist who painted this picture, is your half-brother.'

On that the Second Viscount boxed Arthur Sangrail on the ear.

I don't need to describe the tumult that ensued. Arthur and the Second Viscount went into the garden, each with a revolver in his hand. A few of the men from the party followed them. The rest stayed with the women, in the silent house. Some of the women were sobbing. Uncle Jack Sangrail, Arthur's brother, poured himself a little champagne; the neck of the bottle clinked nervously against the rim of the glass.

Then the sound of the shot from the garden.

The ladies screamed.

'If they haven't shot one of the seconds by mistake, then it's worked already', said Clovis. 'They're both related to us.'

After a few moments Arthur Sangrail entered the room. he put the pistol on the table and said to one of the ladies, pointing at cousin Canute, the Second Viscount's son:

'I was just introducing you to Sir Canute Albert Bilberry-Semiquaver when we were interrupted. I must bring you up to date: Canute Albert, Third Viscount Semiquaver.'

The duel had put a damper on the party, as they say, and there was no way of reviving it. Exhausted from the excitement and satisfied with their evening, the two boys took themselves off to bed.

'An unqualified success ... it works on the recorder as well', said Nicholas.

'Yes, one uncle dead and Daddy will go to prison', said Clovis.

'Or be hanged! That's probably the result of playing in two-part harmony.'

Whether it was the fact that polyphony did not just add, but multiplied disasters, or whether the hot summer night was particularly unchristmassy, a few hours later the boys were woken by an extraordinary racket in the house.

'That's Uncle Manda screaming', said Clovis, who had the rare ability – pleasant for him but as a rule tiresome for those around – to be wide awake the moment he woke up.

The boys ran downstairs. Uncle Manda, bespattered with blood from head to toe, was roaring like a bull as a number of policemen tried to keep hold of him and shove him out.

'Where did all those policemen come from?' asked Clovis softly.

'Look over there.'

Julie Flare, stark naked and panting, panting so heavily that at each breath she doubled up, was standing on the stairs, holding on to the banister with both hands. She gave one more gasp, then gurgled and tumbled down the stairs. There was a rather long knife sticking out of her stomach. A number of other people, servants and policemen, were carrying another naked and bloody body out of Aunt Julie's room.

'Daddy!' said Clovis.

'He seems to have managed to skewer the pair of them with one thrust', said one policeman to another.

'And the eiderdown', said the other, flapping his hand in front of his face to clear away the cloud of feathers that came floating out of the room.

Twenty-five years later two men were sitting in a box at a second-rate night club. That evening it was opening under new management. It was around Whitsuntide, the weather was fine with the promise of a hot summer.

'And Uncle Manda's already dead', said Mr. Clovis Sangrail.

'Yes', said Mr. Nicholas Sangrail, 'two years ago in prison.'

'And dear old Aunt Sarah ...'

'And dear old Aunt Sarah. She was like a mother to us after Daddy ...'

'Ah, yes, Aunt Julie!'

'Who knows', said Nicholas, 'perhaps it's better for Aunt Sarah that she didn't live to see this. He pointed to the stage where a fairly mediocre singer dressed in a carefully-draped feather boa was singing a so-called ballad. It was Dolly Bapik, whose real name was Miss Martha Baffle-Aspik, the daughter of the long-deceased bank chairman, Sir Lanfranc Baffle-Aspic and Aunt Sarah, Arthur Sangrail's sister.

After the family blood-bath Aunt Sarah had taken in the two boys and brought them up with her own children, who were slightly older.

She wanted the eldest of her three own children, Geoffrey Baffle-Aspik, to follow the wishes his father had expressed in his will and take over as Chairman of the bank. However he became a not very successful professional gambler and later he made a living going every evening from restaurant to restaurant telling jokes at people's tables. The second son, the Reverend Humphrey Baffle-Aspik, rose to be secretary to a second-rank bishop. His career was finished when it was discovered that, out

227

of sheer laziness, for his contributions to the General British Encyclopaedia of Churches he had invented numerous mediaeval scholastics, their biographies and even one complete heretical movement. A violent conflict broke out between Nicholas and Clovis over the youngest child, Martha Baffle-Aspik, which she for a while tried to resolve by setting up a *ménage à trois*. It did not last long. The brothers fell out and each tried to win Martha – even then she was called Dolly – for himself. She chose a third who, as they now learnt, had long been a secret fourth in the *ménage à trois*. When the ex-bassoon player, Mr. Anthony Flare, realised his dream and opened his own night club he engaged Dolly, who had meanwhile adopted the stage name of Bapik. And it was out of a certain nostalgia that after all these years Dolly had sent the Sangrail brothers an invitation to her opening night ...

'Uncle Manda was condemned to death but then it was commuted to a life sentence', said Clovis.

'Yes', said Nicholas softly, 'the effect of our two-part recorder playing must have worn off rather quickly.'

'No', said Clovis, 'it was probably because Manda was only a bastard son of the First Viscount with a Malagasy woman; his father had been Consul in Madagascar, you remember. Manda was not a full member of the family.'

At that moment the brothers' attention was drawn back to the stage. Dolly Bapik was announcing an encore. She blew kisses at their box and breathed into the microphone,

'For Nicholas and Clovis.'

Then she sang a Christmas carol.

Among the dead that resulted from the collapse of the gallery and some of the boxes were Nicholas and Clovis Sangrail.

With a sigh the retired bank clerk, Simon Pettifogger, pulled on another new pair of galoshes. He lost them at his nephews' funeral.'

Solveig leant back and sipped her sherry, folding up the family tree she had occasionally consulted and passed round her audience. The writing on it was very small, and the Count had taken out his lorgnon of Russian silver which he now folded and slipped back into his breast pocket."

228

"That story must have lasted until well after midnight as well", said Spring. "And I can imagine what Saturday's niece was called ..."

"Oh you can, can you?" I said. "Did you have the dream or did I?"

"The system by which your castrato or his fine sister named the girls is not particularly abstruse."

"And what is Saturday's niece called?"

"Where does she come from?"

"Venice", I said.

"Oh dear", said Spring, "that's going to be a romantic story. I presume she's called Lavinia."

"No."

"Ladislaia?"

"No."

"Lais, Lamia?"

"She was called Laura. And the drawing-room where we gathered on Saturday was where the old castrato kept his hunting trophies. Apart from the antlers, there was a large painting on the subject, which took up most of the wall opposite the fireplace. It showed a table richly decorated with autumn leaves and piled high with game. The heads of dead pheasants hung over the edge and hares, their legs tied together, lay on a deer. There was a hunting horn leant against the table and underneath a piebald dog was sniffing at a dead boar. The painting was darkened with age and on either side stood tall arrangements of foliage in flaming autumn colours which trailed over the frame of the still life. The real and the painted leaves both seemed to move in the flickering firelight and created the impression of an extravagantly decorated alcove disappearing up into the darkness of the room. I even imagined that the huntsman in the background, whom I had only noticed on a closer look, gave me an occasional wink.

Laura entered in a pink dress and pretended to be astonished when told we were expecting a story from her that evening.

'As Tiffany has stipulated that she should tell her story on the last evening,' said the Count, 'that means there is only you left for this evening. Anyway, you just like making a fuss. I know

229

you had a very special story worked out days ago. Anyone who comes from a city which is so full of stories –'

'Precisely', interrupted Laura, 'only we don't tell our stories, unlike the Neapolitans ..'

'Careful!' said Renata

'We *live* our stories, telling them we leave to others. We Venetians spend all our energy on living and so it's not surprising that all really humorous or moving stories are set in Venice –'

'In opera,' said the Count as he poured us some bright red wine from a slender carafe, 'and that's something I do know a little about, in opera it's different. Real operas are set in Greece.'

'Not at all', said Laura, 'ever since Greece was conquered by the Turks ancient Greece just means Venice. All those *Pomo d'oros* and *Lodoiscas* take place in Venice. Not to mention *Così fan tutte.*'

'*Tosca*,' said Dorimena, 'is set in Rome.'

'And *Der Rosenkavalier* in Vienna', said Mirandolina. 'There are operas set in Norway, *The Flying Dutchman*. And I know of one set in Portugal, *L'Africaine* by Meyerbeer, and another that even takes place in the Garden of Eden.'

'*Adam and Eve* by Rudi Stephan', said Fanny, 'and *The Valkyrie* is set in Iceland or somewhere up there ..'

'*The Ring of the Nibelung*', I interjected, 'is something of a problem from a geographical point of view. But it can be solved fairly easily by a close study of Wagner's stage directions. Do you remember the scene in *Rheingold* where the 'depths of the Rhine' dissolve into mist and Wagner says, 'The billows are gradually transformed into clouds which, as ever brighter illumination breaks behind them, clarify and become fine mist. When the delicate puffs of mist have completely evaporated, the morning twilight reveals an open space on the mountain summit.' There, on the open space on the mountain summit, Fricka and Wotan are having a siesta. But Wagner goes into more detail about the area, 'The growing radiance of the breaking day lights up a castle with glittering battlements standing on a rocky peak in the background; between this castle-crowned peak and the foreground a deep valley is to be assumed, through which the

Rhine flows.' Think, and I beg you to weigh every word precisely: rocky peak, open space on the summit, deep valley, Rhine; there is only one place which has all of those – Switzerland! There is no doubt at all, *The Ring,* at least the greater part, takes place in the canton of Grisons. Wagner, who composed the Ring cycle in Tribschen, localised the seat of the Germanic gods on the Tödi and the Adua. A remarkable parallel to William Tell. And aren't the tubas like sublimated alpenhorns? How often have I come across Brunhildesque dairymaids in the Grisons Oberland, and who has not met a Wotanish cowherd who lost one eye when the cantonal wrestling championships got out of hand ...?'

'It certainly makes sense', said the Count. 'Siegfried's journey goes down the Rhine, of course; perhaps the agitated passage in the middle represents the Rhine Falls at Schaffhausen?'

'And when Siegmund sings 'Winter storms waned in the moon of May',' said Solveig, 'I can just imagine the beautiful scene as the door opens in Hunding's house on the Spluegen Pass and you can see right down the valley to Chiavenna and the magnolias in flower by Lake Como ...'

'Yes, yes,' said the Count, 'if you look at it that way, Wagner wasn't too bad a writer after all. What a pity Offenbach didn't compose the music to his libretti.'

'Offenbach', said Laura, 'knew where to set his operas. Where does the Guilietta scene in the *Tales of Hoffmann* take place? In Venice! And it's the most beautiful in the whole opera.'

'But *Don Giovanni*', said Fanny, '*the* opera –'

'*Don Giovanni*', Laura said, 'from the countless plays down to Da Ponte's libretto and your delightful story, is nothing other than the garbled version of a bizarre and, of course, true event that happened in Venice. It was not without reason that Mozart gave his opera the name 'Don Giovanni' as a subtle reference to the real setting ... And there is nothing very Spanish about the music, but much that is Italian. Of course, lots of foreign elements have become mixed up in the story, but what does 'foreign' mean in Venice?

But the original incident which, since it couldn't be completely hushed up, gave rise to the legend, did not have *one* but two heroes – I prefer to call them main characters – whose situation and experiences were so intertwined that, quite apart from the deliberate mystifications, it took centuries to sort out the true facts, and that even though great minds such as Goethe and Kierkegaard interested themselves in it.

The events did not begin in Venice at all, but that does not signify, since even if they started out on the periphery, they gradually converged, as if by drawn magic, on the hub of the world, that is, Venice, where – where else? – they reached their climax.

Who or what one of the two characters was – the one I will introduce second – is still unclear. But the other we do know: he was, as they used to say in those days, one of the Paladins of Christendom. He was of Swiss origin, but had a Bavarian mother, and in his veins ran Spanish and French, not to mention, if I am not mistaken, Polish, Bohemian and all other sorts of blood: it is Don Giovanni I am talking of, the famous Don John of Austria. Fanny has explained to us the plausible theory concerning the historical Don John in some detail ...'

'And there we are with the story which Laura has doubtless prepared', laughed her uncle as he sluiced the wine round his palate and settled his large body more comfortably in his high-backed chair.

'Successful improvisation', said Laura, 'is always a matter of careful preparation. My improvised story begins on the day during the reign of Doge Luigi Mocenigo when the unfortunate poet, Don Miguel de Cervantes Saavedra lost his left hand. He lost it through a Turkish bullet – a further two left his arm crippled – whilst he, for his part, was on a Spanish ship on that 7th October 1571, firing at the Turks. It was – what else would one expect at that time of the year in that Arcadian region? – a glorious day, but the smoke from the huge cannon on the five hundred ships veiled the sky until it was as dark as night over the straits. The thunder of the cannon reverberated from the cliffs of the Straits of Naupaktos – in Venice we call it Lepanto. Burning galleys full of chained slaves screaming unheard for help turned the awful, artificial darkness back into blood-red daylight. It had begun as an orderly naval engagement but, as that had not brought about a decisive result, it had turned into a brutal and disorderly combat at close quarters, no holds barred, ship against ship, man against man. In that echoing night of gunsmoke and ash both sides were fighting for death or glory, for cross or crescent.

The two immense flagships had collided, and Spaniards and Janissaries were fighting on the blood-soaked decks as if they were on a large wooden citadel, whilst all around the waves, whipped up by the hectic manoeuvrings of this last great battle between galleys, broke over them as if in a storm. A burning Turkish galley exploded and sank in a whirlpool. A Turkish soldier, mouthing awful but inaudible curses, whirled his curved sword until the furious waters engulfed both him and the crescent flag. Just as two equally matched opponents can fight to the point of exhaustion when, breast to breast, their swords crossed at the hilt, they gather their last reserves of strength, to the point when some tiny factor in favour of the one causes the other to falter, the faltering gives the first a slight ascendancy so that the other, now as good as defeated, gradually abandons his resistance until he takes flight or throws down his arms – so the whole outcome of the battle was concentrated in the duel between the two flagships, although through the smoke and spray they could only be seen indistinctly by the other ships. One bore the standard with the three crescents, its commander was Ali Muensisade Pasha, the Capudan Pasha, which means the same as Admiral of the Fleet. The other was commanded by Don John. Oars splintered, the towering vessels were locked in combat, like two beasts with their teeth into each other's throats. The slightest touch might decide the battle. Perhaps it was a trumpet-call making one of the forward janissaries retreat just one step that set off the Spanish avalanche. The janissaries were forced back onto their own ship with the Venetians in pursuit; even ancient Sebastiano Venier, hero of a hundred battles, put on his armour once more and followed his grandsons onto the Turkish ship. The Turks were still resisting on the afterdeck and one or two other raised platforms, but the unstoppable momentum of an avalanche once started sent them to their destruction.

The Capudan Pasha fell, the mainmast was taken, the standard with the three crescents came down and terror paralysed the nearest Turkish ships. The first turned in flight, the Venetians and the Spaniards, the Papal ships, the Maltese and the Savoyards and the Genoese – though the latter less enthusiastically as they had beforehand made arrangements to quietly change sides if the Turks should win – pursued their wounded prey into the bay of Corinth. They found it easier and easier to board the Turkish ships or to set fire to them. It was a horrible, deadly round-up of the wildly fleeing mass of ships which only that morning had been the largest naval unit in the world, the Sultan's fleet.

30,000 Turks had been cut down, shot, captured or drowned. 130 Turkish galleys were taken, 12,000 Christian slaves liberated. The Christian victory was complete, the rejoicing indescribable. A threat which, ever since the conquest of Constantinople, had been hanging over Europe like an executioner's axe, had been blunted. Christendom breathed again. The tension was released in an unending outburst of joy which greeted the victors when they returned to Venice a few days after the battle, plunging them into a whirl of celebrations that lasted for days and days.

Each of the great Venetian families counted it an honour to fête at least one of the heroes in their palace: Duke Emmanuel Philibert of Savoy, known as 'Ironhead', the Grand Master of the most courageous Order of the Knights of Saint John; the noble Pietro del Monte; Duke Don Ottavio Farnese of Parma; even Gian Andrea Doria, the Genoese Admiral; but above all the glorious focus of the triumph himself, Don John of Austria, who after that day was called 'Victor of Lepanto', and, by the ladies of Venice, Don Giovanni.

Some time before these world-shaking events another stranger came to *la Serenissima*. His arrival went unnoticed, just as he, at first sight, was inconspicuous. The stranger, old but clearly still sprightly, and accompanied by a factotum, arrived by land, that is at Mestre he took one of the clumsy dark brown barques that daily cross the lagoon in their hundreds. The size of the tip, his polished manner, his elegant, but at the same time elegantly restrained, dress all told the ferryman that he was not dealing with a pauper. And it was only when he entered and left the barque, in which he had to be assisted by his servant and the ferryman, that one could see that he was much older and more frail than he at first appeared.

The stranger was taken to the *Fondaco dei Tedeschi,* the officially-recognised chamber of the German merchants. There he asked for the representative of one of the wealthiest merchant houses and presented a whole bundle of letters of recommendation from the highest personages which requested any assistance for a Doctor Digitalis from Böblingen in Swabia. The Fugger agent himself sought a suitable lodging in one of the more reputable inns of the city and offered the stranger his services, of which, however, Dr. Digitalis, as we can now call him, hardly availed himself. The Doctor, always dressed in grey, spent most of his time during the initial part of his stay on an exhaustive inspection of the remarkable monuments of our city which, even in those days, were known the world over. At every church or palace he visited he wanted to know the name of the builder, architect, patron saint or owner and all other details that travellers like to hear when they have nothing better to do. But that was nothing unusual when one remembers the incredible number of Germans, French, Poles, Spaniards, yes, even Finns, Arabs and Croats who were coming and going all the time; moreover in those days the whole city was in turmoil over the imminent departure of the fleet of the Holy Alliance, and when it did actually sail out of Messina every Venetian trembled for the success of Don John of Austria upon which – that was obvious even to the poorest beggar outside St. Mark's – the fate of the golden city of the lagoon depended.

It was a few days before the decisive battle of Lepanto – rumours and counter-rumours followed one upon the other in the fearful city – at the time of the great services of intercession in the churches and processions round the city, when Dr. Digitalis came to the *Fondaco dei Tedeschi* for a second time, this time to ask the agent of the Fuggers for some information, an address. The merchant was of course ready to supply, or obtain, any information. But when he heard the name of the man whose residence he had been asked for, he went pale.'

'The authors of certain historical novels', continued Laura after a short pause – a servant had come with the news that one of the Count's favourite cats, Ramses, had been bitten by a neighbour's dog – 'like to give the appearance of knowing things which are not recorded in any historical sources and which may well not even have been known to contemporaries. More intelligent authors avoid things that can be checked. What I find particularly objectionable is when they give conversations between historical personages word for word. In the story that follows I have no intention of joining such authors; I claim neither that the conversation between the two Venetians ever took place, nor that the two reverend gentlemen even existed. It is merely to satisfy the requirement that a story should not only amuse, but also instruct that I introduce Signor Marc Antonio Moro, Canon of St. Mark's, whose mouth had been so compressed by the surrounding fat that his voice had difficulty finding its way out:

'Does *anyone* know why that disgusting beast Peretti has been made a cardinal?'

The two theological gentlemen, as you see, were talking shop. The second, a certain Don Albano Sagredo, Prefect of the School of San Rocco and almost fatter than his friend, rubbed his bluish nose and said, after thinking for a long time, 'Last year, it was last year that he was made a cardinal.'

'And does anyone know why?' repeated the first reverend gentleman.

'He talks a lot', said Don Albano, 'he talks an awful lot; if I were to talk that much', he snuffled like a pig rooting for truffles, 'I would have been made cardinal ages ago.'

'I bet four of my mother's pig's cullions braised with bay-leaf', Don Marc Antonio's tongue flickered with remarkable rapidity round his chin, 'to a hazelnut, that that chatterbox from Ancona will finish up by becoming Pope.'

'The next but one perhaps, but definitely not the next', said Don Albano.

'Why not?'

'Because there's an R in his name.'

'Oh, of course', said Don Marc Antonio, 'he has an R in his name. Who will be the next Pope?'

'Before his election the present one was called Michele Ghisleri, with an R –'

'A disgusting beast of a Milanese', said Don Marc Antonio.

'– the previous one, Pius IV, was christened Gian Angelo dei Medici, without an R –'

'Another Milanese, a disgusting whoremonger, they say he had portraits of noble ladies painted completely naked!'

'– before him on St. Peter's throne was Paul IV, whose real name was Gian Pietro Caraffia, with an R –'

'A Neapolitan, disagreeably overpious – was he not even a monk?'

'With an R, without an R, with an R, without an R –'

'Regular as clockwork', said Don Marc Antonio and yawned, 'it must be the work of the Holy Ghost.'

'Indubitably', said Don Marc Antonio.

'I bet two young gondoliers to the old woman who cuts out corns by San Tommaso that the Cardinal of San Sisto will be the next Pope.'

'Ugo Buoncompagni?'

'Yes. In the first place he's from Bologna. It's ages since a Bolognese was Pope. The last Pope to come from Bologna was –' Don Albano's little mouth made twittering noises as he looked up to heaven '– was Lucius, yes, Lucius, elected in 1144. In 1145 a stone fell on his head.'

'Very interesting', said Don Marc Antonio.

'Yes. And then Buoncompagni was Legate at the Court of Spain. If a Pope were to be elected today, that alone would secure Buoncompagni's election. But he will be one day.'

'Isn't he the madman who is always talking about the same thing, I can't remember what it is, but there's something he wants to introduce or abolish. Clocks, isn't it?'

'The calendar', said Don Albano. 'After him Peretti will be Pope – with a R – and then I tip Giovanni Battista Castagna.'

'He's not even a cardinal.'

'He will be. He's already been Archbishop of Rossano for twenty years. And anyway, it's high time someone from Rome was Pope, otherwise the fishwives will foulmouth the Conclave; the last Roman was –', again the Canon twittered with his eyes turned to heaven as he counted, '– Otto Colonna, that is Martin V, from 1417 to 1431.'

'Let's hope he doesn't want to abolish anything, pig's cullions, say –'

'Nonsense! Then it could be Niccolò Sfondrato's turn – with an R – and after that, there's no way round it, Antonio Facchinetti, Bishop of Nicastro, will be elected. The last time he knelt before Pius, when the Pope bent down his tiara fell onto his head. An infallible sign. Stop that!' The young priest pushed the hand of his spiritual brother gently but firmly from his knee.

The gathering where this conversation between the two youthful nephews of the old Procurator, Contarini, took place was another of the festivities to celebrate Don John of Austria. It was not one of the more fashionable gatherings, even though the organisers had taken great pains to ensure that it was no less resplendent than the balls and receptions in the palaces of the great families. There was certainly no lack of money, and application had been made to the authorities for permission for the celebrations to last for five days. Permission had been granted, but in spite of that the guests who turned up in the Great Hall of the Fondaco dei Tedeschi – for it is the festivity organised by the German merchants that we are talking about – were from the lower ranks of the nobility. Four days had passed during which the drunkenness had increased as the festive spirit decreased, when at last the umpteenth humble petition of a delegation of the German Merchants was finally successful in persuading the great hero himself, Don John of Austria, whom the merchants, not without reason, regarded as a fellow-countryman, to agree to honour the celebrations in the Fondaco dei Tedeschi, as well as a number of other entertainments of a public and private nature, with his presence.

Like lightning the news that Don Giovanni would attend the festivities of the German Merchants coursed through the network of channels carrying information to all those who feel that they must be everywhere anything is going on. And so for an hour, or perhaps half an hour, before the arrival of the hero, the Germans were astonished to see their celebrations, which had gone somewhat flat, submerged beneath the froth of the cream of Venetian society – or at least of those who considered themselves the cream.

Then Don John arrived. Sixteen hired 'pifferari' blew their trumpets so loudly that one would have thought the Fondaco would collapse, and the bosoms of the ladies heaved, even when their owners forgot to breathe. Don John was a little shorter than those who had never met him before imagined, he was dressed in white brocade and around his neck he was wearing the gold chain the Republic had presented to him. He was accompanied by his nephew, the heir to the throne of Parma, Don Alessandro Farnese, who was two years older and dressed entirely in crimson.

Neither the two rotund prelates nor Don John noticed the bearded old man in grey who sat in a corner quietly observing the proceedings. But he did notice Donna Anna Contarini, instantly ...'

A servant who had been waiting in the background until Laura paused, now announced that the injuries to Ramses were not as serious as had been originally thought. The Papal Count ordered the wound to be bathed in old French brandy.

Laura continued:

'I said that Don Giovanni would scarcely have noticed the dignified old man, even if he had not been unknown to him. The old man, however, none other than Dr. Digitalis of course, would have recognised Don Giovanni unannounced, although he had never seen him before, neither in the flesh nor in a picture – at least not in a physical picture ...

The Fugger agent had not found it difficult to procure for Dr. Digitalis the address of the man whose very name had made him go pale. I will call him Messer Simeone – but he probably went by many names – and he lived far from the centre in one of the many side streets off the Rio della Misericordia. Dr. Digitalis had certainly assumed that he would not give himself away by living in a palace on crystal columns, but he had not expected such a miserable abode. On the ground floor a cheap butcher's shop spread a noxious stench. Hunks of meat hung outside. The sun burnt down on them and the yellow fat had run into disgusting rancid little globules. Messer Simeone's private entrance was clearly next to the shop, for he waved to Dr. Digitalis from the first floor and pointed to a small door. It was not a stairwell, rather the borehole of a gigantic stone-grub that had eaten its way into the house, and it wound without landing or window up through a narrow tunnel to a door. There Messer Simeone, short, plump and clean-shaven, was waiting for his visitor. Kicking aside a pile of rags, he led Dr. Digitalis through a small room that was stuffed full with old garments – there was an unmistakeable smell of rats – into the next, somewhat larger one that was full of copper and earthenware vessels as well as countless fragments of pottery. There followed a kind of gallery with inches of dust everywhere. To the left a row of begrimed windows let in a dull half-light. On the right were tall glass cabinets with stuffed fish goggling out of the dusty shadows. Spherical and snake-shaped monsters with square eyes or no eyes at all, with whip-like fins, brightly-coloured, bone-pale or transparent, stared out at the Doctor. They were creatures from the lowest depths of the oceans, often consisting solely of spines, bladders or rings, like figures from the sick dreams of a dissolute mathematician. They were horrible creatures, unnameable and indescribable, creatures such as are sometimes depicted on the penultimate pages of certain books, on those pages one is afraid to turn; they are like guards at the limits of knowable space: if one were to open the very last pages of those certain books one would plummet past them into the nameless unplumbed abyss, which is alien even to God.

With the smile of an aquarist inspecting his pets, Messer Simeone tapped on the glass: a sluggish puff of dust rose and fell ...

The next room, at the end of the gallery, was less squalid: it was a kind of storeroom with bottles of iridescent liquids, essences which seemed to glow from within, golden elixirs, with shelves full of skulls arranged according to size, embryos preserved in spirit, tubes with flies of different species, dried frogs, wolves' ears, horses' eyes.

Adjoining the store was a laboratory with the usual array of glass and copper implements and vessels. The commonest magic formulae were written on the walls, though some were covered up with curtains.

Finally they reached their goal, the library. (You must realise that such houses or, rather, accretions of buildings, in which one can go for hundreds of yards from room to room, along passageways, through cellars, vaults and over covered drains, are not uncommon in Venice.) The library, then, a high room with a gallery, was tolerably comfortable. A globe – not of the earth, nor even of the heavens but a topography of hell – stood under an eleven-armed candelabra by two comfortable chairs in which Messer Simeone and his guest sat down.

'What can I do for you?' asked Messer Simeone.

'It is not something I can put in a word or two. I hope you have a little time to hear me out.'

'If it does not last too long', muttered Messer Simeone.

'Very good of you. I, as you can see', began Dr. Digitalis, leaning back in his chair, his hands placed together in front of his lips and his eyes raised to the ceiling, 'am an old man. My body is bowed with the weight of years and my spirit has been broken by the realisation that that which I have spent my whole life seeking: the meaning of life, the very source of all being, does not exist.'

'Dreadful, dreadful', said Messer Simeone.

'Dreadful indeed, in the true meaning of the word.'

'Dreadful', muttered Messer Simeone, 'the things these Germans worry about. But continue. I'll listen. It's all contained in the price.'

'I was a spirited youth. But from my earliest childhood all my striving was devoted to higher things or –' Dr. Digitalis sighed, '– what people call higher things. At an age when other boys spent their days in childish games, all my zeal was spent on the study of Latin, Greek and Hebrew. It was my proud boast that I knew every line of Ovid that has been preserved. Whilst other youths sighed for women, I sat the whole night through over my books; and when my fellow-students, with whom I no longer had anything in common, sang and caroused in the inns, I quenched my thirst for knowledge at the fountain of mathematics. My only relaxation was a comedy by Plautus or a polished disputation with a scholar on fundamental questions. Although initially this was merely an unconscious striving after knowledge, the more I learnt, the more it became a compulsive search for insight. I wanted to fathom the system of the universe. Convinced that meaning must be concealed somewhere, I thought I would find it when I had gathered the whole store of human knowledge. I thought if I could comprehend within my mind everything accessible to human understanding, then it would not be difficult to comprehend the structure of creation.'

'Excuse the interruption', said Messer Simeone, 'but I hope you intend to pay in cash?'

'Oh – er – what? No; I have bills of exchange.'

'Bills of exchange.' Messer Simeone grunted. 'I don't like them. Which houses are they drawn on?'

'Please allow me to tell you everything in the order in which it happened, my dear Messer Simeone. As I said, the system of the universe seemed comprehensible, if one were to know everything there is to know. Once one had arranged all human knowledge, the system would appear as clear as day and it would be simple to insert whatever was missing or unknown, like numbers in an equation. Even the final mystery, the secret of our existence, would be revealed. I was, it is true, a Christian ...'

'Yeuch!', Messer Simeone spat all over the floor. 'Excuse me, a hair in my mouth.'

'... and so all I needed to do was to *believe*. But I wanted to achieve belief through a miracle, through the miracle of intellect. Therefore I began to collect knowledge in earnest. The prime of my life was spent in extremely painstaking and systematic studies.'

'You never slept with a woman?' asked Messer Simeone with a yawn.

'The experience of physical love seemed to me to belong to

the body of knowledge I wished to assemble. At the age of forty-one, at the time I was studying medicine, I married my housekeeper and fathered several children. As the act of procreation is extremely informative as regards the source of being, I always performed it with due and earnest attention.'

'The poor girl', said Messer Simeone. 'I would imagine you also assembled the experience of cuckoldry?'

'I pursued my studies' – Dr. Digitalis ignored Messer Simeone's question with a wave of the hand – 'from the internal to the external, so to speak, from the narrower to the broader, from the specific to the general, from the physical to the metaphysical. At the beginning of my systematic studies was mineralogy; that took me on the one hand to geology, geography and astronomy, and on the other to botany, zoology and medicine; medicine led to chemistry, chemistry to physics; then after those specific studies I went on to the general sciences: philosophy, political economy, history, jurisprudence and –'

'O Faustus, lay thy damned book aside,

Read, read the scriptures ...' quoted the Count.

Laura laughed.

'Yes, well, I'm sure you guessed long ago who Dr. Digitalis really was. He in fact continued, '– and, unfortunately, theology as well. Though actually I was not unhappy. On the contrary, soon I had quite a reputation among scholars. I was appointed to a chair at the University of Freiburg and even if I did not amass a great fortune, I was comfortably well-off. Free from cares and not without recognition in the world – I need only mention the gold chain and pendant sent to me by the late, most noble and most generous Electoral Prince of the Palatinate, Otto Heinrich the Munificent – I had an ordered existence, everything was as regular as clockwork in my well-appointed house and my library contained all available treasures of the human spirit. When, after a glass of vintage port and with unploughed acres of time before me, I retired to my study at the usual hour and sat down in the pool of light at my desk, the world could storm and rage outside, I felt secure in the eiderdown of scholarship I had drawn around me.'

'That gives me a good idea', said Messer Simeone. From a

concealed cupboard he took a decanter of port and poured himself a glass full to the brim. He set a glass before Dr. Digitalis as well, poured a few drops, paused for a moment to think, and then filled it at least half-full. Groaning with the effort, he brought a plate with four biscuits, of which he immediately ate two. 'My dear sir', he said, spraying biscuit crumbs over the table, 'help yourself.'

Dr. Digitalis took a sip of the wine.

'There was no specific event that changed my mind, I could not name a particular day when my doubts began. They came like an insidious disease, like old age even. At first, of course, I refused to believe the path I had pursued led nowhere; I continued to follow it ever more obstinately. But with time I could not remain blind to the fact that the more knowledge I gathered, the more fragile the edifice I had built out of it became. In irritation, then desperation and finally with an insane fury I tried to disperse the doubts that Hell –'

'Hm, hm', coughed Messer Simeone.

'I'm sorry?'

'Nothing, nothing, please continue.'

'I felt like an insect trying to climb out of a hole in the sand – the more it thrashes about, the quicker the sand slips down. It was inevitable that the day would come when I would force myself to accept the ultimate insight of my scientific studies, no, not a day, a night, a whole series of nights during which horror racked me like a fever. I summed up all the knowledge I had gained. In one mighty effort of the mind which reduced me to a skeleton and sent me wandering through the house and garden like one demented, I drew up the balance sheet of my researches: nothing! I had not succeeded in comprehending the system of the universe; I had not even established a system for understanding that system. On the contrary: everything I had learnt pointed to the fact that the world had no meaning. This insight was, however, less devastating than the awful, inescapable fact that it came too late – I was an old man! All my nights, nay, all my days and all my years I had wasted chasing a phantom. I had squandered my virile strength, I had ruined my eyes, and all for nothing. I had not lived ... In that night I was close to drinking a phial of poisonous liquid. But my spirits revived. I wanted to live! My life up to that point was a mistake for which I refuse to accept responsibility. I want to live. I don't want it to be too late. I want to start again. How much will it cost?'

'You want to become younger?'

'Yes. By not less than forty years.'

'That will not be simple, not in your case. That is, it won't be difficult to make you forty years younger. But all you would do would be to start pursuing your crazy ideas again. You will have to become a different person.'

'I am willing to accept anything that is necessary.'

'You might be!' laughed Messer Simeone, 'but where am I going to find the other person. What do you think it will take to persuade a thirty-year-old to agree to be transformed on the spot into — you'll excuse the expression — a senile old dodderer?'

'I have brought two bills of exchange, both drawn on the bank of Aaron ben Mordechai and both to the value of one thousand ducats.'

'Aaron ben Mordechai!' said Messer Simeone with interest, 'not bad. Let me see.'

'It is all I have in the world. I will give you the first one now, you will get the second afterwards.'

Messer Simeone took the bill to the window and checked the signature. 'Genuine', he said. 'Follow me.'

Through a secret door and up a spiral staircase he led the Professor into a windowless room over which stretched a dome-like iron structure. The walls all around were covered with tapestries.

'The room is a sphere', said Messer Simeone, 'with a floor through the middle. The tapestries are just there for ... you go mad if you stay in a sphere for too long. You are presumably aware that the two thousand is *my* payment?'

'It is your fee, I assume.'

'But you have to pay *Him* in another currency. You know what with?'

'I know. It will be a pleasure. I can't see what I would want with the useless thing after my death.'

'In your particular case there is one awkward snag', Messer

Simeone placed the eleven-armed candelabra on a small table. 'You can speak Hebrew, you said?'

'Yes', said Dr. Digitalis.

'Do you know Coptic as well?'

'Yes, Coptic as well', said Digitalis.

'Babylonian? Persian? Chinese?'

Digitalis nodded.

'I assumed that from what you told me before. Is there any language you don't know? Czech, Finnish, Welsh?'

'I'm sorry', said Digitalis.

'Basque, Buryat?'

'I am unacquainted with Buryat.'

Like lightning Messer Simeone grabbed the candelabra and ran towards Dr. Digitalis, screaming incomprehensible words at him, at the same time watching his eyes.

The Doctor jumped, 'I'm sorry?'

Messer Simeone calmly replaced the light.

'You're not pretending; you really don't know Buryat. I'm not so stupid as to call up *Him* in a language the customer can understand. And have him remember the formulae and do it for himself in future! It's a dreadful language, Buryat. I hope I won't stammer.'

Messer Simeone began to mutter to himself, as if in prayer. He kept on referring to a little book,

'A dictionary of Buryat', he said apologetically, 'one does forget the vocabulary so quickly.'

Suddenly a gap opened between the hangings and a delicate little box slid out. Messer Simeone put on a tall pointed hat and continued his litany, now and then cursing the Buryats and all their words and blowing his nose on a large handkerchief. The box sprang open and Messer Simeone took out a fat tome. Turning to Dr. Digitalis, he said,

'You can sit over there now. Don't worry, whatever happens.'

'Is that a book of magic?'

'That? That's my ledger.' Messer Simeone made a couple of entries, opened a drawer in the casket and put the bill of exchange in. He waved the Professor over, 'Would you be so good as to countersign here?'

Dr. Digitalis signed. While he was doing so Messer Simeone carefully covered up the opposite page with his sleeve, all the while murmuring phrases in Buryat.

When Dr. Digitalis returned to his seat he saw a golden egg roll out from under one of the tapestries.

'Look', he shouted.

'Don't touch', said Messer Simeone, without turning round.

The doctor leant back in his chair and watched with interest as the little egg grew. Soon there was something else that caught his attention: although all the candles were still burning, the whole room was growing darker, apart from one place behind the tapestry. The hanging seemed to become transparent and a bright figure could be seen moving behind it. Messer Simeone was observing the movements as well. He spoke more words of Buryat and then waved Dr. Digitalis over, pulling aside the tapestry. A mirror appeared and in the mirror the naked back of a young woman who was just pulling on a pair of lacy Florentine silk stockings. The background to the scene was the lady's charming and luxurious bedchamber – there, stretched out on a chaise longue, was a man. The woman slipped her shoes on and went over to him. The Doctor could tell that they were conversing, but could not hear what was said. The man gave the woman a casket, apparently a present. When she turned round they could see that it was a long gold chain, richly decorated with pearls and precious stones. Now the young woman posed in front of the mirror, holding the jewellery in the most sensuous manner against various parts of her body and winding it around her limbs, then she twirled round, danced a few steps and ... presumably indicated to the man, who was still reclining calmly on the sofa, the form her gratitude would take. Messer Simeone had taken out a magnifying glass. 'Moorish work', he said, 'the pearls are good, but the stones don't appear to be genuine. Not worth more than eighty sequins.'

Dr. Digitalis had no eyes for the chain. 'Helen of Troy!' he exclaimed.

Messer Simeone laughed. 'That is Zenobia, the courtesan, though one of the most expensive in the city, it is true.'

'And the man?'

'Don John of Austria.'

'But Don John of Austria is at sea commanding the fleet of the Holy Alliance?'

'What you see here will happen in a few days time.'

'What a woman!' said Dr. Digitalis, turning back to the mirror.

Messer Simeone rubbed his hand over it. The glass went cloudy and the image disappeared.

'Soon you will be forty years younger', he said with a suggestive leer. Dr. Digitalis turned round ...

(Supernatural, uncanny or even gruesome events lose much of their terror when they occur in what one might call their natural habitat and when, in addition, they are not unexpected. If you are in a charnel-house at midnight it might not be exactly pleasant to see a skeleton rise from a coffin, but a reasonable person will hardly find it surprising.)

Dr. Digitalis' keen mind was not at all shocked by the appearance in the demagnetised sphere of a cock about eight feet tall sitting with its legs crossed in more or less human posture, not even when he reminded himself who it must be.

Messer Simeone was busy sweeping up the shattered fragments of the gigantic shell.

'I assume', said the cock – it spoke in a pleasant though somewhat high human voice and observed Messer Simeone with, if Dr. Digitalis' knowledge of the physiognomy of poultry was anything to go by, a look of mild amusement on its feathered face – 'I assume, my dear Professor, that good Master Negrocephalus –'

'The name is Simeone', he said.

'– has squeezed a juicy fee out of you.'

'That is none of your business', said Messer Simeone.

'The eggshell', said the cock to Dr. Digitalis, 'is his perk. Pure gold. That's why he likes me to appear in outsize form. Today's shell is worth a good ten –'

'You keep your big beak shut!' snapped Messer Simeone, adding a few choice words in Buryat.'

Once more Laura was interrupted. Gently, the servant carried in Ramses, the wounded and bandaged tomcat, which gave off an aroma of fine cognac. The ladies passed it from one to the other, stroking and kissing it, to which the cat visibly objected. Finally the Count handed it back to the servant and ordered him to take Ramses to his basket. The servant left.

'Because of all the interruptions I will pass over the details of Dr. Digitalis' visit. The fact that the Devil had chosen the form of a cock for his appearance did have the advantage that, once the conditions had been agreed on, all he needed to do was to pluck out a feather and peck open a vein in the Doctor's arm for him to be able to sign the pact in the approved manner.

So it came about that a few days later, at the celebrations of the German Merchants, the face of the Victor of Lepanto was not unknown to the Professor. This was the last evening of Don Giovanni's official visit. That very night he boarded his ship, which left the harbour next morning to anchor off Ancona, a Papal city. But without Don John! Before the departure from Venice a small launch was let down from the flagship in which a cloaked figure accompanied by a servant was rowed ashore by a few trustworthy sailors – none other than Don John. The bells, guns and flags that accompanied the departure were a farewell to the admiral's ship, but not to the admiral himself, who was applying his usual tactical skill to the organisation of a little adventure for the coming night, and whiling away the time until twilight in the company of the celebrated Zenobia. When night fell he had himself smuggled by servants he had bribed into the Palazzo Contarini in the guise of a 'crayfish seller'.

Whether Don John's secret visit came as a surprise to Donna Anna Contarini, who was not the daughter but the grand-niece and ward of Bernardo Contarini – it was not usual, at least in Italy, for a Commendatore to have a daughter, at least not a legitimate one –, or whether she had been party to the planning of it was, and still is, a matter which has exercised the sharpest minds. It is not the object of my modest narrative to throw light on that. Whatever the case, the Commendatore turned up at an awkward moment and there followed the unfortunate duel that ended with the death of the dignified old man who, a few days before at Lepanto, had fought on the side of Don John.

Don John managed to escape from the palace but he was undoubtedly in a tricky situation. His fame would work to his disadvantage, since as 'Victor of Lepanto' and a state visitor who had just been the object of a public celebration he would stick out like a sore thumb. Although he was staying incognito in Venice, Donna Anna knew of his presence, and the Contarini family, one of the most powerful in Venice, would certainly have means of finding the man who had murdered one of its number and violated the niece of the Commendatore.

He went back to Zenobia, who was discreet by profession and who gave him shelter for a few days. His loyal servant Leporello slept under the stairs in the entrance hall and brought his master the news from the city, how the Contarinis had buried their Uncle Commendatore with a great show of tears and that the sbirri of the Council were combing the whole of Venice for the murderer. At night, so that Zenobia's business would not suffer, he had to leave the house. His hat pulled well down over his face, he wandered through the alleyways.

'I feel like a pimp', he said to Leporello. Leporello, who shared his master's discomforts in Zenobia's house but none of his pleasures, was irritable from lack of sleep:

'For that Your Excellency only has himself to blame.'

'As if I didn't know', said Don John.

'We could be on board ship off Ancona, lying quietly in our own beds, Your Excellency.'

Nights in Venice are usually quite cool in October and damp the whole year through. Don John shivered.

'At the same time I've often wondered whether we could really call those uncomfortable bunks on Your Royal Brother's ship *our beds*.'

Don John said nothing, although certainly not because he was not listening.

'Is there anywhere on earth where you have a bed of your own, Your Excellency?'

'The sun never set on my father's empire; my brother still

rules over half the world. Everywhere that owns his sway I can lay down my head', said Don John wearily and not very convincingly.

'At the moment, yes, Your Excellency; at the moment Your Royal Brother happens to need you because you have just thrashed the Turks. But what if things change?'

'What do I care, Leporello. I'm living now, not later.'

'Excuse me, your Excellency, but my father has a little inn near Valencia, in Torrente; it's a one-horse town, Your Excellency won't know it. There, in the bodega in Torrente, there is a room under the eaves, and whenever I return home and *however* I return home, rich or poor, honoured or persecuted, I know that there is a bed and a plate of bacon and beans waiting for me. Wherever I am, Your Excellency, I know that that is where I belong. But where does Your Excellency belong?'

'I belong to the world', said Don John. It sounded like an excuse.

'Does Your Excellency not even have *one* ramshackle bed in an attic in some Torrente or other, one lousy sweet little bed?'

'Where would I have something like that, Leporello?'

'There you are, Your Excellency! I often watch you: you fly from one day to the next, and time flies for you more quickly than for an old man. All those battles and balls, the social whirl, the glory, the women, it's all a hollow sham. The fetid breath of a Contarini – what is a Contarini? – can blow you out like a candle. And here we are, living like pimps.'

'We should try to take a gondola across to Mestre.'

'That is precisely what the sbirri are waiting for! They know very well that is what you will try.'

'Or to Chioggia and then take a boat, a sea-going boat ...'

'And sail to Ancona? Through the equinoctial gales? Count me out!'

'I'll bribe one of the guards.'

'There is a price on your head which is more than all the cash you have on you.'

'Or I'll go to the Doge and simply apologise and send a letter to my brother ...'

'Do you think your brother will risk a war with Venice for

your sake? Your Excellency should be happy if he hears nothing of the whole affair. He would have you thrown into a dungeon compared with which the prisons under the lead roofs would seem a pleasure-house ... Remember Don Carlos!'

'What time is it, Leporello?'

'It will be getting on for two, Your Excellency.'

Don John sighed. 'Three hours to go. We can go home at five.'

'Yes, home, Your Excellency. And a fine home it is!'

'You don't know how right you are, Leporello. I wish I had an attic room and a bowl of bacon and beans, but I don't even know who I am. You're Spanish. Me? I'm half German, a quarter Portuguese, one eighth French, almost a prince and almost a gypsy, I am a little of everything and nothing of anything.'

'Excuse the liberty, Your Excellency, but Your Excellency must have been born on the cusp of two hours, between two planets. There is no planet that rules your life.'

'Sometimes I even believe it myself, Leporello. I am a fool, yes, a fool.'

'If Your Excellency says so –', said Leporello, not without a certain satisfaction.

'What I say, Leporello, is ... *I wish I could change it!*'

'Sh! Your Excellency, someone is coming.'

'Let's disappear.'

On the third night Don John took a gondola to San Michele, the island of burial. During the day, following a whim of his master, Leporello had sought out the freshly-dug grave of the Commendatore, so that now they quickly found it in the bright moonlight of the autumn night. The cypress trees swayed in the breeze which rippled the waters of the lagoon. Trails of dull silver cloud flitted across the face of the moon.

At the grave, that was already dominated by an immense monument, Don John was just trying to decipher the grandiose inscription calling for vengeance when Leporello screamed:

'There! Look!'

Don John drew his sword. A few steps away from them a calm figure stood between the moonlit gravestones.

'Who are you?' called Don John.

'The Devil, the Devil', moaned Leporello.

'Good evening, Your Excellency', said the figure, coming closer. 'It gives me great pleasure that the Victor of Lepanto, the Hero of Christendom –'

'Stay where you are or I'll cut you down.'

'That I do not believe, Don John. If you did, your journey here would have been in vain.'

'What do you mean?'

'It was I who invited you here, without your knowing, of course. Or could you say why you felt you had to visit the grave of your victim? Murderers are usually drawn to the scene of their crime ...'

'Who are you?' repeated Don John.

The stranger had turned to go and just gave them a mute sign to follow. At the jetty a gondola was waiting. Don John, Leporello and the unknown man stepped in and sat down. The gondolier pushed off. Neither he nor Leporello could understand the conversation that took place during the journey.

'You had a German mother', the stranger had said in German. 'I assume, therefore, that you can speak German?'

'Yes', said Don John.

'Have you read the inscription on the Commendatore's grave?'

'Something about vengeance –'

' 'Dall'empio, che mi trasse al passo estremo/Qui attendo la vendetta' is written on the gravestone. No power in the world' – the stranger emphasised the word *world* – 'can save you from the dungeons under the lead roofs. The Contarini will find you sooner or later.'

'They would not dare to imprison the brother of the King of Spain.'

'They will be very careful not to throw the *Brother of the King of Spain* into the *piombi*; they will merely punish the *unknown murderer of Commendatore Contarini* ... They have trumpeted abroad that they find the deed particularly reprehensible because the unfortunate victim was a bold and loyal companion-in-arms of Don John of Austria.'

'But Donna Anna knows –'

'All the Contarini know. As a precaution they have sent a somewhat bombastic despatch to you.'

'To me?'

'Well, to *Don John of Austria on the flagship that lies at anchor before Ancona*. It runs – I have already quoted the text –, 'No power in the world will save the murderer from our just revenge'.'

'And who are *you*?' asked Don John for the third time.

'If you want to escape from Venice alive', said the stranger as he stepped out of the gondola, which in the meantime had moored in a narrow backwater by a dark house, 'then you must become a different person.'

In contrast to Dr. Digitalis, Don Giovanni passed the sea monsters in the dusty gallery without hesitation or deep reflections. Leporello, to his nameless horror, which was only slightly lessened by a greasy sausage from the butcher's shop below, was made to stay there and wait. Don Giovanni also spent much less time in the library with Messer Simeone than the German professor had. And in his case things were reversed and it was Messer Simeone, who seemed changed out of all recognition, who did most of the talking.

'I have long known of you, Your Excellency', hc said, 'and your problems with the murdered Contarini and his debauched niece' – the ironic ambiguity of *debauched* was unmistakeable – 'are merely, though far be it from me to underestimate their seriousness, an excuse for me to carry out my long-standing intention of contacting you. How old are you?'

'Next February I will be twenty-five.'

'Twenty-five! and you have already done much to ensure your immortality.'

'That's for others to say.'

'That, heehee, is for others to say – you have certainly made sure that the Spanish line of the House of Habsburg will not die out, even if your brother, His Venerable and Most Catholic Majesty, should refrain from procreation. Your efforts have allowed countless, at the moment quite young, ladies and gentlemen entry into the House of Habsburg even if – please excuse the somewhat forthright expression – by the tradesman's entrance.'

'Quite a literary prophet, your Messer Simeone', said the amused Count.

'Not surprising at all', said Laura, 'given his connections. But I will omit his further comments on the subject if all it does is lead to interruptions. –

'And there is talk', continued Messer Simeone, 'that you have driven the pirates out of Tunis and that you intend to complete the work of your great father, His late Imperial Majesty, the Fifth Charles, and establish a kingdom there, whose ruler you would yourself be. But leaving that aside – three years ago your unfortunate half-nephew, the good Infanta, Don Carlos ... died, and up to the moment the recent marriage of your royal brother has not been blessed with a son. Who knows...?'

'I'm afraid', said Don John, 'there are still all my nephews in Austria who will make sure a bastard does not inherit the Spanish throne.'

'Would it be the first time that a ... well, if you care to take it, the Governorship of the Netherlands is yours. You will rule in Brussels like a king and the Spanish provinces there are richer than all your brother's other possessions, including India. And all those buxom Dutch women –', Messer Simeone sniggered.

'The one thing I would like to know', said Don John, 'is what you want of me and who you are?'

'Your Excellency', he said, 'you are almost a king; you are the complete hero. You are rich, you are handsome. Women worship you, the world is at your feet, but have you a goal? Indeed, have you really lived at all in your life so far?'

Don John was silent.

'Come!' Messer Simeone hurried his guest up the stairs and into the magic sphere, where he threw the curtain aside.

The mirror shone brightly and then revealed a sunny valley between vine-covered slopes. A narrow path led past an old house and up the hill. Nestling up against the wall of the house in the shade of a tall tree was a stone seat and table. At it sat a man in neat attire, full of years and yet still active. The sun shone through the branches and made his wine-glass sparkle; with delicate precision he was carving a pheasant that lay on the plate before him on a bed of golden and, doubtless, aromatic leaves. When he had finished the pheasant, he tore a piece from a loaf of bread and then slowly, with two fingers, picked up his glass and emptied it. The gnomon of the sundial painted on the wall of the house showed that it was four o'clock in the afternoon. The old man stood up and went into the house. Through a window they could see him enter the library.

'That man', said Messer Simeone, 'has given up all concern with trifles. He is writing a book on logic which will influence the development of human thought for centuries to come. He spent years in study before he started it. The length of the work is so calculated that, as far as it is possible for a human being to judge such matters, if he completes his quota each day the completion of the book will coincide with the completion of his life.'

The moon had risen above the valley. The roof of the house almost vanished in the shadow of the hill.

'And tomorrow', said Messer Simeone as he let the curtain drop back over the mirror, 'tomorrow he will go out for a little easy hunting and will come back with a little game – which, incidentally, he does not actually need – and, more importantly, a feeling of pleasant fatigue. His sleep is deep and refreshing.'

Now it was Laura who broke off.

'Well?' we asked.

'You can work out the rest of the story for yourselves.'

'Not at all', said her uncle.

'Then you haven't been listening properly.'

'Or you haven't told the story properly', he teased.

'Hah!' said Laura. 'I told my story very skilfully. It contains all the components necessary to complete it. You only need to listen properly and use your imagination. A good story, once it has reached a particular point, continues under its own impetus. The earlier that point is reached, the better.'

'That may well be true within its own terms', objected the Count, 'but there are stories whose characteristic it is to jump backwards and forwards: no one can predict how they are going to end. Then there are others whose point is kept back until the very last moment and which keep the listener on tenterhooks until the tension is suddenly released at the end. Then, finally, are those which seem to be a ragbag of all kinds of things that do not appear to make sense or to hang together at all: the listener is confronted with a tangle of coloured threads until with one little twist the storyteller – so far he has done everything to make sure we don't catch on too soon – turns the whole thing over and it suddenly dawns on us that what we have been seeing is the back of a tapestry; now the front with the splendid 'design' is plain for all to see, the sense of the story is not only artfully arranged, it is easily understood by all. There was only one storyteller like that –'

'We know', said Laura 'and it does not worry us at all that we cannot match up to Chesterton. Who can? Well, I suppose you want it all spread out right under your lazy noses: the golden egg rolled in again, the outsize cock appeared, – but you must make up your own minds whether Don John signed the pact because he really wished to become another person, or because he felt compelled to by the deadly situation he had got himself into.

The rest is simple: Messer Simeone interchanged Don John and Faust.

Faust, who had just been reading a book in an inn, dropped off in his chair. The warm afternoon sun shone through the window. Don John, who had just given Zenobia the chain we have already seen, fell asleep on the sofa, exhausted by the strain of a night during which he had hardly slept a wink. Both only shut their eyes for no more than a second or two before they were woken up again, Don John by his book falling onto the floor with a thump, and Faust because Zenobia was tickling his nose with her nipples ...

It must be an indescribable experience to shed one's life like an old skin and slip into a ready-made new life. Every step, every gesture must be a breathtaking adventure. However well one knew the world, it would seem created in a new light.

Faust, now Don John, immediately plunged into all kinds of amatory adventures which naturally meant that the Contarini tracked him down and cornered him in Zenobia's house. As the agreed time was not yet up, Messer Simeone had to intervene. To the horror of the pursuers, he appeared as the living monument of the Commendatore come to fetch the evil-doer. 'Don John' occasionally told the story himself and pointed out how difficult it had been for him not to laugh at the lines, *Pèntiti!* – *No!* He got Messer Simeone to whisk him – and Leporello – off to Ancona. In the months following he fought the odd skirmish for the Genoese and then took up the Governorship of the Netherlands where the pretty, plump Dutch ladies in their starched lace collars were already working themselves up into a fever of – justified – expectation.

Don John, the new Faust, returned home to Freiburg, worked at his treatise on logic and ate his pheasant on vine leaves at the little stone table under the tall tree.

And that is really the end of the story', said Laura. 'However, so that it will also satisfy my uncle's theories, I will add a conclusion that could not be expected from the foregoing ...

Some years passed and the two transformed characters enjoyed their new lives. However, if God's work is never complete, how much truer is that of the devil's: each retained a trace of his former self. 'Don John' began to ponder and Leporello shook his head in disbelief at his master's command to 'bring me that pretty little whore from Bruges who can prattle on so charmingly about death'. 'Faust' found his deep reflections on logic increasingly disturbed by some of the merry wives of Freiburg. One spring, when one of the maids was removing the upper double windows, he gave her shapely calf such a pinch that not only the window, but also the Aristotle open on his desk tumbled to the floor.

Thus it came that a few years after the Battle of Lepanto both of them, Don Juan and Faust, arrived, independently but simultaneously, in Venice. Each demanded his original form back from Messer Simeone, who was not at all pleased, but then what businessman is happy about a complaint?

In a side-canal off the Grand Canal, no more than a small inlet leading to the Jewish quarter, two gondolas met: in the one sat an old man with his beard trimmed and dyed, his eyes red-rimmed and his dress much too gaudy for his years – inside his tight trousers the old dandy was little more than a skeleton! In the other sat a young man with aristocratic features. More than anything else, melancholy can render a handsome man irresistible; this young man however was not melancholic but desperate, pale, unkempt and wasted by illness, both mental and physical – an old man before his time. 'Faust' stood up, shaking, in his gondola and opened his lips to give expression to his feeling, 'What have you done with me?' 'Don John' took a step back, the gondola rocked, the gondolieri gave a loud cry of warning. 'Don John', too, opened his lips to cry, 'What have you done with me?' But then each paused for thought: what is 'you' and what is 'me'? Who am I? Who are you? Who is Don John, who is Faust? What right have I to my own person?

For a moment the gondolas swayed, as if locked together, but then the gondolieri, with a choice oath apiece from their professional store, thrust their long oars into the canal bed and drove them apart. For a second 'Don John' and 'Faust', or Faust and Don John were only an arm's length away; they faced each other and said – nothing.

The worthy magus, Messer Simeone Negrocefalo, was sitting in his magic sphere checking the entries in his ledger. When he turned round he saw the cock preening itself in one of the chairs.

'What a great honour for my wretched hovel', said Messer Simeone. 'I find it rather childish of you to appear in that ridiculous get-up when there are no customers here.'

'Don John was here a minute ago.'

'Yes, Don John or Faust, you can take your choice. And do you know why?'

'The other's coming, too.'

'It wouldn't surprise me.'

'Are they not satisfied?'

'I'll tell you something', Messer Simeone turned to face the cock and pushed his spectacles up onto his bald pate, 'you made a mess of that job! To swap their external forms, well, that's not much more than an above-average conjuring trick. I think I could almost manage that myself.'

'Hah-hahaha', crowed the cock.

'It's their *souls* you should have exchanged. For a while the force of habit in their new bodies helped them maintain the thrust or direction of their new lives, but deep down they remained what they had been all along. And now their spirits are literally tearing their bodies apart.'

'A Faustian Don Juan and a Donjuanesque Faust – priceless', said the cock.

'I don't find it at all funny', said Messer Simeone. 'How can I throw out two such worthy gentlemen when even I have to agree that their complaints are not without justification?'

'You're not going to start on about business eckis-kiki-theckis ...?'

'Ethics', said Messer Simeone, enjoying the way the cock squirmed as he tried to get the word out, 'ethics, ethics: *ethics*.'

'Yes, yes, yes, yes! You only need to say it once, I'm not deaf', the cock ruffled his feathers and one fell out. Messer Simeone snatched it up and put it in the cupboard.

'If we turn Don John back into Faust and Faust into Don John', said Messer Simeone, 'I bet it will just get worse. They have been almost seven years in their other forms. Something of it is bound to stick; I'm pretty sure you'd mess it up again.'

'I have a quite different plan.'

'Ah, that's my pretty little Beelzebub of Campoformio!' said Messer Simeone. 'And what plan would that be?'

'Let's combine the two of them.'

The cock leapt up and fluttered round the room. 'It'll be dynamite! Don Juan and Faust in one and the same person; action and doubt combined. A doubting man of action, a frenetic doubting Thomas! It's never been seen before, Negrocefalo! The old boy up above was very careful to keep those two human qualities well away from each other. A compound of action and doubt, it'd be pure evil!'

'Stop flapping around like that', shouted Messer Simeone, 'you're knocking everything over.'

'Don Juan and Faust in one and the same person. That'll take power over the world out of the old boy's hands. Don Juan's superhuman force and Faust's superhuman mind – that's the key! I was speaking only recently to some cardinals. They were not averse, if my plan should succeed, to the idea of electing Don Juan-Faust Pope. And with a little effort it should not be difficult to make him King of Spain once that Holy Willie in the Escorial has kicked the bucket. Then there's the Holy Roman Empire, hm, I'll have to think what to do about the Electors. Negrocefalo – Don Juan-Faust will rule the world!'

And so the pair of them, the great cock and his magus, set about preparing the grand union. Messer Simeone sent for Don John and Faust. It was 1st October 1578. An autumn storm was blowing across the Adriatic from Istria. The waters of the lagoon rippled ominously. Outside the palaces the gondolas nudged each other like restless horses. There was still no wind, but the palaces and the tower of St. Mark's shone bright with an ominous light against the background of black clouds. Scarcely anyone was out, only two gondolas, making their way to the Rio Misericordia, one from the top, the other from the bottom end of the Canal Grande. The consecrated bells of the city had just begun to defy the storm when a blinding flash of lightning descended from the sky like a flaming hand and demolished a house containing a low-class butcher's shop. Seconds later an unexplained spring tide shot forward like the paw of a mighty tiger and put out the fire. But there was nothing left of the house, not even a smoking beam.

Then the actual storm broke and raged over the city for a while, without doing any further damage. If, in the days after, anyone had asked the people of the Rio Misericordia about the house, they would have found scarcely a single person who would admit to knowing anything about it. A number would certainly even have informed him that such a house had never existed.'

Again a servant entered and gave a soft cough to indicate that he had something to say.

'My story will be over in a moment', said Laura. 'There are just a couple of sentences to go.

It was, as I said before, the 1st October 1578. Don John was found dead in his tent in the camp before Namur. It is said he died of the plague ... Faust was lying under the stone table where he had started to pick rather listlessly at a pheasant.

So far, so good. But the works of the Devil also leave their traces. Two mechanical dwarves, one from Namur and one from Freiburg, set off hurriedly. They had twelve hours time in which to come together, for each was the only one who knew how to wind the other up ... No doubt', said Laura, 'you know how the story continues.'

'I not only know how the story continues', I said, 'I even know the dwarves.' The Papal Count turned to the servant who brought the news that Moses, a brother of Ramses, had bitten off an ear of the neighbour's dog, thus avenging Ramses.

'A most satisfactory ending', said the Count, turning back towards us.

The following Sunday we heard mass together in the Count's private chapel. It was read by a Monsignore, a friend of the family, and the Count sang an Ave Maria by, if I remember correctly, Leonardo Leo. Afterwards we all, Monsignore included, retired to the silver drawing-room – so called because of its white carpet with a pattern of silver daisies. There a particularly festive meal had been set out as it was the birthday of Tiffany, the St Petersburg niece. She came in wearing a necklace of opals, heliotropes and diamonds that her uncle had given her.

During the meal the Count said:

'As we are to travel back to the city this evening, I suggest Tiffany should tell us her story after lunch, over coffee.'

'I will not tell a story', said Tiffany, 'I will read you one. I discovered it recently in a little book. I will tell the servant who is going for news of Ramses to bring it with him –'

– "and that is the end of my dream", I said. "Did you notice that the last words of my dream were 'with him'?"

"So what?" said Spring.

"The last words you read from your Oedipus were 'with him'. Perhaps", I said, "the whole of my complex dream was sparked off by those two insignificant words 'with him'! But off you go now, Spring. I have something to do. Go out and wait until I call you."

I had a bath, dressed and called Spring back.

"Your Eminence?"

"Now, Spring ..."

"Excuse me, Your Eminence, the President has summoned your Eminence."

"Remind me that I am to visit her when we get back. But now we're going to the dome."

"To the dome?" Spring drew back.

"Why not?"

"It's forbidden!"

"For a servant", I said, "even speaking is offensive. Thinking is worse, it's superfluous and possibly dangerous. Off we go."

We reached it without being challenged. Everywhere I was greeted with salutes. If Spring did not have the key to a door it was opened at my order. Either the ban was not strictly enforced or the people up here were not aware of it, or perhaps they were taken in by my self-confidence.

At the next sitting of the Senate, I thought to myself, I will propose that every Senator should have a quartet of trumpeters attached that will precede him and blow a fanfare now and then. The privileges open to a Senator should surely amount to more than a purple ribbon for his jacket and yellow livery for his valet.

I asked to be taken to the duty officer commanding the highest observation post. He was a major in a red uniform who was sitting in a small but comfortably-furnished cubby-hole at the top of the 'dome' sorting out some papers.

He leapt up when I entered.

"In what way can I be of service to Your Eminence?"

"I would like to look out."

"It is not very nice outside ..."

"I'm quite prepared for that", I said.

"If you insist, Your Eminence –" He rang a bell.

"Are we above the surface of the earth here?"

"No", said the Major.

A soldier in a green uniform entered. The Major gave some orders. A captain in a pink uniform sat down at the Major's desk and we – the Major, Spring and I – went higher up, up above the earth, the old earth from which, because of the dispositional parallax, we were more than a million light years away.

If the earth, once so rich and fertile, still existed, it was a corpse, a skeleton even: as far as the eye could see cones of ash rose up out of a desert of carbonised stone. Outside the entrance which Don Emanuele and I had gained at the very last minute stood a dozen or so bizarre figures – delicate little skeletons with star-shaped panties covered in glitter dangling round their pelvises, ankle deep in dust, the rest of Nankeen's chorus girls who had not managed to reach the opening in time. Fans of faded ostrich feathers were clutched to their ribs ...

The air was suddenly filled with the sound of a faint siren.

"Heavens!" exclaimed the Major, "away, away!"

Before the Major could pull me away from the periscope I just caught a glimpse of tall white, yes, white shadows appearing among the skeletons of the chorus girls.

"An attack ..."

We rushed down a narrow staircase into a dark room lined in black with a silver pentagram on the ceiling. Officers were waiting.

"To your positions", commanded the Major.

Each of the officers sat down at a small table on which was a crystal ball about the size of a man's head, the Major at a slightly bigger one in the middle. In his crystal ball a faint bluish flame began to flicker. The floor was swathed knee-deep in white mist. I held my breath. The siren gradually began to articulate a syllable, something like 'Owm' or 'Oom'; it bounced from wall to wall like the clapper of a giant bell, making the whole room reverberate. Here and there the mist swirled up into a pyramid which collapsed limply in upon itself.

Then one of the crystal balls burst! Ten or twelve pyramids shot up higher than a man around the table of the unfortunate soldier.

The Major jumped up from his seat, threw a dark-blue cloak around his shoulders and took a few steps, as if from an old dance. Slowly the mist dispersed. All that was left was blood-red powder on the floor which the officers, with anxious expressions on their faces, examined – the light had now been switched

264

on – with magnifying glasses. The officer whose crystal ball had burst was carried out on a stretcher.

"Is he dead?" I asked the Major.

"A skirmish, nothing more, they happen ... 'every day' I would have said, if we still had days. I suggest we go to the officers' mess." As he threw the blue cloak over a chair, the hem brushed against my trousers. It burnt a long hole in them, white at the edges; its shape was that of three open rose-crosses.

The officers' mess was like the inside of a tent, though presumably as a result of the designer's whim rather than of any necessity. Here I made the acquaintance of an old campaigner, as he termed himself, whose name was Baron von Schweythauszsz. The two W's, he explained to me, had been granted to the family by the German Emperor in November 1918, in the very last minute before the Republic was set up. That is, the patent granting the family the WW had been presented to the Kaiser for signature. As is well known, however, William II was surprised by the revolution whilst signing documents. He had just dealt with the one before the 'WW' patent when the revolution came and he had to abdicate. Ebert, the first President elected by the Reichstag, took over the imperial dispatch-box and absentmindedly signed the patent that his officials had forgotten to remove. Thanks to this oversight the family, which for generations had been trying to disguise the indelicacy of their name by stuffing it full of consonants, had finally achieved a respectable name. ... He was only telling me all this, he said, in case I should ever come across the widespread but idiotic rumour that his family had bought the two W's from a sausage maker to the Bavarian court who had been created Baron Weißwurst but sold the two W's so that he could call himself 'von Eiß-Urst'. Later on Colonel von Schweythauszsz told me a strange story of something that had happened to him shortly before the attack.

"I tell you, Your Eminence", he said, "people nowadays are spoilt, simply spoilt. It was damned irresponsible of all those states, I mean the politicians and so forth – I don't bother with who's in charge up there etc, etc – in the last few years there have been simply too few wars fought. People, I mean civilians of course, just have no idea what war is like any more. In the old days every generation, more or less, had its own war and so everyone knew that when there's a war on this or that has to happen, and so on. But this everlasting peace, this permanent life of ease – there was simply too much property, too many houses, too much money, and that not for armaments ... Well, Your Eminence, it was no skin off my nose. Only now, Your Eminence, now we see the result! These civilians have no self-discipline, no self-discipline! Deuce only knows, I miss fresh trout too, but what that old witch was doing today – No! I was down in No. IV Command and was just going across the corridor to – excuse my French – answer a call of nature, when what should I meet but an old woman, a civilian. Nature stopped calling on the spot.

'You there!' I said. 'What are you doing here?'

She said nothing, just hid some largish, longish object behind her back.

'What have you got there?' I asked. 'Don't you know civilians aren't allowed down here?'

I dragged her over to No. IV Command and told her to come out with whatever she was hiding behind her back. She refused. I called an orderly. And what did we find, Your Eminence? A casserole. The old witch stormed and shouted, but the orderly lifted the lid ... My word of honour Your Eminence, if I hadn't been an old campaigner with what we saw in that frying-pan I'd have forgotten more than a call of nature, I'd have forgotten to eat for a whole week: there was a child in the casserole, roasted, with sauce.

'Madam', I said, even though she was only an ordinary civilian, 'who gave you permission to roast a child.'

'It's my daughter', the old witch said.

There you have it, Your Eminence: that woman was roasting her own daughter! She said the child was twelve years old. It hardly had any room at all in the casserole, knees drawn up like a chicken. No self-discipline these civilians. She said she was afraid she might have to starve. We have supplies for seven million and there are ten thousand in here. And she roasts her daughter! What do you say to that, Your Eminence?"

"I will bring up the case in the Senate, Baron", I replied.

When we were back 'down below', Spring reminded me that the President had summoned me.

"We'll say we're late because of the dispositional parallax", I said.

I changed. Then Spring took me to the Presidential Office. I told the adjutant on duty that I did not want to interrupt anything. No, he said, he had specific orders to send me through.

The adjutant led us to the President's private apartments. After being announced at every possible opportunity – I had no idea how soon that would all be a thing of the past – I came to a large, comfortable room where, besides the President, were Weckenbarth, Dr. Jacobi, Lord Alfred and a fourth gentleman, who was unknown to me.

The unknown man was talking as I entered the room. He continued talking but gave me a friendly wave like the others. The President – I could scarcely believe my eyes – smiled and blew me a kiss; she must be confusing me with someone else, I thought and gave her a cautious, covert glance. She was still smiling at me. She was wearing a ball-gown of white lace, and it was only now that I realised that everyone was in evening dress – Weckenbarth, Dr. Jacobi, Lord Alfred, whose tails had an unusual striped pattern: chains of tiny grey roses which on one side, on the left by the lapel, came together to form a large heraldic rosette. Only the unknown man was wearing a lounge suit, grass-green, just a hint lighter than his grass-green face ...

The Wandering Jew[*] – the unknown man was none other, though here out of politeness he was addressed as Mr. Ahasuerus – was the guest, I now learnt, whom they had entertained every evening. Usually, as when I had been on the ship, they played cards. It is well known that he is cursed never to die and to have to journey on until the Day of Judgment. However, as long as the ship kept moving, he could sit down and play bridge or tell stories and, above all, live like any normal person. But here in the cigar, they had discovered, Mr. Ahasuerus did not need to keep moving.

"Weckenbarth thinks that might be one of the results of dispositional parallax", Dr. Jacobi explained to me, adding, "*I* am afraid it is the result of something else ..."

The Wandering Jew's fund of stories was inexhaustible since he, who had once been Cain, had seen mankind from its very beginning. However, his interest did tend to focus on the one thing that was denied him down the long millennia, death: he had been there when Plato died, he was at the death-bed of Saint Augustine; he told us of the lonely, bitter death of the German Emperor, the fourth Henry, in Liège, and how he had accompanied the mortally ill Emperor Charles V on the mild late summer's day when he took his last walk round the garden of San Yuste; and Mr. Ahasuerus had been there on the dark and gloomy November day when Hofrat Leibnitz died in Hanover and, of course, on 15th May 1821 he had been on St. Helena.

He told us how he kept putting his immortality to the test. Once he had decided to cross the Arctic on foot. Eight years it had taken him, but his curse protected him like a cruel guardian angel and there had been no mercy for him.

"I'm sure", Dr. Jacobi said quietly to me, "that you must have heard the shot on board the river steamer?"

"Yes."

"It was Alfred who fired the shot. Thanks to Weckenbarth's connections we (you were up on deck talking to Don Emanuele Da Ceneda) had just learnt what was about to happen. At that Alfred drew a revolver and fired at Mr. Ahasuerus. He said that if the end of the world had not yet come, then the shot would not kill Ahasuerus because he could not die before the end of the world. If the end of the world had come he would die anyway."

"And the shot did not kill him?" I asked, pointing to Mr. Ahasuerus.

"As you can see, no. But what did not occur to Lord Alfred was that although Ahasuerus enjoys limited immortality, he does not enjoy freedom from pain. Before, they used to play cards together, now they're not talking to each other. Besides, the bullet ruined one of Ahasuerus' favourite waistcoats — two holes, one at the front and one at the back, not to mention the damage to his shirt and vest."

"We are lucky to have Mr. Ahasuerus and his stories. We were going to be a little short of entertainment with the books only painted on the walls."

"We had planned a library of six million volumes, but like so much else the plan was not realised. A few people, at least, have brought books of their own; a minimal number, of course, and a rather haphazard collection."

"I am against any kind of compulsion, especially in the field of culture", I said, "but I will consider whether I should not propose in the Senate that all books should be publicly registered. That would enable us to set up a card index and introduce a strictly-organised system of lending and borrowing; at least the books would be available to anyone who is interested."

"Not at all a bad idea", said Dr. Jacobi. "One could also incorporate an appeal to all those who know a work by heart, even if it is only a short poem, to come forward and have it recorded by the Literature Office. Perhaps we would find people who could work together to reconstruct the 'Odyssey', say, or 'Faust'."

"There is one poem I know by heart", I said. "It is by the great composer/poet, Otto Jägermeier:

There was a young lawyer from Munich
Whose courtroom appearance was unique:
    He of course wore a wig,
    But the leaf of a fig
Formed the whole of the rest of his tunic."

"Oh yes", said Dr. Jacobi, "dear old Jägermeier. He disappeared in Madagascar, you know. I was acquainted with his first, and only, biographer, Max Steinitzer, a friend of Richard Strauß. I know a Jägermeier poem too:

Great Uncle Otto from Husum
Was possessed of a very fine bosom.
    But those two shapely breasts
    Led to such cruel jests,

He really was desperate to lose 'em."

Weckenbarth had been listening. He turned round. "Do you know the correspondence between Jägermeier and his translator? Jägermeier complained that the 'Husum/bosom' rhyme was not very pure, but accepted the translator's explanation that the Yorkshire pronunciation of 'bosom' would both supply the perfect rhyme and fit in with the Northern setting of the poem. But allow me to make my own contribution to the reconstruction of Jägermeier's poetic oeuvre:

A young organist from Buxtehude
Played his instrument nuder and nuder.
    Said the vicar, verbatim,
    'I shall have to castrate him,
Before his fingering gets any ruder'."

Now Mr. Ahasuerus' sonorous voice joined in as he announced, "An apocryphal poem by Jägermeier:

Herr Johann Joachim Quantz
Composed a ballet for ants.
    But Frederick the Great
    Was very irate
And made Quantz dance with ants in his pants."

"Did you know", I said, "that Frederick II of Prussia was in reality an Austrian lieutenant who had swapped places with him?"

"What nonsense", said Weckenbarth.

"If you permit, I'll explain the theory to you – it's not my own, by the way:

There are many puzzling aspects about both the life and person of Frederick II of Prussia, whom the Prussians themselves call 'the Great', which until recently have remained unexplained. Why, for example, did he only speak French? Why could he play the flute before the Silesian Wars and not after? What about his relationship with his wife? With his brother

Heinrich? What about his symphonies, which he had Graun compose but published as his own, even though in his youth he had composed himself? Why did he become a skinflint after 1742? As I said, it was only recently that the historical researches of Zwi Ygdrasilovic threw some surprising light on the life of Frederick II which still had some blank spots, despite being so well-charted.

The key to the events is the battle of Mollwitz on 10th April, 1741. The battle turned out very well for the Prussians. The military talents of the Austrian General, Neippberg, were hardly a threat to the Prussian victory, but Frederick's obstinate orders were; so much so, in fact, that the Prussian General, Schwerin, in a histrionic portrayal of despair – he is said to have bitten the King's boot – that has gone down in history, led Frederick to believe defeat was close at hand. He begged the King to leave the battlefield immediately otherwise he, Schwerin, would not be able to guarantee his life and liberty. Muttering to himself, Frederick climbed on his horse and rode off towards Oppeln which, however, had been occupied by a squadron of Hungarian Czaky Hussars. The unsuspecting Frederick demanded entry at the gates of Oppeln. According to official Prussian historiography Lieutenant Werner of the Hungarian Hussars is said to have recognised the King but ('Let me go, laddie; me reward you', the King is supposed to have said) not taken him captive. On his way back Frederick is said to have heard the news of the victory at Mollwitz.

Thus the official version. It is a fraud. In fact Werner did capture King Frederick. He was taken to a castle in Hungary. Maria Theresa immediately began secret negotiations with the Prussian High Command. General von Schwerin, who was not at all unhappy to lose His Royal Hindrance and had as far as possible hushed up Frederick's capture, refused to ransom the King. As a result the Austrians were no longer sure whether the dubious character they had captured really was the King, but they still made sure he was closely guarded and that the castle where he was confined was kept top secret.

Charles Alexander, Prince of Lorraine, who had just resigned the Austrian High Command in a fit of pique, racked his brains for a long time over the problem and came up with the idea – apparently brilliant, but, as it was later to turn out, with serious, not to say tragic consequences – of misleading enemy agents by keeping a double of the King imprisoned in a not-quite-so-secret castle. A lieutenant was found in the Austrian army who bore a remarkable similarity to Frederick, a certain Diodat Chaos, Baron von Richtberg. Chaos was deputed to be the pseudo-Frederick and sent to be imprisoned in Schloß Salaberg by Haag, in the keeping of Count Sprinzenstein, who suspected nothing.

The enemy agents were so completely mislead that the Austrians, under the personal direction of the Empress, were able to use the line of communication established by the outmanoeuvred Prussian secret police to transmit highly confusing royal commands to the enemy camp. It almost led to Austria winning the war. Maria Theresa is said to have laughed so much at the affair that it resulted in one of her many miscarriages.

The poor woman laughed on the other side of her face when the enemy agents succeeded – incidentally *against* the express orders of Schwerin, who knew when he was well-off – in liberating the wrong Frederick. Maria Theresa immediately offered them the genuine article, which was rejected with sneers of derision, and a pamphlet explaining the true course of events was promptly declared a piece of crude Austrian propaganda. The impostor was understandably careful not to give away his real identity of Lieutenant Chaos. He had no idea what the Prussians might do to someone impersonating Frederick. He continued to play the King. But it turned out that the 'King' – surprise, surprise – was now a quite different King. Not only did he gradually start to give evidence of remarkable talents as a military leader, the Prussians also observed in him a thrift verging on the miserly, a hereditary characteristic of the Chaotic family which history has attached to the name of Frederick. The costs of the court household were reduced to 200,000 guilders per annum, an amount that Louis XV of France spent on ironing the shoe-laces of his reserve double-bass players alone. In order to conceal his ignorance of the Prussian dialect Chaos, alias Frederick, spoke only French from that moment on. Although completely unmusical, Chaos did try to play the flute – at first he took it for a kind of billiards cue – but Quantz immediately became suspicious. So Frederick, that is Chaos, declared that a persistent pimple on his lower lip made it impossible for him to play the flute any more and that he had decided to devote himself from now on to literature, an art, as he thought, where lack of talent would not be spotted, or at least not very quickly. He gave up composition. Philipp Spitta dated Frederick's last compositions at 1753, but musicologists, independently of the researches of Zwi Ygdrasilovic, have long since doubted the authenticity of all pieces after 1741. His favourite brother, Prince Heinrich, was sent to Rheinsberg, and the Queen – who would have been better qualified to see through the imposture? – to Schönhausen after which, in the delicate words of official historiography, he renounced married life, never visited the Queen and only saw her on gala occasions when he occasionally waved to her. The precise detail in which the whole affair of the fake Frederick was worked out is shown by the case of Lieutenant Werner, the Hussar who, according to the official version, had let him go at Oppeln. When he entered the service of the fake Frederick, Chaos, in a mockery of the true circumstances, promoted him in recognition of his services to the rank of general.

All in all, a tragedy for Austria: with the authentic Frederick, an authentic bungler, in command, Prussia would never have won the Silesian Wars. It was only through Lieutenant Chaos that Austria, as so often, like an inverted Munchhausen, pulled itself by its own hair down into the mire.

One interesting aspect was the fate of the genuine Frederick who, initially furious, later resigned, was a mere spectator of the course of history. What more natural than – a typically Austrian solution – to fill the vacant person, so to speak, of Lieutenant Chaos with the real Frederick. Frederick was appointed – no one noticed the deception – director of the Linz theatre (this has been established by the distinguished historian of Linz, Ludwig Plakolb), was a failure there as well and ended up as second flute in the Theater auf der Wieden in Vienna. Emanuel Schickaneder, initiated as always into abstruse matters, was well aware of what he was doing when he wrote 'The Magic *Flute*' for that particular theatre. Years after the death of his double he played the second flute at the first performance and lived on for a further five years until his own death in 1796, surrounded by his numerous offspring. In the course of the next two generations a series of almost incestuous marriages made the relationships of his offspring so tangled that even the members of the family were no longer quite sure who was related to whom in what degree, who was the uncle or aunt and who was the nephew or niece. In Vienna it became known as Chaotic family relationships ..."

For a while all were silent. Then Weckenbarth said with a smile, "Is Ygdrasilovic here in the cigar as well?"

"I'm afraid not", I replied.

"Then we at least will be safe from his further researches. He could end up proving that Cleopatra was in reality a transvestite called Leo; or that Hitler was a woman and General Udet only committed suicide out of unrequited love for him – sorry, her."

"No", I said, slightly put out, "he can't do that any more."

"The five acts of *The World*", said Dr. Jacobi, "are over."

"What about us?" said the President, not without a hint of reproach.

"Your official optimism is commendable", said Weckenbarth.

Dr. Jacobi was enjoying the situation. "We are the epilogue, so to speak", he said with a smile. "We are not really alive any more. We are superfluous. Who would deny it? There's no question of any more 'action'."

"But", I said, "if what I heard just before wasn't dramatic action I –" and I began to tell them what Colonel Schweythauszsz had told me about the woman who had roasted her daughter.

"We were already aware of that", said Weckenbarth.

"The woman", said Dr. Jacobi, "is not the mother of the child at all. She is a witch called Bertha ..."

"And now I suppose you're going to tell me she's the witch Bertha from Scotland at the time of King Nathalocus ..."

"Quite correct."

"My God", I said, "Daphnis, the dancer who knew that I

prefer dark beer to light, he'll be dead now too!"

"Bertha the witch – she calls herself Pedauque, 'with the big foot', now; she has a swan's foot like all witches – has been given the position of adjutant in the General Staff because of her great spiritualistic powers. Sabotage has put her *hors de combat*. Just as a hunting dog's nose can be ruined by ammonia, someone has blocked her medial channels by casting an *Uza* on her."

"What kind of *Uza*?" asked Mr. Ahasuerus.

"We don't precisely know. I suspect some kind of animal magic, perhaps by killing a sacred beetle in a magic bowl – there are instructions for that spell in the Harris Magical Papyrus. But the Doctor favours a name-*Uza*, he believes that those outside have learnt her real name ... it's not impossible."

"Whichever it is", said Don Emanuele, "we have locked up the witch and confiscated the child. Who knows what use we might find for it."

"The enemy outside", said the President, "is certainly more dangerous than we assumed. – But now it's time to leave for the premiere."

"Premiere?" I asked.

"Nankeen's Music Hall", said the President.

"The scoundrel promised to send me an invitation", I said. "He hasn't, but anyway, I have no white tie and tails."

"No tails?"

"Where should I get tails from?"

"You don't need to get any. The wardrobe supplied to all Senators contains evening dress. Another thing: I summoned you – but that does not mean you had to come immediately – you were not present at the last meeting of the Senate."

"I am terribly sorry, Your Magnificence."

"Call me Carola, chéri – you missed the distribution of responsibilities and so you have no portfolio."

"Dreadful", I said.

"It doesn't matter", she said, "I have a real task for you. You know Alfred?"

"Our Alfred?"

"Yes. Do you know who he is?"

"No."

275

"Lord Alfred Coenwulph Herbrand Plantagenet Waldegrave, second son of the fourteenth Duke of Glenfinnan and Marquess of Broadford."

"Yes?" I said.

"It's a very tricky question. Lord Alfred is the only scion of the Waldegrave family that managed to make it to the cigar. As it is to be assumed therefore that his father and brother – the eldest son and heir to the title – are dead, he, as second son, will inherit the title."

"What is tricky about that?"

"The tricky part is to decide which Duke of Glenfinnan Lord Alfred becomes. His father was the fourteenth Duke; if Lord Alfred's brother died before their father, then Lord Alfred will be the direct heir, that is the fifteenth Duke. If, however, their father died before his eldest son then the latter, even if only for a few seconds, was the fifteenth Duke, and Lord Alfred would accordingly be the sixteenth Duke of Glenfinnan. You see the problem?"

"Hm", I said, "it will be impossible to decide."

"You'll find something, chéri. And since you have been entrusted with this critical task, chéri, it is naturally impossible for you to remain a mere Senator. I hereby appoint you Gentleman of the Bedchamber. That gives you the right to wear a navy blue shoulder-ribbon, and your servant gloves of the same colour. It also confers the privilege of opening and closing my zips – a kind of echo of the original significance of the title. I'll see you in the box, then?"

I went, accompanied by Spring, back to my apartment.

"Spring", I said as we walked along, "do you by any chance also know this Mr. Daphnis and all that?"

"Whyever not?"

"And Bertha the witch?"

"At your service, Your Eminence."

"The dancer did not quite finish the story of King Nathalocus of Scotland –"

"I know. Up to what point do you know the story, Your Eminence?"

"To the point where Good King Nathalocus in his ignorance

sent the friend of his bosom, Findoch," — I found I was imitating the style of the dancer's old book, — "to seek out the Witch Bertha, in order that she might by her powers of divination reveal what the fates held in store for him; the point, therefore, when the witch saw that the hour of her vengeance was come."

"Then Your Eminence is acquainted with almost all the facts, there is not much more to tell. The witch thought up an audacious and extremely effective means of destroying the King, and his friend as well. When Lord Findoch entered her bothy and asked what the future held for the King, she replied that ere long the King would die at the hand of one of his Lords. And when Findoch, in deep distress, asked, 'By the hand of which Lord?', the witch replied, 'By yours'. As this was an answer the loyal Lord Findoch could not well take back to his King — it would like as not have meant his own death — and as, on the other hand, he would never have ventured to lie to his King, his only expedient was to kill the King for answer, although he had served him faithfully his whole life long.

This made it uncertain whether the witch had merely foretold the murder or carried it out by subtle means. The line of Findocus however, who became King after Nathalocus, was to come to an extremely troubled end. During the reign of his great-grandson, King Crathilind — son of his grandson Donaldus III, grandson of his son Donaldus II — in the year CCCVIII AD, the King's favourite hound was lost and ran across the border between the Scottes and the Pictes, with whom there was constant feuding, and when a keeper sought to find the hound a war broke out because the keeper did cross ye bordere without ye consent of ye Pictische Kyninge, and Crathilinde, his sonnes and all his thanes were done to dethe by ye Pictes."

"And the witch?"

"She's managed to keep going to the so-called present."

"How do you come to know all this?"

"Ach weel", said Spring, "translated into Old Scots, Spring is 'Findoch' —"

We were outside my warren. Over the door a red light was burning.

"What does the light mean?" I asked.

"As a Gentleman of the Bedchamber Your Eminence has the right to a red light over the door."

"Oh", I said, "Carola didn't mention that, I almost thought this was a brothel. Or that I had been made a midwife instead of a Gentleman of the Bedchamber. They both have red lights. It led to an unfortunate mistake in my family: when my mother was about to give birth to me, my father went to the wrong red light ... Evening dress, Spring."

The trousers fitted perfectly. Over the shirt front and waist-coat a six-inch navy-blue sash with white marbling at the edge ran from shoulder to waist. Instead of the Senatorial ribbon, Spring told me, a purple rosette was worn on the left sleeve. Then he handed me the coat and a top hat.

"What for?" I asked.

"It looks bad if we have nothing to hand in at the cloakroom."

We set off. And Nankeen had remembered me after all. At the apartment I found a letter from him with a programme attached, inviting me to the premiere.

At the front of the middle box (it was a different theatre, larger than the one I had seen through the mirror whilst I was washing my hands) sat the President, on her left Dr. Jacobi in violet robes with a white Latin cross over his heart on his cloak; then came Don Emanuele in evening dress with black shirt, tie and waist-coat, and on Carola's right-hand side Alfred, Fifteenth – or was it Sixteenth – Duke of Glenfinnan. The end seat was free. I took it and looked down into the stalls. In solitary splendour in the front row sat Herr Uvesohn. He waved to me.

Not all the instruments were there yet and the orchestra was tuning up and chatting. There was the clatter of people coming and going in the upper circles, the open doors let in a hint of the splendour of the foyer filled with golden light. Someone was hammering behind the curtain.

I glanced at the programme, and my head spun. It said:

"For the very first time:
ENDYMEON
and (or)

THE BASS FIDDLER OF WÖRGL
or
AND OR OR
Subtitle: A pantomime for the blind

A more precise designation of the manner of the piece:
1. Serenata notturna teatrale o radiofonica.
2. Serenade for Wireless Operator.
3. Serenade for Sparks.
4. Sparkling serenade.
5. Serenata notturna brillante.
The characters and actors: ..."

"You look pale?"
I gave a start. The President had leant across Lord Alfred
Coenwulph etc Plantagenet etc – who remained as silent as ever
– to address me.
"The play ..." I said. "I would never have thought that this
play –"
"The play by your friend Uvesohn?"
The theatre suddenly went dark. My blood ran hot and cold
– that Pomeranian scribbler had had the cheek to put on my play
– the devil only knows how he got hold of the manuscript – as
his own!
But there was an even more devastating surprise, if that were
possible, in store for me: in the darkened theatre my – my! –
voice rang out from a loudspeaker:
"As announced, it is a pantomime for the blind; in order,
therefore, to preserve the illusion, throughout the performance
the theatre will remain dark –

dark –

dark –"

Then voices were heard from the stage:
Acurator-Fiscal: Yes?
Muttering
Acurator-Fiscal: Speak clearly, if you please.
*Muttering from which the words 'Please ... petition ... cru-
saders ... first of August ...' can be heard.*

279

Acurator-Fiscal: Everyone mumbling at the same time doesn't make it any more audible.

Several voices: It concerns ...

Several others: ... the first of August ...

Third group: ... Peter of Amiens ...

Acurator-Fiscal: One at a time please. You there.

Coughing, then: It concerns two questions, Your Honour, which, at the stroke of a pen so to speak, can decide the fate of two enterprises ...

Acurator-Fiscal: Will you be so kind as to inform me whom I have the pleasure of addressing?

1st citizen: Visigoth Schniller.

Acurator-Fiscal: And the others?

Schniller: I only know half of them.

Further muttering.

Acurator-Fiscal: Are we going to have some silence, or aren't we? Someone from the other half step forward. You there.

2nd citizen: Anonymus Rosenbein is my name.

Acurator-Fiscal: Hm, hm. A strange first name.

Rosenbein: Actually, it's not an actual first name. Actually it's a non-first-name, Your Honour.

Acurator-Fiscal: What is it, then?

Rosenbein: I do not possess an actual one, a real first name. It's all the result of an unfortunate accident. At that time, at the time of my birth, that is sixty-nine years ago, the law governing the registration of births in the old Crown Province of Lodomeria required a new-born child to be given a first name within four weeks on pain of disembowelment. Do you know what disembowelment consisted of, Your Honour? In Lodomeria, in those days? Apart from people who broke the registration laws it was only applied to those who broke the forestry laws. The felon's belly was slit

open just enough for one end of the gut –
disinfected, of course – to be fixed to a tree
with a treasury tag. Then the offender was
obliged to walk around the tree – usually it
was a beech – until his or her guts were
threaded onto the trunk. If, as usually happened, the punishment led to the death of
the offender, the gut became by law public
property and was traditionally sent to –

Acurator-Fiscal: To the Court butcher's?

Rosenbein: Not at all, Your Honour – that would be
cannibalism, even if they only used them
for horsemeat sausages. No, they were sent
to the Philharmonic Orchestra to reduce
expenditure on strings for the bass fiddles:
it is well known that fiddlers refuse to play
on anything other than sheep gut.

Acurator-Fiscal: I see. So at the last moment your father –

Rosenbein: No, no, not my father – the Lord have
mercy on his soul – it would more like have
been my mother, but it was not her either;
my mother, God rest her soul, had already
been condemned to disembowelment –

Acurator-Fiscal: Ah! Your brother then is also called –

Rosenbein: No, for breaking the forestry regulations.
You see she –

Acurator-Fiscal: Keep to the point!

Rosenbein: Of course, your Honour. It required the
agreement of the Archbishop of Kalocsa
before the punishment could be carried out
on a pregnant woman. But just at that time
there were two circumstances which coin-
cided. The one was that the Archiespicopal
See of Kalocsa happened to be vacant and
remained vacant for some considerable
time because the candidate favoured by the
Emperor had not yet been received into
holy orders, while the candidate favoured

by the Lodomerian Estates General, a certain Szlypczod, had not yet been baptised. The second circumstance was that my mother, before she became my mother, had – there is no other way of putting it – had her wicked way with a prison warder, of which I am the fruit, so to speak. His name was Rimpel. He had a certain talent as a painter and became famous for his peasant nudes, which had a tendency towards the gynaecological and which earned him the nickname *Titian Bums*. For his pains – and given the fact that the act took place through the prison bars, that was probably the right word – the warder was transferred to another prison. But the vacancy of the See of Kalocsa did at least make it possible for my mother to bring me into the world. It was with tears in my eyes that later, on the occasion of my confirmation, I told His Excellency Baron von Schlippschott, who had finally managed to assume the archiepiscopal mitre as Anthony of Padua XIII, that I regarded him as my real, my actual father. After an initial and quite natural misunderstanding, he took me in his arms and embraced me.

Despite the pleas, the entreaties of the whole of the staff of the Lodomerian Registry Office my mother could not be brought to give me a first name within the time limit. Not even the affecting words of His Imperial Majesty's personal Aide de Camp – at that time one Luitpold-Agamemnon, Count Saint-John-Zamoyski of Pimodan, the one who was so well-known because of his wooden leg that he always used to beat his wife with, she came from the Almássy-Bretzenheim family – who finally went to see her, could shake her out of her obstinacy. She stuck to the view that as she was to be disembowelled anyway she could not give a fig for the fact that she would be given the same punishment for breaking the registration law. Since, for reasons that will be obvious, it is almost impossible to disembowel a person twice, the whole of the Lodomerian Civil Service was at its wits' end.

Acurator-Fiscal: A recalcitrant subject, your mother!

Rosenbein: They eventually found a solution, though not a very satisfactory one: the court decreed that my mother had to feel one half of the pain of disembowelling as a punishment for breaking forestry regulations, the other half as a punishment for breaking the registration law.

Acurator-Fiscal: The only result of that would be to make her laugh at being disembowelled!

Rosenbein: And I still had no first name. As, once the legal time limit had passed, no one can be given a first name, there was nothing for it but to call myself Anonymus.

Acurator-Fiscal: A dangerous precedent. It could lead to irresponsible parents ignoring the legal time limit – to cock a snook at authority or simply as a joke – and then, whilst they are being disembowelled, wallowing in the discomfiture of the poor civil servants at the fact that there is one more Anonymus to be dealt with. Is Anonymus a first name or is it not? If it is, then it is ruled out by law, so it can't be ... I won't even start to go into the problem, but I feel for those who have to. I hope, Herr Schniller, that your no less remarkable first name is not the result of a

	similarly anarchistic attitude?
Schniller:	By no means. But perhaps I might be permitted to leave the – unsolved – problem of my first name on one side for the moment to return to the problems which have brought us here –
Acurator-Fiscal:	Oh what a lack of imagination! To return to problems with a first name like yours, Visigoth. Do you know what I was christened? Rubicon!
Schniller:	Just Rubicon? Not even Rubicon-Maria?
Acurator-Fiscal, *shyly:*	
	Rubicon Theseus Ansegisil Salvator.
Schniller:	That's nice.

Deafening thunder. Rain. Files get wet. The muttering turns to screaming. A sonorous bass voice:

	STOP!
Acurator-Fiscal:	That'll be the Goddess Minerva, God bless her.
Minerva:	I will not put up with it any longer. It's time something happened! The audience has been sitting here for an hour already and still there isn't the slightest sign of a dramatic development. I will take matters in hand myself.

Two bearded cherubs bring an embroidered cushion which, by means of artfully placed buttonholes, they attach to two buttons on the rear of the Goddess, at hip height. The Goddess then sits down, in the process automatically cushioning the chair of the Acurator-Fiscal.

Minerva:	Who are you?
Acurator-Fiscal, *shaking his head:*	
	So direct!
Rosenbein:	We are the ballet group of the Emperor Francis Joseph Memorial Old Folks' Home.
Minerva:	And you over there?
Schniller:	We are the choir of the State Sanatorium for

	the Tubercular.
Minerva:	And what is your request?
Rosenbein:	We have been mixed up, Your Deity.
Schniller:	And we don't know whether the first of August is according to the Greek or the Roman calendar.
Minerva:	One thing at a time. Who mixed you up?
Rosenbein:	The typesetter of the Official Gazette.
Minerva:	Hm. What can we do about it?
Acurator-Fiscal,	*in desperation, though actually more in irritation:*
	Once a thing is set, it is set.
Minerva:	With whom have you been mixed up?
Rosenbein:	They with us, us with them. We, that is the Ballet Group of the Emperor Francis Joseph Memorial Old Folks' Home, were supposed to present a mime show for the inmates of the Deaf-and-Dumb High School on the nine hundred and fifty-sixth anniversary of the arrival of the First Crusade at Constantinople, whilst they, the Choir of the State Sanatorium for the Tubercular, were supposed to perform a cantata in the Hostel for the Blind on the self-same occasion. And the typesetter has mixed up the announcements -- we are to dance for the blind, while they are to sing for the deaf and dumb.
Schniller:	Added to which we do not know whether the first of August, the day on which the auspicious event falls, should be worked out according to the Greek calendar, because the Army of the Crusaders arrived in *Constantinople,* or according to the Latin calendar, because the *Army of the Crusaders* arrived in Constantinople?
Minerva:	It was the typesetter who mixed you up?
Rosenbein:	Yes.

285

Minerva:	Hmm. We could make him take compulsory retirement.
Acurator-Fiscal:	Or have him disembowelled?
Rosenbein:	What about our mime show?
Minerva:	If it's in the Official Gazette ... I don't know.
Acurator-Fiscal:	I have my doubts too.
Minerva:	STOP! – again. Where are these performances to take place?
Rosenbein:	In the Great Hall.
Minerva:	In which Great Hall?
Rosenbein:	That of the institution concerned.
Minerva:	Does it say so in the Official Gazette?
Rosenbein:	Well, it's implied.
Minerva:	Naturally we cannot tamper with the arrangement for them to take place in the Great Hall, but we hereby decree that both events shall take place in the same ...

Rejoicing

Minerva:	Quiet, if you please! ... Great Hall. I stipulate that the blind must commit themselves to try as hard as possible to see the ballet and the deaf and dumb to hear the cantata.
Schniller:	And on which first of August.
Minerva:	That will be decided by the Rota Romana.

'Terrible', I thought – the lights went up in the auditorium.

I found myself in the seat next to the President, where Lord Alfred had been sitting – now he was sitting at the end on the right – and my head was resting in Carola's arms and on her breast. On my forehead was a lace handkerchief soaked in eau de cologne ...

"Ah, you've come round at last, chéri", said the President, "I was just about to send for an ambulanceman!"

I sat up.

"You fainted", said Dr. Jacobi. "Do you feel sick?"

I was bemused.

"Endymeon –" I said.

"Sorry?" said the President.

"Do I feel sick?" I laughed. I may have felt sick before, but now I felt better than ever.

'Thank God', I thought, 'I never wrote a play anything like that!'

On the stage Nankeen's chorus girls were dancing in a red light, turning round in a circle, one leg in the air, smiling at the audience.

"Did I miss anything?" I asked the President.

"Hardly anything at all", she said. "In the first scene a girl came onto the stage and took a poster out of a dustbin. She unrolled the poster. On it was another girl wearing a bikini. Obviously that made the girl on the stage want a bikini. She took two scraps of cloth out of the dustbin, undressed, crouching behind the bin, and put her clothes on a bench. Then came a man with another dustbin. The girl hurriedly jumped into the first bin. The man saw the clothes, that appeared not to belong to anyone, and threw them into the bin he was carrying, then he found the two scraps of material, threw them into the same bin and heaved it onto his shoulder. He was probably from the Refuse Department. He also took the other bin, but that had no bottom – the girl was left sitting naked in the street, stripped by her own initiative. The audience clapped."

"And the girl?"

"Didn't move. The curtain fell."

"Hm", I said, "at most that could have been the exposition."

Now the chorus were dancing in a green light, smiling all the time. Then they jigged off the stage.

The curtain came down, but rose again immediately to reveal a snow-covered landscape with eight snowmen standing in a semi-circle. A man and a woman were dancing round the snowmen and pretending to skate, it looked amazingly genuine, and then played tag – presumably a kind of courtship, the orchestra was playing Tchaikovsky – and when, finally, the couple danced together, Cupid appeared on a swing and shot an arrow. The male partner caught the arrow and tore it apart, and it turned into a huge heart. The heart began to shine with a dazzling light, at which the snowmen melted and out of each snowman leapt a chorus girl clad in scraps of snow. The ex-snowmen danced on with a sleigh, the couple sat in it and were hauled off by the chorus.

There followed a scene in which the chorus, dressed as Dutch girls mainly in bonnets and clogs, danced round a windmill from which a cow sang 'Mammy'.

Then followed the interval.

Weckenbarth was whispering to Lord Alfred, Dr. Jacobi was listening and looking serious. Don Emanuele had gone out.

In all innocence I went up to Dr. Jacobi and asked what had happened.

With a few dismissive, cutting words Weckenbarth put me in my place, as if I were not a Senator, not a Gentleman of the Bedchamber, but any Tom, Dick or Harry from the gallery, a schoolboy who had had the temerity to enter the staff common room. I prefer not to record his actual words.

The President took me by the arm and drew me, as if to comfort me, back into the box. We sat down.

"Don't get angry", said Carola. "They are doing it to protect you."

"What from?"

She was silent.

"It seems to me that something must have happened. Tell me the truth."

"Nothing has happened", she said, turning away from me, "nothing."

"Is it serious?" I asked.

"Sorry?"

"I ask for a straightforward explanation of what's going on and why Weckenbarth is behaving in such a mysterious manner, and you pretend you don't understand. If anyone has a right to be puzzled, it's me."

"What a tone of voice, chéri."

"I'm sorry, but I feel I'm slowly going mad – don't you feel the same?"

"I feel quite normal."

"I miss time in here, the resistance, the frictional heat generated by the fear of growing older, when we struggle against it; it was pointless but nevertheless refreshing. I'll not even bother mentioning fresh trout, which we have presumably seen the last of for the rest of our lives, or a good night's sleep. What I feel is missing is any necessity to demonstrate *élan vital*. What is life down here? I hardly know if you could still call it life, this damned eternal day-in-night, without hours, without dates, without seasons, perhaps even without death ... Is the life of the Wandering Jew really *life*? You see! Do you realise now what it means to say 'It is death that gives meaning to life'? We will make any kind of effort as long as we can see that it has some point, that it proves our identity. Time stretching out before us is the claypit from which we form bricks to build our stronghold against death. Once the stronghold is built, the clay that was our life has been all used up. To raise an eternal stronghold, we have to cast the clay of our mortality into the fire, lump by lump. We cannot have both, the stronghold and the clay. We cannot combine immortality and eternal life in this world. Chérie, I feel as if I am about to burst with lethargy, don't you feel the same?"

"That was the first time you said 'chérie' to me ..."

The bell rang. The interval was over, but the others did not come back. I asked where they were.

"I don't think they will be able to see the second part of the show", said Carola.

"Why not?"

"Ssh, the lights are going down."

After a short overture Nankeen's chorus girls reappeared and hopped around the stage in constantly-changing multi-coloured light.

Then a conjurer came on and did a few card tricks. From a distance one could not see how they were done. After some short applause he asked a young lady from the audience to come up onto the stage. The young lady was in evening dress with which, rather oddly, she was wearing a riding hat. First of all he magicked away her evening dress, then her petticoats – she was wearing three – then her shoes, which made her do a nice little hop and a skip, and then her stockings. Finally he set to work on her underwear, item by item, until the young lady was standing there on the stage, her arms just about covering her breasts, the riding hat on her head, wearing black panties. The conjurer witched away her panties; like lightning the young lady snatched the riding hat from her head and, leaving her breasts unguarded, held it over her *pudenda*. The conjurer made a grand gesture, the girl looked around anxiously, there was a rumbling of basses and drums, everyone held their breath, there came a resounding crash from the orchestra – and the conjurer had made the girl disappear, only the hat still hung motionless in the air on the same spot. The girl came back on stage in a golden dressing gown, put the hat back on and took her bow with the conjurer.

"Well", said Carola, "still in a bad mood?"

"If it wasn't all prearranged, it must have been devilish embarrassing to be undressed without warning on the stage like that. I am delighted that you are in a box and cannot be dragged on stage by the conjurer for such a performance."

"Well, you know, with such a close-fitting dress I would have had to grab my hat after the very first *abracadabra* and, as you can see, I haven't got one on ..."

There had been a hurricane of applause. The conjurer had to agree to repeat the scene. He asked a very old woman from the audience to come up. The audience hissed and booed, at which the conjurer tried to send her back, but the lady insisted on making her appearance on stage. With a sigh the conjurer made her disappear immediately.

Then he persuaded another young girl to come up. She was wearing a red dress, but the conjurer had obviously been distracted by the incident with the old lady and instead of the girl's red dress, he magicked his own trousers away. He dashed into the wings to fetch his trousers and put them on again amid expressions of regret. Then he made the girl's clothes disappear in the right order, one by one. When he had reached her black and white striped lace basque a man dashed up onto the stage claiming to be her fiancé and shouting furious threats. The conjurer watched him for a while and then made a pass with his hand and the man was turned into an aspidistra. With an imperious smile but no further interruptions he reduced her wardrobe to a pair of – lime-green – panties. The girl was not wearing a hat but she had the presence of mind to turn her back on the audience who, with no thought for the girl's embarrassment, were going wild with enthusiasm. The conjurer obliged them by laying bare her buttocks, then he bowed and started to leave the stage. The girl gave a little scream. The conjurer stopped, clutched his brow with a smile of apology for his absent-mindedness, made a magic sign and in place of the girl a mouse darted across the stage and into the prompt-box. With a scream of horror the prompter leapt out of the box. The prompter was also a young woman.

The conjurer, who was now well into his stride, made her dress vanish as well. The prompter shrieked and ran to and fro, trying to get down from the stage but, with baying encouragement from the audience, her clothes were whipped off mercilessly. In desperation she held tight to her herring-blue panties, but it was no use – they whirled away as if sucked up by a whirlwind. Stark naked, she climbed up the curtain and hid in the folds. The conjurer made another magic sign. There was a crash of thunder and lightning, the curtain swung to, and there on it was the image of the naked prompter embroidered in pearls.

The audience was beside itself with applause.

The conjurer came out in front of the curtain, bowed, made a sign and four ladies from the audience fled squealing to the cloakroom ...

I looked across at Carola: she was still wearing her glove-tight, honey-coloured evening gown. However the conjurer was forcibly dragged behind the curtain before he could make anything else disappear.

Understandably the acts that followed found it difficult to retain our attention. Nevertheless, by the time the show came to a close in a frenzied finale I had forgotten Weckenbarth and the others.

They had not put in an appearance at all during the whole of the second part of the show, not even those wretched mechanical dwarves who had been hanging around at the back of the box until the interval. Now, however, after Nankeen had bowed time and time again to the audience and the frenetic applause had finally died away and we came out of the box into the foyer, I found them assembled there. They said nothing and made a great show of being occupied: Weckenbarth was uncorking a bottle of champagne, Dr. Jacobi was winding a laurel wreath round a goblet, Don Emanuele and Lord Alfred were unrolling a red carpet out through the double doors into the promenade area. From baskets the dwarves were scattering rose-petals – artificial ones presumably. Outside a group of onlookers had gathered. Spring was busy with other liveried colleagues keeping the crowd under control and a narrow passage free. My fellow-writer, Uvesohn, waved to me from the excited throng.

Through a side door the two horns, the trumpets and the three trombones from the orchestra slipped in, spat into their mouthpieces and quietly tried a note or two before Alfred positioned them at the back of the foyer between two columns.

Now the cheers could be heard. The musicians took up their instruments. Weckenbarth filled the glasses and handed each of us one. His own and the wreathed goblet he placed on a tray. We arranged ourseles in a semi-circle, and then Nankeen arrived ...

A flourish from the brass; 'Hip hip hurray!' from a thousand throats. Weckenbarth handed him the laurel-wreath goblet, the dwarves threw the rest of the rose-petals in the air so that they rained down on the hero of the evening. Don Emanuele crowned the impresario with an olive branch. Now Weckenbarth raised his glass, the brass played a long fanfare and everyone drank Nankeen's health. I was still unaware of the depths of hypocrisy my friends were at that moment descending to ...

I had the idea of dashing my glass to the floor when I had emptied it. Everyone followed suit, last of all Nankeen who first kissed the laurel wreath.

Then we shook him by the hand and he presented his artistes: the conjurer, the dancers, the bandleader.

Dr. Jacobi turned to me, "Terrible. At this moment he is surely the happiest man alive."

"Why terrible?" I said.

He looked at me in surprise. The others had formed a procession to leave. At the head went Nankeen, then Weckenbarth, followed by the President and Lord Alfred, then came Dr.

Jacobi, Don Emanuele and myself, the dwarves and all the rest. We had to form Indian file to push our way through the rejoicing crowd, then everything came to a halt. They had lifted Nankeen up on their shoulders. Once more the cheers rang out and the uniforms had to step in to separate the crowd a little. Finally we made our escape with Nankeen into a side passage. The musicians were dismissed and we went to the room with the club chairs where I had been reunited with my friends after we had escaped into the cigar.

There was a cold collation and here, too, the champagne had been put on ice.

Gradually things calmed down. I was talking to the bandleader, a Herr Franzelin from Brunico, when Weckenbarth joined us.

I do not easily bear a grudge and I forgot the hurt he had caused me the moment he spoke to me with all his old friendliness:

"My dear *Conpater* and Gentleman of the Bedchamber, could I have a word with you in private?"

We went over to the fireplace.

"I have some secret information to pass on to you which neither may nor should be kept from you, as Senator: a spider – *a living spider* – has been found inside the cigar. And what is worse, we haven't caught it yet. It may already have young ..."

He gave me a tap on the shoulder and went off.

The party was beginning to break up. The guests left until we, the President's associates, were the only ones left, plus Nankeen.

No one spoke.

Nankeen, who had been talking to Don Emanuele, suddenly found himself alone. He looked around in alarm. The two mechanical dwarves were approaching. He retreated, dropping his glass. Then he screamed. The dwarves hit him on the hip with the flat of their hands. Nankeen fell to the ground, still screaming. I did not know whether I should help Nankeen and looked over to Weckenbarth. He was looking at Nankeen and the dwarves; his expression was not just serious, it was that of a priest officiating at a solemn rite. I no longer knew what to think.

The dwarves seized Nankeen. At first he struggled, but once the dwarves had a stranglehold on him he gave up. Then they dragged him out by the feet. Weckenbarth, Don Emanuele and Dr. Jacobi followed with funereal faces. I was about to join them, but Carola held me back.

"We go that way." She pointed at the main door. Outside Spring was waiting with two of the President's attendants.

"Tell me, what does it all mean?"

"*Gardez aux serviteurs* ..."

We came to Carola's rooms, which had the same fox's lair layout as my own, only they were more extensive and more expensively furnished.

Spring and the attendants saluted and stayed behind. We crossed a wide state room at the end of which a maid was waiting; Carola sent her away. Then we entered the central room of her suite. It looked like the setting for the first scene of a particularly lavish production of *Der Rosenkavalier*. In the middle of the room, like a great galleon riding at anchor, was a four-poster bed with purple drapes. On the wall I noticed a small copper-engraving. It showed a fat old man surrounded by seven young girls. The man was wearing decorations and sitting in an armchair.

"I know that man", I said.

"A family heirloom", said Carola.

"Did you manage to save your heirlooms in the rush or did you just happen to have it on you?"

"This girl here is my great-grandmother. The others are her sisters. The man is their uncle. He was the famous castrato, Torroni. His sister, my great-great-grandmother, was a singer, perhaps even more famous than he – Giuseppina Torroni, known as La Forlisana. Unfortunately her seven daughters do not testify to an irreproachable life; you see, each one has a different father."

"The story seems familiar", I said.

"But now to your official task."

"What task?"

"I told you: as Gentleman of the Bedchamber it is your privilege to undo my zips. It is your duty even."

The curtains of the four-poster slid apart. It was not Carola who woke me, but Spring.

"Spring is here!" he said.

I got up. I was alone. Although I had slept well it put me in a bad mood – as always – not to wake to a fresh new day, but to artificial light. Spring had brought a lounge suit. Several times I had to tell him off for making suggestive remarks. I had him lead me to the dining room.

Weckenbarth, Lord Alfred, the dwarves and, to my surprise, Colonel von Schwweythauszsz were there. As there was a free place between Weckenbarth and the Duke I sat there. Weckenbarth turned to me and said:

"Well then?"

"What do you mean, 'well then'?"

"How was it?"

"How was what?"

"You're a shy one! How was it with Carola?"

"Has word got around already?"

"We'd have to be blind. Anyway, it's nothing to be ashamed of."

"She's very ... very eccentric ... At the ... how should I put it ... at the moment of ... at the very moment when ... you know ..."

"I know", grinned Weckenbarth. "Well?"

"Well, just at that moment she raised me to the rank of a 'Knight Commander of the Dragon Order of the Resurrection of Lazarus' ..."

"Did she now!" said Weckenbarth. "And in bed?"

"Of course. Where else?" I said. "With the Honey-coloured Ribbon, I think."

"Aha", said Weckenbarth with a chuckle, "with the Honey-coloured Ribbon. That confers a hereditary baronetcy – perhaps that explains it."

"Does it?" I said, "and what do you mean by 'perhaps that explains it'?"

"Well, perhaps Carola was afraid – or hoped – that at that very moment ... You understand. And in that case the father should be at least a baronet. She's very particular about that."

Some time later – I can only say 'some time later' since absolute time no longer existed, of course – I retired to my apartment.

There was no regular rhythm of waking and sleeping. We went to bed when we were sleepy and got up when we awoke and did not need any more sleep or, as now, when we were woken.

Weckenbarth was standing beside my bed. I noticed immediately that he was different from usual. The clannish, ironic, bored tone we had adopted had been replaced by serious concern:

"I climbed in through the emergency entrance – you didn't know of its existence. Your valet doesn't need to know about this. Come along with me, please."

I leapt out of bed and dressed quickly.

"What is it?" I asked.

Weckenbarth was engrossed in a small handkerchief and did not reply.

"Ready", I said, at last.

Weckenbarth looked up, put his little handkerchief away and led me into one of the rooms surrounding my central parlour. The ceiling rose concealed a kind of trapdoor which had been opened. A narrow iron ladder came down from the dark opening. We climbed up. At the top Weckenbarth operated a mechanism which drew up the ladder and closed the trapdoor. We were in a wide room with a fairly high ceiling which, as far as the eye could see, was supported by countless aluminium columns in regular rows. Both the ceiling and the floor were like polished mirrors.

Weckenbarth climbed into a small electric buggy, I jumped on behind and clung tight as it sped between the pillars. Finally we came to a lift. Dr. Jacobi was waiting there, holding the door open. He too had a worried look on his face.

"Quick", said Weckenbarth and went straight into the lift without the usual courtesies. The door closed behind us. When it opened again Weckenbarth rushed off in front of us along a panelled corridor. We ran round several corners then came upon

Lord Alfred, who was waiting for us by an open door. We went through without even saying hello.

In a half-lit room which had been given the appearance of a chapel Don Emanuele was kneeling before a catafalque saying the prayers for the dead according to the Roman Church. The figure-of-eight painters, Schizion and Pythicles, were standing on his right and left, dressed in cassocks and surplices and swinging censers. On either side of the catafalque three tall candles were burning.

Following Weckenbarth we rushed in at the double. At the sight of the scene I have described I stopped in surprise. Weckenbarth nodded to me to come close to the coffin.

In the coffin lay the Wandering Jew.

"Is he dead?" I whispered.

Weckenbarth said nothing.

"Did the dwarves kill him, like Nankeen?"

"No", said Weckenbarth, also in a whisper, "he would not have been a suitable victim. Come."

He led me past the catafalque – I glanced at Ahasuerus' face: the green colour had almost all gone, he looked more alive than when he was living – through another door into a small, bare antechamber.

"You know what this means", said Weckenbarth, after we had closed the door.

"Yes", I said. "The end of the world."

"Let us sit down, my friend. That must be it. Ahasuerus was found dead in his room. We do not know what he died from, nor have we tried to find out; we could not find any external injuries, but it doesn't matter. The death of Ahasuerus is not the only worrying sign. The spiders have penetrated the cigar!"

"Are we at war with *spiders*?"

"Of course not", said Weckenbarth irritatedly, adding in a more conciliatory tone, "of course, you can't know about all that. We have no idea with whom we are at war. However, that is not the most difficult problem, though of course the military do recognise that the fact that we do not know who the enemy is makes strategic planning considerably more difficult. You remember what people a few decades ago used to call 'conventional warfare'?"

"Yes", I said, "with artillery, tanks, aeroplanes and such."

"After that came atomic warfare; that was even put into practice just a tiny bit. Then, in theory, came chemical warfare, then biological; now we have spiritualist warfare – it is merely a logical development."

"I suspected something of the kind when I was up in the 'dome'."

"Our military have certain procedures which compel the enemy to become visible. Then we can destroy them. We have had several successes but so far no decisive victory. A spider forced its way in just before the premiere of Nankeen's show – you remember? The assumption is that these spiders are instruments of the enemy. The fact that a spider could penetrate the cigar represented a considerable danger – not so much because of the spider itself as because it showed that the enemy clearly had ways and means of getting past the dispositional parallax, which we had thought an insuperable barrier. We have since then managed to establish that the spider did not enter from above, through the dome, but penetrated directly to the heart of the cigar. We repulsed the attack by means of – please do not be shocked", Weckenbarth stood up and turned away so that I could not see his face, "– a human sacrifice."

"Nankeen", I said.

"Yes, Nankeen. That's why we made sure his show was such a triumph – with that kind of human sacrifice the victim has to be happy."

"And how", not surprisingly my voice croaked somewhat, "was he sacrificed?"

"Horrible, I tell you", Weckenbarth now looked at me again, "horrible. You'll see."

"God forbid", I said slowly.

"And now more spiders – not *a* spider, *spiders* – have entered the cigar. They have cut us off from the upper section, that is, we fear the upper section no longer exists. Four-fifths of the army has gone, all those who were up there. The measures we have taken have managed to keep the spiders quiet, but we are convinced they are preparing a further attack. We must make another human sacrifice."

"Who?" I asked.

"We have reason to believe the enemy in some way incorporates the female principle, therefore we must sacrifice a woman. I assume you now realise why I have brought you here?"

"Carola", I said.

"The spiders have managed to interrupt the electricity supply from the main power station, perhaps even destroyed the power station, but we still have an emergency generator. It will keep us going for so long that we do not need to worry, not even if the lighting for the ball I have had organised is lavish in the extreme – it's our last chance!"

"A ball now?" I said.

"A ball for Carola", said Weckenbarth. "The person who is sacrificed must be happy, and it is your task to see that Carola is happy."

I stood up. "What is happiness?" I said.

"We have no time for discussions of theory at the moment. Go and change and then collect Carola."

"I –", I said, "I am sure ... I am certainly not a happy person ..."

Spring had been called. He was waiting at the door outside the chapel, where Don Emanuele was still saying the exequies for the Wandering Jew, and led me back to my suite where the light, there was no doubt about it, was dimmer than before ...

The ball took place in the theatre. The seats had been removed from the stalls. A magnificent buffet was spread out on tables in the boxes and the circles. Spring accompanied me. One of Carola's personal bodyguards took me to the central box. I was in evening dress with my various decorations. Among other things the Senate had awarded me – though it is true that the purpose was merely to curry favour with me – the Star Cross for Gallantry in the Face of the Enemy. Don Emanuele, Weckenbarth, Lord Alfred and Dr. Jacobi, who were already seated in the box, were wearing rather strange scarlet cloaks.

"Is it a masked ball?" I asked.

It was understandable that everyone was in low spirits. Weckenbarth looked up.

"All that is left of the army after the enemy's great breakthrough are the guards who were stationed down here and a few remnants who were not in the dome for some reason or other. There are hardly any officers left, all the generals are dead. This here", said Weckenbarth, opening his cloak and revealing the scarlet uniform he was wearing, "is a general's uniform."

"So you are all generals?"

"We are all generals", said Weckenbarth, but no one laughed.

Don Emanuele sighed. Weckenbarth said, "I told her that I had worked out that outside it would be her birthday today."

"But it's not true?"

"Not at all – that is, who knows, maybe it is her birthday. It's impossible to work out."

"But it is her death day", I said softly. No one spoke.

As Weckenbarth had promised, the lighting from the emergency generator was lavish. A symphony orchestra was playing.

Dr. Jacobi leant over to me. "The situation is the same with music as with literature – you remember our conversation all that time ago? – a musical archive was planned, but there was no time to carry it out. I'm sure only very few people brought music with them – if anything then probably books – and perhaps one or two musicians have brought parts along with their instruments. On the other hand we are much better off as far as musical memory is concerned: our team of musicians managed to reconstruct all of Beethoven's symphonies, apart from the second, Schubert's Trout Quintet, several Haydn symphonies, Brahms' B flat major piano concerto with the help of a pianist and with that of a cellist the Dvorak concerto. At the moment they're even working on Bruckner's Eighth. And that chap there, the young conductor, knew a series of Strauß waltzes, including the orchestration."

"I would be happy to put myself at the team's disposal for a reconstruction of the score of 'Don Giovanni'."

"I'm sure the team would be honoured", said Dr. Jacobi, "but I always carry a score of 'Don Giovanni' around with me."

The orchestra had already played some waltzes. No one was dancing, however. Then, in the middle of *Tales from the Vienna Woods,* the conductor stopped the orchestra and turned round. The orchestra played a fanfare. The door to our box was thrown wide open. We stood up and stepped to one side. Carola entered, dressed all in black. Everyone turned towards the box and clapped and cheered and flowers – artificial ones again, of course – rained down from the ballroom ceiling. In a dignified posture the President stood at the edge of the box and greeted her people warmly. Weckenbarth slipped out unobtrusively. We had hardly sat down again when he appeared below before the curtain and made a speech. There was no doubt that he was a man of great self-control. I may be doing him an injustice, but I cannot get away from the idea that the degree of self-control, even self-denial, that he showed while reading his speech, would be impossible without a certain cynicism. Once he even spoke of the sacrifices Carola had made for us all and at the end he said, "I cannot wish Your Excellency 'a long life and a happy one', as is usual in birthday addresses – with our corrupted time what does a long life mean, since we have no days or years to measure it in? But I wish you, Your Excellency, the thinking person's fulfilment: to be used as best befits your natural endowments."

Again the people clapped and cheered without suspecting the terrible double meaning. Outside the door to the box I had already seen Schizion and Pythicles, the executioners, waiting.

Weckenbarth's speech was followed by a ballet, a classical ballet with Nankeen's chorus girls in white tutus. They danced the *Congratulation Waltz* that Johann Strauß had written in Boston for the hundredth anniversary of the Declaration of Independence.

"Johann Strauß wrote something for every occasion", said Dr. Jacobi. "A.W.Ambros once said – it would be very topical just at the moment – that for the end of the world Johann Strauß would have composed a 'Last Trump Quadrille' without batting an eyelid. There is something about this music which is beyond understanding. There is a magic in the waltzes to which no one is immune, even if he spends the rest of his time wallowing in

Parsifal, like the late lamented Knappertsbusch. And it is a magic that is unfathomable – the tunes are simple, sometimes even simple-minded, in strict four-bar units, their structure is crude – a straightforward stringing-together of waltz themes of the same length; it is true that the variation between lively and tranquil sections, between flowing and staccato, deeply-felt and majestic is always masterfully done, the orchestration is skilful and full of effect – but that alone cannot explain it ... they have something of the magic of perfection."

"I assume" – how long ago was it since it last came up? – "that you have written a book about it?'

With an expression of horror in his eyes, Dr. Jacobi regarded me. "Yes. Or do you think I would have fresh ideas on things like that *now*?"

After the ballet came the presentation of birthday wishes. For this ceremony we went into the spacious anteroom to the presidential box. Guards accompanied those who were to offer their congratulations. The Senators, the surviving officers, the conductor and the chorus girls all came to wish the President 'Happy Birthday'.

During the presentation we stood behind her. Carola was wearing a dress that reached to the ground; it was wide at the bottom, close-fitting from the hips up, closed at the neck with a high collar of fine lace. In contrast to the severe lines of the dress, the sleeves were very wide, ornate and made of lace, through which her shapely arms shimmered. In her hands she held a closed, black fan.

I decided on a madcap plan. The ball proper, so Weckenbarth had informed me, was to follow the presentation. Carola and I were to open it with the first dance, her *valse d' honneur*.

'I know', I said to myself, 'that it's ungrateful to Weckenbarth, and to Dr, Jacobi and the others. But what is ungrateful?' Don Emanuele had saved me, perhaps I should even add 'without thought for his own safety'. And it was Weckenbarth whom we had to thank for the 'cigar'. But what was that if it was only filled to a hundredth or a thousandth of its capacity? And not finished. Anyway, it was ridiculous to entrust the construction to an architect of ruins, even if he was a person of F.

Weckenbarth's intelligence.

On the other side: had they tried at all to negotiate with the enemy? I was not aware of it, I had to say, and I was a Senator, a Gentleman of the Bedchamber, a Knight with the Honey-Coloured Ribbon and goodness knows what else! I had gone aloft, to the front on my own initiative and contrary to Weckenbarth's orders – those orders certainly came from him. Everything came from him. What gives an architect of ruins the right to give orders to ten thousand civilians and an army? I – I, with the dignity of Senator – was occasionally informed, but then only of trivial matters or when everything was over. I had no influence. I was no Eminence, I was a low buffoon, or both.

Ungrateful or not, I decided to warn Carola. The two dwarves, wearing the ridiculously tall hats they were so proud of, had just entered the foyer – but not to join in the congratulations.

They were standing hand in hand, casting glances at Carola that were both lascivious and malicious.

I would warn Carola during the dance, I decided. She would doubtless have been informed about what happened to Nankeen and why. A word would be enough to make the situation clear. She was the President, after all. Power in the cigar was, at least nominally, hers. In reality – or were truth and appearances just as corrupt as time in here? – she probably knew as little as I did. But she had her Guard and I had the faithful Spring. We ought to be able to seize power in a coup, if necessary by the lightning elimination of Weckenbarth, Jacobi, Lord Alfred and... perhaps we could spare the aged Don Emanuele.

At least we could try to flee from the cigar ... It was all pointless – negotiation, flight – I knew. But at least I was not going to be one of Carola's butchers. We had to act immediately. Spring was waiting outside. I stole out of the room to let him in on the plot, as far as necessary, and give him my orders.

The dwarves scrutinised me with a hostile glare as I slipped past them.

(Who was it who invented the ridiculous figure of the tailor with the wispy beard? The spindly little man who had to carry an iron everywhere with him so as not to be blown away by the wind. I know a tailor who is six foot six and as strong as an ox;

there are fat tailors and thin ones, just as there are fat and thin bakers or locksmiths and plumbers.

It was the dwarves who, having been forced by the tailors to reveal their true measurements, spread the fairy-tale of the scrawny tailor. A cheap trick to get their revenge. That all went through my head when I saw the dwarves. The things one thinks of, even when everything is humming.)

The corridor was empty. The people were crowding around the buffet in the presentation room. Spring was not where I had told him to wait. I took my revolver, slipped the safety catch and ran from door to door. All the doors were locked. "Spring!" I shouted. Dr. Jacobi, Don Emanuele and Lord Alfred were with Carola; Weckenbarth, that much I had seen, was not. If I had met him I would have gunned him down. I called Spring again. For answer I heard groans behind a door. I took a run-up and broke the door down. On the floor of the small room lay Weckenbarth, his hands tied behind his back. A broad strip of elastoplast was stuck over his mouth.

A moment ago I was ready to shoot him ... I didn't know where I was.

I knelt down beside him and pulled the plaster, a painful procedure, off his mouth.

"The dwarves", he groaned.

I put my revolver away.

"I presume you were going to shoot me", said Weckenbarth, "to escape with Carola, or something? That was to be expected. It had even been worked into the plan. But *that* was something no one could have foreseen."

"What?"

"Would you be so kind as to undo the rope?"

I hesitated.

"I tell you: your anger with me, with us all, had been taken into account, was part of the plan. I don't hold it against you. Undo the knot, but be quick about it. We haven't a second to lose."

"I don't understand anything any more", I said, and began to loosen the knot. With a last flash of anger I said, "Nobody ever tells me anything, of course."

"Calm down; we had no idea that Carola was having an affair with the dwarves, either."

"Oh –", I almost choked on the words, "and – and me?"

Weckenbarth had one hand free and we undid the other knots together. "You idiot – I'm sorry, we were all idiots. That was just put on. What I don't know is: did the dwarves and Carola want to seize power for themselves, perhaps sacrificing one of us ... or are they traitors, have they been bought by those outside?"

Weckenbarth was free. He massaged the blood back into his limbs. "You will naturally want to know what precisely was going on between Carola and the dwarves. I'm afraid I don't know either. Though for quite some time now there have been rumours going round of an artificial penis the dwarves had which was supposed to perform miracles ..."

"Do you have to tell me that?" I said.

"You are right. We have no time to lose."

Weckenbarth sent me back into the ballroom. He himself hurried off in another direction. My orders were to avoid any disquiet among the people. I hurried over to Franzelin and told him to keep the orchestra playing. Four of the chorus girls had to improvise a dance to distract the attention of the guests. For the time being the shouts and disturbance from the presidential box and behind it were drowned. As an extra precaution I ran backstage, had the auditorium darkened and the curtain raised. I chased the rest of the chorus girls out into the limelight, just as they were: in outdoor dress, in their underwear, in the nude – which certainly had the desired effect. I had hurriedly sent a props man looking for dummy revolvers, and now I equipped the girls with them. On the stage was the set for the third act of Parsifal. Just the thing! I thought. The girls performed a pistol dance and shot the blanks in the air, making a fearful noise. Franzelin and the orchestra very skilfully improvised on 'Twinkle, twinkle little star'. The audience was beside itself. When I heard shots from the box I grabbed a couple of fireworks, skipped – I saw myself as Fred Astaire – onto the stage, danced a few steps, blew kisses to the girls and set the rockets off into the ballroom. The audience went wild. When the decorations burst into flames they fled. Those who were not quick enough were soaked by the fire brigade hoses. The place was in utter chaos, no one was bothering about the President's box any more. Later on Weckenbarth told me I had done a good job.

In all the confusion I saw Spring on the lighting bridge, waving to me vigorously. I climbed up. From the bridge an iron door led to a corridor. Carola was coming down the corridor, tall and proud in her black gown. She walked straight past me without a glance. Now I could see that she was being escorted by two muscular, bearded men with machine guns, presumably troops of Weckenbarth's. Little slips of paper – I later learnt that they had magic formulae written on them – were woven into their beards. Behind them came Weckenbarth and Lord Alfred. Both had drawn their revolvers. Weckenbarth signalled to me with his eyes to follow them and I joined the procession.

In a wide, tiled hall filled with cold steam about a dozen men were waiting – naked, all of them, apart from red rubber aprons. The slatted wooden floor was slippery. From the channels below came gurgling noises. Massive iron girders ran diagonally across the ceiling; hanging down from them were chains with gleaming hooks.

When Carola saw the twelve men in rubber aprons she screamed for the first time. Then I heard inhuman screams from behind me. I turned round – the two mechanical dwarves had been led in, bound hand and foot. They heaved and screamed like madmen ...

The sacrifice of Carola was not in vain. Afterwards – presumably it was Weckenbarth's doing – I was left alone with, as they say, my feelings, so it was only through Spring and later through Weckenbarth that I learnt that the situation had been normalised to a certain extent. The lower part of the cigar, the inhabited section, had been cleared of enemy troops. A surprisingly large number of soldiers in the dome had not been killed, only cut off, and they had been freed. The dome had had to be evacuated, but on the other hand we had succeeded in capturing some spiders alive. They were at the moment being examined by experts.

When I had rejoined the others around the table, they were in a worried mood. No one mentioned Carola, so I did so myself.

"Who is to be Carola's successor?" I asked.

Dr. Jacobi, who was sitting next to me, shrugged his shoulders. "Presumably the Senate will elect him."

"I am more concerned about who should take over as Supreme Commander", said Weckenbarth. "I think it would be a good idea", he turned to me, "if you were to take command of a division."

"But I heard that lots of soldiers were liberated. Were there no generals among them?"

"There certainly were", said Weckenbarth, "but, as the enemy intrusion indicated, they failed completely. It will all have to be examined by a court martial. In the meantime, they are in prison."

"Colonel Schwweythauszsz too?"

"I think so."

"No", I said. "I prefer to stay a Senator. I will call a meeting of the Senate so that we can vote on Carola's successor. My idea is to have a Presidial Council composed of both civil and military representatives which will take over the office of President for the time being."

"As you like", said Weckenbarth – like Dr. Jacobi, Lord Alfred and Don Emanuele he was wearing the scarlet uniform again – "it might even not be a bad idea. You see, I'm thinking – it would be your job to get your Presidial Council to push the bill through the Senate as an emergency decree – I would like", this very softly to me, "Lord Alfred to become Supreme Commander and be made Field Marshall."

"The one I miss most", said Dr. Jacobi, not realising he was interrupting, "is the Wandering Jew."

"Now that it's getting darker and darker", said Don Emanuele, "his stories would be doubly welcome."

"How are we off for electricity?" I asked.

"The emergency generator is operational", said Weckenbarth.

"And the power station?"

"Some technicians are seeing if it can be got back into working order."

"We will presumably never learn the end of the instructive story of the punctual man that Ahasuerus started to tell shortly before his death", lamented Don Emanuele. "And I wanted to ask him the question", his voice became even sadder, "you know, my question –"

"Didn't you ask him about Stellidaura long ago?" asked Weckenbarth.

"I never got round to it, he never stopped talking himself. And he had journeyed so far and wide. If anyone –"

"Perhaps I can help you", I said.

"You?" said Don Emanuele. "But I told you the story and you had never heard of her."

"I have heard something since then."

"In here? You can't hear anything new in here."

"Don't say that", I said.

"Is Stellidaura here in the cigar?" asked Don Emanuele quickly. "Have you seen her? I thought right away, one of –"

Weckenbarth laughed out loud. Don Emanuele's enthusiasm immediately deflated, he spoke haltingly, "– one of the – of the chorus girls – looks like her ..."

"No, Don Emanuele", I said. "I have dreamed of her, or rather: dreamed about her."

"Why do you make fun of an old man?" he asked sadly and in a slightly irritated tone.

"What was that story of the punctual man that Ahasuerus started telling?" Dr. Jacobi suddenly interjected, not without ulterior motive.

"It is the story of a man called Albert Gaunt", said Don Emanuele, "and it goes roughly as follows:

Albert Gaunt had probably turned a particular corner on his way to the office every working day for six months before he noticed the clock. Albert Gaunt was a middle-aged man. He was not short, had the typically skinny figure of a man with stomach trouble and tried to conceal his more than incipient baldness by growing his hair longer on one side and carefully training it across his head, to which end he used large amounts of unperfumed hair lotion to keep one hair neatly alongside the next, like sardines on a slice of toast. Albert Gaunt had an iron sense of duty, used nothing but his own personal lavatory paper at the office and had to be supplied by one of the secretaries with a cup of special herb tea, which had a bluish shimmer, at certain precise times.

The street corner with the clock was fairly close to Gaunt's office. It was where a busy main road was joined by a somewhat quieter side-street, and in a side-street off this side-street was Gaunt's firm. The corner had a certain significance for the office because it was there that a cheap snack-bar was situated which also sold carry-outs. The clerks in Gaunt's department ordered simple meals from it which were collected by an office-boy or messenger. Gaunt also sometimes had something brought. He did not fetch it himself, of course; his sense of duty was such that he always had something important to get on with, even during the lunch break. Gaunt only passed the corner once a day, in the morning, on his way to work. In the evening, Mondays to Thursdays at five, on Fridays at half past four, he went in the opposite direction to the tram stop. That was connected with his stomach trouble. He was convinced there was only one kind of special health bread that agreed with him and this bread was sold in a bakery not far from his office. Even though it meant a detour Gaunt went there every day to buy bread, and, so that it would be as fresh as possible, just sufficient for his supper and breakfast.

If I talked of 'Gaunt's firm' I did not mean to imply that the firm belonged to Gaunt, far from it. Throughout his life Gaunt had been such a model of solid respectability that any spark of fantasy or imagination, if such a spark had ever existed, had been stifled. He was a 'man of principle'. He felt most at home in a rigid system where unquestioned commands were obeyed unquestioningly. Such a system showed off his good qualities, which amounted to no more than dogged perseverance and unconditional conscientiousness, to their best, and only in such a system were these qualities any use in helping Albert Gaunt to get on in the world. His best years therefore had been in the army and the war, even the years after the war, for Gaunt was not only a good soldier, he ws a model prisoner-of-war. Looked at like that, he would, all in all, have been a born civil servant.

Gaunt, however, lacked certain certificates necessary to enter the civil service and as those responsible for appointing civil servants were themselves civil servants, that is, men of approximately the same qualities as Gaunt, they were not unsurprisingly blind to his in-born suitability for the civil service. Gaunt was a qualified insurance clerk with some knowledge of bookkeeping and after the war he worked for twenty years in a firm that sold building materials. He was 'promoted' each time they found, when looking for a replacement for his immediate superior, that they could, with the best will in the world, no longer overlook him. Thus in the course of time he entered the ranks of middle management. His great moment came when a firm in another town was taken over and made into a subsidiary. A wealthy partner in the firm was made boss and offered Gaunt a position as departmental head. After overcoming his own moment of inertia, Gaunt accepted, packed his special herb tea and his personal lavatory paper and moved to the other town. After some time his family, of course, joined him, for Gaunt – they knew that in the wages department from his tax code – was married, although the ladies above all whispered that they could not imagine that he was married, nor what his wife might look like. He naturally kept his work and his private life so strictly separate that no one from the firm ever met Mrs. Gaunt, neither on the firm outing, nor at the Christmas party. The more scurrilous members of the staff used to joke about his presumed punctuality in enjoying his marital rights – punctuality, that hardly needs saying after what has gone before, being the be-all and end-all of Gaunt's existence.

Thus every working day for six months Gaunt turned that corner in the city, where he was no longer a complete stranger, until the day when he noticed the clock for the first time.

The buildings in that area were mostly grey. Middle-sized firms, wholesalers stocking dull but serious and important articles, lawyers' chambers and mail-order businesses were situated there. Any tourist who entered those streets was certainly lost, and people only went to that district, if they did not happen to work there, if they had connections which allowed them to purchase material for a suit or floor tiles at wholesale prices. A jeweller's or a fashion boutique in that area would have been condemning itself to bankruptcy. And the clock above the snack-bar was as mundane as its surroundings. When Gaunt noticed it, it was showing one minute to eight. That meant he would be in the office on the dot of eight. His feeling of satisfaction was not so much at his punctuality than at the fact that it was a matter of course.

From then on Gaunt glanced at the clock each time he went past it – or rather went under it, since the clock was attached to a sign that protruded from the side of the building. And every day he was filled with a deep sense of satisfaction that the clock stood at precisely one minute to eight.

Now Gaunt's firm was not one where there was anyone to check on the punctuality of the staff, no doorman, no boss who, suffering from senile insomnia, was always there at the crack of dawn. There were no time-clocks since the staff were not wage-earners who were paid by the hour, but salaried. Their working day began at eight, and in the quarter of an hour from 7.55 to 8.10 they trickled in. There were some who lived out in the suburbs and were allowed to arrive a little later, depending on the most convenient train. Before the day on which he first noticed the clock Gaunt had not been so pedantic in his punctuality that he always arrived at work on the dot of eight. Of course he was not one of those who always slipped in hurriedly at ten past eight, but he did sometimes arrive three minutes earlier or later, something which was inevitable because he travelled by tram. But all that changed from the day on which he noticed the clock, or, to be more precise, from the following day when he again passed it at one minute to eight. From then on he arrived in the office on the dot of eight. Initially he relied on chance and his own well-developed sense of punctuality, but gradually he began to take more and more care to ensure that he passed the said clock at one minute to eight. He observed every clock he could find on his route, occasionally backing this up with a glance at his own watch, which was naturally always set according to the radio time-signal, and then hurrying up or slowing down as necessary. If he was too early, he would glance into one or two shop windows; if he was behind time, he would accelerate his metronomic step. At first the clock and his punctuality was a kind of sport that only came to mind when he got off the tram at his usual stop nearest the office. Gradually, however, the clock began to dominate his thoughts – he started thinking about it in the tram, then when he got on the tram, then at breakfast already, until finally his mind was completely in the grip of his mania for punctuality from one one-minute-to-eight until the next one-minute-to-eight. We must grant him that, in the early days at least, he was aware of how irrational his behaviour was. But that did not stop him from racing like mad against the clock when time was short or, on the other hand, inspecting completely uninteresting shop windows if he still had time in hand. Once, because he was in a hurry, he even denied himself the spectacle of the ambulance collecting a woman who had been run over by the tram, something he would not normally have missed for anything.

So it went on for three months. Since he was in a permanent state of mild excitement, his stomach trouble got worse, but never, not even once, did he pass beneath his clock at any other time than one minute to eight.

Then came the catastrophe ..."

Don Emanuele stopped.

"And?" said Weckenbarth.

"I have tried to tell the story as the Wandering Jew told it to me. That was the point he had reached."

"Well now you have another story", said Dr. Jacobi, "that you can tell everyone you meet until you find someone who can tell you how it ends."

"Now you are being silly", said Don Emanuele, and his eyes were immediately clouded with tears, "the two stories are worlds apart."

"I can imagine what the end would be", I said quickly. "It is one of those stories which, once they have reached a certain point, continue of their own impetus along their predetermined path. I am sure I have the basic idea although I cannot guarantee that the story of Gaunt's clock would have worked itself out in this precise detail.

One day someone – let's say it was the boss' secretary –

would have a birthday. Her colleagues give her a bottle of expensive perfume. The next day the secretary brings it back: the top, a roughened glass stopper pushed into the neck, will not open. Gaunt has a go at opening it like everyone else and he it is who has the idea of heating it. An apprentice provides a gas lighter. The bottle explodes – perfume contains alcohol, of course – filling the whole section with an overpowering smell. But Albert Gaunt is caught in one eye by a splinter of glass. At first they try first aid, but when the convulsions start and blood runs down from his eye they send for the ambulance, which takes him into hospital by the shortest route. The shortest route goes past the clock. With his uninjured eye Gaunt sees that it stands at one minute to eight when in fact it must be close on four o'clock. The clock has been stopped for months.

In order to round off the story I could add that Gaunt dies a few days later, either from blood-poisoning, from his stomach trouble suddenly becoming acute, perhaps brought on by the blood-poisoning, or from the collapse of what, with a man like Gaunt, we are justified in calling a 'world-view'. At his funeral the staff see Mrs. Gaunt and the two children for the first time. As far as can be judged through the black veil, her appearance corresponds roughly to the way people in the firm imagined her – a colourless creature who had spent her life suffering the unconscious torture of a pedant."

"Yes", said Weckenbarth, "I imagine you're probably right. But I think it is going too far to make a clock that has stopped the cause of poor old Gaunt's death – that's the point you want to make, I suppose."

"Do not forget", said Dr. Jacobi, "that Ahasuerus was a specialist in death. He knew every possible way of dying. Perhaps he told the story to show us what tiny things have led to death."

"Whilst he", said Don Emanuele, "could cross the Antarctic on foot and still death would not come, until ..." Don Emanuele paused.

"Until now", said our architect of ruins and stood up. He left, saying he had important business to attend to.

My fellow Senator, Uvesohn, paid me a surprise visit when

I returned to my apartment. He was very polite, waited for me to wash my hands and offer him a seat and asked, in German, how I was. Then he went on in his Pomeranian dialect. I listened for a while and tried to guess what he was talking about.

He talked calmly, with his eyebrows raised well above the upper rim of his spectacles. The effect was to throw his face somewhat out of kilter. His spectacles, as an inanimate object, did not join in the facial gesture and thus created a certain amount of tension between the three points on which they rested – the bridge of his nose and his ears. As the bridge of his nose did not give way, every time Uvesohn wrinkled his brow, the hooked ends of his spectacle frames made his ears flap like wings. His ears were large and thin, and the lamplight shone through them. The longer he spoke, the more the writer wrinkled his brow, and I began to hope he might fly away like a moth.

The idea made me laugh out loud.

He stood up, smoothed his brow – his ears folded neatly – bowed and went.

I called Spring.

"Spring, were you listening?"

"No, Your Eminence."

"I couldn't understand a word the man said. It was just too Pomeranian."

"Eminence Uvesohn, if Your Eminence will pardon the liberty, was talking about Eminence's parents."

"About my parents."

"No, not about the parents of Your Eminence, Your Eminence, but about the illustrious parents of His Eminence, Senator Uvesohn."

"I hope you realise that I only put up with all your eminent nonsense because my reputation as a Senator and Gentleman of the Bedchamber demands I have a personal valet."

"As you wish, Your Eminence."

"Couldn't you just simply say, 'he was talking about his parents'?"

"He was talking about his parents."

"Good. You understand Pomeranian, then?"

"One of the hounds of Spring was a pom."

314

My hand reached out for the volume containing Sagredo's tragedy. "Spring!" I threatened, "Spring ..."

Spring ducked. I put the book down again.

"What was he saying about his parents?"

"He belongs, he says, to the parentophagi."

"What on earth does he mean by that?"

"They are people who eat their parents."

"What?"

"That's why they call themselves parentophagi."

"Funny times we live in!" I said. "Parents eat their children, children their parents. Had he just come from dining on his parents?"

"No", said Spring, "a long time ago, when he was still in Pomerania. First of all he and his mother together ate his father, and then he gobbled up his mother alone. – There's a lot of eating in a Pomeranian father. – Unfortunately, Senator Uvesohn said, it gave him an inverted Cronus complex. That was when he started writing books."

"Was it, indeed."

"And then Your Eminence laughed."

"Decidedly in the wrong place. What a pity, it was more interesting than I thought. Spring, you must always listen in when Uvesohn is visiting."

A little while later the news reached me – I was asleep, Spring received it from a Senatorial deputation in my stead – that the Senate had passed an old bill proposing that each Senator should be accompanied by a trombone quartet, with one modification, namely that this privilege should be restricted to members of the Presidial Council and the three oldest members of the Senate and should only be granted when a formal motion requesting the privilege had been put.

When I woke up I heard Spring's report and immediately sent him with a note containing the motion – I was the only Senator to make use of this privilege – to the Senate business sub-committee. He returned accompanied by four trombonists: doubtless the Senate was trying to assure itself of my favour because I was intimate with Weckenbarth.

315

The trombonists had brought their instruments with them. I would very much liked to have had an alto trombone, but unfortunately no such instrument was available. I immediately ordered an alto trombone to be made. I wanted to see how far the Senate would go to win my favour.

Then I composed my fanfare:

It already happened now and then (Senators and the like were for the moment spared such measures and lacked for nothing) that one would meet a troop of evacuees in the corridors. They had begun moving part of the population down to the lower levels, mainly families with children. There were even already children who had been born in the cigar – another effect of the corrupted time. Not that the women took less than nine months to give birth, it just sometimes seemed to the fathers as if it were no more than that many hours. It is understandable that this circumstance encouraged the spread of promiscuity, which, however, did not worry anyone in our marginal situation where all values had disappeared (or rather, where so-called values had been reduced to bare essentials).

The deprivations suffered by the evacuees were minimal. They complained about interference in their private affairs and demanded special payments as refugees, but otherwise were provided with all necessities. The stores, which had been calculated on the basis of much larger numbers of inhabitants, had not noticeably diminished, even though the evacuation of the upper storeys had meant that for tactical reasons dozens of repositories had been left to the enemy – who could probably not make any use of our food ... For this reason when I met a group of refugees whilst on my way to Dr. Jacobi, together with my trombone quartet (Spring walked in front bearing a gilded plaque with my name surrounded by a gilded laurel wreath), their grumblings about extravagance left me cold. I was going to Dr. Jacobi to play him my fanfare.

He was sitting in his drawing room with Weckenbarth. They were playing patience against each other and talking about politics. In the meantime Jan Akne Uvesohn had become Chairman of the Presidial Council.

"No one whose first names are Jan Akne can be any use at all", said Weckenbarth.

"That is prejudice", said Dr. Jacobi. "Is it *his* fault?"

"Of course it's not his *fault*," said Weckenbarth, "but why call it prejudice? Is it prejudice to say someone is stupid? But it's not his fault that he's stupid. First names have an enormous influence on character. If some poor unfortunate person has the forenames Jan Akne hammered into his mind from earliest childhood, then he won't come out of it unscathed; eventually his mind will identify with 'Jan Akne'. A Jan Akne will inevitably end up intellectually stunted."

"What's so bad about Jan Akne?"

"Its brevity", said Weckenbarth, "I refuse to believe that a dramatist who calls his tragic heroine Elsa is anything other than untalented. One-syllable or very short names always smell of the servants' quarters. It's only logical – servants and kitchen maids are called all the time, their names get worn away. Kings and Princes on the other hand are never called, not even addressed by name. They can quite happily call themselves Salomanassar or Ferdinand-Weiprecht-Maria-Balthasar. Elsa is odd for a duchess because it's unsuitable, just as Nebuchadnezzar or Shionotulander would be for a valet."

"But you yourself have a one-syllable name", I said to Weckenbarth, "which you share with two Habsburg Emperors."

"True", said Weckenbarth. "Has it never struck you that precisely those monarchs had a menial air about them?"

"That may well be", said Dr. Jacobi, "but that still leaves you with the name."

"In the first place", said Weckenbarth, "through its use by the aforementioned monarchs and countless archdukes it has become gilded with tradition. No emperor, no king, not even the most dubious, non-canonically elected antipope was ever called Bengt or Uwe. Secondly, I have a number of further forenames; and thirdly, since earliest childhood I have been known to my family and friends as Memoraldi."

"So a child", I said, "whose irresponsible parents christened him Jörn could be saved by the nickname Svetovzar?"

"Indubitably", said Weckenbarth.

"Then it has been proved beyond any possible doubt that the Chairman of the Presidial Council is an ass", said Dr. Jacobi as he took a card from the pack. "He will have to be deposed."

"God forbid", said Weckenbarth. "Where would we be if being a complete ninny was a sufficient reason for a head of state to be deposed." He took a card.

"Before you continue with your game, gentlemen", I said, "I would like to put on a little performance for you. That's why I came, actually."

"Is it?" said Weckenbarth. "Have you been practising ventriloquy or something?"

"No", I said, and called my four trombonists and made them stand in a line. "You are about to witness the first performance of one of the last compositions in the history of Western music: Fanfare macabre in C for four trombones, opus 1, by myself."

Weckenbarth and Jacobi applauded. I raised my hand and brought them in. At that very moment the lights went out and the room was immediately filled with a high-pitched, unpleasant metallic noise. Although my trombonists blew till their lungs were bursting, not a note could be heard. On the other hand, their instruments did glow with a blue and yellow light and out of the bells came cascades of magnificent flames, curlicues, exploding balls that combined to produce dancing figures, pulsated from wall to wall in waves of garish colour and then died away the moment the horrified trombonists took their instruments from their lips. I tried to give the order, "Blow on!", but all that came out of my mouth was a green, iridescent ray. Weckenbarth leaped up and knocked over his chair, sending a silent, golden bolt of lightning to the ceiling where it ricocheted back and sank slowly to the floor in a thousand silver motes. In the light of the silver rain I saw Spring take out his pocket torch. When he switched it on it gave out no light, but a dull rattling sound. The phenomena lasted for a short time only, then the unpleasant pulsating noise stopped. The lights stayed out. Four bemused trombonists stood there in the beam of Spring's torch. We could talk again. Weckenbarth ran out. Dr. Jacobi said, "Congratulations, congratulations, a magnificent composition. Scriabin, who had so little success with his own 'keyboard of light', would have been enraptured by it."

We soon learnt that the enemy had attacked once more and destroyed the emergency generator; for a few seconds in the course of the attack light waves had been transformed into sound waves and vice versa. In spite of feverish activity on our part, it was impossible to repair the generator. 'Night' had fallen and the situation was now definitely serious.

They pushed ahead with the evacuation of the upper storeys. Columns of men, women and children led by a military police-man with a lamp stumbled down to ever deeper levels of the cigar. Since spatial parameters were irrelevant for spiritualist warfare, the measure was pretty pointless, but it calmed the population and gave the government the opportunity of actually doing something. A group of engineering specialists were still working on the emergency generator, but any hope of ever repairing it was slowly receding. Everything in and around what had been the emergency generator crumbled into tiny, damp grains not unlike semolina. Eventually that was the fate of the engineers working on it as well. As we could imagine the chaos the enemy would cause by interchanging sound and light waves, if they should succeed in doing so again, we had the phenome-non analysed. It had been observed everywhere in the cigar, although for different lengths of time and with different degrees of purity – if that is the right word. All members of the popu-lation were asked to describe what they had seen and the results analysed; the phenomenon seemed to occur according to certain laws. The statement of the excellent Franzelin, our conductor, was of particular value: at the crucial moment and with great presence of mind he had used his tuning fork, which spread a strong red, almost brick-red, light. The results of the research were used to work out a colour code for commands. All common orders, even salutes and prayers, were translated into colour signals so that we could communicate if the light-sound transposition should occur again, perhaps even become permanent. It was decreed that everyone should learn the colour code and courses were organised so that people could practise using them. The weakness of the courses was, naturally, the fact that they remained on a theoretical level. And in the confusion that soon set in, the decrees were not really carried into effect. I doubt whether the system would have worked, had it come to it. Anyway, the interest of the general staff was soon directed towards other plans.

"A counter-offensive is being planned", Dr. Jacobi told me.

"Aha", I said, "another human sacrifice?"

Dr. Jacobi nodded.

"And where do you think", I asked him, "you will find a happy person in all this confusion?"

"One is not enough any more, they say."

"That makes it all the more difficult."

"It is not a matter of a happy person – what is happiness, anyway –"

"A rather rapid change of mind."

Dr. Jacobi shook his head. "That was all for show. It wouldn't have been logical. How could it be a sacrifice if a happy person ... unless he were to sacrifice himself; no – someone had to be sacrificed who was *needed*; that is a sacrifice."

"And the ball for Carola?"

"Nankeen was sacrificed when he had proved that he was an outstanding director. He was worth his weight in gold to take the people's mind off things."

"And Carola?"

"We gave the ball for *you*. We assumed you needed Carola, you understand? The loss of Carola was to bring you to the

320

depths of despair."

"Thank you very much", I said.

"The episode with the dwarves ruined everything – almost. It was only at the very last minute that we realised the dwarves had a much greater need of Carola –"

"Then I propose that now we should sacrifice the general staff."

"Are you serious?" Dr. Jacobi laughed.

"Who is more needed?"

"You must turn the question round and ask, who is the least burden to us?"

"And who would that be?"

"The chorus girls."

"Because of the female principle", I said, "or was that put on as well?"

"Naturally", said Dr. Jacobi.

"And how many chorus girls will ...."

"All of them", he said, "the quantity alone should do it."

My presence was not required at the sacrifice of the chorus girls.

"But we can go if you would like to, Your Eminence", said Spring.

We were sitting in my apartment by the meagre light of a paraffin lamp. "I would rather not, Spring", I said.

"But just think of it, Your Eminence, all those girls will be stark naked, if you'll excuse my French –"

"– and then killed, Spring."

"Women always bring bad luck", said Spring.

"How can you say that, Spring; wasn't your mother a woman?"

"My mother wasn't a chorus girl."

"All right, all right", I said. "But I'm still not going."

"Twenty-five pretty girls in lace-up boots! Think of it, Your Eminence!"

"No, Spring."

Spring's voice had taken on a pitiful whining tone.

"Your Eminence", he said shamefacedly, "Your Eminence

... may I go?"

"So that's it", I said. "If you like."

It was no more than five minutes later – for me at least, presumably because of the dispositional parallax – that Spring returned.

"It was magnificent, Your Eminence ..."

"I don't want to hear anything."

"I was almost at the front, right behind His Excellency Field Marshall Lord Alfred .."

"Weren't you listening: I don't want to hear anything, and anyway I need a shave now" – after the destruction of the emergency generator I could not use my electric razor any more – "I have to go to see Weckenbarth to rehearse our string quartet."

"You want me to shave you while my hands are still trembling with excitement, Your Eminence? My hands will go on trembling until I can tell someone about it."

"I don't want to hear about it. Your hands can tremble as much as they like whilst you're applying the soap. By the time you've finished you'll have calmed down."

"Oh, Your Eminence –", said Spring, "twenty-five girls, pretty girls, and immediately after they had been brought into the huge tiled chamber they were stripped naked ..."

"If you don't stop immediately ..."

"But I'm getting the shaving things ready, can't you see, Your Eminence? Sit down in this chair, here, take the napkin – ... of course they realised what was going on, more or less anyway, when the heavy iron door closed behind them ..."

"At least spare me the gory details – look! the water's boiling dry on the primus stove."

Spring ran out and kept up his chatter as he ran:

"They were hopping about all over the place, just like hens when there's a hawk overhead –"

"Didn't they have the lace-up boots on?"

"No, it would have been too much bother. And anyway, there weren't enough pairs. Those big chaps in their rubber aprons kept plucking out one of the naked, pink little things; they held them tight and tied them up with string so that they couldn't move. When they'd finished the girls all lay there in a row, and then the Padre came – you know, fat old Reverend Schwerdtauer with the bald head – and blessed them –"

"Watch out, you idiot, you've just filled my ear full of soap!"

"Sorry, Your Eminence; yes, well, the Padre blessed each one of them, just as if he were blessing a consignment of shells, and", Spring gave a snigger, "he was very careful where he put the holy water, the dirty old devil –"

"You can talk", I said.

"Then he consecrated the spiritualist gun as well."

"What?"

"Because it takes less time than the method that was used with Nankeen and with – and with Her – er – Excellency ..."

"Spiritualist gun?"

"It was like a huge stone barrel, with strings of glass beads all round it and with levers and wheels."

"And they shot the girls with it?"

"No, of course not, Your Eminence. They loaded the gun with girls. In they went, one after the other, head first – a kind of spiritualist muzzle-loader – the spiritualist gunner fired the gun and each time there was an enormous bang."

"Do we know yet whether it was successful at all?"

"No, not that soon, Your Eminence. But the Padre fainted from the excitement of it all."

Then Spring, calmed down at last, started to shave me.

'Night' had fallen, then. We agreed, therefore, to hold regular – as far as, with the dispositional parallax, one can talk of regularity with respect to time – rehearsals for our quartet. We met in Dr. Jacobi's apartment. The salon was lit by some thirty torches that gave off thick smoke – they were rolled-up carpets that had been drenched in an inflammable liquid. We had had to make do with them since the loss of the emergency generator, but we were well off; for everybody else carpets were strictly rationed, but we could burn as many as we liked.

In those technological surroundings the soot on the walls and the reddish light seemed almost 'natural'. The awareness that things were not going well any more, brought back the sense of discomfort, which I had missed up to now, by which we knew that we were alive. The atmosphere was similar to that amongst shipwrecked mariners or soldiers in the field. I regarded the privileges which, in spite of everything, we still enjoyed, as the little comforts of an outpost –pleasantly out-of-place, almost slightly decadent but definitely acceptable. We had become a Noah's Ark, if immeasurably more comfortable than the original one. Now we were on the borderline, at the crossover point, at the wellspring, if you like, of our real lives.

Dr. Jacobi was alone. In the middle of the room were five chairs and five music stands.

"Why five?" I asked.

"Oh yes", said Dr. Jacobi, "you don't know yet. We want to let Lord Alfred join in, so we are not going to play the D minor quartet but op. 163. Have you anything against that?"

"I have long since called that quintet 'Farewell to the World'."

I opened the music. "Who is playing what?" I asked.

"Weckenbarth first and Lord Alfred second violin, Don Emanuele the viola. I leave it to you whether you play first or second cello, I'll take the other. Both parts are difficult."

"Second", I said.

"So that you can start with ten bars rest? Don't be misled – we are going to practise the second movement first. You'll spend half an hour playing pizzicato."

"As a pupil of a pupil of Mainardi I am used to the so-called two-finger pizzicato ..."

Weckenbarth entered, followed soon after by the other two who made up the quintet.

"Apart from the late Ahasuerus, all those from the riverboat are here again ..."

"Yes", said Weckenbarth and dreamily tapped his tuning fork against the music stand. Dr. Jacobi handed out the instruments, which he took out of a large black chest. We sat down.

"How far have you got", Lord Alfred asked me, "with your memorandum on the question of whether I am the 15th or the 16th Duke of Glenfinnan?"

"It is still at the preliminary stage, Your Grace. One fact that my preliminary researches have unearthed, and of which you are possibly not aware, is that you have the right to the title of Hereditary Lord High Comptroller of the Salt of the Dukedom of Ragusa and the princely House of Remisl. You should be addressed as 'Your Saltship' and you have the privilege, not a very real one any more, when you attend mass in the presence of the Austrian Emperor, or of more than four male members of the Imperial House who are of age and in line of succession and have not been made wards of court, of taking a consecrated salted gherkin instead of the host."

We tuned our instruments and started with the second movement.

"Hmm –", said Dr. Jacobi when we had finished, "let's go through it again straight away." He cleared his throat, felt in his pockets and leant over to me while the others were retuning their instruments, "You know, my friend, we cellists have one advantage over all other instrumentalists – we can decently smoke and play at the same time."

I thought about it.

"Wind players are automatically excluded", he continued. "The organ ... you can't smoke in church! Can you imagine a harpist with a cigar? Or a timpanist?"

"Pianists", I said.

"I said decently", he said. "A jazz pianist can smoke, of course, but I call that neither music nor decently."

"What about double bass players?" I said, or rather asked.

"They wag their heads too much. No, it's for cellists alone. That was Casals' secret, he told me himself: to smoke a pipe while playing the cello."

Dr. Jacobi had filled his pipe and was lighting it.

We started the movement again. At the difficult latter part of each bar, with precise regularity and accompanied by the familiar puffing noise, a mushroom of smoke rose from Dr. Jacobi's pipe.

The worrying news came that the sheath surrounding the lift shaft on which the 'droplet', where we lived and which we had to defend, had been seriously damaged in one place. In an audacious sally, General Weckenbarth flew out in a small aeroplane, a kind of helicopter, and inspected the damage from close to.

On his return he looked very concerned. The possibility could not be ruled out, he said, that the enemy was employing negative matter against us. If they were to succeed in cutting through the lift-shaft the 'droplet' would float aimlessly around in the cigar and we would be helpless to prevent the enemy driving us *en bloc,* or *en goutte* rather, against the inner wall of the cigar. If that were to happen, however, the energy released would cause the 'droplet' to vaporise in an incredible explosion.

The laboratories that were undamaged were working at fever pitch to develop counteragents to negative matter.

Uvesohn, as Chairman of the Presidial Council, called an extraordinary meeting of the Senate in which a punchy slogan to encourage people to keep their chins up was agreed, and an emergency committee was granted special powers.

Field Marshall Waldegrave – Lord Alfred in a deep purple uniform – reviewed the troops and gave out a spirited order of the day (in the short time available we had been unable to find a more fitting expression for order of the *day*). As long as no counteragent to negative matter had been found, it ran, we would have to do our best with traditional methods, that is with spiritualism, to keep the enemy at bay at least until we had developed better weapons. The Field Marshall gave the order to sound the attack.

The aim of our counterattack was to reach the place where the lift-shaft had been damaged in order to forestall any further attempts to cut it, at that same time, however, retaking the human slaughterhouse, that dreadful chamber that was coyly referred to as 'General Staff Tent no. XII'. It was, they maintained, obvious that no permanent success – if that were possible any more – could be achieved without further human sacrifices.

Without being able to put up a fight the defenceless soldiers burnt to death as a pulsating white star burst upon them at the point where the sheath around the lift-shaft had been damaged. In a contemptuous gesture, one soldier had been left unharmed to report the final defeat back to the Field Marshall. Any remaining doubts were resolved a short while later when the lift-shaft was severed. We were drifting towards the wall of the cigar. Spring, who, like my four trombonists, as personal attendant to a member of the Presidial Council had been exempted from service in the final sortie, brought a message calling me to Uvesohn. The members of the Presidial Council met in one of the side rooms of Uvesohn's apartment. When we were all assembled the Chairman entered with Lord Alfred. It was his duty, Lord Alfred said, to inform the Presidial Council that we had suffered a decisive defeat. Further resistance was not only pointless, it was impossible. Our destruction was only a question of time. The Field Marshall saluted and left.

Then Uvesohn slowly rose. "I hereby", he said, "take over sole and absolute power." He took a revolver out of his pocket and laid it on the table before him. "Is there anyone who dares to contradict me? I would like to point out that this is a *coup d'état*. For the moment – and until the contrary is proved – I regard those present as prisoners ..."

What a good thing it was that Spring was so punctilious in obeying my order always to listen at the door when Uvesohn was speaking. The door flew open and Spring rushed in with a revolver in his hand and, with a fearsome roar, let off a few rounds into the carpet. The other members of the Presidial Council scrabbled under the table. Uvesohn shook his revolver, presumably in an attempt to release the safety catch. My quartet came running, instruments at full blast, and hit the Chairman over the head with their trombones. Uvesohn collapsed in a heap. Immediately the Senators scrambled back out from under the table and fell upon the failed usurper. At the same moment a mighty tremor sent us all tumbling. We held our breath, but no explosion came.

"Has the time come?" I asked Spring.

"With Your Eminence's permission I would just point out that we are to hurry as quickly as possible to Your Eminence's rooms", said Spring.

He ran so quickly that I could hardly follow him. Repeated tremors of varying strength, and at intervals which were irregular but obviously getting shorter, threw us to the ground or made us stumble along the passageways. At one point one of the trombonists caught up with me. He was an NCO, the senior of the four, and in breathless tones he asked permission to fall out. I granted it. Before I could say a short word of thanks for their loyal service, he had disappeared.

We reached my suite. The interval between tremors – still silent but each accompanied, if I was not mistaken, by a small, scarcely noticeable electric discharge – was by now a matter of seconds. The fact that the acceleration in their frequency had been constant wherever we had been in our dash home suggested that the dispositional parallax had been destroyed, presumably when the lift shaft was severed.

Spring handed me some clothes.

"Do I need to change as well?"

"These are the clothes you were wearing when you came in from outside, Your Eminence."

"Oh, yes –" I quickly changed. Then I ordered Spring to take me to Weckenbarth. "I can't", said Spring, "I don't know where he is."

That came as something of a surprise. Then I remembered the iron ladder ... I ran to the room in question and searched everywhere, but I could not find the mechanism for opening the ceiling rose.

"What are you looking for, Your Eminence?"

"No more Eminence, Spring, that's all over."

"What is there supposed to be in here?"

"There's a ladder that comes down from the ceiling rose."

"Impossible. I would know about it." The tremors were now coming in such quick succession that there was a constant rattling.

"How do we get into the room above?"

"That I don't know Your ..., they are secret rooms."

"I thought so", I said. "Is there a ladder or some kind of steps anywhere around?"

Spring brought a table and put a chair on it. There was so much vibration from the tremors that I could hardly climb up onto it. Spring ran out.

"What is it, Spring?" I screamed.

"A knock at the door", he said.

I searched for a crack or gap around the rose, but there was none.

Spring returned. "Come and see", he said, "there is someone to see you." – Weckenbarth will have sent for me, I thought. Outside was a soldier carrying a trombone.

"With your permission, Your Eminence", he rasped, "the alto trombone is ready. I am the alto trombonist, reporting for duty, sir!"

I gave him immediate permission to fall out.

When I returned to the adjoining room the blasted rose was hanging open but the ladder could not come down because the table and chair were in the way. Don Emanuele was peering down from the hole, waving vigorously. "Quick! Come up! It's almost too late again!"

I climbed up. Spring stood at the bottom hesitating. Don Emanuele waved to him too.

This time there were no electric buggies, we had to run. The interminable forest of aluminium columns, or whatever they were, was giving off a phosphorescent glow in the dark.

"Don't touch any of the columns! They give us some protection against negative matter."

I looked back. Out of the opening above the rose there climbed, yes *climbed,* a blinding, white, pulsating star which used its five points like limbs.

Don Emanuele had seen it too. "It won't be long before they find out how to overcome the obstacle."

We hurried to one of the columns that was not glowing and ran round it a few times. Don Emanuele knocked on it.

"Too late?" I asked.

Then a door opened in the column. The room was rocked with a deafening explosion – the pulsating star had burst, but already another one was crawling out of the opening. We slipped through the door and closed it behind us. Outside I had run round the column a few times, so I had a good idea of its circumference and I thought it would be a little tight for the three of us. Inside, however, it seemed somewhat roomier but, as I told myself, that could well be an illusion as it was pitch dark. Spring lit his cigarette lighter.

"Thank you", said Don Emanuele. He looked upwards. the hollow column seemed endless; high above us there was a reddish glow. "We will have to be quick", said Don Emanuele, fiddling with the lock on a door.

"That glow up there, is that the enemy?" I asked.

"That is the molten plug to fill the column. It's already being poured in."

We were crushed together; it was getting hotter. The molten plug was presumably rushing towards us at 32 feet per second per second. At last Don Emanuele managed to open the second door, we pushed our way through and found ourselves in a room that, by all appearances, was used as a storage or lumber room. There were rubbish bins everywhere. In one corner lay a bundle of antlers and a pram.

"Watch out!" We jumped away from the column which glowed red. Immediately there was a wave of heat given out, then the colour paled and the column turned white. Don Emanuele walked round it, fingering it and muttering to himself, clearly satisfied.

"Ah –", I said, "the vibration has stopped."

Don Emanuele headed for a stone staircase without a banister which ran diagonally up the longest wall. We followed him. At the top we went through a door into a spacious winter garden where a number of people were gathered. The sun was low in the sky and cast the luminous pattern of the three high, coloured glass doors with round fanlights onto the parquet floor. It was afternoon. The heat of the summer day already held a hint of the cool of the coming evening. The ladies and gentlemen of the company had doubtless risen not long before from a refreshing afternoon nap and were now gathered for tea. Weckenbarth was sitting with his back to me, Lord Alfred waved when he saw us come in, and Dr. Jacobi was talking to the castrato – softly, so as not to interrupt Tiffany who was sitting with her sisters, a little book bound in white silk in her hand; she was just saying:

"Even though I am reading you a story, instead of telling you one I have made up or even lived through myself, I do not need to worry that anyone here might have come across it before.

There are probably no more than half a dozen copies left of this book here which contains 'my' story, which has the curious title 'The Murgan'. There were quite a lot printed, but almost all were pulped. The author was an extremely wealthy man and an extremely unsuccessful writer, Count Clement Karatheodory. Thanks to his wealth and his connections this Count Karatheodory occupied a dazzling array of honorary posts. He had also distinguished himself as the author of expressive poems. You know how people say of an ugly girl, 'She has beautiful eyes' ... well you can say of any poem that has no good qualities at all that it is 'expressive'. Though 'distinguished himself' is probably the wrong word: Karatheodory had managed to press the odd poem on this literary supplement or that little magazine ... enough, anyway, to warn publishers to be on their guard against his literary ambitions, all the more so because there were rumours going round that the Count had completed a substantial verse epic on the subject of German prisoners-of-war in Russia. One careless publisher, however, wandered into his sights at such close range as to allow him a pot shot – the Count was, of course, a huntsman, so the image is not inappropriate. Once he had strayed within the Count's territory the publisher found himself so entangled in a net of hospitality and obligation that the only way out of it was to promise to print a manuscript. That was after the banquet on the Count's country estate, a banquet that was given in honour of the publisher ... Magnificent wines of legendary vintages, saddle of venison, pheasants, two nieces – no expense was spared for the publisher, countless toasts were drunk to him and at the end all the glasses and the piano were smashed – the whole works. The publisher could not worm his way out of it, he had to accept the manuscript.

The next day the publisher appeared at his office with a considerable hangover, dropped the manuscript on the desk of his senior editor and disappeared into his office, leaving two instructions: 1. The manuscript was to be typeset immediately; 2. An ice pack was to be sent in. 'Let us hope', said the publisher, trying with difficulty to gather his thoughts, 'that at least it isn't the verse epic!' The editor looked at the manuscript with distaste. He leafed through it, annoyed that his employer had accepted a book without even asking his opinion. He decided that if it was going to be a fiasco, it would be a spectacular one. He would send the manuscript to the printer as it was, without the slightest change, without even correcting the typing errors. He ordered a run of 100,000 copies. The secretary had qualms. Secretly she crossed out one of the noughts. But the messenger thought even that was a mistake. He crossed out another nought. Eventually one thousand copies were printed. They managed to persuade a number of bookshops to accept two hundred on sale or return. One hundred and ninety-eight were returned. It was not without a certain sense of satisfaction that the senior editor passed this information on to the Count who was interested to know which two bookshops had sold a copy. To his delight, one of the shops was even able to tell him who had bought the book – an eccentric who collected books by aristocratic authors. It was from him, incidentally, that it came, by way of inheritance, into my hands, together with the whole collection of noble literature. It proved impossible to establish the identity of the other purchaser until one day, years later, when the Count was visiting a friend. This friend lived in one of the new estates on the edge of the town which consist of nothing but ugly high-rise buildings. The friend, who was also a keen huntsman, talked about the ugly houses and about how the estate had been built and also the remarkable fact that – as a conciliatory gesture on the part of Mother Nature – a pair of kestrels were nesting in the block opposite his. The friend fetched his telescope and went onto the balcony with the Count to show him the kestrel. The building opposite had eight stories. The kestrel's nest was right at the top, above the eighth. But the Count did not get higher than the eighth floor itself for there, on the balcony, was a man reading a book – *his* book, Count Karatheodory's book, *The Murgan*. One purchaser was known to the Count and this was not he. As the known purchaser, the eccentric, did not read books, only collected them, he did not lend them either. Ergo, the man on the balcony of the eighth floor must be the purchaser of the second copy!"

"I hope", said the castrato, "that the book is as exciting as its background."

332

"Habent sua fata libelli"; I indulged myself in a little Latin.

"I have made the observation", said Weckenbarth, "that the *fata* of interesting books tend to be interesting. In contrast to people. People with interesting lives are usually boring *at bottom*."

"Well, yes ... and no", said Tiffany. "I read the book a long time ago. I liked it very much then. I liked it so much that I not only read it, I ..."

Tiffany stopped.

"You ...?" asked her uncle.

"Nothing, nothing", said Tiffany. "Perhaps I won't like it any more. We all change with time. When I took it out of the library just now I had a quick glance at it — stylistically it is rather overloaded, if you know what I mean. The instrumentation is too full, the solo voice is sometimes drowned. When I read it I will omit some passages."

"Now we really are looking forward to your story", said Don Emanuele with a slight grunt.

"Well, now that I have brought it down from the library I might as well read it", said Tiffany.

Tiffany opened the book. Before she could begin, however, a strange sight drew our attention to the park outside: three people were cycling slowly across the park. One was slightly in front, the other two the servant's obligatory yard behind. The two at the rear were the mechanical dwarves, the one in front was wearing a green suit, its green just a touch lighter than his grass-green face ... Just as he rode past the glass front of the winter garden he waved to the dwarves who pedalled furiously to catch up with him; one handed him a cup of tea whilst the other popped a sandwich into his mouth. The dwarves then retired to a proper distance and Ahasuerus gave us a friendly wave.

We all waved back. Then Tiffany looked down at her book, but added first of all:

"The story begins with a dialogue. I will try to give the voices some characterisation:

'As Your Highness will doubtless remember, Your Highness forbade me to play the organ less than a week ago.'

'You have not obeyed my command.'

'Your ban hurt me too deeply for me not to comfort myself by playing the organ.'

'And why, if I allow you your music in future, do you refuse to help me ...'

'I am not going to play for your birthday. I don't know why, but I do know that the musicians cancelled the engagement because Your Highness could not pay them ...'

'You are becoming spiteful, Leon.'

'No, Your Highness, just hurt; since last week.'

The servant, Leon, turned away and began to arrange the volumes of French novels (one was missing, one from the pen of Madame Gyp) on the mantelpiece over the porphyry Empire fireplace. His mistress, Princess Beniamina Karatheodory, also turned away and straightened the chairs – which were already neatly in line – at the table in the middle of the room.

'Unless, Your Highness –'

The old Princess turned round. 'Unless what, Leon?'

'Unless Your Highness works the bellows for me.'

'You must be out of your mind. I'm sorry, but it goes without saying that I will never work the bellows for you. You may go now.'

'I will go now', said Leon softly, twirling the cloth, with which he had just been dusting the large leaves of the rubber plant, round like a windmill, 'and not say another word on the matter, although it will be taxing my patience and my pride to the utmost, but – are you listening, Your Highness? – I am still prepared to play during the banquet provided ... provided Your Highness will tread the bellows.'

The servant left. The Princess returned to her chairs; with a sigh she adjusted the position of one or the other by a fraction of an inch, then left the room by a door which was always kept open because at the slightest touch the grey rotten wood would have disintegrated, and went to the music room. She sat at the spinet and played a note which flew quivering from wall to wall of the large room and, filled out by its own harmonics to a full chord, seemed to make the spider-webs on the high ceiling reverberate. The Princess played a second note, and then a series, which she was about to make into the opening of a delicate *invention,* which would have poured balm on her wounded soul, when the walls began to shake with sounds that made not only the fine spider-webs but even the floor tremble – an organ thunderstorm from Leon, an interweaving of Gedackts and Flutes with the strength and intensity of the reed pipes, complemented in the upper and lower octaves by Mutations and Octave-couplers, all accompanied by the rhythmic hammering of wind supply like a musical smithy.

Denied her balm, Princess Karatheodory let her hands slip from the keys. Her eyes turned to the wall where the once mauve paper was gently vibrating to the sound of the organ with the plaster trickling down behind it; where the wall-covering was split, the fine powder puffed into the room and the motes swirled up in the delicate, slanting rays of the setting sun.

The organ of Castle Confetti – that is the Karatheodory Palace – was an unknown masterpiece, one of the few still extant made by Zaparini. It was completely dilapidated when the servant came across it. Like all early castle organs, it was a secular instrument, not intended for use at divine service. It had been installed in the Banqueting Hall or rather, the former Lord of the Castle, Field Marshall Baron Hercules Confetti had had the banqueting hall built around the organ. The neglect of the hall and the organ probably began during the Rococo with its sonatas for transverse flute, viola d'amore and harpsichord. When, at a later time, people were once more prepared to put up with the brute physical effort of playing the organ, the hall was already in such a state of disrepair that the draught alone ruled out any question of gathering round the festive board there. It was a vicious circle in which the organ led to the neglect of the hall, then the state of the hall to that of the organ.

The walls were hung with tattered remnants of tapestries. Most of the stonework – interrupted by figures of Titans supporting columns – was bare. The Titans, carved in wood and formerly marbled, had been painted over in the previous century in the course of a rather amateur attempt at restoration and that paint was now peeling off. The colossi were now naked and wormeaten, most of them lacked some member or other, all of them had lost their noses.

Leon had found the organ soon after he entered the Princess' service. The Princess had been happy to allow him to have the old banqueting hall as his servant's quarters, though she did so with a shake of the head: one thing the castle did not lack was rooms. In the years following Leon had cleaned the instrument of dust and vermin, freed the pipes from corrosion, replacing many of them, taken out the action, carved new parts for most of it, repaired the bellows and finally removed the bronze grille with the Confetti coat of arms and a number of deities playing instruments which, although very decorative, did not fit in with Leon's plans for the organ. For Leon had installed a number of new stops, about five in all, and these stops were remarkable in the extreme ... They were not connected to their sliders, but regulated a mechanism for emptying a number of small wooden tubs which he had installed behind the pipes. Later on, when he built the branch off from the bellows, some of the pipes had to be sacrificed and replaced by mute pipes. This branch led to a separate valve and to a kind of pressure chamber or reservoir. The reservoir had the appearance of a small central-heating boiler: heavy metal, steel bands and a screw lock. With great technical ingenuity Leon had fitted it into the organ below the pipes so that it was concealed behind the carved scroll-work. A new pedal had been inserted to regulate the branch from the bellows to the reservoir.

These innovations – once the work was finished they were completely invisible – were to turn the source of divine or, in this case, worldly music, into an instrument of the devil ...

It so happened that Leon had completed the restoration of Zaparini's masterpiece a mere week before the aforementioned birthday of Princess Karatheodory, on the stroke of midnight

He ran to wake Silverswan, the gardener (a young man who had been employed *against* Leon's recommendation, whom Leon therefore treated roughly and who, for that very reason, treated the latter with respect) and ordered him – in his nightshirt as he was – to tread the bellows; he played right through the night until the early morning.

The Princess, whom the sound of the organ (less the sound, in fact, than the spiders which fell on her from the ceiling) had robbed of the sleep which she needed more than ever, decided to forbid her servant to play the organ, at least at night. But on the morning after the completion of the restoration Leon was not to be found. He slept right through the day. As the gardener could not be woken either, the Princess had to get her own meals. She went to bed early.

But in the evening Leon got up and without dressing, in his nightshirt like the gardener the previous evening, sat down at the organ and began to play.

One great advantage of the pressure reservoir, though not the one Leon had in mind, was that the wind supply could be stored. The gardener's efforts on the bellows the previous night had filled the reservoir as well. Opening some of the valves of the reservoir very cautiously – opening them incautiously would have led to the whole instrument being demolished by the pressurised air – the organist could play for two or three hours, depending on how many stops he used, without the bellows needing to be operated.

Pianissimo and sparing in his use of registers, Leon started to play one of those remarkable melodies by the early Spanish masters.

After a few notes he stopped playing, stood up from the organ, put his slippers back on and fished papers and drawings (the technical plans for the improvement of the organ) out of various drawers and compartments. Then he fetched a frying-pan, piled up the papers on it, set light to them with a candle and, holding the pan by its long handle, quickly thrust it out of the window. The flames cast their light as far as the pomegranate trees in the park and illuminated the frogs and duckweed of the pond where once the tall jet of a fountain had splashed.

After the paper had been burnt up he crushed what was left to a fine ash which he poured into one of the wooden containers installed behind the wind supply. Then he sat down at the organ again. Softly, he took up the melody he had been playing before, but his attention was divided; he was mainly concentrating on a small pressure-gauge at the side of the manual. The gauge rose.

The indicator reached a red mark. Leon opened a valve: with a hoarse whistling noise the ash, which the pressure in the reservoir had ground to a powder, sprayed out from a very fine nozzle. The nozzle was at about chest height in the upright, coffin-like box for the person treading the bellows.

'Aah –', said Leon with a satisfied air, turning back to the manuals as his plans and sketches, transformed to dust, whirled around the room before finally joining the thick layer of dust already in the cracks and corners of the hall.

Without inhibition, Leon pulled out all the stops and played until the wind reservoir was exhausted, so that the Princess, having been robbed of her precious sleep once again, furiously decided to ban his organ playing once and for all. Leon, however, was once more unavailable. He slept until the red of the evening sun pierced the Venetian blinds and awoke all kinds of phantasmagoria from the faded tapestries above his bed. Then he got up. With a reproachful look on his face – the gardener, Silverswan, had gleefully passed on the message – he went to face the Princess.

The ban had no effect whatsoever. Urgent pleading and imploring reminders of how much the noble lady needed her sleep did produce some change of mind in her servant – he agreed not to play the organ *in the middle of the night*. It won't be long now, anyway, he told himself. On the following days, therefore, he stopped playing at ten o'clock and did not start again until just before six in the morning. On top of all that he went about in a particularly good mood, did his mistress' bidding, chatted to her and even treated her to an informal lecture on Shakespeare. What particularly fascinated him about the man, said Leon, was that he was privileged to reach a fabulously precise age, that is, to die on his birthday. The Princess was delighted at her servant's affability.

It was the gardener who mostly looked after the household, when he wasn't required for working the bellows. At that time the Princess lived on potato sorbet. It was strange, then, that Leon, without being asked, should suddenly offer to do the cooking for the Princess' anxiously-awaited birthday celebration. What was even stranger was that he still refused to put his annoying hobby to its proper use and play while the guests were at table.

Less because of the music, without which, after all, the celebration could still go ahead, than because she was afraid that her abrupt rejection of his suggestion that she tread the bellows might decide him not to prepare the food, the noble lady began at least to consider the humiliating proposal. She rang for the gardener and told him to call Leon. An observer who was aware of the significance of the slightest occurrence would have found it extremely significant that, when the young gardener brought him the Princess' summons, he immediately stopped playing and went to her.

'There is no use saying anything if Your Highness still refuses to work the bellows.'

'Leon ... I thought perhaps that if the gardener ...'

'If the gardener treads the bellows, then who will serve up the dishes which I will prepare, though only, as Your Highness can imagine, if I am in a good mood?'

'I was afraid of that.'

'What, Your Highness, do you think would seem odder to your noble guests: if the gardener works the bellows, I play the organ and *Your Highness* serves the food? Or if Silverswan — we'll have to see if we can't clean up my livery somewhat and find some coloured string from Christmas presents to stick onto it — that is, if the gardener serves the meal, I play the organ ...'

'Could we not do without treading the bellows altogether? Silverswan tells me you have installed something in the organ that means you can play for a while without someone working the bellows.'

'Only for a while, Your Highness.'

'You don't need to play for that long.'

'With the thing I've built in you cannot play very loud, and not all registers. But it is my intention to celebrate Your Highness' birthday with a performance of 'Musiquiana', a resonant composition of my own, which is very loud and needs all the stops.'

'A composition of *your* own?' the Princess asked. Silverswan giggled. Leon turned away.

'Stay here, Leon. Silverswan, what is there to giggle about; be quiet. In God's name, Leon you mean ...'

'All I want to say is: it will seem less odd if the gardener serves, I play the organ and Your Highness insists on working the bellows for her favourite nephew.'

'For which nephew?'

'I thought that for the evening Your Highness could pretend I was Your Highness' nephew.'

The Princess gulped and looked at Silverswan.

'Your Highness is silent', said Leon. 'My pride has not quite exhausted my patience yet. Your Highness may command me, provided – provided what, Your Highness knows.'

Leon left. The Princess, with one hand on the chair she had positioned down to the last fraction of an inch, twisted her necklace round the other tighter and tighter, as if she intended to strangle herself.

Towards midnight, surrounded by silence – Leon, as we know, had given up playing after ten – the Princess was sitting in her library. On her knees she had a book of which every year since it appeared she had read six or seven pages: *Bob au salon de 88* by Countess Gabrielle de Martel de Jauville, née Riquetti de Mirabeau, who wrote under the pseudonym of 'Gyp'. Every year Princess Beniamina was outraged by Countess Martel and her *Bob au salon de 88* and every year she decided not to read any more.

Today she had not read more than four lines of *Bob au salon de 88* when she let the book sink and abandoned herself to her thoughts. On the highest shelves, scarcely visible in the darkness of the huge room above the zone illuminated by the Spectral Multiplex Biform Reading Lamp, were the oldest works in the library of Confetti Castle. The rarer and more valuable ones had been sold years ago, leaving cavernous gaps between the parchment and pigskin spines out of which the bats were now swarming.

If only they would eat all the spiders, the Princess was thinking, when Silverswan entered..

'You forgot to knock', said the Princess.

The young gardener was standing silently by the door, wiping his hands on his green apron.

'You have forgotten to knock, but it's not your fault; you see my staff treat me like a monkey, like a wild animal.'

Silverswan was still wiping his hands on his gardener's apron. He was just about to say something when the Princess stood up and threw '*Bob au salon de 88*' onto the table, where it slid across the top and fell to the floor, pulling the black silk tablecloth with it. The Princess leant with both hands flat on the marble tabletop.

'You were going to say, Silverswan ...', the Princess sat down again, '... you were going to say ...', she repeated in a soft, tired voice, '... that a knock is not usually audible in this house. And why is your friend not playing, so that one would not hear you knock – or forgetting to knock – or might assume ...' she took her hands from the table and stretched out an arm in an attempt to reach the book she had thrown away without getting up from her seat, '... or might assume that one had missed the supposed knock or rather, not ... Why do you let an old woman like me go on talking when you can see that I can't finish my ... I don't know what I meant to say. Give me the book.'

With two bounds – on tiptoe, and yet some bats were disturbed and immediately fluttered out of the highest shelves and only went back to rest after flying around for some time – Silverswan was at the table, let go of his gardener's apron and handed the Princess the book.

'Your Highness knows ...'

'Of course I don't.'

Silverswan picked up the tablecloth and wiped his hands on that.

'Your Highness knows that Leon is no friend of mine. Your Highness, I could tell you a story about how I thought Leon was behaving like a friend to me ... how I accepted a favour from an *enemy*, from Leon, he was my enemy, you see, that is even today ...'

'It seems to me you don't know what you want to say, either.'

'No, Your Highness, Your Highness is right, it wasn't the story of my enemy, Leon, and how he arranged that I came here to Your Highness' castle ... and so on, that I was going to tell you, but something else.'

'I'm not int ...

aaaaaa!

eeeeek ...'

The Princess clutched her wig, ducked her head and slid from her chair to the floor.

'A ... A ... A ...

eeeek ...' she screamed, an octave higher. 'Look ...'

One of the disturbed bats was dangling from the shade of the Spectral Multiplex Biform Lamp. With three further bounds Silverswan was round the table, holding the silk tablecloth like a toreador, and staring the bat, which was hanging head down, in the face. Both, the bat and the young gardener, blinked. Finally, cautiously, Silverswan began to blow in the bat's face. The only result was that the bat blinked more rapidly.

'You're an idiot', said the Princess from under the table. She snatched the tablecloth from the gardener and flapped it at the bat. The blow loosened its grip on the shade so that it was swinging by one claw. After a second blow with the cloth it fluttered back up to the old books on the top shelves.

Young Silverswan took the Princess by one hand – she pushed herself up from the floor with the other – and drew her back to her chair, then retired a few steps to where he had been standing before.

'We ought to get rid of Leon', he panted, 'before it's too late.'

'Silverswan', said the princess, glancing with a shake of the head towards the top shelves again, 'oh, Silverswan.'

Silverswan bowed, took a further step backwards out of the light of the Spectral Multiplex Biform Lamp and stood there in the darkness. The Princess picked up her book and opened it. Silverswan gave several nasal snorts.

'You have not gone yet, Silverswan?'

Silverswan intoned like a voice from the grave, 'We should get rid of Leon before it is too late.'

The Princess put her book down. 'I'll be dead before I've read the book ... although, of course, the whole book ... I would like to know if other books are different. And then', she raised her voice, 'I would like to know what gives you the right to join yourself and myself together in the pronoun 'us'?'

'I apologise ...'

'Good. You may go.'

'But *why* can't we get rid of Leon?' the gardener had put his hands together as if in prayer.

Then the Princess began to cry, with her head raised and her eyes wide open, without burying her face in her hands; she cried in a deep, hoarse voice. Like the captive Cassandra dishonoured by Locrian Ajax, between sobs she uttered curses, mainly directed at Leon, but also at the gardener, herself, the day and the hour of her birth and being born in general."

"Like the captive Cassandra, dishonoured by Locrian Ajax ..." repeated her uncle, not without a hint of mockery in his voice, "are you sure, Tiffany, that it's not the verse epic you're reading?"

"No", replied Tiffany, "you would be able to tell because of the lines. But if you want me to stop ...?"

"No, no", said Weckenbarth, "we have reached the same stage as your princess with *'Bob au salon de 88'*."

Tiffany continued:

"Without moving a muscle, the young gardener waited until the Princess' curses gave way to sobbing once more.

'Why can we not get rid of Leon?'

'Tomorrow is my birthday.' After each word the Princess dabbed at her eyes and nose with a twisted corner of her handkerchief.

'And without Leon it would not be Your Highness' birthday?'

'But I am having guests.'

'The guests are coming because of Leon?'

'Good God, no; but the cooking ...', the Princess twisted another corner of her handkerchief into a pad.

'And Leon', recapitulated the gardener, 'is refusing to cook for your guests.'

'And the musicians have called off.'

'If the musicians had not called off –'

' – Leon', the Princess was furiously twisting the third corner of her handkerchief, 'would not have been able to offer to do the cooking.'

'So far I understand, but not the rest. May I sit down, Your Highness?'

'I am to tread the bellows.'

Silverswan leant back in his armchair. Starting with the fourth corner, with which she had just dried her last tear, Princess Karatheodory began to make a long roll of her handkerchief.

'Aha', said the gardener, 'he wants Your Highness to tread the bellows.'

'I', nodded the Princess, 'am to tread the bellows.'

'And that's why we can't get rid of him?'

'No. We cannot get rid of him because he is going to cook for my guests.'

'And why shouldn't *I* do the cooking, Your Highness?'

'Can you make potato sorbet?'

'... well ... no ...'

'There you are.'

'I see', said Silverswan, and furrowed his brow in furious thought whilst the Princess converted the roll she had made of her handkerchief into an even larger and more awkward knot.

Silverswan leant forward. 'I have a plan. We must get him to a point where he is still willing to play the organ and do the cooking, but cannot compel Your Highness to work the bellows, or', he added softly, 'go around giving orders at all.'

'... a *plan*?'

'Yes, I have a plan.'

'A plan?' said the Princess with a sigh of incredulity.

'Yes, a plan; we must *put a spell* on Leon.'

'Silverswan', said the Princess, 'you're being a bore.'

Ignoring the reproach and the pointed yawn with which it was accompanied, Silverswan sat down on the table, right next to the Princess, his whole weight resting on one arm so that that shoulder was pressed close to his ear, and revealed his plan, his free hand wandering over the veined marble of the tabletop in presumably explanatory but in fact completely incomprehensible illustrations.

'Leon must be able to play the organ, Your Highness, that is the first thing, because he is to entertain your guests at dinner; secondly, he must also be able to cook; therefore he must still be able to use his brain the same as ever, the same as now, I mean, that is, not quite the same, a bit less — or not less, just a little more slowly and ..., but he has to be able to cook and — just a minute, he mustn't be able to attack us, he must be smaller, but not much or he won't be able to reach the pedals or the plates on the cooker, but he could be a bit smaller, smaller than me at least, and weaker, and stupider; and ugly as ... So, Your Highness, how can we make Leon smaller, weaker and stupider, but just so stupid and small and weak that he can still cook?'

The question was meant rhetorically; the Princess answered, 'Silverswan, you are so stupid that ...'

'No, Your Highness', Silverswan's fingers drew further explanatory illustrations, 'no, we must change him into something.'

'Indeed!'

'Yes. Into a chimpanzee.'

The Princess looked up at Silverswan.

'Into a chimpanzee? And how do you propose to do that?'

'With minced fish-gut', said Silverswan, pleased at having aroused his mistress' interest.

'Is that possible?'

'Yes. With fish-gut from a carp. Because the intestinal bacteria ...'

'The intestinal bacteria?'

'The intestinal bacteria of the carp ...' said Silverswan, '... anyway, with minced carp-gut.'

'But then he will become a carp?'

'No', said Silverswan, 'a chimp.'

'Good', said the Princess.

'I read it in a book', said Silverswan. 'The fifth Earl of Howbergh ate minced fish-gut and lived to be two hundred years old, more or less — and a chimp.'

'The late eighth Earl of Howbergh was a chump, a *chump*, I know that. Something fell on his head during the First War, a grenade or something, or he was grazed by a bullet; since then he fell asleep every time he felt like laughing. You're sure you're not mixing up a chump and a chimp?'

'The fifth Earl of Howbergh was a real chimpanzee.'

'With hair?'

'With hair all over.'

'Did you see him?'

'No, I just read the book.'

'You read a book? Here?'

Silverswan refused to be diverted. 'We must give Leon some minced fish-gut, and quick.'

'And then Leon will turn into a chimpanzee straight away, like the fifth Earl of Howbergh?'

'Straight away?' said Silverswan slowly. 'Oh, not straight away, of course not.'

'How long did the fifth Earl of Howbergh take to turn into a chimpanzee?'

'Well', said Silverswan even more slowly, 'roughly one hundred and fifty years.'

'Silverswan', said the Princess with a sigh, 'you may go.'

The young gardener slowly slid down from the table and was about to walk away dejectedly when the Princess called him back in a hoarse voice:

'Silverswan, it doesn't have to be a chimpanzee.'

'How do you mean, Your Highness?'

'We could turn him into something else that works more quickly.'

'For example?'

'For example, for example ...', said the Princess irritatedly, 'into something or other.'

'Into something or other. Hm. Into a *coney*.'

'Into a what?'

'A coney.'

'Isn't that some kind of rabbit?'

'No. No one knows what it is. It occurs in the Bible.'

'In the Bible? Are you sure?'

'Quite sure. At school we had a scripture teacher who was called Coney, and quite naturally he had a soft spot for the animal. He often got us to read the passage in the Bible where the coney is mentioned. And he was sad that no one knew what a coney was.'

'There would be one advantage', mused the Princess, 'of turning Leon into a coney – the world would finally learn what a coney is, wouldn't it?'

'Well, yes, but it might bite.'

'That is true. Into what then?'

'Into a trout.'

'A trout can't cook', said the Princess.

'But a trout can *be cooked*.'

'Aha – you really are a marvel, Silverswan, a marvel! My guests should eat their fill on *one* trout?'

'We'll turn him into twenty-four trout, then.'

'Or into twenty-four pheasants?'

'No Your Highness, please, no. Not pheasants.'

'Why not?'

'Because –'

'Because?'

'Because you have to chop a pheasant's head off. A trout dies just by being taken out of water. I wouldn't like to have to chop Leon's head off twenty-four times.'

'Quite right', said the Princess, 'quite right. That's decided on then. And now I'm going to bed, Silverswan'

'But Your Highness', said Silverswan, 'how? *How* are we going to turn Leon into a trout?'

'A spell', said the Princess, 'a spell.'

'Can Your Highness do magic?'

'Am I a witch?'

'Then how are we going to ...'

'One can learn how, Silverswan. We'll just have to learn how to do magic. There!' she pointed to the top shelf of the library, 'there are bound to be a few books on magic up there, for God's sake. Don't you think so? Wait a moment', the Princess stood up, 'we'll have a quick look before I go to bed, so that'll be done. Climb up and have a look, I'll wait here a while.'

The Princess twisted the lampshade round. The light shone in a great semicircle on one wall of the library, right up to the top shelf of books. As if sucked out by the lamp, a swarm of startled bats scattered into the darkest recesses of the library, making a noise like a gentle siren. Silverswan climbed the ladder until his head was almost touching the ceiling. When he took out the first volumes from the dusty shelf he found that, with the centuries of spider-webs and bats excrement, they had almost fused with the wood. Numberless tiny mummified bats fell down, little greyish-violet bodies as hard as stone, like dried plums with ears.

'Get on with it', said the Princess, 'throw the books down onto the sofa, all of them.'

One after another Silverswan threw them down. The wide old sofa embroidered with silver roses deadened their fall somewhat.

Clipping her pincenez to her nose the Princess, in danger of a fatal blow from one of the volumes Silverswan was still throwing down, examined the pile of volumes that was rising up, as if for an auto-da-fé:

The Memoirs of Johann Zacharias Dase, Rapid Reckoner to His Highness the King of Prussia; including a description of his celebrated feat in Wiesbaden of multiplying two 60-digit numbers in two hours fifty-nine minutes whilst engaged in lively conversation.

Baron Johann Theodore von Trattner: *The Gentleman's Medical Companion.*

Of Mid-Wyves; a Most Christian Instruction in their Art. Thereto appended a Compendium of Comforting Wordes that may most expeditiously be used for the Solace of Those in their care. By Christopher Voelter of Stuttgarde in the County of Wirttemberg.

The Canting Deceiver, or the most cunning, amorous and martial Adventures of that dangerous and hypocritical Arch-Rogue, Sir Tartuffe Mealymouthe.

The Mirrour of Knyghthoode, wherein are reflected divers Artes pertaining to that estait, to wit the science of Construction and Fortification, of husbandry and venery.

Hieronymi Delphini Eunuchii conjugium, sive the Capon's Marriage.

Karl von Knoblauch, *Anti-Traumaturgy or the Miracle-Doubter.*

The political confession of Joseph von Wurmbrand, former Minister to the Emperor of Abyssinia, regarding the recent revolutionary events in France, with particular regard to their further consequences, by Baron Knigge.

Erasmus Darwin, *A Plan for the Conduct of Female Education in Boarding Schools*.

Success at last:

Daniel Bortolomaei termini magici iconibus illustrati, seu, Specula physico-magico-historico notabilium ac mirabilium scientiorum, seu Doctor Alexis Gzmaroq's Rare and Wondrous Boke of ye Secrete and Occult Magicke Arts, wherein is shewn ye incantations by which divers spirituall creatures may be conjur'd; to which is attached speles for the Transformacioun of both menne and wommen into Bestes of the field and Fowles of the air by the hand of the Learned Magus Caius Morisote. Given to be printed in Mumppelgarde by the order of Eleanore Charlotte, most noble and Serene Duchesse, Dowager of His most Serene Highness Duke Fredericke Sylvius of Wuerttemberghe and Oelse in Silesia.

'Look, look, come down right away'; the Princess read out the title.

'That's it', said Silverswan.

'That's it', said the Princess, '... the transformacioun of both menne and wommen into bestes ... and now I can go to bed. Keep the book on one side and put the rest back up on the shelves. Good night.'

'Your Highness' – it was less curiosity than the desire to avoid having to carry the heavy tomes back up again straight away that made Silverswan detain his mistress. 'Is there anything about turning people into trout in it?'

'In that book?'

The book was almost square, roughly a yard square and a foot thick. Silverswan heaved it onto the marble table. When he opened it a book-scorpion quickly scuttled across the tabletop. The young gardener stared at the book in horror, but not because of the scorpion, which was only the size of

349

his little fingernail. He riffled the pages with his fingers as he said in an expressionless voice:

'Does Your Highness know Greek?'

'Greek. Of course not. Why?'

'The book is written in Greek.'

'All of it?'

'All of it.'

Not bothering that his mistress was standing, the young gardener sat down in the chair by the lamp and gazed at the agitated book-scorpion.

After a while he said, 'Leon. Leon knows Greek.'

Princess Beniamina Karatheodory straightened up, gave her dress a vigorous tug to pull it back down to the proper length, shook her head and began to curse in a barely controlled voice:

'Leon ...!' she said and broke off. It was a long time since the wick of the Spectral Multiplex Lamp had been trimmed; it began to smoke and the stem to glow, surrounding the figure of the Princess with oracular fumes and bathing the whole scene in an infernal glow.

'Leon ...', the Princess' ancient bosom heaved, the scorpion ran to and fro over the table, 'Leon ... the scurvy bumscratcher ...' there was an audible creak of corsetry as her bosom heaved, the Spectral Biform Lamp began to hiss. 'Deuce take that bumscratcher Leon', she screamed.

The Spectral Multiplex Biform Lamp exploded. The moth-eaten net curtains flew in an arc across the room like a fluttering banner as the door was flung open. In the moonlight that illuminated the room after the brief darkness, stood Leon.

It left the Princess breathless. Mobbed by twittering bats, Leon had to wave his arms about like a navy signalman as he made his way across the room towards the Princess.

The Princess recoiled. Silently, Silverswan slid under the table.

The Princess, trembling with fear but not without dignity, decided that attack was the best form of defence, 'Ah, Leon, I was just about to call you. I need you to translate some

Greek for me.'

Leon stood still. The gardener under the table expected something extraordinary to happen, a catastrophe from which, protected by the black marble, he hoped to emerge unharmed. Even more extraordinary than what he had expected was the sound of the normally so recalcitrant servant speaking in a normal voice and with proper respect:

'Greek ... we will presumably need some light. Silverswan!'

Silverswan stood up. Leon told him to go down to the ground floor and bring a new Multiplex Biform Lamp.

'To translate some Greek', the Princess repeated when Silverswan reappeared bringing the soft light of a new Spectral Biform Lamp, 'from this book.'

Leon walked round the table, subjecting the pile of books and the gaps in the shelves to a brief scrutiny. Without touching the tome, he looked at the open pages. 'Who says that it is Greek?'

The Princess shot a glance at Silverswan; he shrugged his shoulders.

'Of course it isn't Greek', said Leon. 'It's Coptic.'

'Coptic?'

'Yes. What am I to translate, the whole book?'

'Leon', said the Princess, 'Leon, my dear. Before I tell you what you are to translate: please do not ask me *why* I want you to translate it. It is a very odd text and I am sure you ...'

'Your Highness –'

'No, please, Leon, please don't ask; it's for ... it's for nothing, nothing at all ...'

Silverswan came up, the Spectral Multiplex Lamp in his hand, and said,

'Allow me, Your Highness. Ask nothing, however suspicious the Greek ...'

'Coptic, you ass.'

'– the Coptic text might seem. Ask nothing. Translate and be silent ... and don't even *think* anything, anything at all – isn't that so, Your Highness?'

'And if', he went on, 'you translate the Coptic text nicely ...' – Silverswan smiled and gave the Princess a wink – 'if you translate it nicely, the Princess will work the bellows for you tomorrow.'

Leon said:

'Good. Only, am I to translate the whole book or what?'

'Does the book have an index?' asked the Princess.

'No', said Leon after he had leafed through the last pages.

'Then it must be in the contents. Trout, you are to translate the chapter on trout.'

'There is no table of contents. What does Your Highness require to know about trout?'

'You won't ask any questions?'

'I have already said I won't.'

'Right. I want to turn a person into a trout.'

'Into twenty-four trout', said Silverswan.

'Trout', said Leon. 'Hmmm. I see that, as you would expect, the book is arranged according to planets. As the trout is sacred to Venus I imagine ...', he leafed back and forward through the book and after a while he found a page with a crude illustration of a fat fish with the caption – in Coptic –: *Trout*.

'As far as I can see', reported Leon after a short perusal, 'there are some sixty spells for turning a person into a trout.

... ertha athrak koyth Salpiel Tabithia parek chiao
Amanu, Phurat, Phurani,
O watchers three, strong in your strength!
Adonai Ermusur,
that liveth within the six curtains,
Zartheel, Tarbioth, Urach, Thurach, Armuser, Jecha,
and the six ineffable stars
that burn within the tents of the sister!'

'Terrible, terrible', moaned the Princess.

'I thought it wasn't anything important?'

'Keep on reading' whispered Silverswan; the Biform Multiplex Lamp in his hand trembled.

'Adon Abrathona', declaimed Leon, seeming to grow taller all the time,

'who sent sleep upon Abimelech for four and seventy years,

go Thou to the West
beneath Thy mountain,
beneath the cover of Thy mountain,
down to Eluch, Beluch, Barbaruch.

Then call out six times:

SATOR
AREPO
TENET
OPERA
ROTAS

Th-'

Then the second Spectral Multiplex Biform Lamp exploded as well.

Whimpering, Silverswan fell to his knees. He did not let go of the glowing stem of the broken Multiplex Biform Lamp. Soon the stench of burning skin could be smelt. The Princess had fainted.

Leon, whose hair had been blown stiffly out to one side by the explosion, took Silverswan's arm, shook the slowly cooling lamp out of his hand and said,

'That, Your Highness, would have been the formula to turn *someone* into twenty-four trout. I wish you a very good night. Silverswan is coming with me.'

Like a monkey led by one of its front legs, the babbling gardener hobbled along on three limbs in Leon's powerful grip; the wind, blowing through the broken panes, made the dress of the unconscious Princess billow out like a sail.

After a few minutes all was quiet. A tiny trumpeter above the face of an ornamental clock on the mantelpiece put his instrument to his lips and gave one single

'Ting.'

This might not be the best moment, but unfortunately it is necessary to insert some technical explanations into the course of the action:

A jet of liquid, squirted under high pressure from an extremely fine nozzle (such as the one Leon had installed in the coffin-like box for the bellows-treader) has the effect of an injection. Such a fine jet penetrates the skin without causing any pain, almost unnoticed, and the liquid enters the blood-stream directly. Clothes, even leather clothes, are no obstacle. No trace is left. If the liquid squirted out of the nozzle is a toxin, then the effect is that of an injection of poison. With petrol, for example, unconsciousness would be instantaneous and death would follow in a few minutes.

In the manner already described, Leon dragged the unresisting gardener across indistinct shadows thrown by high mullions onto the worn marble floors of long passages. The wan September dawn took over from the pallid moonlight and slowly filled the castle rooms with the sobering grey of morning. Down the stairs, which faced east and were thus in almost full daylight, Leon dragged Silverswan, whose nose and chin occasionally slapped against the steps, into the Banqueting Hall with its Titans.

Leon had brightened up the thirteen noseless colossi with a coat of paint: the bodies a childish flesh colour with a little too much red in the skin, beards black, eyes rolling white and garments gaudy in reds and blues.

The post of the bellows-treader, the narrow box, had been decorated with two yew trees. Leon pushed Silverswan upright and crammed him into the bellowsman's stall. Like an automaton the young gardener obeyed the order to tread the bellows. Leon did not play at first, and thus Silverswan's exertions filled the wind reservoir of the mechanism. As he trod, he stared, understanding nothing, with a fixed, imbecilic expression at the tiny nozzle directed at his chest.

Leon sat at the console and kicked off his shoes. He began with the tremolo. From the glittering notes *Isoldes Liebestod* gradually emerged, making the garish Titans quiver. Leon extended the *Liebestod* – given the structure of the piece, this was no problem – over four and a half hours.

At the end of it Leon was exhausted almost to the point of unconsciousness. Silverswan, on the other hand, had gone mad. He claimed to be twenty-four pheasants and asked permission to go to confession.

'Out through the middle door', barked Leon.

Silverswan hopped out and climbed a tree in the park, crowing quietly to himself.

When she entered the Hall of the Titans unannounced the next morning – her birthday – the Princess almost dropped dead with shock at the unexpected change in the wooden colossi.

Leon, in flannel pyjamas with a flat bonnet on his head, sat up in bed. The bed, surrounded by a simple wooden balustrade, stood on a three-foot high dais.

'Leon', said the Princess, 'Leon, I admit it quite openly: I wanted to turn you into a trout. But you can't abandon me now.'

Still half asleep, Leon scratched himself.

'Today is my birthday.'

His eyes scarcely open, Leon said, 'Happy birthday.'

'Thank you. But you can't abandon me now that Silverswan's gone mad.'

'Silverswan's gone mad?'

Leon sat up. He picked up a pair of sprung dumb-bells, squeezed them a few times, jumped out of bed and stood with his legs apart, with his arms in position 1.

The Princess turned her eyes away.

Holding the dumb-bells, Leon stretched his arms out horizontally to the side and then bent them at the elbows again. Each time he bent his knees slightly as well, so that the dais shook and the nearest Titan began to nod its worm-eaten head.

'One, two-two, two-three, two ...' said Leon softly.

'I am to do the cooking for Your Highness?' Leon spoke in short gasps.

'Yes.'

'And play the organ?'

'I will tread the bellows, but ... it takes strength. An old woman ... like me ...'

'It won't, two-two', said Leon, 'take long.' He sprang
back into position 1 and stopped, panting.

'And for today', said Leon, 'I will be your nephew.'

'My nephew? – Hm ... my nephew too ... what do you
think you should be called?'

'Karatheodory.' Leon put the dumb-bells back under his
bed.

'Karatheodory? Wouldn't you perhaps prefer to be related
by marriage?'

'No. Karatheodory. Your Highness can let me know the
Christian name in the course of the day. And now may I ask
Your Highness to leave me by myself. I am going to say my
prayers.'

Leon took off the flat, lilac knitted bonnet the shape of an
ice-pack and knelt down by his bed.

So Leon was not turned into twenty-four trout, but into a
young nobleman, Prince Laioté Karatheodory, Pasha of
Samos – as they agreed during the course of the day. Even
when he was preparing the banquet, which consisted of three
courses of potato sorbet, he wore his evening dress, though
protected by a rubber apron. There was an addition to his
evening dress, a flamboyant little touch that he had designed
himself and that the Princess did not dare to criticise: some
braid with pink stitching on the waistcoat, just hinting at a
hussar's uniform.

Besides that, Leon had found time to decorate the Hall of
Titans with garlands of yew. Stretching from the mouth of
one colossus to the next, the streamers went right round the
hall. It looked as if the wooden giants were clenching a huge
green sausage between their teeth.

Towards half past nine the first guests arrived. Nineteen
places had been set.

The Princess and Leon greeted them at the castle portal.

'Chère Béatrix – chère Christine', the Princess greeted her
cousins, 'this young man is my nephew – yours as well

therefore – the organist Karatheodory.'

'Did you know', said Princess Béatrix to Princess Christine, 'that we had an organist in the family?'

In all, seventeen of the Princess' cousins appeared and all, of course, from the very best families. Even Frau Aliënor Gruber was there, the illegitimate daughter of the penultimate Austrian Emperor from his brief but passionate liaison with a sea-nymph which the Khedive of Egypt had brought with him on a state visit in 1897. Later – the Archbishop insisted – the sea-nymph was baptised and became abbess of a specially founded convent, *Our Lady of the Star in the Sea* in Dubrovnik. Frau Gruber had the right to the title of *Privy Imperial and Royal Majesty*.

The ladies wore gowns with trains in pale violet, beryl green, scarlet or black, but all of them interwoven with gold, like the blooms of limp, gigantic and perhaps just slightly poisonous orchids.

They were already seated at table, when, wearing a white coat, Princess Thamara Makrembolitissa-Bagration Porphyrogenete, Despotissa of Epirus and Sevastokratissa of Thessaly, Imperial Princess of Byzantium appeared.

None of the ladies could match her for beauty. 'Please do excuse me', she said with a slightly nasal, incomparably aristocratic accent, 'for being un peu trop tard, but what on earth is that monkey you have sitting crowing in the tree out there?'

The ladies sat in tall chairs of dark, heavy wood and decorated with carved canopies like choir stalls or niches for statues of saints. The silks and brocades of the spreading gowns rustled softly as they were forced into folds between the arms of the narrow chairs.

Since Silverswan was hors de combat, Leon could not start playing the organ immediately, as he would have liked to, but had to condescend to serve the potato sorbet himself, accompanied by a long, complicated and incomprehensible explanation from the Princess. Afterwards Leon led his 'aunt' to the bellows and began the prelude to his 'Musiquiana'. Such potpourris of other composers' works are known, although of a much more limited nature – 'Scarlattiana', 'Mozartiana', 'Smetaniana'; in a similar, only much more comprehensive manner, Leon had composed a potpourri of the whole of music and given it the title 'Musiquiana'. Ignoring a chronological, geographical or musicological arrangement, the cohesion of the pieces Leon used in his 'Musiquiana' was more profound, more intrinsic. It began with a fugue by Ozingas on the 32 foot Sub-bourdon into which, like a spider weaving its web, it soon began to weave themes from 'The Trumpeter of Säckingen' and the hymn 'Laudant pastores' by Max Hildebrandt the Younger.

Pianists (male pianists, that is, though there is a lack of research into the phenomenon) tend either to churn up the piano, to knead the keys like dough, to hammer away ecstatically at them, or to sit hunched over their instrument, stroking it like a piece of ethereal silk, or even to clasp it to them in uncontrollable lust like the body of a harlot. An organist, on the other hand, always sits calmly at his instrument, in stockinged feet, as we know, the better to feel the pedals, his upper body still, upright and majestic. Thus Leon sat at the dark Zaparini organ, which towered above him like the canopy above a throne. The Princess groaned in her box.

The prelude to 'Musiquiana' ended *organo pieno* in a mighty fugal finale including several more recent tunes, 'Tea for two', for example. Then Leon served the second course, sorbet of marinaded potatoes served on cabbage leaves.

After a few transitional chords the main part of the work began. A host of melodies and themes of all kinds, hardly recognisable individually, but magnificently effective in combination, were intertwined so that just occasionally there was a glint of a bar from a hornpipe by Handel or the mad scene from Lucia di Lammermoor, here in the Super-octave, there in the Großgedackt. A wave of incense, from a harmless nozzle on the instrument, filled the room, mixing with the scent of yew and wafting over the eighteen noble ladies who, half embarrassed, half excited, were eating their marinaded potato sorbet with silver spoons from plates that were quivering from the violence of the music. When the delicate echo sounded with a myxolydian sequence over the ostinato of a Bohemian furiant, the Princess could be heard groaning once more.

'Léon, c'est impossible ...', she said as she panted over the bellows. At that Leon pulled out a series of special stops which released a group of his new pipes. Immediately a well-known palm court melody rang out as if sung by hoarse voices, indistinctly and in a foreign language. – Were the noseless colossi bellowing out a primaeval ritual hymn to some forgotten deity? The giants nodded their heads so that the garlands between their gleaming white teeth were thrown up and down, as if in a whirlwind ...

The reactions of the ladies varied. Whilst some of them, notably the rather lumbering Countess Dietrichstein-Proskau-Leslie, retired as gracefully and as inconspicuously as possible to the farther end of the hall, Princess Makrembolitissa stood up with a half surprised, half amused expression, and took a step towards the console, which Leon noticed by the rustling of her white silk dress. Without stopping playing, he turned his head and looked into the face of the Princess who, motionless, was staring mindlessly straight through his forehead.

Forgetting that the last course, potato sorbet in the Karatheodory colours, was still to be served, without even noticing his mistress' tentative reminders, Leon pulled out stop after stop and entered the finale of his 'Musiquiana'; above the five or six contrapuntal lines he improvised here and there an exultant descant, or even two, spurred his aunt on with cries of 'plus vite, ma tante' and gave only half a glance at the pressure gauge at the edge of the console where the indicator was slowly rising and already approaching the red line.

Letting all the lines, even the exultant descant, swell into a chord, Leon now combined all the registers into one voice. A surging, rolling, primeval melody poured out of the instrument like an avalanche.

The indicator on the pressure gauge had reached the red mark. With one hand Leon let the resplendent melody dwindle into a babble of chords. On the pedals he started a tune of a unique character (the only one in the whole of 'Musiquiana' that he had written himself) whilst his hand moved casually towards the stop marked 'Petrol' ...

The old Princess sank to the ground, was hurled back into the air by the treads as they flipped up again, and then fell out of the bellows-box. The ladies screamed, even Princess Makrembolitissa. Frau Aliënor Gruber said, 'What, no dessert?' The door burst open and Silverswan hopped in, crowing. He tried to mount some of the august ladies, but they fled without exception.

Leon put his shoes back on, gave Silverswan a thunderous box on the ears, then opened a window. By the light of the moon the pomegranate trees swayed in the soft breeze. The surface of the pond moved in gentle ripples. The crunch of the coach wheels as the ladies fled, died away. Leon caught a glimpse of what might have been the white coat of Princess Makrembolitissa disappearing through the gate at the end of the avenue."

"Is that the end of the story?" asked Weckenbarth.

"The end of the first chapter", said Tiffany.

"Hm", came from Dr. Jacobi.

"It is getting rather late", said the Count.

"The story is supposed to be true?" I asked.

"That's what the author told me at least. He said it was about the death of his aunt."

"What I find lacking is the motive", said Weckenbarth, "but perhaps the other chapters reveal that. How many are there?"

"About twenty", said Tiffany.

"Then I suggest", said Dr. Jacobi, "that we make do with that one chapter and try to guess the end. What is your opinion, Weckenbarth?"

"Leon is evil", said Weckenbarth. "He murders for pleasure."

"Or", said Don Emanuele, "he is a socialist and wants to eradicate the aristocracy."

"Perhaps", I joined in the debate, "he was so carried away by the perfection of his murderous instrument that he lost all moral restraint?"

"There is another possibility", said the castrato. "The author was the Princess' nephew and he is said to have been very rich."

Tiffany was silent; the book sank to her lap.

It was almost evening. The sun was low above the trees in the park. The luminous pattern of the three glass doors stretched right across the room. The tall potted palms were bathed in the rich gold of the evening light and their shadows cast lengthened and etiolated images across carpets and furniture.

For a time it was quiet. Then Weckenbarth said:

"Why didn't he help her? And, anyway, why isn't he a prince if his aunt was a princess?"

"That was a different line, that had been granted the title of prince. The Count and the Princess were relations, but only distant ones. Count Karatheodory had acquired his wealth through marriage and the Princess was the last of that branch, which, I believe, had already become separate from the main Karatheodory line by goodness-knows-what century before Christ —"

"Stop! Stop!" said Weckenbarth. "With all due respect to the age of the noble lines, whether princely or countly, I think before Christ is going a bit far."

"Well after the birth of Christ, then", said Tiffany and put the book, or rather gently threw it, onto the stool beside her.

"And why did the wealthy Count not help her?"

"Apart from the princely line", said Tiffany quickly, "there are numerous others: counts, margraves, earls, barons and the devil knows how many other collateral lines of the Karatheodorys, all of them impoverished. If he had tried to help them all, simply because they were called Karatheodory, he would have soon been impoverished himself."

"But that eternal potato sorbet", said Dr. Jacobi, popping a biscuit into his mouth, "would melt even a heart of stone."

"What happened to Silverswan? Was Leon brought to trial?" said Weckenbarth.

"Silverswan died in a lunatic asylum not long after. Leon was not brought to trial because nothing could be proved."

"Perhaps", said Weckenbarth, "Leon's condition that his mistress was to pretend he was her nephew might lead us to the motive."

"You mean to suggest", said Lord Alfred, "that Leon also forged a will making over the castle to him after the death of the Princess."

"I can't remember how it ended any more", said Tiffany, picking up the book and leafing through it.

"Perhaps he even put an adoption in the forged will", I suggested.

"Adoption by will is not possible", said Weckenbarth.

"Augustus was adopted by Caesar in his will."

"That was a forgery, too", said Dr. Jacobi.

"You have written a book about it?"

"An article", said Dr. Jacobi with a smile.

"I have a vague idea there was a Delphina Martini who played some role in the later chapters –"

"– who in reality is a Princess Makrembolitissa?"

"And Princess Beniamina was a man and the agent of an international conspiracy –"

"At the end Leon marries the Princess and becomes Emperor of Byzantium."

"Then he would have been Leon VIII."

"If he had become Pope he would only have been Leon IV."

"What I'm interested in", said Lord Alfred, "is the coney. Does it really come in the Bible."

"Yes", said Dr. Jacobi. "And to anticipate certain questions: no, that is one of the few subjects on which I have not yet written a treatise."

"But who", asked Weckenbarth, "was the other purchaser of the book? The man on the balcony of the house with the kestrels?"

"Leon, of course, permanently on the run from the police ... The author is the detective."

"Perhaps the author is the same person as the murderer?" I said. "The author only called himself Karatheodory, but that wasn't his real name. He wasn't called Clement, either, but Leon."

"It would be even better", said Dr. Jacobi, "if the reader were the murderer. But it would be very difficult, I imagine, to portray him."

"My assumption is", said Weckenbarth, "that *the publisher* is the murderer. He followed it up by killing Count Clement Karatheodory by hitting him over the head with his verse epic."

The general discussion about the sad story and the surmises as to how it might continue broke up into different conversations, filling the large room with the sociable murmur of voices.

A thought had come to me during Tiffany's story.

I went over to Renata and said, "You remember the story you told on Tuesday about the unfortunate musician Orlandini?"

"Yes", said Renata, "have you been thinking about it all this time? You shouldn't, you know. At most it will be half as true as Tiffany's story."

"I know that your story is true!" I said. "Perhaps you changed some of the names, but the story is true."

Renata's expression became somewhat more serious. "How do you know?"

"Would you be so kind as to repeat your story, at least in broad outline, to that gentleman over there, Don Emanuele Da Ceneda?"

"Why should he be interested in my story?"

"You will be surprised", I said, took her by the hand and led her over to Don Emanuele. He was just pouring grappa into his coffee.

"This young lady", I said, "will tell you a story which I am sure you will be pleased to hear –"

"Miss Renata?" he said in surprise, but ever the gentleman.

"It is more than a story, it is a piece of news for you, news of ..." I bent down and whispered in his ear the name that had, in so many ways, cast a spell over his life.

He gestured Renata to the seat next to himself. It was plain that the old man's heart was beating faster. The coffee spoon he was holding rattled against the saucer, but he did not notice – Renata had started her story.

I went out into the mild evening air. The party had broken up. Some of the ladies went to change. They were getting ready to return to the city. After dark a ruin that Weckenbarth had built was to be ceremonially opened with a grand firework display. It was, anyway, a great day for our Senior Adviser on Ruins. It was his fiftieth birthday, he had been made Director of Ruins and awarded a distinguished decoration. On top of all that, one of his ruins had collapsed on the very day it was supposed to.

I had offered him my congratulations before I went out onto the terrace.

"Are you coming with us to the firework display?" he had asked.

I got him to tell me where it was to take place and said I might come along later.

It was the hour of the swifts, that short hour of their silent ecstasy when day has almost departed, twilight not yet fallen. There was still not a cloud in the clear sky. The sun was sinking behind one of the many gentle, wooded knolls. The knoll was picked out in a golden halo whilst the tops of the trees on the western slopes glowed a delicate orange. Almost the whole of the park was in soft shadow. Only one bright green meadow in front of me had a broad strip of light running across it. One single tree stood in the middle; it was bathed in a reddish-golden glow and cast an immensely long, slim, deep violet shadow over the grass, clinging with supple grace to even the slightest bumps and hollows in the meadow.

Daytime in the park belongs to the pigeons and sparrows, to the ducks and swans in the ponds, and to the peacocks. But now, just before twilight, the hour of the swifts had come.

Swifts do not sing. The harsh little screeches they give out as they fly, seem more like mechanical noises, like the sound from the friction between the torpid air and the arrow-swift bodies. – No, the song of the swift is something else. They hunt alone, in twos or at most in threes, to and fro between the invisible boundaries of their hunting grounds in the high airy hall of the sky; sometimes they fold their wings and shoot along a small segment of a huge circle or away in a perfect straight line: this, when they glint in the sunlight, for up there the sun is still shining, and draw the mysterious counterpoint of their fugitive geometry on the pale sky, this is the silent song of the swift. But their short, golden canon for a hundred and twenty-eight voices quickly dies away – when twilight falls and the long hour of the nightingale begins.

Spring was standing behind me.

"There, Your Eminence", he said as he pointed to the left, over the one still sunlit meadow, "there is the temple. If you look carefully, you can see the roof between the treetops."

I turned round in surprise. "How do you know that?"

"I know the park very well."

"That's not what I meant. How do you know what I am looking for?"

Spring was silent.

"Are you all actors playing out your parts for me? Even if you are just doing it for fun, it's going to too much trouble just for me."

"I don't understand, Your Eminence –"

"It's all right, Spring. I don't expect any of you to give the game away."

"I really don't understand, Your Eminence. I just wanted to ask whether Your Eminence needs me any more?"

"No", I said, "no, Spring. Thank you."

"And I thank you, too, Your Eminence. If you take that path over there, along the meadow, you will come directly to the lake."

From the far side of the building came the sound of the others leaving, engines starting up, car-doors slamming shut. The path led me into the silence of the park.

In the last light of evening the round temple stood on a treeless knoll rising from the midst of thick deciduous trees by the lake. Under the columns sat Daphnis, the dancer. He was sitting at an elegant little portable easel, painting. I walked up the knoll to him. He noticed me and gave me a friendly wave. Then I saw that he was not, as I had assumed, painting the twilit park around the lake but a King of Hearts. Several completed sketches lay on a folding chair beside him. He took them off and invited me to sit down. "Oh, yes", he said, taking something out of the depths of a bag, "here is your hat."

He handed me my hat, which I had left on the bench beneath the weeping willow on the other bank.

"It is extremely kind of you to remember such a trifling thing after so long a time."

"Half an hour is not that long a time", he said, "it's just that I don't get on with the mechanical dwarves."

"No one gets on with the mechanical dwarves", I said.

"They are a design fault. – I rowed across. If you are still thirsty ..." with a smile he pointed down at the boat. Two strings hanging tautly down from the tiller indicated that two bottles were being kept cool.

"Yes", I said, "but the only thing I cannot understand is how you can talk of half an hour?"

He gave me an astonished look, then went down through the soft, knee-high grass and brought the two bottles.

"Are you still interested in your Nameless Mourning Spirit?"

"I don't want you to go to any trouble at my expense."

"It's not a secret", said the dancer and laughed. He took a

grubby, crinkled piece of paper out of his pocket and handed it to me.

"I know this", I said, "I've seen this drawing or writing or whatever it is before —"

A tiny memory, like the memory of an almost forgotten dream was rising in my consciousness, but before it broke the surface, Daphnis said:

"Of course you have seen it before; the holes on the marble plinth of your Nameless Mourning Spirit are arranged like that."

"Holes —", I said and tried to think.

"But they probably mean nothing at all. The monument is just a joke. It was never completed. The letters never existed, it always had one wing missing. The monument is the work of a certain Weckenbarth."

"Him I do know", I said, "F. Weckenbarth, architect of ruins."

"He had the ruined monument erected for a friend a long time ago, when he was still a probationary Adviser on Ruins, today he's already a —"

"Today he's been made Director of Public Ruins", I said.

"Yes", said Daphnis.

The twilight was falling quickly. Here under the columns it was already dark. I closed my eyes and, since I had been staring at the piece of paper for a while, I saw the dots as white on a black background. — And suddenly I had the solution ... But like every solution of a true mystery it just led to a new mystery.

"The inscription", I said, my eyes still closed, "is:

SATOR

AREPO

TENET

OPERA

ROTAS"

"Give me the piece of paper, please", said Daphnis.

I opened my eyes and was dazzled by the sudden brightness.

"I forgot to take it before", said the police inspector, "we need it for our records. Who knows, perhaps it's a secret code and friend Einstein is a spy ..."

I handed him the scrap of paper and was about to say something when the train slowed down as it pulled into a brightly-lit station. The inspector said a hasty goodbye and left. I opened the window and looked out. While the loudspeaker droned its incomprehensible message, nun upon nun descended from the carriages and swarmed across the platform to a tunnel; the connection to Lourdes was standing at the next platform.

THE END